Nowhere Else

Nowhere Else

Fiona McCallum

MIRA

First Published 2011
First Australian Paperback Edition 2011
ISBN 978 192179436 0
Reprinted in 2011

NOWHERE ELSE © 2011 by Fiona McCallum
Philippine Copyright 2011
Australian Copyright 2011
New Zealand Copyright 2011

This is a work of fiction. Names, characters, places, and incidents are either the
product of the author's imagination or are used fictitiously, and any resemblance
to actual persons, living or dead, business establishments, events, or locales is
entirely coincidental.

Published by
Mira® Books
Level 5
15 Help Street
CHATSWOOD NSW 2067
AUSTRALIA

MIRA® and the Star colophon are trademarks used under license and
registered in Australia, New Zealand, the United States Patent & Trademark
Office and in other countries.

Printed and bound in Australia by Griffin Press

MIX
Paper from
responsible sources
FSC® C009448

Fiona McCallum spent her childhood years on the family cereal and wool farm outside a small town on South Australia's Eyre Peninsula. An avid reader and writer, she decided at the age of nine that she wanted to be the next Enid Blyton! She completed her final years of schooling at a private boarding school in Adelaide.

Having returned to her home town to work in the local council office, Fiona maintained her literary interests by writing poetry and short stories, and studying at TAFE via correspondence. Her ability to put into words her observations of country life saw a number of her feature articles published in the now defunct newspaper *SA Statewide*.

When her marriage ended, Fiona moved to Adelaide, eventually found romance, and followed it to Melbourne. She returned to full-time study at the age of twenty-six, and graduated with a Bachelor of Arts (Professional Writing) from Deakin University. While studying, she found herself drawn to writing fiction where her keen observation of the human condition and everyday situations could be combined with her love of storytelling.

After brief stints in administration, marketing and recruitment, Fiona started Content Solutions, a consultancy providing professional writing and editing services to the corporate sector. Living with a sales and marketing executive and working on high-level business proposals and tenders has given Fiona great insight into vastly different ways of life.

Fiona continued to develop her creative writing skills by reading widely and voraciously, and attending short courses. In 2001 she realised her true passion lay in writing full-length fiction, and in 2002 completed her first manuscript.

In early 2004 Fiona made the difficult decision to return to Adelaide alone in order to achieve a balanced lifestyle and develop a career as a novelist. She successfully re-established her consultancy, and now enjoys the sharp contrast between her corporate work and creative writing.

Nowhere Else is Fiona's second novel.

Acknowledgements

Thank you to Haylee Kerans and Cristina Lee at Harlequin Australia for believing in me, for granting me this opportunity, and for giving me access to a great team of talented and lovely people. Special thanks to Amanda Gitzel and Gabby Maait for their assistance and support.

A lot of work goes into turning a manuscript into a book. I feel truly blessed to have again had the privilege of working with the fantastic Lachlan Jobbins — a technically brilliant editor and all-round nice guy. Sarah Hazelton, thank you for your eagle-eyes as proofreader. Thank you to designer Romina Panetta for another gorgeous cover and Lauren Roberts, Kita George, and Lilia Kanna for all your work in turning my plain A4 pages into such a lovely looking book, and making my dream a reality. For anyone else involved whom I have missed, please accept my sincere thanks.

Huge thanks to Deb McInnes, Amy Milne and Alana Sun of DMCPR Media for spreading the word and to the media outlets, booksellers, libraries, and readers for your interest and support of me and my first novel *Paycheque*.

I have a handful of very special friends who have never wavered in their support of me and my dream of being a novelist. Thank you for sharing the joys, the disappointments, and being there for me during my roller-coaster of a life. You know who you are — please know you mean the world to me.

The story of *Nowhere Else* includes a plane crash. On 31 May 2000, Whyalla Airlines flight 904 crashed into Spencer Gulf killing the pilot and seven passengers on board. Among the passengers were two friends I knew from my days living on the Eyre Peninsula:

Wendy and Peter Olsen. They were lovely, welcoming people with warm hearts, and I will always remember them fondly.

While flight 904 served as inspiration for *Nowhere Else* and I used some online media articles, Australian Transport and Safety Bureau and coroner's reports to add some authenticity, *Nowhere Else* is a work of fiction.

In memory of my beloved feline friend, Calvin, who gave me fourteen wonderful years of companionship and unconditional love.

Prologue

Walkley Awards presentation
'And the final nominee is Nicola Harvey, *Life and Times*, for her investigation into the crash of SAR Airlines' flight 519.'

> *Tonight we spare a thought for the families of the victims of flight 519, which the coroner has found crashed as a result of mechanical failure and not pilot error, contrary to the initial Australian Transport Safety Bureau investigation.*
>
> *'Mayday Mayday Mayday...two engine failures...we'll be ditching... Request someone come out and help us please.'*
>
> *Pilot Matt Berkowitz, Ruth and Paul Harvey, Elizabeth Gibbs, Violet Patterson, Mark Neilson, David Richards, and Stewart Cope perished when the Piper Navajo Chieftain aircraft in which they were flying suffered twin engine failure, and plunged into Spencer Gulf.*
>
> *During an investigation spanning three years and two continents, Life and Times journalist Nicola Harvey made a number of crucial discoveries.*

Not only did she uncover a raft of questionable business practices by operator SAR Airlines, but she found that the Australian Transport Safety Bureau had itself played a significant part in the disaster, and then tried to cover it up. This discovery changed the course of the investigation and helped clear the young pilot's name.

'...And the winner for television current affairs feature, documentary or special longer than twenty minutes is...'

Chapter One

'Me, me, me,' Nicola yelled into the pillows, beating them with her fists, the announcer's words bouncing back and forth between her ears.

Leaning back into the plush pillows, hands clasped behind her head, she couldn't wipe the grin from her face. Not that she was trying to. *Stuff being humble*, she thought. *I deserve this.*

Steam drifted from under the ensuite door, rolling towards the end of the bed like a fog, accompanied by the damp musky smells of masculine body wash and shaving foam. She could hear the heavy beat of water on the glass screen, the occasional stomp of wet feet and squelch of a soap-filled sponge rubbing briskly on skin.

'And the winner is...Nicola Harvey,' Nicola whispered. A Walkley *and* a Gold Walkley – could life be more perfect?

She could hear Scott padding about on the smooth, damp Carrara marble, the opening and shutting of vanity cupboard doors, the buzz of his electric toothbrush. Scott always followed the same routine. Soon would come the brief roar of his hairdryer – there it was. And finally the slap, slap of hands as he applied aftershave.

Nicola imagined the astringent stinging and wondered why you'd bother every day. But it did smell damn good, she thought, as it accompanied Scott past the wardrobe and around to his side of the bed.

She rolled over for a better look as he bent to retrieve his Tag Heuer watch from the bedside table, admiring the muscles of his smooth, toned back and strong shoulders. Damn he was in good shape; almost forty and not an ounce of fat in sight.

Nicola fixed her gaze on the section of olive skin that disappeared under the roll of white towel around his waist, licking her lips hungrily. God she wanted to tear his towel off. What better way to celebrate than to make love with the man you loved?

She sighed. How long had it been? Nicola had tried to coax him when they'd got home from the ceremony, but he'd said he was too tired. And she really had been too drunk.

Though as he inspected himself in the mirrored door of his wardrobe, she saw that he hadn't been too tired to hang up all his clothes.

Of course he hadn't, she thought, feeling a little annoyed.

In the early days, Nicola had questioned whether two people with such diametrically opposed views on tidiness could happily cohabit. When they'd moved in together Scott had stated that as long as everything was out of sight he could put up with her untidy ways. Compromise; that was what love was all about, right?

She was impressed the first time she saw his carefully ordered wardrobe.

The mirrored doors hid carefully lined up rows of shirts in blocks of stripes, then checks, and then all the solid colours in ascending order of brightness like a rainbow. A bank of dark grey suits separated business and casual wear. Highly polished brown and black pairs of shoes were lined up in neat rows beneath, and belts and ties were rolled up in sets of timber boxes above drawers of carefully folded socks and jocks.

She'd pushed aside her concerns about what it potentially revealed about him as a person, telling herself she was just jealous, and that it was actually quite adorable. Well-ordered, controlled people were reliable and good with money, weren't they? They'd certainly done well with their property and share portfolios.

By contrast, her own wardrobe held jumbled piles of clothes, and shoes stuffed into shelves wherever they would go or on the floor when they wouldn't.

Nicola regularly marvelled at how ordered her work life was by comparison; it certainly went against the tidy mind, tidy life concept. Anyway, results were what mattered, and she'd won a Gold Walkley!

Scott finished re-adjusting the already impeccable Windsor knot of his navy and gold striped tie. He patted his side-parted, glossy black hair into place, and turned back towards her.

'Aren't you getting up?'

'I think I've earnt a sleep in. Why don't you come back to bed,' she said, raising her eyebrows and pushing the thick down-filled quilt back slightly to reveal a hint of breast. She patted the plush thousand thread count sheets and beckoned to him with an expensively manicured nail.

'I have to get to work.'

'Aw come on, it's not even seven-thirty. Surely they won't mind you being a little late…'

'I mind, Nicola.'

'But it's not every day I win…'

'I'm pleased for you. I really am.'

'This might never happen again.'

'All the more reason to keep it business-as-usual.'

With his charcoal pinstripe suit jacket now hung in the crook of his elbow, Scott walked over to the bed and bent down to peck her on the lips.

'Pleeeeaaaase,' Nicola groaned, clasping her hands behind his neck while she kissed him, trying to part his stubborn lips. 'I'll make it worth your while.'

'I'll hold you to that,' he laughed, pulling away after a brief struggle and instinctively wiping his mouth with the back of one hand and smoothing his shirt and tie with the other.

'Whenever that will be,' Nicola muttered under her breath.

'If you get bored you could always sort my shirts – Carmel is still ignoring my instructions.' He paused in the doorway and shook his head.

'Right,' she said, rolling her eyes.

She hadn't really expected him to pause, rip his clothes off and ravish her – she knew him too well – but there was that human desire to want what one couldn't have.

Nicola sighed deeply. She'd just have to hope his golf went well on Sunday. A bad round would see him disappear upstairs to sulk and work on his swing. A good one and she might have a chance. She had learnt early in their relationship that replacing pouting with encouragement was the better course of action.

Nicola lay in bed listening to the coffee machine downstairs – the grinding of the beans, and then the gurgling and spurting as it finished Scott's double-strength latte; his answer to breakfast. She knew she should join him for the few moments before he left, but still felt a little miffed at his rejection.

She glanced around the large, white painted room with its charcoal grey short pile carpet, sleigh-style bed and pair of chocolate coloured leather tub chairs. They were entirely decorative; not for sitting in, and Scott certainly hadn't intended hers to be a clothes horse. But she hadn't been able to resist draping her clothes over them, much to his annoyance.

There lay horrendously priced black lacy Victoria's Secret underwear, stockings, dainty black Manolo Blahnik high heels with diamante straps, and a slinky black Alex Perry evening dress, all of which she'd stepped out of less than four hours before.

At the far end of the room was the expansive ensuite decked out in charcoal and white marble. It was the warehouse conversion's main bathroom, and had a shower, a huge central freestanding bath, and a large vanity with double basins. *Maybe I'll take a bath.*

The thought was interrupted by the downstairs front door clicking shut, and the hum of the automatic garage door opening.

Damn. Not even a goodbye kiss?

That was another thing that had stopped in the past few months; they were usually so caught up in their morning routines.

Feeling a twinge of sadness, she rolled over, pulled Scott's pillow to her, breathed in his comforting musky scent, and tried to ignore the ache of frustration.

But she really shouldn't complain; you couldn't have everything all of the time, could you? Life itself was a compromise. Didn't people say the romance slowed down over time?

No, she really was truly blessed: she had a wonderfully successful stockbroker fiancé, a gorgeous sparkling solitaire diamond engagement ring, a fantastic warehouse conversion, Mercedes convertible in the garage, and a comfortable, stable relationship.

And now, after years spent slaving over dodgy plumber stories, miracle diets and anti-ageing potions; her very own pair of Walkleys! No one could dispute her journalistic credentials now. Never again would she be considered just a pretty face. *No siree!*

Chapter Two

Nicola stood in the kitchen in her bathrobe, staring out the window at the tree-lined park and wondering what to do next. She couldn't remember when she'd last had a weekday off.

She'd tidied the bedroom, packed up last night's clothes for dry-cleaning and spent ages in the shower washing the lacquer from her hair. While she'd loved how the hairdresser had put her hair in a chignon for the awards, leaving wisps of hair to frame her face, she preferred to have the stiffness gone and her blonde, naturally wavy locks back soft and bouncing about her shoulders. She shook her head back and forth a few times to test it before going to the coffee machine and setting it make her latte.

Leaving the after-awards party, Bill, her boss, had told her to take the day off, waving his arm in a dismissive, drunken gesture of goodwill. Nicola thought she deserved more than a day.

Her success would affect the whole station. *Life and Times* now had credibility; it could no longer be seen as limp attempts at serious journalism or mere stuffing between the news and prime-time.

And there was no doubt a host of doors would be opened for her – not that she wasn't perfectly happy where she was.

But it was a bitter-sweet victory, Nicola thought, looking at the silver framed photo of Ruth and Paul – her adoptive parents – taken for their fortieth wedding anniversary just a few months before their deaths. She felt heavy as she sat at one end of the flat, expansive couch. She wrapped her hands around the black and white striped mug for comfort.

Why did everything have to be a double-edged sword? Why did she have to lose her entire family for her career to seriously take off? It wasn't exactly the lucky break she'd overheard rival journos saying it was in the bar of the Rose and Thorn the night the story went to air.

★★★

She'd fled back to her desk, where Bill had found her mopping up her tears and trying to tidy her smudged mascara. 'They're just jealous,' he'd said, after she'd finally sniffled her way through an explanation. Much as it was nice to have her boss with his arm around her shoulder saying 'there, there', she'd been mortified to have lost it like that – in public.

But Bill was right. It was just a release after keeping it together for so long, especially given the personal nature of the story. His words stayed with her: 'I'm really proud of you for seeing it through – lesser journos wouldn't have.'

Nicola knew Bill had been reluctant to have her on the story to start with; knowing there was a risk of her falling apart in the middle of it all and leaving the station in the lurch and his job on the line.

Nonetheless, he'd called her into his office to say *Life and Times* was doing a piece on the crash and did she want in, knowing full well what her answer would be. Apprehension didn't even get a second beat – the desire to learn, as an outsider, the truth about her parents' deaths had her by the throat. Even if it was just a simple accident caused by an inexperienced pilot, she wanted the facts; all of them, no matter how gruesome.

It was when she first spoke to the young pilot's fiancé that she realised it wasn't as simple as both SAR Airlines and the ATSB were trying to make it out to be. Olivia Smith told her that Matt had been complaining for months of doing more than the required hours. Nicola had been disbelieving until Olivia had gone on to produce Matt's diaries as proof that SAR had been doctoring the logbooks.

Six months after the accident, the ATSB still hadn't interviewed Olivia; it made sense if they were trying to lay the blame solely at the feet of a young and relatively inexperienced pilot. But as Olivia said, she wasn't a qualified pilot, what did she know?

Nicola had warmed to her immediately, and the feeling seemed mutual once Olivia learned of her personal connection to the story. She was impressed at how brave Olivia was through it all, and only rarely did she allow herself to believe the same of herself.

Even more sensational were the revelations from another pilot sacked by SAR for apparent insubordination. Olivia had given Nicola Tim Manning's number after he'd contacted her to offer his sympathy. Manning had also let on that SAR had questionable business practices, which tallied with her knowledge of logbook tampering. He urged her not to accept any finding that laid the blame on Matt.

Nicola thought her eyes might drop out of her head when Tim told her about SAR's cost-cutting measures, which included experimenting with fuel mixes, and running tanks as low as possible. He'd had a number of close shaves, one time almost running out of fuel as a result. When she'd asked why he hadn't come forward, he'd said he had, only to be dismissed by the ATSB as biased because of his history with SAR.

The ATSB had picked up on the fuel and raked SAR over the coals for it, suspending their aviation licence pending the outcome of the investigation. But they seemed set on laying the majority of the blame on Matt; saying he'd over-revved the second engine when the first had failed. They'd added the patronising footnote that it was an understandable error, given Matt's low number of flying hours.

But what Nicola hadn't been able to shake were the incredible odds of two engines failing on the same flight – that couldn't have been pilot error. And as it turned out, the odds should have been nearly impossible. But all the experimenting with fuels had exacerbated damage to a defective piston and caused it to fail after the extra exertion placed on it.

If they hadn't done that, they might have limped home on one engine and the story would have been an exciting holiday tale for her and Ruth and Paul to discuss over Sunday night roast dinners. But it wasn't to be.

She sighed. She still missed them terribly, but slowly, over the past four years, the wracking tears and sadness had been replaced by a dull ache.

It had been a tragic web of mismanagement, error and coincidence that had taken her and the team ages to unravel. And it had been worth every sleepless night, every heartbreaking detail she'd had to learn to get the closure she had. She'd been relieved to have been partially responsible for clearing pilot Matt's name.

But perhaps most of all, Nicola was pleased the coroner had managed to get the regulations changed to require all flights across water to carry life jackets – previously they were only necessary on flights with more than ten passengers, or those that travelled further than thirty nautical miles from land.

Yep, they'd all done a good job; producing a well-balanced presentation of facts and humanity. And now the industry had spoken.

Despite drinking far too much bubbly to counter the nerves, Nicola had managed to react appropriately. The first time her name had been read out she'd nearly missed it. She'd been too busy trying not to give in to the tears that always threatened when she heard the pilot's mayday call.

She'd given a startled cry at hearing her name, and stumbled dazed up onto the stage. The story was good, but she'd never thought the industry would award her with a Walkley. As a consequence her speech was a bewildered mumble of thanks. At least she'd remembered to say it was a team effort.

The second time her name was called up – for the Gold – she'd been sipping champagne nonchalantly, barely even listening for the results. Her shock had been genuine. She'd paused to take a few deep breaths and still her racing heart before sliding her chair back and walking slowly to the stage pondering what to say.

She'd started off shakily thanking the industry and fellow journalists for their support before remembering to name every member of the team. She'd then looked Bill in the eye as she thanked him for his faith in giving her the opportunity. His nodding back had served to give her strength, and she'd gone on to pay tribute to her parents and all the other passengers on flight 519. She'd then bowed her head for a few moments of silence. Looking up again out to the sea of faces, she'd given a final nod, said 'thank you', and calmly walked from the stage amidst loud applause.

When dressing for the occasion, she hadn't for a second thought she'd be the centre of attention. She was pleased she'd gone with safe. She looked good; nothing the glossies could pick on for being too glam, too dowdy, or 'out there'.

Boy was she glad she'd ignored three new designers offering to dress her in exchange for free publicity, and instead settled for a simple yet elegant strappy number that showed off her slender arms but hid her long but sturdy legs. She'd hoped the diamantes on her new Manolos would be more visible – why spend eight hundred dollars if no one saw them?

She closed her eyes and relived the night.

'And the winner is…Nicola Harvey, *Life and Times*.'

When she'd seen the clip slotted alongside the other five contenders up on the massive plasma screen, it had seemed different, almost unrecognisable as her own. It was as though she'd distanced herself from her personal connection and was watching a story about people she'd never met.

She supposed she had to a certain extent; the raw emotion had left her when she'd become focussed on finding out the truth. There was nothing she could do to bring Ruth and Paul back, but she could do something for Matt, and in turn Olivia and his parents, Grace and Peter.

The more time she'd spent with them, the stronger the feeling that she had to find her own truth had been.

Halfway through the assignment she made the decision that when the story was finished she would start the search for her biological parents; when she was satisfied she'd done all she could for Ruth and Paul, who had been such good parents to her. She knew Scott wouldn't approve; he thought the past should be left in the past. She'd given up trying to explain how it felt to be the child of adoptive parents. He'd just told her she was being silly and feeling sorry for herself. But the feelings weren't that easily explained away.

The morning after she filed the story she'd been unable to get out of bed. She'd felt so emotionally, mentally and physically spent. Scott told her to fight it – no pain no gain. Of course he meant well, he just didn't understand. But how could he? He only spoke to his parents out of polite obligation, and he'd never even been to a funeral.

So Nicola had put on a brave face and waited until he was at work before dissolving into tears. For a whole week she'd moped around the house.

Without saying as much, Bill seemed to understand what she was going through. When she phoned him in desperation and told him she thought she was having some kind of breakdown and might never be able to return, instead of telling her she was being ridiculous and to get a grip (like Scott had) he'd left the office and come straight over.

His explanation, that what she was experiencing was probably a mixture of delayed grief, shock, and relief, made sense. It also made sense that it was occurring now she'd stopped after being so driven, so focussed for so long; her brain now had the time and energy to process the trauma. He'd finished by telling her he thought she just needed some time and to take as much as she needed; 'After all,' he added with a lopsided grin, 'you've accumulated a shitload of leave.'

When the Walkley nominations were announced six months later, Nicola had spent the first week smiling sweetly and agreeing that yes, the nomination alone was enough, while all the time desperately hoping for success. She knew that many in the industry saw her as little more than a well made-up clothes horse with ample cleavage.

That Scott was so dismissive of her nomination hurt. He seemed to share the view of many of her peers, and clearly didn't think she had a hope in hell of winning. She consoled herself that he knew nothing about journalism, let alone the magnitude of what a Walkley nomination really meant. If he did, he'd be reacting differently.

This was her chance to prove she had both brains and beauty; that Nicola Harvey was a journalist to contend with, not just a glorified presenter with impeccable hair and makeup.

Though of course she'd give up the chance in a heartbeat if it meant having Ruth and Paul back. How the hell would she keep it together if she did win? It was such a personal story.

'Stop with this false modesty crap – winning's everything, Nicola Harvey, and you can. You did a bloody good job, and don't you forget it!' Bill barked one morning after overhearing her reply to one such well-wisher. At least someone believed in her.

That afternoon Nicola had drafted a response that adequately expressed her joy at being nominated while remaining humble about her talent. In truth, she wanted to scream that she bloody well deserved to win.

Just before the first announcement, Scott had squeezed her hand to offer support, luck, and probably sympathy – he'd told her enough times not to get her hopes up.

Nicola let out a slightly pained sigh, remembering his obvious discomfort at having microphones, cameras and spotlights thrust in his face and being asked how he felt.

'Proud. Yes, obviously very proud,' he'd replied awkwardly. No wonder he couldn't wait to get to the safety of his office.

But at least Scott hadn't been uncomfortable in his attire – that was one of the first things that had attracted her. She had always been a sucker for a man in Armani pinstripe.

It felt a little cruel to be enjoying his unease, but it reminded her he was human after all. Anyway, he deserved it for not believing in her.

As a stockbroker he'd had his share of hairy moments but somehow he'd always managed to land on his feet. It was as if he had a crystal ball.

He'd even managed to dodge the global financial crisis and make enough to pay off his BMW convertible before everything went pear-shaped. She failed to see how he could remain so calm when there was so much at stake.

★★★

As much as Nicola liked the idea, aimlessly hanging about the house during the day just wasn't in her nature. She got up, put her mug on the sink and went back upstairs to get dressed.

Forget the day off; it was high time Bill coughed up her next serious assignment.

Chapter Three

Nicola stood tall and proud outside television headquarters, her two solid, twenty-centimetre fountain-pen-nib inspired statuettes tucked under her arm. Shoving the frosted glass foyer door open, she strode across the polished stone floor towards the lifts.

'Congratulations, Ms Harvey,' Barry the doorman-cum-security-guard-cum-general-dogsbody said. 'I knew you'd do it.'

Nicola turned and walked over to where he sat behind a long timber veneered reception desk. She grinned. 'Thanks Barry.'

'Thought his lordship would have at least given you the day off,' Barry continued, tossing his head up to indicate above them.

'He did. I'm just not cut out for sitting about.' Nicola shrugged. The lobby phone rang and Barry waved a dismissive arm as he picked up the receiver. Nicola repositioned the slipping awards and started making her way back to the lifts.

As she ascended, Nicola felt kittens doing tumble turns in her stomach. What should she say? How should she act? Would everyone be pleased for her or be catty and jealous? The men would probably be cool and gracious, but women were always a different story.

In her acceptance speech she'd been very careful to emphasise that she was accepting the award on behalf of everyone involved with *Life and Times*. She was sure she'd named everyone who'd played a part.

The lift doors opened, and she stepped out onto the sixth floor.

As she strode down the narrow corridor in front of the wall of chest-high office partitions, heads bobbed up from desks, bums swivelled chairs around and there was a chorus of 'here she is,' and 'congratulations!'

Within seconds the office had formed a crowd around Nicola and someone shouted, 'Round of applause for our star reporter.'

Wild clapping and cheering followed and Nicola felt the kittens in her stomach claw their way up to the back of her throat.

'Um, thanks guys, but you all deserve one of these,' she said. After carefully unloading her lunch, handbag and satchel onto her desk, she thrust the gleaming sculptures towards the nearest two people.

Paul Cox, the copy boy and most junior of staff, received the Gold, his pimply adolescent face reddening right up to the ears. His hands were hesitant when he reached out to stroke the object that every serious journalist aspired to.

'Go on, have a decent look,' she encouraged, pushing the object firmly into his chest. Paul stared down at it, mouth open in awe, then back at Nicola like it was the nicest thing anyone had ever done for him.

Nicola's chest pinged in sympathy. She too had started at the bottom. Under Paul's lack of confidence she could see some of her own tenacity.

She smiled warmly at the lad, then turned slightly at hearing an uneven thudding tread coming down the hall to her right.

Bill Truman's stout legs struggled under a belly that had grown considerably in the two years since he'd joined executive ranks and swapped pounding the pavements for lunch meetings.

'Heard all the commotion and knew you'd be at the centre of it. Didn't I tell you to take the day off?' he added, waggling a scolding finger.

'Too quiet at home.'

'Well in that case, the station had better fork out for a bit of a celebratory lunch. Nothing flash; pizzas in the boardroom at noon.

'All I ask is that I get a couple of hours work out of you lot before then. In return you can all have the afternoon off.'

There were whoops and squeals of delight.

'So now if everyone can return to work it would be much appreciated – we can celebrate later.'

Nicola smiled. Bill was one of the best bosses she'd ever had – tough but fair. He'd cracked his fair share of whips but could still appreciate the need for the occasional slack attack.

Nicola watched the crowd slowly dissipate. Within seconds the office had returned to its loud, lively pace; masses of people made phone calls, tapped hard on keyboards, raced between cubicles, and hurried to and from the lifts weighed down with clipboards, tripods, sound booms and backpacks full of cabling and camera gear.

She turned her attention to her own desk. An array of pens, pencils and textas were jammed into an old coffee jar. Four beige plastic in-trays were stacked up to the left of her computer screen, the top one almost overflowing. To the right sat her only personal items; three matching silver photo frames.

One contained a posed, formal picture of her and Scott taken at his brother's wedding the year before.

The second was a shot of Paul and Ruth paused from work in their treasured garden, leaning on rake and shovel. Nicola had taken it for fun, only months before the disaster that claimed them – her entire family.

The third contained a faded polaroid of a bundled newborn baby with only a shock of blonde hair and wrinkled sleeping face visible. Nicola picked it up and stared at the photo given to her the day she learned that her whole life had been a lie.

***

That's how she'd felt when they told her she'd been adopted. She remembered how her five-year-old world had melted like the chocolate chips in the biscuits they tried to placate her with.

They'd joined her where she was drawing on the lounge room floor of the house that had been her childhood home; the home of Paul and Ruth Harvey until the day they left to go on holidays but never came back.

They'd sat in a circle and all held hands. Nicola had got excited, thinking they were going to play a new game. And with Daddy who rarely sat on the floor with her; Mummy always said he was too busy for games. They held hands, the three of them.

They'd started telling her a story. Nicola remembered how, frowning, she'd stared at them. It was a very strange story, not a fairy story like in her books. It was a real story – about her, they said.

What were they saying? That she wasn't theirs; that she hadn't come out of her mummy's tummy like the baby of the lady next door. No, she'd come out of another lady's tummy.

'Did someone drop me off then, like Father Christmas?'

They'd given a chuckle. She'd been pleased to make them laugh; maybe it meant everything was okay. But they were being so serious. They looked at each other and then told her she was a gift, even more special than those Father Christmas brought, because they'd gone and chosen her.

'At a shop?' she'd asked.

'Well no, not a shop.'

She thought they'd looked a little angry. She didn't want to make them angry; she wanted to make them laugh again.

'Oh,' she'd said, feeling totally confused. They'd told her how special she was, and how lucky they were to have her. They couldn't have a little girl or boy of their own because there was something wrong inside Ruth. Nothing would change; they just wanted her to know the truth.

'What if the mummy whose tummy I came out of wants me back?' She didn't want to go away from here. They were her parents; she didn't want anyone else. Her bottom lip had started to wobble and then she burst into tears.

Ruth dragged her onto her lap and spent ages stroking her hair, saying that she was their little girl; she was staying right there with them.

But what about the other mummy and daddy; didn't they want her? Why not? Everyone said she was so pretty, and she was a good girl, wasn't she? She'd stared up at them and some more tears ran down her cheeks.

They'd shaken their heads and said that her other mummy had been sick and wasn't able to take care of her.

'But what if she gets better; will she want me then?'

'No,' they'd said, shaking their heads. The adoption papers proved it.

They showed her the papers, but to her five-year-old eyes they meant nothing.

'Okay,' she'd finally said with a shrug and taken a homemade chocolate chip biscuit from the plate on the floor nearby. She'd nibbled around the edges of the biscuit, separated out the chocolate chips and watched them melt in her hands, all the while pretending to forget the conversation.

After a while Paul and Ruth had unfolded their legs, got up, and gone off to do other things, leaving her there with her plate of chocolate biscuits. She put her half-eaten biscuit aside, went to her bedroom, threw herself on her bed and cried. She was careful to be quiet because she didn't want to upset Mummy and Daddy; they'd been sad before and she didn't like it when they were sad.

They said nothing had changed; that she was their little girl and would be theirs forever. But something was different. She didn't really know what it was; it was just a weird feeling inside. Like when you felt a bit sick after eating too many chocolate chip biscuits, or maybe empty after you'd thrown up those too many chocolate chip biscuits.

The odd, slightly empty feeling never really went away, but she never discussed it with Paul and Ruth. They were wonderful, loving parents, who had always been supportive, caring and encouraging. The last thing she'd ever want to do was hurt them.

But as much as she'd told herself over the years that they were her real parents, there was always a question mark. Sometimes it was a deep pain; the rest of the time it just sat there as a feeling of being somehow incomplete, hollow.

★★★

To their credit, Paul and Ruth had always encouraged her to search for her biological roots if and when she felt the time was right.

But she'd always thought starting the search while they were alive would be disrespectful. What had also stopped her was knowing she wouldn't be able to let go, would be totally consumed. It was the same wilful streak she'd channelled into a successful career in journalism. She could never stop at just knowing names of people and places.

The deaths of her parents had caused the itch of curiosity to become a strong ache of needing to know. The investigation had kept her distracted for over three years, and had given her a certain sense of closure. But three months after its completion, the questions that had been burning inside her could no longer be ignored.

Returning from her week off after the plane crash story had gone to air, Nicola had been mortified to find herself back covering the crappy stories of old; shock mobile phone bills, used cars that turned out to be lemons, pensioners struggling to make ends meet.

It wasn't that they weren't worthy of coverage, it's just that she needed something she could really get her teeth into, do some serious research and groundwork on; something really gritty.

When Bill had tersely reminded her that these stories were the bread and butter of *Life and Times* – 'It's what the audience wants' – Nicola had wondered if it was time for a career change.

Three months ago, she'd decided that she'd put off her own story long enough; she really had to start the search that might lead nowhere, might lead somewhere – somewhere she might or might not like.

One lunchtime she'd gone into the South Australian government adoptions website where she found a link: 'Searching for birth relatives'. She'd quickly scanned the screen, pausing at a line that said to consider other parties involved.

What if her biological parents didn't want to be found? What if she was setting herself and others up for heartbreak? Scott always said you should look ahead in life, not back. But life wasn't that simple.

Anyway, she might not even get that far. She might not even have enough information.

Nicola had selected the form for an 'Adopted Person' from the list, pressed print, and raced to the printer to collect it before anyone else in the office did. Back at her desk, she hadn't been able to quite believe how straightforward it was; ironic really that something so important could be put so simply. Just five questions were all it took.

She'd picked up the frame containing her birth photo, turned it over, and copied the details from those in blue biro on the back of the polaroid:

Baby Nicola
Born 16ᵗʰ April 1977
Port Lincoln Hospital

Nicola had paused at the two options underneath 'What information are you seeking?' and shaken her head. How would anyone be satisfied with just a birth certificate? She ticked the box for 'All information relating to the adoption', and then with her hand shaking even more, inserted her signature and the date.

She'd got out her cheque book, pausing with her pen hovered above the printed form to acknowledge the further irony of such a plain, uncomplicated number (fifty dollars) for something that was anything but.

She'd torn the cheque from its stub, placed it in the middle of the two A4 sheets of paper and folded them into three. She'd dragged an envelope from her desk drawer and slid the wad inside. Nicola had then returned her baby photo to its normal position and sat staring at the envelope.

She'd done it; taken the first step. But could she take the next one and actually send it?

Nicola picked up the silver frame containing the picture of Paul and Ruth. 'You'd approve, wouldn't you – say I'm doing the right thing?' she whispered. She'd planted a kiss on the glass between their smiling faces and held it to her chest. Then she'd filled out the address on the envelope and posted it.

Three months on and she was still waiting for information to arrive.

Chapter Four

The tightly packed room of round tables draped in white linen reminded Nicola of mushrooms grown in boxes. *Kept in the dark and fed on shit*, she mused.

Another boring dinner with an information session about the stock market was the last thing she felt like tonight. In fact, she'd been on her way home, picturing a steaming bath full of bubbles and a glass of wine, when Scott had phoned to ask her to get him a clean shirt and tie; he didn't have time after all. Nicola had managed to hide the fact that she'd completely forgotten about his industry function; had thought it was next week. 'Yes, fine, I'll meet you at your office at six,' she'd said and hung up.

Nicola had finished her drive home in a huff and four hours later, having showered and dressed in a black pantsuit, wasn't feeling any more congenial. 'Oh well, fair's fair,' she muttered to herself, as she stood just inside the doorway looking for Scott.

They'd left his office in separate cars, and she'd had trouble finding a park; he should already be here somewhere, she thought, scanning the mingling crowd.

God she hated turning up to these things alone. She didn't mind introducing herself to strangers, just the initial awkwardness of standing alone surveying the room for someone familiar.

Men stood around in grey-suited clusters – plain and pinstripes – their ties the only splashes of colour. The uniformity went further than their dress-sense; the younger ones were trim and muscular, probably gym junkies like her Scott. But once they hit their mid-to-late-forties it seemed there was a collective giving up on trying to keep pot bellies at bay. And there must be some kind of weird agreement over hair as well; in all the younger men, not a speck of grey in sight, but plenty of grey and even white amongst the older set. Regardless of age, they all seemed to have the same style, short back and sides, slightly longer on top with a neat but sweeping fringe parted on the side. The younger lot had their fringes up and spiky, the elders low and soft.

Nicola grabbed the last glass – a tumbler of water – from the tray being whisked past by a twenty-something waiter in white shirt and black trousers. She sipped at her drink in an effort to have her people-watching seem less conspicuous.

As usual, segregation had occurred and the women stood in their own small groups. Their preferred uniform was the pantsuit – in any colour as long as it was dark; grey, black, navy, occasionally burgundy or even teal. One of the few things Nicola liked about these events was not having to agonise over what to wear.

Nicola politely smiled and shook her head as tray after tray of canapés were offered to her. She was always careful to avoid the greasy morsels at these functions. Dessert was usually worth saving space for and the last thing she needed was to be the butt, so to speak, of any wide-screen jokes making their way around the office.

Where the bloody hell was Scott? She couldn't stand here on her own for much longer. Ah, over there by the far wall. He saw her at the same time she saw him, and raised his glass in acknowledgement. She returned the gesture, with the addition of a forced smile.

He was clearly occupied; she'd have to fend for herself.

★★★

'You must make more effort to join in, dear,' was something Ruth would have said, and had many times, bless her.

It was only when she was older that Nicola realised how worried Ruth had been about her being an only child, and the impact it would have on her social skills.

They really had been great parents; they'd got along better than any of her high school classmates, who could barely stand being in the same room as their parents. Nicola would nod in agreement when they rolled their eyes at how clueless their parents were. What she'd wanted to say was 'actually, my parents are really nice'.

And they were; she'd loved hearing about Ruth's job at the library, but Paul's work as a structural engineer she found fascinating. She would have gone down the engineering path herself if only she'd inherited his maths brain. But of course the thought was ridiculous; she had none of his DNA. They got on well, but they were very different.

Nicola had realised that very early on, and had been plagued with a thousand questions along the way; like, did her biological mother prefer to be alone too? As she'd gone into puberty the questions had tended towards the more personal; did they have the same hair or eye colour? What about body shape?

But she shoved every question back down as quickly as she could. Ruth was the only mother she had or needed; it didn't matter that they were different. To think otherwise was hurtful.

★★★

Nicola forced her thoughts back to the present and the masses of people mingling around her. The room had filled considerably and she could now hear the conversation of a nearby group of men:

'So, Toby. Win, lose, or even outcome today?' asked a man with dark grey hair circling a bald head.

'Up today, thank Christ; shocker yesterday,' said Toby, mid-forties in charcoal pinstripes.

'Futures or CFDs?' asked a younger chap with a hideous green paisley tie.

What the hell were CFDs? She'd ask Scott. On second thoughts, she didn't care enough to bother.

Finally, Nicola recognised someone she knew, a woman with sharp square spectacles and spiky dark hair. She'd met Yvonne several times before and instantly liked her. She was a fellow career woman and – unlike most of the women she seemed to meet at these things – hadn't spent their first evening boring her about what her kid had done that day in childcare. Actually, Nicola didn't know if Yvonne and her husband, a senior manager at a rival firm to Scott's, even had kids.

'Yvonne, hi,' she called from just outside the group. The etiquette was to wait until invited by someone stepping aside to give you space to physically join.

'Nicola, great to see you,' Yvonne said, placing her glass on a passing tray and pulling Nicola into a hug. 'Thank God you're here,' she whispered near Nicola's ear before releasing her. She turned back to the group who had resumed their chatter, smiled at them and said, 'I'm really sorry, girls, but there's something that I just *have* to discuss with Nicola.'

Before Nicola knew what was happening she'd been gripped by the elbow and dragged over to the nearest table.

As she went, she noticed two of the other women in the group had confused looks on their faces; as if they were trying to figure out why she was familiar. She got that a lot. What the hell was Yvonne up to?

'Thanks for rescuing me,' Yvonne said, flopping into the nearest chair. 'I swear, the next time someone asks me if I went to the opening of that new boutique today I'll scream. As if I have time to shop during the week!

'Hey, fantastic news about your Walkleys. Congratulations!' Yvonne said, slapping Nicola on the knee.

'Thanks,' she said, beaming back. 'It was…' she started, but was interrupted by the emcee tapping his glass into the microphone and booming that it was time for everyone to be seated.

'Good timing,' Yvonne said.

As the table filled up around them, Nicola put her handbag on the next chair to save it for Scott. She removed it when she noticed he'd sat at the next table over. Bastard.

She smiled at a nervous looking young woman in a dress with shoe-string straps who claimed the seat.

'I'm Bianca,' said the young thing in barely more than a whisper.

'Hi, I'm Nicola,' Nicola said, offering her warmest smile as she gripped the limp hand. The girl couldn't be more than twenty; still a child, she thought, suddenly feeling very old.

She was about to ask if it was Bianca's first time at one of these functions. The answer was obvious but she wanted to help erase the startled rabbit look from the poor kid. Who was she with?

She peered past Bianca and offered her hand to her companion, an equally startled looking young lad. 'Hi, I'm Nicola.'

'Tim,' he said, 'Tim Robinson. I'm with KLR – started a month ago. Learning the ropes of futures at the moment; mind blowing.'

Nicola nodded and smiled while wishing he'd shut up and let go of her hand, but at the same time feeling a surge of sympathy for

him. If he didn't toughen up quick he'd get eaten alive. She'd heard
enough from Scott to know what a cut-throat world share trading
was. Perhaps he wasn't going to be an actual trader, but someone's
assistant.

'Hey, aren't you on television?' Tim asked with a flushed face.

'Yes I am. Excuse me,' she said, as she felt a gentle bump from
Yvonne. She sat back to allow the waiter to put a bowl in front of
her.

'Thank you,' she said, picking up her spoon to tackle pumpkin
soup, complete with an artistic swirl of cream and sprig of parsley.
Standard mass-produced convention centre fare. No doubt the next
course would be a choice of either chicken or beef. She pitied the
vegetarians; their meals always looked like ghastly afterthoughts.

***

While they waited for dessert, a fifteen minute presentation was
given. Nicola and Yvonne couldn't see the screens from where
they were sitting, and neither could be bothered shuffling around.
But both Tim and Bianca dutifully moved their chairs. *You'll learn*,
Nicola thought to herself.

While everyone's attention was fixed on the speaker, Yvonne
gave Nicola a gentle nudge and whispered into her ear. 'Hey, have
you got yourself one of these yet?'

Nicola peered down into the handbag Yvonne was holding open
below the edge of the table, out of sight from everyone else. Inside
was a long glowing green stick. It was on the tip of her tongue to
ask what it was, but then she realised, and had to clap a hand to
her mouth to stop herself from laughing out loud. Of course! This
was one of those 'little friends' she'd overheard a couple of the girls
talking about in the office toilets a few times.

'Jesus, put that thing away,' she wanted to cry, but at the same
time she was curious to get it out and have a damn good look.

But that just wasn't something you did in a room full of boring old accountant types. And, ew, it had been, ew! She cringed at the thought.

'Don't worry, it won't bite.' Yvonne chuckled. 'My friend's selling them; apparently they're the best thing since sliced bread. Even comes with batteries so you can put it to use right away. Thirty-nine ninety-five including postage,' she added with a wink.

Jesus, Nicola thought, she could be talking about Tupperware. Were lots of women really buying them? Was no woman being sexually satisfied anymore? She leaned over for another look, trying not to attract attention.

'Um, have you…?'

'Not yet.' Yvonne snapped her handbag shut just as a waiter appeared beside her carrying a tray full of wedges of lemon meringue pie with generous knobs of thick cream. 'I'll let you know when I've given it a whirl.'

Turning to her dessert, Nicola dug her spoon in. 'Yum, one of my favourites.' And a fine example it was. Hmm, a perfect balance of sweet, savoury and bitterness. Not that she could cook; she just knew what she liked.

As she ate, her thoughts were still with Yvonne and the 'little friend'. God, wouldn't Scott freak out if he found one in her bedside drawer – especially if she went with one of the extra-large versions. It would almost be worth it to see his reaction, she thought, running her tongue around the spoon in her mouth.

Perhaps there was a story in the waning of sexual interest in upwardly-mobile corporate couples. Maybe it wasn't a conscious decision at all for her demographic to be putting off having children. She looked at Tim and Bianca, wondered what they saw when they looked at her: a successful career woman? Or someone who had let the chance for a family slip through her fingers?

★★★

Finally the tempting aromas of coffee were wafting around the table – a sure sign the evening was winding up. She longed for a cup of the silky, bitter tar but knew she'd never get to sleep if she did.

'You wouldn't happen to have peppermint tea, would you?' she asked the waiter.

'Oh, peppermint tea, yes please,' a chorus around the table chimed.

'I'll check,' the young man said through gritted teeth.

'I'd really appreciate it,' she said, beaming her best television smile. Thank God the night was almost over; Nicola wasn't sure she could play partner and interested wallflower much longer.

Scott hadn't said two words to her all night; why the hell had he insisted on her even coming?

Chapter Five

Nicola woke to a headache of disappointment. She'd always felt that a hangover was only worth suffering if a worthy investment had been made, but last night she'd only had two glasses of white with dinner. That was the trouble with bad wine.

She rolled over to find further disappointment. Scott's side of the bed was empty.

Kitchen clatter informed her he was making coffee. The small carriage clock confirmed she'd managed to sleep in. It was eight-thirty.

She picked up the small wooden picture frame from beside the clock. It held a copy of the same faded polaroid as the one in her office. She stroked the baby's innocent sleeping face, her face, which showed nothing of the impending abandonment.

Why had her mother given her up? Had she done it voluntarily or under duress? What about the man or boy involved: did he know he had a daughter who had been given up? Maybe her mother had been raped. Jesus, Nicola couldn't bear that thought.

When her adoption information eventually arrived, it would only give her names; not these more emotional details. For that she'd have to meet her, whoever she was.

The thought sent a shiver down Nicola's spine. But what if she was dead? Nicola had always refused to believe that. No, somewhere out there she had another mother, and hopefully a father too. She'd felt sure of it right from the start, and would continue to believe it until she knew otherwise.

Scott's frame filled the doorway. 'Don't forget we're meeting Bob and Sandy for breakfast at Becco at ten – you'd better get cracking.'

'Come back to bed,' Nicola cooed, patting the emptiness beside her.

'There are some emails I need to deal with.'

'Surely they can wait.'

'No, Nicola, they can't – they're important.'

And there it was; that tone she hated. Nicola felt like pointing out that she was important too, but cautioned herself. The effects of last night's below-average wine were probably making her overly sensitive. It was easier just to let it go.

She climbed out of bed, and as she padded naked to the bathroom, Scott started making the vacated bed. Personally she preferred to air it – as Ruth had taught her – but again it was easier to bite her tongue and not be subjected to another jibe about her lack of tidiness.

Bob was a golf buddy of Scott's; Nicola adored him. He and his wife, Sandy, who was an absolute hoot, ran their own business importing high-end Asian furniture and homewares. Nicola wasn't keen on the style of furniture, but had bought a pair of lovely paintings for the lounge room wall.

There were rarely any customers in the shop and Nicola didn't see how they made enough money to sustain their lavish lifestyle.

Yet somehow they managed to have Sundays *and* two days off a week; Bob so he could achieve a single-figure golf handicap and Sandy so she could shop with the girls.

Nicola loved spending time with Sandy; she was real. Well, as real as a boob job, liposuction, collagen lips and an incredible fake tan.

Shopping with Sandy meant you'd never end up with something the tabloids could poke fun at. 'No, no, *no* sweetie,' she'd say. 'You look like an old Jersey cow in that.' Or, 'That colour makes you look seasick.' And she was *always* right.

Nicola once suggested she get into the fashion industry. Sandy's reply: 'And have to deal with morons who think they look two sizes smaller than they are? At least furniture can't tell you it looks fine when it doesn't.'

No, there was no arguing with Sandy – she had the world and her place in it well and truly sussed. The bluntness could be upsetting, but you always knew where you stood.

★★★

'Daaarling,' Sandy cooed, standing and embracing Nicola and kissing the air somewhere near her ears. She gave Scott the same treatment before sitting down.

'Great to see you guys,' Bob oozed. He rose, kissed Nicola firmly and gave Scott's hand a solid pump.

'Took the liberty of ordering you coffees,' Sandy said. 'Thought you might be a little shabby after a night on nasty wine. Hope it wasn't too ghastly,' she whispered to Nicola, now seated beside her.

'It was a great night, wasn't it?' Scott said. A bit too defensively, Nicola thought. 'Very informative.'

'I bet. Lots of gorgeous specimens to perve on, eh Nicola?' Sandy said, nudging her.

'Sandra,' Bob warned.

'Get with the program, Bob – everyone knows these things are a veritable smorgasbord. Just look at Scott here.'

Scott blushed right up to his ears.

'Sorry Scott, hadn't noticed,' Bob said, grinning cheekily.

'Thank Christ for that.'

'You're in fine form this morning, Sandy. What's been happening?' Nicola said, fighting the urge to snap that there was no point having gorgeous if it didn't put out.

If Sandy knew the truth she'd say that it wasn't bad wine but not enough sex making her cranky. Nicola had been horrified a couple of years ago when Sandy had volunteered – totally unprompted – that if Bob didn't make love to her at least three times a week she was like a bear with a sore head.

'Hey, have you got the new iPhone yet?' Scott suddenly cried.

'Um, I'm actually thinking of sticking with the current model,' Bob said.

'You'll change your mind when you see it; here, check it out,' he said, sliding his phone across to him. Within seconds they were both engrossed.

Nicola and Sandy exchanged withering expressions.

'Well, let me show you *my* new best friend.' Sandy reached into her Louis Vuitton handbag.

Please no, Nicola thought. *Not in public.* But she edged closer just the same.

To Nicola's relief (and just a tinge of disappointment), Sandy pulled out a small embossed silver pump pack a little larger than a lipstick.

'Essential oil,' she said proudly, taking the small lid off. 'This one's orange – take a whiff.' She squirted a dose into the air. 'Makes you feel all bright and chirpy. Give it a whirl on your temples – you look like you need *something*.'

'Thanks,' Nicola said sulkily.

'You'll have to excuse Sandra. She's gone all hippy on us,' Bob said.

'Where's that waiter? I'm starving,' Sandy suddenly announced.

'So, where did you get it?' Nicola asked, turning the object over in her hand and sniffing the nozzle.

'China – came as a sample with a heap of incense sticks and burners. Different fragrances for whatever mood you're after.'

'Hmm,' Nicola mumbled, idly wondering if there was something she could give Scott.

'So, Scotty,' Bob finally said, putting his knife and fork down on a yolk-smeared plate. 'Ready for a thrashing tomorrow?'

'Are you? That is the question.'

'Come on you two. I thought golf was a battle between mind and little white ball,' Sandy said.

'Well, you thought wrong,' Bob said.

'Got a new driver this week – two-seventy-five right down the middle,' Scott said, throwing an arm across the table.

'You haven't seen me around the green with my new lob wedge. Anything from fifty out and it's all over red rover,' Bob countered.

'You have to get that close first – bit of a struggle with that slice you're nurturing.'

'I seem to remember a little trouble with a certain creek the other week – was it three or four balls?'

'All right, you two. That's enough,' Nicola scolded.

'Yeah, would you put your dicks away?' Sandy added.

'Well, may the best man win,' Bob said defiantly, offering his hand across the table.

'Indeed he will,' Scott said, giving the hand a robust shake.

'All too much for me,' Sandy said, rolling her eyes. She reached for the essence spray still on the table.

'So, what are you guys up to for the rest of today?' Nicola asked, of no one in particular.

'Driving range,' Bob said quietly into his raised coffee cup.

'Driving range,' Scott said through clenched teeth, glaring at Bob.

'Sandy?' Nicola asked.

'Shopping – you?'

'Same.'

'Where are you heading – want to go together?'

'Well, I'm supposed to be going down Melbourne Street with Joanna – you remember her from that New Year's Eve toga party at the Wharf.'

'The one with the stunning race car boyfriend, right?'

'They split up.'

'Oh, poor thing; he was yummy.'

'Maybe, but the bastard ran off with one of the grid girls from the Melbourne Grand Prix – had been seeing her all year apparently.'

'Dirty rotten scoundrel. She'll need your undivided attention – I won't intrude.'

'Actually, she might like the diversion – not to mention someone else to tell her he's a piece of shit not worth wasting tears over.'

'Hope she got a chance to knee him in the balls,' Sandy said quietly.

'She needs to start being sociable again,' Nicola continued, ignoring Sandy. 'I'll give her a quick call, but I'm sure she won't mind.' She picked up her iPhone and dialled.

'Listen Bob, since we're both going, want to go to the range together?'

'What? And get a look at your secret weapon ahead of the comp?'

'Watch and weep,' Scott said.

'You ain't seen nothing yet, Scotty boy.'

After a minute, Nicola put the phone down.

'So, is she up for blowing a hole in his credit card?' Sandy asked, rubbing her hands together.

'Not sure whose card, but let's just say she's in therapy – retail therapy,' Nicola said, grinning.

'Listen to them, would you?' Bob said.

'Yeah, let's get out of here,' Scott said, putting some cash on the plate with the bill and rising. 'See you tonight.' He pecked Nicola on the cheek. 'Don't have too much fun – either of you,' he added, waving a warning finger.

'And I want that card back in one piece,' Bob said, patting Sandy on the back.

★★★

Scott was tapping away on his laptop at the coffee table when Nicola returned home. She dumped her pile of shopping bags on the floor, went over to him and draped her arms around his shoulders.

'Good day?' Scott enquired, not looking up from the screen.

'Okay, you?'

'Showed Bob a thing or two – he'll be shaking like a leaf come tee-off tomorrow.'

'Fancy a bath?' she asked, kissing his neck.

'No, I had a shower earlier,' he said absently, with his eyes still straight ahead.

Not exactly what I meant. She undraped her arms, retrieved her shopping from the floor, and stomped off down the hall.

Chapter Six

On Monday morning, Nicola was easing herself into the week by flicking through the collection of newspaper and magazine cuttings she kept for potential story ideas. She was staring into space when her phone rang, startling her. 'Bill Truman' flashed on the screen. She picked up the handset.

'Hi Bill,' she said.

'Nicola. My office, thanks.'

'Oh, right, okay, thanks, I'll be there...'

There was a click.

'...in a sec,' she finished, but he'd already hung up.

Nicola got up and made her way out into the empty hall. She preferred to get in early on Monday mornings; liked the peace before the other journalists arrived.

★★★

'Have a seat.'

'Ta.'

It was a large office. Not by executive standards, but definitely compared to the four-to-a-cubicle squeeze of the *Life and Times* team. At least he had a window, even if it did look out over a depressing industrial wasteland.

Like the rest of the office it was showing its age; decked out in dark stripy fake woodgrain and the same threadbare and dirty mid-brown carpet that plagued the whole floor. In the corner stood a large round planter pot filled with potting mix but with no sign of plant life.

As usual, there was a lingering mustiness underneath Bill's fresh morning scent of Brut, Imperial Leather soap, and toothpaste. He always wore a white shirt and conservative tie – this latter article would be shed sometime during the day, depending on which meetings he was booked to attend, and when.

It was a running office joke that Bill often left the place looking like he'd had to physically wrestle the powers-that-be to prevent budget cuts or fight for more airtime. Although he invariably started the day clean-shaven, hair carefully arranged into a sweeping comb-over, by the afternoon his shirt would be wrinkled and half-untucked beneath his pot belly, his hair flopping over his eyes, and a fine grey stubble on his chin.

'Latte?' Bill enquired from the bench that ran around the wall under the window behind his desk. His shiny aluminium coffee machine looked to be the only addition since the office's last refurbishment in the early nineties.

'Yes, thanks.'

'Right,' Bill said, after taking a deep slug of coffee and putting his mug down heavily on the desk. 'How would you like a little trip out to the country?'

'Are we talking day spa country?'

'Fussy now we're hot property, are we? And no, not quite; you'll be lucky to find a latte.'

Yeah right.

'I'm offering it to you first. We want a story on the ongoing drought out bush. I'm thinking you'd go out there for a couple of weeks – month tops. I'll even throw in an airfare for Scott to visit.'

A weekend together in a quaint B&B, fossicking about in art galleries and antique shops – maybe it was just what she and Scott needed. Meanwhile, a change of pace and scenery might be nice for her too. The more Nicola thought about it, the more she liked the idea.

'All right, so where am I off to?' she said, sitting up straighter in her chair.

'So you'll go?'

'Sure, why not?' It was a month, tops, right? Bill looked a bit surprised. 'Where am I going?'

'Nowhere Else. Ever heard of it?'

'You've got to be kidding – someone did not name a town Nowhere Else!' Nicola cried.

'Someone did indeed.'

'Cute. So, what's my angle?'

'Thought I'd leave that up to you.'

'Okay. When do I leave?'

'You fly out tomorrow, 6 p.m.'

'Righto. But what's the hurry? The drought's been going on for years, hasn't it?'

'It's the only booking I could get before next week. Oh, and um, there's one small catch…'

'Isn't there always?' Nicola said, rolling her eyes at him.

'It'll probably be a smallish plane. And you'll be crossing the Gulf – flying to Port Lincoln and hiring a car from there. You're welcome to drive the whole way around, but it'll take you best part of seven hours,' he said with a shrug.

'Oh.' Shit. *The* Gulf – the Spencer Gulf; the same one that had claimed Ruth and Paul. Jesus, just how small a plane was he talking? At least it wouldn't be operated by SAR Airlines – they'd had their licence suspended after the crash and closed their doors not long after that.

But *seven hours* in a car? No bloody way. She didn't even like to do the Clare Valley and back in a day.

No, she'd have to face her fears; get on a small plane, cross the Gulf. Anyway, he did say it was 'smallish': the plane her parents perished in was *tiny* – only an eight seater. A completely different kettle of fish. And he had said 'probably', which meant he didn't know for sure; for all he knew it would be a 737. Yep, it would be okay.

She, Nicola Harvey, Gold Walkley winner, was certainly not going to pass up the chance because of being a pathetic scaredy cat. It was only when Bill cut in again that Nicola realised she'd been silent for ages.

'Well it's either that, "How much fat is really in a Big Mac?" or "Does price equal effectiveness in the world of women's anti-wrinkle cream?"'

'I've said I'll go.'

'Good. I'm sure it'll be a lovely place to chill out. Who knows? Maybe there are day spas,' he said with a shrug. 'What would I know; never been there. Go and find me a knockout story, there's a good girl.'

The words 'day spas' and 'chill out' rang in Nicola's head. That was what this was all about – a break, not a story at all. Of course Bill was too cunning to say so; he knew she'd never fall for the 'take some time off, you deserve it' line. Also, this way she was still strictly working for the station and Bill could balance his budget and keep everyone happy.

'Well, Scott's off to a conference – one of those cushy bonding soirées. I may as well go on holiday too,' she said brightly, and got up.

'This isn't a story for *Getaway*, Nicola,' Bill warned.

'Doesn't hurt to dream, now does it?'

'Whatever works,' Bill said absently, flicking through some papers on his desk. 'Right, I'll get the final arrangements sorted. You let me know the angle when you've sussed the place out. Not just dead stock and foreclosures…'

'What?'

'Remember, Nicola, I'm expecting gritty.'

'Yeah, no worries,' Nicola mumbled. She too was expecting "gritty" – in an expensive jar awaiting her arrival.

Chapter Seven

Nicola looked around at the other passengers standing beside the bus on the tarmac, feeling very overdressed in her navy Perri Cutten pantsuit. Everyone else was in trackies and jeans, t-shirts and polo tops.

She always liked to look presentable when flying, in case there was a chance of an upgrade. She'd worn this particular suit – one of her best – rather than risk crushing it in her suitcase.

But if she'd known she'd be traipsing up and down stairs she would have selected more sensible shoes – certainly not the chocolate Ballys with the five inch heels.

Oh well, too late now. Nicola sighed and brushed a few escaped blonde strands from her cheek.

There were a few sidelong glances from her fellow passengers: some admiring her well-turned-out presence; others trying to work out just where they recognised her from. Dark Gucci sunglasses kept her identity a mystery.

She wasn't trying to be incognito; she still hadn't sufficiently recovered from last night's dinner – a fundraiser at the zoo – to contemplate naked eyes. And she certainly did not need crows' feet spoiling her smooth television face.

After a few moments she was handed her suitcase from where it had been stowed under the bus. It was the only one; everyone else seemed to just have cabin luggage.

'Now if you'll just follow me, folks, staying within the yellow lines for safety,' called the gentle, cheery voice of the baby-faced pilot as he led the way. His name badge read Mark.

Nicola glanced around. The little group made its way around the bus to where a number of aircraft, large and small, were parked. Pairs of yellow lines showed the way to each craft. Nicola looked along their particular set to see where they were heading.

Shit! It was one of the *really* small ones. Her heart began racing. Her feet stopped short and her mouth dropped open. Someone's carry-on bumped the back of her right knee and she would have been sent toppling if a man hadn't grabbed her by the elbow.

The other five passengers pushed past, bumping her like a buoy amongst whitecaps.

'You okay?' mumbled the stranger by her side.

Nicola lifted a long, lightly tanned hand and pointed a clear varnished nail. The solitaire diamond on her ring finger sent rainbow arrows across the barren pavement. She tried to speak but it was as though her jaws had locked open.

'It's…it's…a Piper Chieftain.'

'Could be, I wouldn't know,' was the reply.

'Come on, folks.'

About fifteen feet away, the young, crisp-shirted pilot was efficiently ushering the other passengers up the flimsy foldout steps and into the plane.

Nicola's four-hundred-dollar heels felt glued to the sweltering tarmac.

'I know she looks small but, trust me, she's solid as a rock,' the pilot urged.

Nicola was damn sure she didn't like the idea of a small plane being 'solid as a rock'. The last thing she wanted was to be crossing two shark-infested gulfs strapped to a rock.

The pilot checked his watch. 'Look, we really have to get going. You're either coming with me or you're not.'

Nicola pictured Bill becoming purple with rage upon hearing he'd lost an airfare from his already stretched budget.

'You'll be fine. I understand small planes are a lot scarier than big ones, but trust me, I haven't lost one yet.'

Yes, but I lost both my parents in one just like this – and on the same route.

She felt like sitting down and having a good cry. 'For Christ's sake; it was four years ago, get a grip,' she heard her inner voice say.

On the inside of the tiny bubble windows, the other passengers were twisting in their seats and peering out. They all had places they were trying to get to. And the poor pilot had a schedule to keep.

The coroner's report on flight 519 had told of the enormous pressure pilot Matt Berkowitz had been under. One of the criticisms of SAR Airlines was their tight turnaround times; schedules which were at times barely possible to make without factoring in delays due to booking problems – another thing pilots were expected to deal with.

While the coroner wasn't prepared to say these tight turnaround times contributed to the accident, it was stated that the young pilot of flight 519 took off almost eight minutes late.

Having already been raked over the coals for being late the week before, and threatened with losing his job as a result, he was under considerable pressure to make up the time.

Nicola had no desire to put that same burden onto this young man, who was probably the same age.

'Right,' she said, gritting her teeth and jerking her large trolley case forward.

She was sweating; soon her suit would be ruined.

'I'll take that – it's too big to go inside,' the pilot said, nodding at Nicola's suitcase. Nicola pushed down the handle, left it where it was, and scrambled up the narrow steps. She half-expected him to pat her behind; he seemed that sort of guy.

The interior of the plane was even smaller than it looked from the ground.

'Sorry,' she muttered to her fellow passengers, waiting patiently to get to wherever they were going.

Sympathetic smiles followed her to her allocated seat, not the arctic stares and exasperated sighs she expected.

She sat, snapped the heavy ends of her seatbelt together and pulled the strap tight. She then checked under the seat for the life jacket the coroner had insisted be added to these flights since the tragedy. Good. She sat back again.

Outside her tiny perspex window, the first engine spluttered and sneezed and finally the propeller flicked back and forth then became a blur of spinning metal. The second engine went through the same procedure. The whole cabin vibrated as the engines were revved. Talking would be difficult; Nicola could barely hear herself think.

Fighting to ease her gasping breaths, she looked across at her neighbour. The stranger beside her offered a sympathetic smile, then the sick bag, indicating her to put it to her mouth and breathe into it slowly and deeply.

The other passengers were busily inspecting safety cards and complimentary magazines, and seemed not to notice her.

She tried to listen to the safety instructions, but could barely make them out over the sound of the engines.

If she wasn't so terrified she might have been amused at being told to keep her belt fastened when seated; there was no toilet to visit, and no aisle to stroll.

Sitting there in the same make and model of plane, waiting to fly the same route, and – shit! – at the exact same time, Nicola wondered how Paul and Ruth must have felt. But of course they were off on holidays; would have been chattering excitedly about what they expected to do and see. They wouldn't have had a clue about their impending demise – thank God.

If only she'd insisted on leaving the office early to take them to the airport. But they hadn't wanted to burden her; said a taxi was a lot less hassle. They had agreed to let her pick them up on the Sunday night, but of course it wasn't to be.

Her last words to her parents had been: 'Have fun, love you!' She couldn't imagine how people lived with the guilt of their last exchange with a loved one being a fight.

★★★

When Nicola heard about the anonymous letters the ATSB had received regarding SAR Airlines, she knew there was a major story to be told. While nothing would bring back Paul and Ruth and the other six who had perished, she owed it to them to at least learn the truth. If not, what was the point of having a journalist in the family?

She'd been prepared for Bill to refuse her request to lead the investigation, on the grounds that she was too close, too emotional, and not objective enough. Instead he agreed.

Had he seen something in her as a journalist or just understood that the best thing she could do for everyone was be at the heart of the story, no matter how painful? It no longer mattered.

It had taken all of her strength to sit and listen to the pilot's transmissions, knowing her parents had done the same for a full five minutes before the eerily calm mayday call was issued. For weeks she'd had nightmares about them frantically searching under their seats for life jackets that weren't there; being plunged into icy, shark-infested water at over two hundred kilometres an hour; and finally, the hopeless struggle to survive while calling to searchers overhead who couldn't see or hear them.

Four years on, it still made Nicola shudder to think about.

★★★

As the plane jerked and rolled forward, she felt her neighbour's hand give a squeeze, or maybe it was an attempt to regain some blood flow. She offered an embarrassed grimace and released the hand. To her further dismay, Nicola realised her good Samaritan was around her age and decidedly attractive.

Even more frigging embarrassing! Without making it too obvious, she snatched another look at the biggest, brownest eyes and possibly the longest lashes she'd ever seen. Wow, and those strong, tanned arms disappearing into rolled up blue and white striped shirt sleeves... Yum.

Jesus, Nicola, stop it!

She quickly stuffed the sick bag in the seat pocket in front, noting the length of his legs as she did, and set about studying the emergency card again.

Damn it; she could just kill Bill for putting her in this situation.

Maybe he thought she'd dealt with everything and had sufficiently moved on; perhaps he had no idea she was booked on a Piper Chieftain.

Or could it be his fatherly way of shoving her over the cliff to really get on with her life? Bill was perceptive when it came to human emotion – the main reason he'd been an award-winning journalist himself.

One thing was for sure; she'd definitely need a couple of weeks of massage and pampering after this.

Nicola watched the large jets taxi past the end of the runway while their pilot patiently waited, flicking switches, poking buttons and muttering into the headset in a tone that couldn't be heard over the bone-penetrating drone of the engines.

Suddenly she wished she'd told Scott she loved him when she'd rung him to say goodbye; both rarely uttered the words these days. When had he last said them? When had she?

Nicola closed her eyes and gritted her teeth until her jaw ached.

And then the vibration beneath her feet ceased and her stomach did a weightless lurch. They were finally airborne. The houses got smaller and smaller below them and then they were suddenly out over water – Gulf St Vincent. The dark blue was littered with whitecaps.

The little craft bobbed and twisted, throwing them against their seatbelts.

'Sorry folks, bit of a crosswind,' came the voice over the loud-speaker.

★★★

'See, not so bad, eh. All safe and sound,' the man beside her said, winking.

As Nicola alighted from the hatch onto the first step, the pilot said, 'Thanks for flying Air SA.'

Outside the plane Nicola's legs were not cooperating. She stopped and tried to stretch the cricks from her neck and back before trying to walk.

She took a deep breath of the brisk, fresh air coming straight off the nearby sea. The salt was instantly noticeable in her mouth. It made her thirsty. She hated to think of what it was doing to her hair's perfect body and shine.

Theirs was the only plane in the harsh white light of the terminal.

None of the passengers spoke and the only voice was that of the pilot uttering, 'Watch your step – thanks for flying Air SA,' as each passenger alighted behind her.

His voice had an obvious country drawl to it now, so different from the official tone reeling off safety instructions back in Adelaide.

Nicola, after a lifetime devoted to people-watching, recognised it at once. Pilot Mark might have been in the city at private school for a couple of years to get the grades for aviation and a plummy voice for the right circumstance, but he was never going to settle there. The lad was *country* country.

'Thanks,' Nicola replied. 'I really appreciate it.' She tried for a friendly smile, but was so intent on willing her legs to regain their feeling that it came out as a pained grimace.

'Life's too short – don't stress so much,' he offered kindly.

'Too true,' Nicola muttered, finally summoning the grin she was after.

They wandered the fifty metres over to the cream brick building where eager faces peered from backlit windows, searching for friends, relatives and business associates.

After settling into her room, Nicola planned to have a long soak in a steaming bath before ringing Scott – and this time she'd remember to say she loved him.

Standing by the counter of Brown's Rentals, Nicola fished her mobile from her pocket and turned it on while absently watching the tarmac goings-on.

A short, fat attendant was hauling the trolley piled with luggage back towards the building, a small fuel tanker was driving across to the plane, and Pilot Mark was striding purposefully about, green clipboard tucked under his arm.

Suddenly her stomach grumbled, reminding her how little food she'd had that day and the unhealthy choices made since the awards night. What a whirlwind it had been.

She was a little disappointed – but at the same time grateful – that local media hadn't turned up. She could just imagine the caption below an unflattering grainy black and white image: Nicola Harvey, *Life and Times* – Needing Her Own Makeover.

'Someone picking you up, or can I call you a cab?' Mark enquired, stopping next to her.

'Yes, a Mister Brown from Brown's Rentals. I'm driving to Nowhere Else – an hour away according to this,' she said, reading from the printed itinerary Bill's assistant had provided.

'That'll be Bob – he'll be here any minute. We were a touch early. I'll wait with you, if you like.'

'Thanks but that's not necessary – I can always call a cab or stay the night in town.'

'Public phone's out of order.'

'That's okay, I've got a mobile.'

'Take extra care on the road; there are bound to be roos about – they graze at night.'

'Okay, I'll be sure to keep a good look out,' Nicola said, thinking that she couldn't take much more care than trying to navigate unknown dark country roads in an unfamiliar vehicle. She checked herself; she was being tired and snippy. He was just being friendly.

They lapsed into silence. Mark shifted from one foot to the other. She listened to the sounds of the country – the thick, eerie silence punctuated by the howls of dogs and hum of traffic on a distant highway.

'This must be him now,' Mark finally said, nodding to his right. She followed his gaze towards two sets of bobbing lights negotiating the speed humps and winding course of the car park.

The first vehicle to halt in front of them was a four-wheel-drive wagon that looked slightly outdated with its squarish profile. At least she'd have half a chance in an accident. A burly man in bulging workman blue overalls got out and strode over.

He introduced himself and went over the particulars of the vehicle, and then showed her how to flick the lights between low and high beam, how to adjust the mirrors, and where the horn was – 'in case there's a roo sitting in the road or something.'

God, how bad was the roo population? Was she even safe driving? Should she stay the night in Port Lincoln? No, she was expected in Nowhere Else; if she didn't arrive tonight and someone phoned Bill – the other name on the booking – all hell would break loose.

'Know where you're going? Just follow the signs,' he added. Not waiting for an answer, he pulled open the back door, tossed her suitcase inside and slammed it shut. He then gave her a wave and walked to the small hatchback idling behind.

As Nicola got into the four-wheel-drive, she wondered how she would manage this huge tank after her sleek little convertible. Feeling self-conscious with the other car still behind her, she searched for the seat levers and made herself as comfortable as she could.

A far cry from her leather seats, she thought, grinding her bum back and forth to get a better position. She adjusted her mirrors, pulled her seatbelt over her shoulder, put the vehicle in gear, and drove slowly from the curb.

Chapter Eight

Nicola was still chuckling at the Welcome To Nowhere Else sign at the edge of town when she came across the Hotel Motel. She steered the vehicle into the large gravelled parking area, turned it off, and got out. Her legs were a little stiff after the drive, and she was exhausted from concentrating so hard on the unfamiliar road.

Her Ballys protested at the gravel. She struggled to get traction, and with every step, cringed at the thought of what the sharp stones were doing to her precious heels. Damn not changing into something more appropriate for the drive; they were comfortable, but not *that* comfortable. If they were ruined, Bill would have to pay for their replacement, she thought with a huff as she finally stepped onto solid pavement and rounded the corner to find an impressive stone façade stretching above and away from her.

To the left was a door – the top half glass, the bottom half shiny aluminium. Across the glass in large gold letters were the words Front Bar. Surrounding the doorway was old red brickwork, and above that, carved into the stone, the date – 1883. There's something really lovely about old stone, Nicola thought as she cast her eyes back over the building.

Now she saw the main entrance, flanked by large glass panels. The place had definitely had a nineteen-sixties makeover.

Oh well, the good with the bad; at least the sixties had seen ensuites added to most hotel rooms. The thought of traipsing down a long passageway to use a shared loo made her shudder.

Nicola tried to push the door forwards before realising there was a sticker saying Pull. She suddenly felt a whole lot more tired. The stress of the journey had obviously caught up with her; the sooner she got settled into her room and ran a bath the better.

★★★

She stood on red and black carpet in front of the reception desk. A label next to a plastic black and white doorbell read Press If Unattended.

It was unattended, but Nicola thought she'd give whoever it was a minute or two – she was probably being viewed on a monitor somewhere anyway.

On the wall behind the desk was a large blackboard with a menu scrawled on it in white chalk. Nicola's mouth began to water as she quickly read through the list of entrees and light offerings and then the cuts of steak and varieties of seafood and fish – all with chips and salad or chips and veg.

She'd planned to call into a fast food outlet to break her journey, and wouldn't have believed anyone if they'd told her there wouldn't be one McDonald's, KFC, or Hungry Jack's along the way.

God, I'm starving, she thought, staring at the menu. *I really should have something light – soup or a salad, or even the bruschetta.* But her gaze kept being drawn back to the t-bone.

When she looked back down she found a lanky teenage girl

with glossy but slightly limp mid-brown hair standing in front of her. The girl wore a navy blue polo top with an image of the building's facade and the words Nowhere Else Hotel Motel printed in white over her small left breast.

'T-bone, mushrooms, chips and salad – medium rare,' Nicola blurted, barely giving the lass a chance to open her mouth.

The girl blushed. 'Sorry, but the kitchen's closed,' she said.

'It can't be,' Nicola whined, and had to consciously stop herself from stamping her feet in protest.

The girl, whose name tag read Tiffany, shrugged apologetically and said, 'Kitchen closes at nine.'

'But it's only ten past,' Nicola protested.

'Sorry. You can get snacks and toasted sandwiches in the front bar,' she said, pointing back towards the door Nicola had come in.

Nicola wanted to beat her fist on the faded West End bar towel and tell this kid just who she was – none other than Nicola Harvey – yes, *the* Nicola Harvey of *Life and Times* and Walkley fame.

'Is there another restaurant in town? Maybe a café, hotel?'

'No, this is it. Hey, you're Nicola Harvey, aren't you?'

'Yes, I am,' Nicola grinned, suddenly brightening. So the girl *did* recognise her.

'Was beginning to wonder if you'd show.'

'Sorry?'

'I've got you in room eight...'

Nicola realised she'd forgotten all about checking in.

'It's all paid for; just sign this and I'll take you to your room,' Tiffany said, pushing a clipboard under her nose. 'Just the date and your signature is all we need.'

Nicola fleetingly thought Tiffany should be asking for an imprint of her credit card for mini-bar purchases too – a bag of chips in her room for tea was looking likely – but didn't have the energy to point out her error.

'Where have you parked?'

'In the car park around the side – is that okay?'

'Perfect. Where's your luggage?'

'Still in the car – I can get it later.' The words were half-hearted; the last thing she felt like doing when she finally got settled into her warm, cosy room was to have to come back out again. Where was a porter when you needed one?

'We can do a bit of a detour and collect it on the way if you like – save you the extra effort.'

'Thanks, that'd be good,' Nicola said, beaming at the girl and feeling a wave of gratitude.

Tiffany came out from behind the counter, strode to the front door and held it open. It took Nicola a few moments to catch up.

'I can't walk in heels – well, not ones that high,' Tiffany said, staring down at Nicola's feet.

'I don't seem to be able to either now,' Nicola said with a pained smile. She was suddenly aware of just how sore her feet were – the soles were burning and she could no longer feel her toes.

Nicola followed Tiffany outside and around to the four-wheel-drive as quickly as she could, grateful for the girl not showing the least sign of frustration with her slow pace.

Tiffany didn't let out so much as one exasperated sigh when Nicola spent ages fossicking in her handbag for the keys, only to realise she'd put them in the pocket of her suit jacket. Finally they wrestled her suitcase from the back.

'Round the back here – you can also get to your room through the pub,' Tiffany said, leading the way.

They rounded the corner of the hotel and Nicola stopped when she saw that surrounding her were not quaint old stone outbuildings but something that looked more like the concrete ablution block in a caravan park.

Two things told her the expanse of beige concrete was in fact motel accommodation: the black plastic numbers on a series of regularly spaced mission-brown doors, and the net curtains visible in the aluminium framed windows. She was careful not to show her disappointment; it wasn't Tiffany's fault – it was bloody Bill's!

At least it didn't look like the building was made from asbestos; thank God for small mercies. And the way she was feeling, she didn't care what the bed felt like as long as she could take these bloody shoes off and get out of the suit that was now starting to feel stifling.

Anyway, it's what's inside that counts, Nicola reminded herself, wheeling her suitcase along the concrete path.

'Here we are,' Tiffany said, putting the key in the lock beside the number 8 and throwing open the door. Turning back she added, 'You can get back into the pub from that door over there – see?'

Nicola followed her pointing finger and nodded.

'Breakfast is from seven to ten. I'll leave you to it.'

Nicola watched her make her way towards the back door of the hotel, which she now noticed was almost identical to the entrance at the front.

She closed the door behind her, dumped her bags and looked around the room. It was like the set of a low-budget porno: a sagging bed covered with a faux patchwork quilt, a white vinyl studded bedhead, and a dusty plastic floral arrangement glued into a vase on the TV.

Her nose twitched. The obnoxious scent of cheap rose deodorising spray unsuccessfully masked the odour of stale cigarette smoke.

She summoned the courage to check out the bathroom, and with fingers crossed, slowly pushed the sliding door aside.

Vitreous china, the colour of caramel, was the only plain colour amid a sea of cream tiles with a fancy geometric design that was probably meant to be floral but to Nicola looked more like fuzzy

monsters top to tail with their mouths open, screaming. God, she'd
go mad if she stared at that too long!

'Bath,' she crooned. 'At least there's a bath.' That could almost
be considered a feature to redeem all, she thought, as she pulled the
clear plastic shower curtain, with strategically placed palm leaves,
aside. Great, she'd have to soak with her ankles wedged under her
bum, it was so bloody small.

Nicola plonked herself askew on the toilet and put a hand over
her mouth to stifle the erupting giggles.

Bloody Bill. This was no doubt his way of stopping her getting
big-headed. She laughed even louder when she caught sight of
the time-yellowed, once-considered-slimline phone by her left
shoulder, and was unable to resist.

'Hey, it's me.'

'Hey,' Scott replied, his voice crackling and hollow through the
ancient handset.

'Just wanted to let you know I arrived safely.'

'Thanks – good to know. How was the trip?'

'Exhausting. But can you believe there was nowhere to eat along
the way – I'm absolutely starving. And of course I get here and
they've stopped serving meals. Missed it by ten minutes.'

'I'm sure Bill's budget will stretch to a meal from room service.'

'There is no room service.'

'Thank God for mini-bars then, hey?'

Nicola began to laugh. Was she becoming delirious from tired-
ness and hunger?

'Scott, you would *so* not believe this place. It's like something
out of...'

'Apparently the place we're going to this week has only four
stars. Can you believe it? The rooms probably won't even have
baths. I hope you'll think of me slumming it while you're soaking
in your tub full of bubbles.'

'Well I'm in the bathroom but…'

'Phone in the bathroom, eh? Bill really *is* taking care of his star these days.'

'Well actually it's…'

'Look hon, I'd love to hear all about your marble and complimentary toiletries but I've really gotta run – sorry.'

'Right, um, okay. I'll let you go… Love you.'

'Yeah me too, bye.'

★★★

Feeling refreshed after her shower, but again reminded of her hunger, Nicola ventured back across to the hotel.

The reception desk now had a cage pulled down over it with a sign that read Closed – All Enquiries To Front Bar.

Swallowing her apprehension, Nicola pushed the door marked Front Bar open and made her way inside.

'Settled in okay then?' Tiffany asked.

'Yes thanks.'

'What can I get you?'

'Um…er…' Nicola frantically searched the menu for something remotely appetising.

'Something to drink while you decide?'

'Do you have a wine list?'

'There's probably one somewhere around here,' Tiffany said, ducking down behind the bar. It didn't bode well.

'Don't worry, I'll just have a beer thanks.'

'Hey Tiff,' a loud voice called from around the corner. 'Dry argument around 'ere luv.'

'Come on,' another called.

'Just bloody hang on,' Tiffany muttered, thumping the glass in front of Nicola and accepting her money.

Nicola had been staring at the menu a full minute when a voice next to her said, 'The toasted sandwiches are the closest thing you'll get to sustenance.'

'Thanks,' she said, turning. She frowned; the dark features were a little familiar, but from where she wasn't sure. 'Have we met?'

The guy smirked. 'Yep.'

'When?'

'Oh, about three hours ago,' he said, looking at his watch.

Nicola blushed furiously as she realised he was her flight companion – the one who'd held the sick bag for her – the one whose hand she'd held. *Oh my God*, she silently groaned, *could the day get any worse?*

'Um, I'm really sorry about all that,' she muttered, waving an arm casually, feeling anything but casual.

'Alex. Even though we've already been somewhat intimate, it's a pleasure to meet you,' he laughed, thrusting his hand at her.

'Nicola, highly embarrassed,' she mumbled, shaking hands.

'Ah, don't be.'

'Right, can I get you anything to eat?' Tiffany asked, reappearing. 'The ham and cheese toasted sandwiches are almost edible,' she offered.

'Great, I'll have one thanks,' Nicola said.

'Care for a game of pool?' Alex asked.

Why the hell not? Nicola thought. Things could only get better.

Chapter Nine

Nicola scowled at the crude sketch of the hotel motel in cream on the gleaming chocolate brown plastic placemat. Despite scanning the Yellow Pages and finding a caravan park the only other option, she was still in denial. Surely there was *somewhere* else to stay.

She was also in denial about the amount she'd had to drink. Disconnected images flickered through her mind, vague and grainy like an old silent movie. It couldn't have been the drink – the ham must have been off.

'Good morning.' It was Tiffany from the night before.

The kid was sweet enough but far too bloody cheery when one was suffering a hangover and stiff back. Nicola glowered in response.

'Bread, butter and spreads over there by the toaster, cereal and milk on the table, plates and cutlery on the bench,' Tiffany rambled. 'Help yourself,' she added. 'Can I get you a coffee, or perhaps you'd rather a tea? I've just put a pot on.'

'Coffee, thanks.' As Tiffany bounded away, Nicola wondered if the pot she'd referred to was for tea, and instantly regretted her request. In her experience coffee that came in a pot was rarely drinkable.

Maybe there was a coffee machine hiding out in some back room and it wouldn't be so bad. She hoped so, because the only thing she could see making her feel better was a decent latte or three.

She got up for a closer inspection of the breakfast offerings. The cereals were all in little boxes, brightly adorned to attract the attention of children. She sighed and stuck two pieces of grain bread into the nearby toaster, more for something to do to pass the time.

Nicola stared at the toast she'd just cooked. It looked about as nutritious as cement. Tiffany appeared beside her and put down a tray with a plain white mug of inky black coffee, a small ceramic jug of milk and a matching bowl of white sugar.

'Thanks,' Nicola said, and set about doctoring her coffee. Fingers crossed.

She took a tentative sip and almost dropped the cup as her tongue was burnt. She put the mug back on the table with a grimace.

'Sorry, is it too hot?' Tiffany asked.

'Not your fault.'

The beverage's temperature was the least of its shortcomings, but Nicola curbed her desire to point out its flaws. It was bitter, watery, and had almost no depth of flavour. Could it actually be the worst cup she'd ever tasted? It was a little hard to tell now that she'd burnt the taste buds off her tongue. Bad or not, she thought, it *is* caffeine; a vital ingredient for the treatment of the common hangover. She lifted the cup again and took a couple more sips.

Nicola put the mug down and looked at Tiffany who was still hovering – why, she had no idea.

'Tiffany. Um, is there a B&B anywhere nearby, or maybe a…?'

Tiffany looked mortified.

'No offence, it's just that...'

'We may not be all the frills floral but we're clean and comfortable,' Tiffany said defiantly.

'Sorry, I didn't mean to...' Nicola began.

'Anyway, there *is* nowhere else,' Tiffany said.

Nicola wanted to know if the pun was intended, but was far too peeved to give Tiffany the upper hand by praising her wit.

As she stared at her mug, weighing up its drinkability versus her desperation, Nicola felt a slow sinking feeling take hold. If there was no B&B, did that mean there was no day spa either? It was all too awful to contemplate.

'Is there by any chance a day spa nearby, or a masseuse?' Nicola asked hesitantly.

Tiffany thought for a moment. 'Well, there's an old retired shearer does a bit of work on the footy players.'

Nicola stared at her, horrified.

Taking great joy in Nicola's obvious discomfort, she chuckled. 'Though I'm guessing that's not quite what you're after.'

'Could it get any worse?' Nicola mumbled, thinking aloud. She laid her head on her arms on the table.

★★★

Nicola was wondering just what the town did have to offer when Tiffany again materialised at her side and dumped a wad of photocopied and glossy brochures beside her.

'This place might not have all the city finery but we're an honest, down-to-earth bunch of good people who do our best with what we have,' she said a little indignantly.

Tiffany looked like she was waiting for applause. Well she'll be waiting a while, Nicola thought, sitting back in her chair and folding her arms tight across her chest.

'You can get paracetamol at the chemist or supermarket. Both are down the street and open at nine-thirty,' Tiffany said, before turning lightly on her heels and walking away. A door marked Private slapped shut behind her.

Nicola steamed in her chair. The place was a hick town full of country bumpkins and she hated it already. Damn Bill. Boy was she going to give him a piece of her mind! Right bloody now!

She got up and stormed out the door and across the courtyard. By the time she got to room eight she was a little out of breath.

Inside she grabbed her mobile from the bench, remembered there was no signal, and put it down again. Bloody thing; what's the point of an iPhone if you can't get any reception? She'd have to do something about that. If she was staying that was.

Nicola reached for the phone by the bed and was about to dial Bill's office number when she stopped and put the handset down again. What the hell was she going to say, anyway? 'Get me out of this shithole because I'm drowning in bad décor and crap coffee?' She'd just sound like a petulant child; not an award-winning reporter prepared to get down and dirty for a great story.

And had he actually promised her a quaint chocolate box village? Hmm. What had he said exactly? Nicola nibbled at her bottom lip. 'For all I know there'll be day spas…'

He'd actually only asked her to go out to a town called Nowhere Else and do a story on the drought, hadn't he?

She'd been the one who had assumed the accommodation would be a posh little B&B. Just heard what she wanted to hear. Fine journalist she was!

Well, she should at least let him know she'd arrived safely. She picked up the phone and dialled his office.

'Bill Truman.'

'Hey Bill, it's Nicola.'

'Where the hell are you calling from?'

'Nowhere Else – I'm on assignment, remember?'

'Of course I bloody remember; your mobile didn't come up.'

'Oh yeah, right. There doesn't seem to be any reception out here.'

'Right, might have to change you over to the national carrier – I'll check the coverage.' Nicola could hear him scrawling notes. 'Everything else okay?'

'It's fine,' she said with a sigh.

'What? What's wrong?'

'It's just not what I was expecting.'

'Have you had a good look around yet?'

'Not yet.'

'Well, you never know what you'll find; it might surprise you with what it has to offer.'

A fleeting image of Alex from last night passing through her mind caused Nicola to smile. That had certainly been a pleasant surprise.

'Oh well, you got there safely; that's all that matters.'

She told him about the lack of food stops on the road in.

'It's *that* remote? Who would have thought?'

'Came as a bit of a shock to me as well,' Nicola said with a chuckle.

'Accommodation okay? Too bad if it's not 'cause I hear there's nowhere else.'

'Ha ha. I'll be fine, Bill. I'd better go before I blow your budget.'

'Well, keep in touch. I'll let you know about the phone.'

'Thanks.'

'And Nicola?'

'Yes?'

'Go find me a killer story, there's a good girl.'

'I'll do my best, boss.'

'Oh, and be friendly to the locals. See ya, kiddo. Take care.'

'See ya.'

★★★

Nicola hung up and sat smiling, thinking how lucky she was to have a boss like Bill. She felt so much better. But she did feel a little guilty for her behaviour towards Tiffany earlier. She hadn't been rude, had she? Not quite. But she hadn't exactly been gracious.

With the words, 'Be friendly to the locals' in her mind she got up, left the room, and pulled the door shut behind her.

As she crossed the courtyard back to the pub, Nicola wondered if she'd been a bit too friendly towards another local she'd met – Alex. She was a little fuzzy on the detail of last night.

The dining room was empty when she re-entered. Her untouched plate was where she'd left it, along with toast, mug, and cutlery. She drained the last of the coffee, which, as expected, had deteriorated as it had cooled.

'Sorry. I wasn't sure if you had finished or not,' Tiffany said, appearing beside her. She nodded at Nicola's plate.

'Had to quickly phone my boss.'

'So do you want it or should I take the plate?'

Nicola looked at the toast. She hated cold toast, but didn't want to add to her already poor standing with Tiffany by wasting it.

She picked up her knife, tore open the packet of butter she'd collected earlier, and started buttering.

'Don't suppose you'd like another *crap* coffee?'

'Another coffee would be lovely, thanks,' Nicola said, smiling broadly up at her. 'Tiffany, look, I'm sorry we got off on the wrong foot – too many late nights…'

'Whatever.' Tiffany shrugged, collected the mug and left.

'Well that went well,' Nicola mumbled to her toast.

After a few moments alone, she looked around to find Tiffany had returned. She put the mug down but remained standing beside Nicola.

'Um…er,' Tiffany stammered awkwardly, her face reddening.

'Yes?' What now? Is she going to tell me where to stick my coffee?

'I'm sorry, I shouldn't have snapped,' Tiffany blurted. The glower was a dead giveaway that the apology was being issued under duress.

'No, I deserved it,' Nicola sighed. 'Bloody hangover,' she muttered, taking a swig of coffee and cringing.

'I'm not surprised,' Tiffany grinned, sitting. 'You enjoyed yourself last night.'

Nicola raised her eyebrows.

'I never expected you to be so…so relaxed. I mean here, of all places. I think Alex was quite… Sorry, I'm rambling.'

Nicola wished she'd keep going. She hadn't been *that* drunk; certainly not drunk enough not to notice the mattress springs poking her in the back and the bathroom tap dripping all night – almost, but not quite.

'Bugger, I must have made a bloody fool of myself,' she groaned and laid her head on the table.

'Nah, everyone loved you,' Tiffany enthused. 'The blokes never thought you'd be so normal. You were great. Pretty pissed, but you were great,' she added, grinning shyly.

'Do I want to know details?'

'Probably not,' Tiffany laughed.

Nicola shot her a quizzical frown. She was actually beginning to like this girl; the cheeky forthrightness.

'Just kidding, nothing to worry about.'

'You'd tell me, right?'

'Promise – cross my heart. So,' Tiffany said, banging the table, 'last night you mentioned you're here to cover the drought. Maybe

I can help. There's practically no one in town I don't know. You just have to ask.'

'Well, I think I'd like to start with the editor of the local paper. Can you point me in the right direction?'

'Easy – I'll mark his office on a map,' Tiffany said proudly, leaping up.

'Thanks,' Nicola said, smiling warmly at her new friend.

Chapter Ten

'Be hard to get lost around here,' Nicola muttered to herself while scanning the map. *Doesn't even look big enough to have its own paper.*

'Quaint,' she said, stopping in front of a row of five pale limestone shops with red brick quoins. Large terracotta planters overflowing with masses of deep red camellia blooms completed a scene worthy of a tourist brochure. Nicola pulled the compact digital camera from her coat pocket and stood back and took a few shots. 'Post Office, Police Station, Newspaper, *and* District Council – must be the CBD.'

She approached the shopfront marked *Nowhere Else Echo*. In the window was a large old printing press, a number of ancient manual typewriters, and wooden boxes filled with pieces of large and small lettering. Black and white action shots of newspapermen hard at work and a yellowed example of a broadsheet headline page encased in Perspex hung from the ceiling, completing the display.

Nicola took a few moments to marvel at how far the world of newspaper printing, and technology generally, had come.

The door had a small bell that jingled when it opened. She smiled. It was like something out of a museum village.

Actually, as she looked around the small reception, which doubled as a stationery shop, it was more like a 1950s movie.

A sea of black and white chequered lino stopped at an imposing timber counter. Pale yellow light barely lit the narrow hallway beyond.

The place smelled strongly of printing: the warm plastic scent of a photocopier, and the unmistakeable earthy and tangy odours of ink, worn metal and industrial oil that belonged to a printing press – probably the one in the window.

To the left were three small white melamine study hutches with a printed sign above them: Public Internet $3 for 30 Minutes.

To the right, a Stationery sign hung over a set of shelving. She wandered over for a closer look, half expecting to see 1950s advertising on the boxes, and was surprised to find a small but wide array of pens, pencils, refills, copier paper, lined pads, printer cartridges, calculator rolls and batteries.

There was a nice looking pen in a hard clear plastic display box she wouldn't have minded taking a closer look at, but she didn't want to embarrass herself or the newspaper manager by having a sneezing fit – there was a fine layer of dust over everything. Obviously not a huge turnover.

At home she kept her allergies under control with a daily antihistamine and weekly visits from the cleaner, but out here anything could happen.

'Hello?' she called, leaning over the counter towards the hall. Waiting for a response, she traced the dark scars in its worn surface and wondered at the stories the furniture held.

A gruff voice echoed down the passage. 'Sorry, we're not open until ten.'

Heavy leather soles clack-clacked on the lino, as a figure emerged slowly from the gloom.

Nicola's jaw dropped and she felt the colour drain slightly from her face. 'Richard? Richard Watkins?'

'Nicola Harvey, what the hell are you doing here?' The lanky man had a pair of reading glasses on his forehead, beneath a dark tousled mop streaked with white pepper. He threw back the hinged timber barrier and pulled her into a tight hug.

'Visiting an old friend, apparently,' Nicola muttered. It was nice to be hugged, but she was distracted. Why was Richard Watkins out here, of all places? And why was he hugging her like a long lost friend when he'd been the one who'd left all those years ago? She shook the questions aside; it was nice to see him, even if it had come as a shock.

'Seriously, what's a journo of your calibre doing way out here?' Richard asked when they broke apart.

'I could ask you the same question – you topped our year and you end up out here?'

'Hey, it's not a bad little rag. I'm in charge, remember.'

'Sorry, I wasn't suggesting it was – it's just…well…why out here? Last time I saw you you were off to London. Didn't you have a job with *The Times*?'

'Things changed,' Richard shrugged, obviously keen to change the subject. 'So, Gold Walkley. Well done. But I'm sorry about your parents – they were a lovely couple.'

Nicola found herself blushing. 'Yeah, thanks. How did you know, anyway? About the Walkley I mean.'

'Oh, you know, we get the odd carrier pigeon through, keeps us in touch,' Richard said.

Carrier pigeon – do people still use those? Nicola's brow knitted with confusion.

'We do have TV, you know, and even mobile phones – though the coverage is still a bit patchy.'

'I didn't mean to...' Nicola started, blushing beetroot.

'Forgiven. I know we're a long way from the big smoke but it's a great place – you might even get to like it.'

Nicola raised her eyebrows. 'Not likely.'

'There's a lot more to do out here than you'd think. But I want to know why *Life and Times* has sent their star reporter to Nowhere Else – anything I should know?'

'Well, nothing major, just a piece on the drought,' Nicola hoped it would turn out to be more, but wasn't really feeling at all optimistic. At least with the plane crash there had been specific leads to follow up.

What she needed now was an angle, no matter how tenuous; just a starting point of some sort. 'Actually, I could probably use your help.'

'Angle?'

'Not yet.' Nicola bit her lip. She hadn't actually given any thought to the story. She was still coming to terms with the fact she was actually here to work; she'd been too busy dreaming of facials, mud wraps, and quaint shopping strips.

'Hmm, come out to my office – better for thinking.'

'Sure you've got time; I'm not imposing?'

'No worries, I'm really just pottering around enjoying the peace I don't get at home. Would never have believed two small children could make so much noise. Though I suppose they are boys,' he added, directing her into a chair.

'Oh,' Nicola blurted, unable to hide her surprise.

'So,' Richard said, leaning back in his chair, 'what *really* brings you here?'

'Well I was actually looking for an internet connection – my motel room doesn't have one.'

'No, Nicola. I mean, what's a city girl like you doing in the sticks?'

'I told you – the drought.'

Richard's raised eyebrows told Nicola he didn't believe her.

'What?' she snapped.

'Nothing. So, I know you got your career on track, what else has been going on – husband, boyfriend, kids?'

'Fiancé actually. Scott; we've been living together almost eight years now.'

'So when's the big day?'

'What? Oh…that… No plans as yet – too busy to even think about it,' she lied.

The truth was she'd spent plenty of time browsing bridal magazines and dreaming of her perfect day. She'd hoped Scott would make the first move – if he really loved her he would. But he hadn't said anything about it since brushing off her last enquiry twelve months ago.

At the time she'd accepted his, 'Honey, I'm really too busy with the research on this new listing – maybe when it's finished we can discuss it, but right now I don't have the headspace'. But since then at least three new listings and five major clients had diverted his attention. She'd given up dropping hints.

'Ah, so you're escaping.'

'What?' Nicola asked, genuinely confused.

'The trip out bush,' Richard said, flapping an arm.

Nicola had forgotten just how nosy Richard was – the trouble with time and a selective memory. Now she was finding him damn annoying.

'And you can talk – avoiding the wife and kids,' she snarled.

'Ouch, walked into that one,' he said, grinning. 'Anyway, this is different. Do you have any idea how rowdy kids are on polished boards with their...?'

'Tell me about your wife,' Nicola cut in. 'Though I've gotta say, I never really pictured you as a family man.'

He'd said as much to her all those years ago. For a few months there Nicola had thought she might have one day become the mother to his children. Their university days seemed to have been yesterday and another lifetime ago. They'd once been highly competitive students, each desperate to beat the other with grades and then into the cauldron of a cadetship.

Both had been equally passionate about becoming great journalists and spending their lives enlightening the public. And of course there'd also been the other sort of passion... She remembered how it ended.

Richard had decided he was leaving for London at the end of the year and didn't want the complication of a relationship. Why did men and women always seem to view relationships differently? According to him, theirs was only casual; the occasional bonk as reward for an assignment well done or other drunken celebration. Why hadn't she had the guts to tell him she had fallen in love?

Something tugged inside – regret, longing, guilt – Nicola couldn't identify it.

'What? Oh sorry, kids? No, wouldn't know,' she stumbled.

'Actually, we'd moved on – I was telling you about my wife, Karen,' Richard said, sounding annoyed. 'Where were you?' he added.

'Nowhere Else?' she said, an attempt at wit to change the subject.

Richard rolled his eyes at her.

What had he said about his wife? Was he happy? 'Sorry, I was miles away.'

'Your turn, what's this Scott fellow like?'

'Oh, you know,' she said, waving a dismissive arm. 'Tall, dark, and handsome.'

'So, what does he do for a crust that makes him too busy to make an honest woman of you?'

'I'll have you know I'm a very honest woman, thank you very much, and it has nothing to do with Scott.'

'It was just a figure of speech, Nicola. You know I'd never question your integrity.'

'Well, since you asked; he's a stockbroker. Very busy and quite wealthy as it happens,' she added defiantly.

'So he's too busy off making money to make you happy by putting another ring on your finger, huh?'

Nicola coloured slightly. 'I didn't say that.'

'You didn't have to. And being wealthy isn't just about money, Nicola.'

'Someone sounds like they're a little jealous.'

'And someone else sounds like they're in denial about gilded cage syndrome.'

'And when did you find time to do a Masters in psych? It might have escaped your attention, but I actually have a fabulous career all of my own. I'm hardly a candidate for the gilded cage. And anyway, we're not married,' she snapped.

'All right, I'm sorry. You're right; I had no right to judge,' Richard said, showing his palms in surrender.

'I'm sorry too, I've had a tough week. Then I get sent out to a dump called Nowhere Else, which really is like nowhere else, to do a story on dirt. I'm allergic to dust, flies and crappy motels. Don't know what I was thinking...'

Well actually, I do, but I'm not going to make a fool of myself by telling you.

'So where's the fabulous Scott right now?'

Nicola checked her gleaming gold watch.

'Probably sitting by the pool sipping something green and foamy with a pink umbrella sticking out of it.'

'Gone on holiday without you?'

'Conference – his fourth one this year,' Nicola said sulkily.

'Speaking of green,' Richard muttered.

Nicola shot him a scowl.

'Sounds like you miss him,' Richard corrected. 'That's good.'

'Yeah,' Nicola sighed, suspecting it was probably the resort and fun he was enjoying that she missed, not him. She shook the thought aside.

They lapsed into an awkward silence. Nicola was desperate to ask about London, but didn't want to look too interested, especially given his jibing about her relationship. Also, she didn't need to be reminded that she hadn't meant as much to Richard as he had to her.

Richard finally broke the spell. 'Well, you'd better get him to come out here for the weekend then.'

'Yeah, like that's ever going to happen.' She regretted the words as soon as they left her mouth. Damn it. How did he still have the power to loosen her tongue after all this time? She'd better be careful if she didn't want to lose her story to him – if she ever found one worthy of stealing…

'Why not?' Richard asked, breaking her train of thought.

'Firstly, he hates small planes…'

'Actually I can't believe you got on one – let alone a Piper Chieftain. I don't think I could have in your position.'

'…I didn't know – but that's another story. Secondly, the accommodation is appalling. And finally, there's nothing here that would interest him.'

'What about you? You're here.'

'Richard, you're sounding like a marriage counsellor, and quite frankly it doesn't suit you. Thanks for your concern but we're fine. Better than fine, perfect.'

Richard cleared his throat. 'Right, about this story of yours.'

Nicola sighed, relieved.

Chapter Eleven

Nicola returned to the pub's lounge bar, her head swimming with the threads of information gleaned from Richard. She sat with her notebook and pen, making notes of story ideas, jotting down questions, and doing abstract doodles. She just had to grab onto one – the right one – and find a decent story.

Did a long-term feud between two brothers over water have enough potential? It would be good to show the human effects of drought – how it tore families apart. Though, she had no idea if the feud Richard had mentioned was anywhere near that bad. She rolled her eyes at the title that sprang to mind: Water – Thicker than Blood. So damn clichéd.

She was now a Walkley winner, not just an ordinary journalist – there were certain expectations. She now had a lofty standard to uphold. God, the pressure. Nicola rubbed her hands over her face and through her hair.

What about government handouts for struggling farmers? She

picked up her pen again and made a note before scratching it out. No, that had been done plenty of times. And what was there to report anyway; that city people don't understand that farmers need the money to survive for the security of the nation – primary production apparently being the key.

Nicola thought that if a business was unviable it should follow the natural course and fold. It's what happened in every other industry.

No, she didn't feel impartial enough to delve into that story – especially from out here. Did they still practice tarring and feathering, or running people out of town with burning pitchforks? That would be one sure way to find out!

What about starving stock? No, it had been done to death. So to speak, she thought, cringing. Actually, she really wasn't looking forward to seeing bags of bones wandering around.

The suffering of people was one thing, but Nicola couldn't bear the sight of animals in distress. She looked away every time an ad about animal cruelty or live export came onto the television. She shook the thought aside. No, she would definitely not do a story covering animals.

Richard had mentioned a couple of road deaths that had the shadow of suicide hanging over them. No, definitely not. It was a worthy story, but she didn't want to risk getting pigeonholed as the 'death investigator'.

No, what she needed was something more upbeat, or at least something that didn't involve death – human or otherwise. She sat staring into space, tapping her gold metal pen against her top lip. Maybe the brothers' water feud thing was a goer. She wouldn't know until she started looking into it.

Suddenly Tiffany leapt into the chair next to her, startling her.

'So, how did you go?' Tiffany asked, helping herself to Nicola's open packet of salt and vinegar chips.

'Sorry?'

'Your *rendezvous* – with Richard at the paper.'

'Tiffany, I bumped into an old friend, end of story.'

'What? You *know* him, like from years ago? Ooh!'

Why was she being so damn defensive? The girl wasn't being nosy; was only being friendly. And she had been the one who'd directed her to Richard's office.

Damn Richard; it's his fault she was uptight. She'd let him get under her skin with his comments about her relationship with Scott. Where did he get off?

'Yes; we were friends at university,' she said. 'Got quite a shock to find him here, I can tell you. Last I knew he was off to London.'

'He *is* rather good looking. For an older guy.'

Nicola could remember being Tiffany's age; when finding love and being in love consumed every living moment; when every date was scrutinised for homemaking, income, and happily-ever-after potential. The kid was in for a rude shock.

'Not that it's any of your business, but he's married, and I'm engaged,' she said, waggling her left hand.

'Wow, what a gorgeous ring...'

'Thanks.' Nicola stared at the round cut one-point-five carat diamond solitaire set above a plain gold band. She loved it; it was modern, elegant, but not overly flashy. And Scott loved it too, but more because it glowed like a beacon signalling his place on the corporate ladder to all who saw it.

'Were you and Richard ever an item?'

'Not really,' Nicola said, still staring at her ring.

'Do you ever wonder?'

'Wonder what?'

'Wonder if you and Richard had got together?'

'No – you move on, meet other people.'

'Right,' Tiffany said thoughtfully, picking at her fingers.

'Are you having boy troubles, Tiffany?'

'Not really,' she said. 'Just a guy who's a mate.' She shrugged.

'Opposite sexes *can* be just friends, you know. You just have to know where you stand.'

Unlike Richard and me, Nicola thought. And of course she *had* wondered what if; had put her life on hold for two months while she did. What if she'd told him she loved him? What if she had pushed for commitment; asked him to stay? What then, what now?

Instead she'd pretended he was just a dear friend; taken him to the airport and waved him off. He'd got his big break – a cadetship at *The Times* in London. Sure she was a little jealous, but what had hurt the most was that he hadn't even once hinted she should go with him, try her luck in the big city as well.

After he left she cried for two weeks and vowed never to be hurt by a man again. He'd called twice; the first time he'd rambled for twenty minutes about how well it was all going, not bothering to even ask about her.

The second time he'd called, Nicola had stood beside the phone, shaking her head and silently begging Ruth to tell him she was out, which she had. Bless her. Although Ruth had always advocated that honesty was the best policy, she'd lied for her daughter. Nicola hadn't thought she'd do it; had hoped beyond hope, but hadn't expected it.

Later Ruth said she'd done it because she'd seen the pain this young man had caused. Whether or not he meant to was of no consequence; what mattered to her was Nicola.

They'd spent hours huddled together on the couch with Nicola weeping buckets of tears and Ruth stroking her daughter's hair and telling her she would get through this. She would be okay.

Finally Nicola had dragged herself out of her chocolate haze, feeling bloated and unattractive, and ventured into a newly opened bar.

When Scott appeared at her elbow she was queasy from the tequila shots curdling the kilo of rich, dark sin. She wanted to tell him to fuck off – no offence but she hated all men – but couldn't open her mouth in case the lethal mix erupted.

At the end of the night, after she'd given a slurred version of her pathetic life and current lament, he'd been the true gentleman and seen her home.

The next morning he'd called to check she was okay. Her heart had melted at his thoughtfulness. Tall, dark, handsome, intelligent, ambitious, *and* compassionate; was this just the most perfect guy on the planet?

He'd wined and dined her, taken her on long country drives in his entry level BMW. They'd spent days curled up on the couch in his shabby flat talking about their careers and ambitions; the cars they'd own, the places they'd travel.

On their eight month anniversary he took her on a picnic where he announced that he'd got a big promotion and a huge pay rise. He pointed across the park. 'See that warehouse conversion over there; that's going to be home.

'Come on, it's open for inspection,' he'd said, dragging her up and hurriedly collecting everything together. Nicola had allowed herself to be led across the park while wondering if he meant home for both of them or just him. She'd wandered through the apart-ment oohing and aahing.

It was lovely; bright, shiny and new, high ceilings, heaps of open space. She'd particularly admired the exposed timber beams above and around them. Nicola liked the idea that the old building had been given a new lease of life; apparently it had once been a butter factory. It was the sort of home Scott dreamt about; he'd told her often enough.

But while she'd nodded along, she'd been dreaming of some-thing entirely different. Her dream was of a more traditional-style home: solid stone, with large bullnose verandah and tessellated tiles, picket or wrought-iron fence out the front. She liked cosy; like plush feather-filled couches upholstered in Laura Ashley, handmade Persian rugs, and open fires.

'So, what do you think?' he'd said over and over during their walk through.

To which she'd nodded and said, 'It's great, brilliant, totally you.'

They'd left with Scott telling the real estate agent he'd be in touch and her still wondering if she was part of this grand plan of his.

They drove away. He was so excited; she loved seeing him like that. She really didn't want to burst his bubble by asking a silly practical question, but she needed to know.

'So are you buying it?'

'No darling, *we're* buying it. Cool huh?'

'Oh! Yes, very cool.' She'd returned his broad smile. He was so pleased with himself.

At that point she realised he didn't have a clue that she dreamed of something entirely different; that he'd never actually asked her.

'So you do love it, don't you? You're awfully quiet.'

'Yes, of course,' she'd said, patting his hand in the car. 'Just getting my head around it all.'

He'd taken her to an upmarket café to discuss it further. It seemed he'd done his sums, and hers. By putting in both their savings they'd have enough for twenty percent deposit and save a shitload in mortgage insurance. On their salaries, they could afford the repayments, he said. At the rate he was going, his salary would double in the next two years. And she had high hopes for her own career in television.

'Okay?'

Okay what exactly? Nicola wondered.

'So I tell the agent it's a done deal then, shall I?' He had his mobile out, finger poised over the keypad. He was a damn good catch, and she'd been very lucky to find him. So what if they liked different house styles? They were the ultimate upwardly mobile couple. She wasn't about to be a stick in the mud and risk upsetting him, or worse, losing him.

'Yep; let's do it,' she said, putting on a broad grin.

She'd been sad to tell Ruth and Paul that she'd be moving out. But she'd also been excited about setting up house together with Scott.

And, as the saying went, the rest was history. They got on well, they were well-off. All was good. But why did love and life have to become so *comfortable*; at what point had the soft fluttery feelings of expectation been replaced by the dull thud of normality?

Nicola sighed inwardly at Tiffany's flushed innocence. *Poor kid*, she thought, and wished she could save her the torment. But it was something millions before her had endured – survival of the fittest, or thinnest, she added wryly, picturing the line of stick thin up-and-coming presenters waiting to take her place at *Life and Times*.

'All right,' Tiffany said, defeated. 'Did Richard help with your story then?'

'I'm not sure yet. Do you know the McCardles?' Nicola asked, consulting her notes.

'Bert has a spring, Graeme wants water from it; been fighting for years – those McCardles?'

Nicola was wide-eyed with wonder.

'Let's just say "privacy" is a word they don't need to teach kids out here to spell,' Tiffany quipped.

'You're far too young to be so cynical,' Nicola laughed.

'Everyone knowing everything doesn't take long to be a huge pain in the arse – you'll see.'

'Just how long?' Nicola laughed.

'About a month – and that's being generous. I have to be; parents managing the pub makes me an honorary town ambassador. Welcome to Nowhere Else,' she added, tilting her head and offering a smile worthy of a toothpaste commercial.

They erupted into hearty laughter that took a few moments to die down.

'You're going to use Bert and Graeme to illustrate the desperation drought brings about – how people are pushed to the edge, right?'

'What are you, an undercover journalist?' Nicola moaned good-naturedly, a little miffed that her idea was so transparent.

'I wish,' Tiffany said.

'Really?'

'Yep, I'm waiting to hear if I've got into Adelaide Uni.'

'That's great.'

'Will be if I get in – I don't fancy another year behind the bar.'

'Want to kick-start your career by keeping me company? I'm going for a drive to check the lie of the land.'

'I'd love to but I'm meant to be on duty – till four,' Tiffany groaned. 'Actually, I'd better get cracking. I'll be chaperone when you visit yummy Richard next though,' she laughed.

'Tiffany!'

'What?'

'You know damn well what,' Nicola said, grinning at the cheeky kid who was smiling back like butter wouldn't melt in her mouth. Suddenly she realised she was starving; must be all that country air. She checked her watch: ten past twelve.

'Actually, before you go, could I order some lunch?'

'You check the menu and I'll get my notepad. Back in a sec,' Tiffany said, got up, and skipped away.

Nicola went over to where the menu was visible. Her mouth

watered at seeing the t-bone steak she'd been unable to order the night before.

She tried to convince herself that the chicken salad was all she needed, but thoughts of a thick juicy steak kept haunting her. She again cursed the country air; at this rate she'd be the size of a horse before she got back to the station and she really would be replaced with a thinner, younger model. *Oh well, one steak won't hurt; I'll diet tomorrow.*

'Right, what can I get you?' Tiffany said from behind the counter, pen poised.

'T-bone medium rare, mushroom sauce, chips and salad, thanks.'

'Ah, the steak you wanted last night, right? Better late than never, as they say.'

'I suppose so,' Nicola agreed with a grin. She really liked this young lass.

'And I'm sure it will be absolutely worth the wait. I'll put it on your room then, shall I?' Tiffany asked, suddenly all business again.

'That would be good. Thanks, Tiffany.'

'No worries. Call me Tiff. All my friends do,' she added, and disappeared.

Nicola returned to her table, looked around at the large empty room and wondered how there would be any profit in serving just one meal. Maybe everyone was eating in the front bar. Or perhaps country people ate nearer one o'clock and an onslaught would occur. Nicola really hoped she'd be on her way to Graeme McCardle's place by then.

She didn't feel like having people gawking at her, the obvious ring-in, like she'd experienced earlier on the main street. Sure, plenty of people had offered friendly nods and mutters of hello, and a few older men had even doffed their Akubras, but it had still been an uncomfortable experience having everyone's eyes on her.

What seemed only moments later, Tiffany was back carrying a steaming plate and small bowl of garden salad. Did no one else work in this place?

'Cracked pepper?' she asked, putting the plate and bowl down, and then taking a large pepper grinder out from under her arm.

'That'd be great thanks. Just a sprinkle.'

'Enjoy,' Tiffany said, after giving the wooden implement two half turns and a final shake.

'Thanks very much, Tiff. I'm sure I will; it looks fantastic,' Nicola said, beaming at Tiffany.

'Great,' Tiffany beamed back, and left.

She speared a cucumber slice with her fork while looking over her meal and wondering if Tiffany was also the establishment's chef. Surely not. But the girl had a sheen to her forehead and lip that she hadn't had earlier.

The t-bone steak covered nearly half the plate. The other half was piled with crispy looking golden chips.

Nicola was pleased the steak hadn't been put on top of the chips – like the trend seemed to be elsewhere. Didn't they know it made the chips soft? Crispy was the point of chips. *And these certainly are*, she thought with glee as she tried her second attempt to spear one.

Fingers crossed it's not overcooked, Nicola thought as she picked up her knife and pushed it through the thick mushroom gravy. She smiled as the knife made its way easily into the meat, then examined the first piece before putting it into her mouth. Perfect.

Chapter Twelve

Nicola eased the four-wheel-drive out of the hotel car park and into the main street.

It was a thoroughfare of two lanes each way, divided by a wide nature strip with sections of paving, lawn and trees at regular intervals. Three hours earlier, cars had been parked right the way along and people had been bustling about or standing, chatting in pairs or small groups. Now the whole length of the main shopping strip was deserted – not a car or person in sight.

Nicola braked from her crawl as a brown kelpie wandered onto the road in front of her. She was forced to a complete halt as the dog stopped in the middle of the road and snuffled at something invisible on the bitumen. She tapped her fingers lightly on the steering wheel and looked around her while she waited. It was actually quite a lovely clean and tidy town.

There were some modern buildings that weren't nearly as aesthetic as the row of shopfronts containing the *Nowhere Else Echo*, but nothing unkempt or particularly out of place.

On the side wall of the newsagent was a large mural painted in browns and creams, like a sepia photograph. It depicted a team of horses harnessed to a dray overflowing with hay. Men were dotted about in a paddock, preparing more hay for carting.

Nicola marvelled at the lack of graffiti. The painting was obviously not new, but there was not a hint of a stray mark on it – nor any sign of patching up.

'No worries, take your time,' Nicola said to the dog as it zigzagged back and forth on the road in front of her with its nose to the ground. Finally the dog moved off the road and the way was clear for her to continue.

She put the vehicle in gear and drove forward slowly towards the office of the *Nowhere Else Echo*. As she passed it, she thought about Richard.

Yes, he is yummy, she thought, replaying her conversation with Tiffany. *But I'm engaged to Scott.*

★★★

Nicola turned left at the RSL Hall and slowly headed west out of town past another group of shops, which she tried to take note of. But her mind was still on Richard. If only she'd let him keep in touch. What would he have told her if she'd taken that second call? And when had he got back to Australia? He hadn't said. And married with children! She wouldn't have believed it if he hadn't told her himself.

It doesn't matter; you got over him years ago, she told herself, forcing her attention back to her surroundings.

The tourist brochure said that Nowhere Else was on a large plain surrounded by thousands of acres of farmland that then gave way to a band of hills stretching like a horseshoe from the south, across the east, and around to the north. A large creek – nearer the size of a river given its status on the map – wound its way around the western boundary of the township and through the 'challenging but picturesque' golf course. *Hmm, maybe Scott would like a golfing weekend*, she thought as she crossed the bridge and passed a billboard.

It was a cold but sunny winter's day, and the cabin flickered with light and dark as she passed large pine trees lining the road. The trees ended at the Thank You For Visiting Nowhere Else sign, and the cabin was suddenly bathed in sunshine. The warmth was instant.

Residential housing became light industrial businesses – a couple of car and machinery yards, a petrol station, agricultural supplies business, and finally a grain and fodder store – and then the white lines stretched ahead on the grey bitumen road, dotted with trees on either side, and farmland as far as she could see.

Suddenly Nicola realised she hadn't taken notice of her trip meter. Fifteen kilometres from the RSL Hall, at a stand of large gum trees, she had to turn right onto a dirt road.

How far had she gone? Probably only a couple of kilometres, though it seemed like she'd been driving for ages.

There were lots of trees, but they were spindly, scrappy specimens in clusters, not large imposing trees you couldn't reach around. The ones she'd passed so far were what the brochure referred to as mallee scrub – apparently it made up the majority of the district on the flats. Taller timber only occurred naturally closer to the hills and the creek.

Looking in her rear vision mirror, Nicola noticed a car travelling very close behind her. She checked her speed. Shit, she was only doing fifty in an eighty zone.

She pulled off the road to let the vehicle pass. The driver gave her a wave. *That's nice and friendly*, she thought. She'd been fully expecting a rude gesture or even the honk of a horn.

Now that she wasn't driving, she took a closer look at the landscape. For the first time she noticed how parched everything was.

It was winter, but not a tinge of green was visible beneath the trees or in the gravel of the roadside.

If she didn't know better, she'd think it the middle of summer. The trees looked literally thirsty. Their limbs seemed to be hanging limply, not stretched out strong.

Checking that no one was coming, Nicola got out of the vehicle. Using the steel bullbar for support, she took off her running shoes and placed them on the bonnet, and then climbed on top of the vehicle.

As far as she could see was a patchwork of cleared paddocks with clusters of trees around their perimeter and at times within. Some of the land was quite dark and some was much lighter. She got her camera out and panned around as she snapped away.

Nicola wondered if the darker patches were where farmers had taken the risk and sown the land in the hope the opening rains would come before it was too late.

Richard had explained that it was very rare – almost unheard of – for nearly the whole district to not sow a crop. This season only a few had taken the punt – the wealthier farmers who could cover such a loss, and some older die-hard religious types who had themselves convinced that God would provide. Nicola wondered what it would take for them to accept that perhaps God didn't always come through.

Richard had also explained that if a decent amount of rain didn't fall in the next week or so the window of opportunity would close for the year. Nicola didn't like their chances. She wondered how they got up day after day and looked over this parched land, knowing they wouldn't be able to do anything with it until next year – and only then if some rain fell. And then it would probably flood; wasn't that what had happened in Queensland?

Nicola's attention was caught by movement to her right. She turned and watched as sheep, all hips and sunken flanks, sauntered in a wobbly trail towards where a farmer tossed hay from a slow-moving ute. A cloud of dust hung above the scene. She took more photos, despite the scene being a little far away for her compact's zoom.

Nicola's knowledge of the land was limited to say the least, but even she could sense the desperation of the man trying to save his stock.

Watching the farmer and his sheep, it seemed they were no longer just anonymous producers of wool and meat. Gathered around, gazing up at him they looked tame, like family pets. The slumped shoulders and slow laborious tossing showed the farmer's burden.

A lump formed in Nicola's throat. She swallowed hard, put her camera back in her pocket, got down off the vehicle, and put her shoes on.

Back in the vehicle she studied her map with Richard's notes scrawled on it, trying to rid herself of the sadness welling up inside her. She had to turn right at the gum trees where the sign said Gum Rise. Then five kilometres further she'd find an old milk can with a sign hanging above it that read G.T. & D.A. McCardle.

'Right,' she said, checking her mirrors and pulling back onto the road.

★★★

As she lashed the heavy chain back around the imposing steel double gates, Nicola was having second thoughts about dropping in unannounced. She told herself it was a measure to keep stock in and not visitors out. Country people were known for their friend-liness, right?

Negotiating the deeply corrugated track was slow going and after five minutes she was beginning to wonder if she'd somehow taken the wrong turn. She had almost decided to turn around when she went over a rise and saw her destination for the first time. Nicola gasped.

On a raised cleared area stood a majestic Edwardian-style lime-stone homestead; the mottled pale creams of the stonework and surrounding mortar, red brick quoins framing it, and the wide verandahs covered in bullnose corrugated iron.

Nicola inched the vehicle forward, its wheels crunching steadily over the white gravelled semi-circular driveway.

Clear fibreglass strips set between the corrugated iron allowed bright streaks of light to strike the front windows. Art nouveau-inspired leadlight gleamed, sending rippling shadows of green and ruby over the cranberry sill and down the pale uneven walls.

Parked under a tall, thick-waisted gum, Nicola took in the view that the occupants of the magnificent home enjoyed.

Miles of farmland stretched down below, flanked in the distance by a haze of sapphire blue mountains. An empty creek bed ran along the left side of the house and snaked its way towards the range; no doubt the reason for the home's elevated position.

Turning in her seat, Nicola could see the tips of gums waving skyward behind the house. For the first time she noticed the absence of sound – it was deathly silent.

Wasn't the country supposed to be teeming with bird life? A shiver tingled up her spine.

A movement in the corner of her eye caught Nicola's attention. She got out of the vehicle. A tall, lean man in khaki Yakka work wear and an Akubra strode around the far corner of the verandah. With an upturned pitchfork swinging by his side, the man cut an imposing figure.

'Can I help you?' His voice from the top step was deep, almost a growl. Nicola felt a slight knot of fear grip her; he didn't seem at all friendly. His eyes were hidden by the shade of his hat and the verandah, but his jaw looked tight and his squarish chin set in a defiant looking jut. He now clutched the handle of the fork in both hands in front of him. Nicola could see white knuckles.

She swallowed. What was the worst that could happen; this wasn't the Wild West. 'I'm looking for Graeme McCardle.'

'Who's asking?'

'My name is Nicola Harvey. I'm a journalist from *Life and Times*, Channel…'

'Suppose that layabout brother of mine sent you.'

'No, I was wondering if…'

'Not interested.'

'But…' Nicola persevered.

'You're trespassing – leave.'

'I need an expert opinion on the drought, and I thought you could help me with my investigation.'

'Well you thought wrong. You hard at hearing, missy?'

'You have a lovely house,' Nicola continued tentatively.

'Keeps us dry,' he snapped, not taking the bait. 'Not that that's a problem lately,' he added wistfully. 'And you can tell that no-hoper brother of mine to bugger off,' he snapped.

'I don't know your brother, Mister McCardle,' Nicola said.

'All the better. Now I've asked you nicely,' he said, and brought the end of the wooden handle down hard onto the verandah.

'Hardly,' Nicola muttered.

'Get off my property,' Graeme warned.

'Okay, I'm going,' Nicola said, holding up her palms as she retreated back into the vehicle. 'But if you change your mind,' she called hopefully from the window, 'I'm staying at the Nowhere Else Hotel Motel.'

'Not bloody likely. Interview the bludger over the hill,' Graeme boomed, waving the pitchfork at her, before turning on his heel.

★★★

'Far too scary,' she gasped, her heartbeat finally settling after she'd closed Graeme McCardle's gate and checked that she hadn't been followed.

Parked back on the main dirt road, Nicola wondered why he was so angry – the drought had been going on for a few years now and, according to Richard, the feud many more than that. *Just wait until I see Richard next*, she silently growled. *And Tiffany – 'friendly' my arse.*

'Well that's the end of that lead – back to square one,' she sighed. There was no way she was visiting the other brother, Bert, now.

She looked at the map for something to take her mind off her defeat. Almost instantly she spied Wattle Falls. The description read 'Small but picturesque waterfalls approximately twelve kilometres north of town'.

It was far too cold for a dip, but it would be nice to sit in the sun, taking in the scenery and fresh air while listening to the running water. Nicola had her indicator on and the car in gear, about to pull away when it occurred to her that drought equalled no water – there would be no waterfall.

She didn't fancy returning to her dreary motel room; if only she could find a find a nice little café-restaurant with an open fire and decent wine list. A glass of bold Barossa Valley shiraz would go down a treat.

But none of the brochures had shown anything classier than the pub, and no other towns nearby. 'There is nowhere else,' she said with a groan.

★★★

Nicola only realised she'd forgotten to take the turn back to town after she crossed the bitumen road onto more dirt. She'd given way, but had forgotten to turn left.

Oh well; she had a map, half a tank of fuel, and it wouldn't be dark for a few hours yet. The road before her stretched for miles ahead. According to the map there would be three cross-roads; any one of them would take her back to the main road that approached Nowhere Else from the south.

By the second intersection, Nicola was tired of the landscape that barely varied except for occasional clouds of dust in the distance; presumably from other vehicles. She took the left turn.

Ten minutes later she brought the vehicle to a halt beside an old fridge with the name B.A. McCardle handwritten across it in black paint. In her roundabout journey she hadn't realised she'd be anywhere near the other farm she'd originally intended to visit.

She shook her head with amusement at the resourcefulness, and remembered a documentary she'd once seen about what country people used for mailboxes. With journalistic instincts threatening to overwhelm her, she put the vehicle back in gear and continued on her way.

She'd already had an encounter with a pitchfork. That was enough for one day; she really wasn't up to being threatened with a shotgun.

'And it's a known fact most farmers own at least one firearm,' she said aloud, justifying her decision. If Bill wanted her to risk life and limb, he'd have to pay her a hell of a lot more than he did.

Melodramatic or not, she'd check with Richard just how dangerous these men were before venturing any further.

Nicola liked the idea of paying him another visit. Seeing him again after so long had stirred up something. She looked at her diamond ring above the steering wheel, twinkling and sending rainbow colours across the cabin.

In the months leading up to her second anniversary with Scott, more and more of her girlfriends had turned up to lunches and shopping expeditions glittering with newly accepted diamond solitaires. While they nattered excitedly about 'the four Cs' – colour, clarity, cut, and carat – Nicola had felt left behind.

She'd fully expected Scott to pop the question at their anniversary dinner. He hadn't, and she'd been so disappointed that she'd quietly cried herself to sleep. The next day, she discussed her options with Sandy, and it was agreed that the only course of action was to issue an ultimatum.

With her heart racing, she cornered him that evening after dinner when he was sitting on the couch with the second of his two customary glasses of red wine. She still remembered the entire conversation, which had started with a deep breath:

'Scott, are we ever going to get married?'

'Probably, haven't really thought about it.'

She wanted to yell at him to look at her and not the television.

'Well I have, and I've decided I want to get married. It's either that or I'm leaving.' There, she'd said it. Her tone had been a lot harder than she'd intended, but she'd finally got his attention.

Scott sat up straighter. 'If it means that much to you, of course we'll get married.'

'Oh, right, well, great. Thanks. Um, does that mean we're now engaged?'

'Guess so,' he'd said with a shrug, turning back to the television. Nicola had stared at him, feeling decidedly let down.

This was meant to be the second most exciting moment of her life. And there it was: 'If it means that much to you...' And he'd bloody well shrugged.

Where was the fairytale for her friends? She should at least phone Ruth and Paul, but instead she'd curled up with him to watch *NCIS*. She'd start telling people tomorrow.

And now, years later, time was running out. The mere thought of marrying Scott made her heart beat against her ribs – and not in a good way. No doubt about it; she, Nicola Harvey, was having second thoughts.

But it wasn't like she had to panic; the topic hadn't been raised in the past twelve months.

Chapter Thirteen

With eyes closed, Nicola focussed on the warmth of the milky coffee snaking its way through her body.

'That's better. God, it's freezing out there.'

'Well it is winter, Nicola. I can't believe you walked,' said Richard.

'It's only up the street, and I need the exercise after the lunch I had. Anyway, the less I drive that bloody tank of a four-wheel-drive, the better.'

'So, did you find either of the McCardle brothers?'

'Yes, and I have a bone to pick with you on that. You could have warned me they'd be hostile.'

'What happened?'

Nicola filled Richard in on her encounter with Graeme.

'So, is there something about all this you're not telling me?' She looked over the rim of her mug in anticipation.

'Well, I don't know a whole lot more than I told you, except that there was a woman involved.'

'Isn't there always.' Nicola rolled her eyes cynically.

Richard shrugged.

'Jeez, when will men learn that they can't…?'

'Can't what?'

'Nothing.' Nicola inspected the bottom of her cup.

'Seems we've touched a nerve with the lovely Nicola,' Richard teased, and playfully stroked her hand.

Nicola pulled her hand away.

Richard pouted and returned to his cup.

'I'm sorry, I just… Look, I really should be going,' she said, and leapt up.

'Don't go. I didn't mean to make you feel uncomfortable. I'll keep my hands to myself, promise,' he said with a grin.

Looking down, Nicola saw the warmth in his eyes – the boyish charm she'd loved, seemingly a lifetime ago. She sat again.

Richard started fidgeting with the corner of his desk mat.

Nicola felt the large room become stuffy. In the silence a clock ticked somewhere.

'Richard, what happened in London?' she asked quietly.

Silence.

She looked up to see Richard shake his head slowly, the brightness gone from his eyes.

A few more moments passed. Nicola was desperate to fill the silence, but the ball was in Richard's court.

'Right,' he said, suddenly changing the subject. 'Well, Beryl Roberts is your best bet for the nitty gritty of the McCardle thing. Monday morning might be best. No bowls. Just pop in, she loves the chance to spread some gossip. Third Street. I think she's twenty-four. Anyway, you can't miss her – she's the one with the lilac picket fence. Loves to be the centre of attention does our Beryl.'

Nicola marvelled at how country Richard sounded – nothing like the man she'd once known.

'Okay then.'

'I can call her if you like; give her a heads up?'

'Oh. Okay, if you think she'd prefer that.' What happened to 'just pop in'? She didn't like the feeling that he was muscling in on her story.

'Was there anything else?' Richard prompted after another short silence. His voice was less steady.

Nicola suddenly felt the desire to have someone, Richard, hold her, comfort her – from what she didn't know.

Seeing the dismay cross her face, Richard spoke softly. 'Are you okay?' he asked, again covering Nicola's hand.

Looking up, Nicola realised her eyes were glistening with the beginning of tears. She nodded her reply, afraid of choking on the lump forming in her throat, and rose again from her chair.

'Come on, it's me, Richard, who you could talk to about anything, remember?'

Nicola nearly snorted – she remembered all right, especially that she'd only ever told him what he wanted to hear. And now here they were – he a married man with kids aged six and eight and she, well…

Eight! That meant… Nicola's inquisitive mind was racing and her non-mathematical one struggling with the sums.

So caught up in her thoughts was she that Nicola didn't notice Richard wheel his chair closer. She wanted to pull back but there was nothing like having your hair stroked, and it wasn't something Scott regularly indulged her in.

Richard's face was so close she could smell the remnants of earthy bitter coffee on his breath. Then he was tilting her chin up ever so gently and she was forced to look into his eyes. They were what she'd first been attracted to all those years ago – his deep chocolate puppy-dog eyes and long dark curling lashes.

She willed her own emerald ones to not give her away and forced herself to hold his gaze. He was scanning her face, every smooth millimetre of it. Was he trying to commit it to memory or conjure up past feeling?

Suddenly Richard had his lips on hers. What! No, what the hell was he doing? Nicola's mind was whirling.

'No. Stop.' She pulled back from him.

Nicola stared at Richard, shocked and surprised.

'Shit, shit, shit,' he was mumbling over and over into the hands he was rubbing across his face. 'I'm so sorry. It just happened.'

Nicola found she enjoyed seeing Richard squirm. He had always been so in control.

'Well,' she teased, 'just like old times – marriage and kids doesn't seem to have affected your form.' She didn't care what she sounded like. There was nothing to lose. 'And they say,' she continued, 'everything changes when you have kids.' Her tone was icy and vengeful, but all the hurt she'd suppressed had suddenly flooded back.

'Hey, that's not fair,' Richard said, genuinely wounded. But Nicola was just getting started.

'I'll tell you what's not fair. Not fair is you dumping me because you don't want to be tied down. Well what the hell is having a kid only a matter of months later? London, pah! You lying bastard.'

Nicola leapt up suddenly, her chair falling to the ground. She stormed out, the shop bell tinkling behind her.

★★★

Only when she got back to her motel door did Nicola realise that in her haste she'd forgotten her handbag and key.

'Damn.' She slumped onto the cold concrete steps, put her head in her hands, and considered her options. Tiffany would have a spare but she wasn't about to face anyone looking like this.

Nicola drew circles in the gravel with her feet. She hadn't acted like this over a man since, well, since Richard — last time.

She could almost hear Ruth telling her — box of tissues in hand — that he 'just isn't worth it', that there were 'plenty more fish in the sea'. They'd spent a whole weekend on the couch, watching chick flicks and devouring block after block of chocolate.

Paul had stayed in his shed out the back, avoiding what he termed 'women's stuff'. Nicola loved that his only involvement was a sympathetic smile or pat on her shoulder. Ruth would have shared all the gory details with him in bed at night; they had that sort of close relationship. Nicola didn't mind; she liked the idea that her dad knew and that he was there if she needed him.

They'd only been a small family, but it had been a good one. They'd had their ups and downs like any family, but they had always dealt with them together — usually through long discussions at the kitchen table. She smiled sadly. God, she still missed them so much.

Nicola looked up at the sound of crunching gravel in front of her. The sad smile still on her face froze.

'Thought you might be needing this,' Richard said, swinging her handbag from his shoulder.

Nicola couldn't help laughing. 'But daaarling, the pink one would be much more you,' she drawled.

'Truce?'

'Truce,' Nicola said meekly, accepting his hand then the handbag. 'Care for a tour of my stunning abode?' she added, after finding her keys and throwing the door open theatrically.

'Honoured,' Richard said, bowing.

'Er, bathroom over there — all the glitz and glamour of the seventies. And well, as you can see, this is bedroom, kitchen, office and lounge — we don't like to have to walk too far.'

'Comfy bed,' Richard said, throwing himself back onto it.

'If you like springs in your back,' Nicola mumbled. Suddenly an embarrassed teenager all over again, she blushed violently.

'Right, coffee?' She quickly turned her back to the bed.

'No thanks.'

Nicola was startled by Richard's whisper close to her ear. She held on tight to the bench with both of her trembling hands.

Then Richard's arms were around her, guiding her back to the bed, gently pushing her into a sitting position.

'It seems we need to talk,' he said.

'It's okay. I just overreacted.'

'Well I want to talk to you.'

Another thing she'd loved about him – his ability to be the adult in the relationship when it counted. Not a bossy, grumpy stick-in-the-mud like Scott, but calm and sensible.

And just what was this comparison with Scott all about? Richard was off limits and Scott? Scott was, well, off – if she was being totally honest with herself, which she wasn't. No, Scott was Scott, her partner whom she loved; end of story.

'Okay then, speak.' Nicola inched away slightly to put a more respectable distance between them.

'Well…um…I'm afraid back at uni I took the term "casual relationship" a little too literally.'

'And?'

'And I got Karen, now my wife, pregnant.'

'Oh. Right.'

'I was being honest about not wanting to be tied down, but…'

'But?' Nicola knew it was cruel but she wanted him to squirm.

'…she told her father and he insisted we get married. Living close to family was important to her, so here we are,' he added with a shrug.

'But I saw you off at the airport, and you rang – were you even in London?'

'Yes, and had to turn around a week later and come straight back. I can't tell you how embarrassing... And I *did* try to tell you.'

'But you were so careful – paranoid – with me, why not with her?' Nicola spat.

'I was...'

'Well, obviously not bloody careful enough.'

'What can I say?' He shrugged. 'Why are you so upset, anyway?'

She took a deep breath. *May as well say it.* 'Has it ever occurred to you I might have been in love with you?'

'Um, no...you never said.'

'Jesus, you men... For the record, Richard, you made your feelings, or lack of, quite clear. How could I have? Look, there's no point. It's all irrelevant now.'

'Yes, I suppose it is.'

'You should be getting back to your family.'

'You're probably right.' Richard got up. Turning at the door, he looked back. 'Look, Nic. I'm sorry, I really am.'

Nicola rolled face down on the bed. She expected the tears to flow but none came. Suddenly she wasn't sure how she felt.

Chapter Fourteen

On Sunday morning Nicola woke feeling a little disoriented. Where was she? Ah, that's right; a dumpy little motel room in a tiny town in the middle of nowhere. She groaned. No lingering over a sumptuous café feast with friends this morning. All that awaited her was another average breakfast and bad coffee.

She rolled over and tried to go back to sleep. But the twenty-year-old bedsprings poking her in the back weren't going to let her, and neither were the birds outside. What right did they have to be chirping like that, anyway? *Shut up! Damn cheery, noisy little birds. Go away!*

Nicola checked her Cartier. Eight o'clock.

'How uncivilised,' she groaned, and threw herself back onto the pillow with a thump.

Suddenly the twittering birdsong was drowned out by an urgent squawking from something clearly much larger.

Nicola leapt out of bed, intent on both seeing what the

commotion was and lending assistance. She imagined one of the smaller birds being pecked to death in the courtyard by a group of magpies or some other species. As much as she hadn't enjoyed their joyous announcement of the morning, it didn't mean she wished them dead.

Pushing aside the drapes, she peered out at the magnificent eucalypt, the only sign of nature within the large expanse of concrete courtyard. The pale grey trunk was almost iridescent in the sunlight striking across it in strips.

Nicola's mouth opened in awe. On the straight, sprawling branches sat hundreds of galahs. The pale pink and grey was like a patchwork quilt thrown over the side of the tree. Large numbers of the birds came and went, giving the quilt a rippling, shimmering effect.

Suddenly a loud deep metal clanging sound rang out.

As she watched, Nicola was both annoyed and amused to see Tiffany banging two frypans together as she strode from the car park into the courtyard and towards the tree. With a flutter of feathers, the quilt rose up and away from the blue green foliage, and was out of sight within moments.

Nicola stepped back from the window and went into the tiny bathroom. What the hell was the girl thinking, shattering her peaceful morning like that?

She stood under a cascade of steaming shower water. Impossible to ignore was the white plaque riveted to the wall, asking guests to conserve water. She sighed, reluctantly turned off the water, and threw the plastic curtain aside.

★★★

Nicola scowled at her cup of coffee and looked with disinterest at her toast. She could have ordered the bacon and eggs and had at least half her favourite Sunday morning treat, but no one did it as well as her favourite café, and she wasn't prepared to take the chance. Anyway, the ambience and décor was as important as the food. Her favourite day was definitely ruined.

Seeing Tiffany bustling about the dining area made her even crankier. When she started to hum while noisily tidying the crockery and cutlery, Nicola wanted to bang the girl's head against the wall, and then her own.

'Ever heard of Sunday sleep-in?'

'Sorry?'

'Those birds were happy until you disturbed them – and so was I,' Nicola said sulkily.

'Oh shit, sorry.' Tiffany put her hand to her mouth and blushed. 'I forgot you were here – you were the only one booked in last night.'

I'll bet, Nicola thought, wondering if the girl was taking the piss.

'I'm usually up at six. Tend to forget that some people like to waste the day lolling about in bed.'

Nicola wanted to tell her that 8 a.m. was hardly lolling about, and ask where she'd left her 'give the customer what they want' attitude.

'So what's with the pots and pans?'

'The galahs are ruining the tree and we're not allowed to shoot the bastards.' Tiffany shrugged and continued lining up rows of cups and saucers. 'God knows why, but they're protected,' she added, coming over and laying a folded napkin next to Nicola.

'Well I think they're pretty,' Nicola stated.

'Well you haven't seen the damage they do,' Tiffany replied, matching Nicola's huffy tone. 'And it's not just the shitting on the concrete – it's only the smokers who brave the courtyard these days. But they're killing the trees by pulling off all the new shoots. They don't even eat them; just seem to pick them off and drop them for entertainment.

'Galahs mainly eat seeds and grasses on the ground. So when there *is* a bit of rain and farmers take a punt and sow a crop, they pick the grain out almost as quickly as it goes in the ground. They're a bloody pain in the arse.'

★★★

Back in her room, Nicola threw herself face down on the still unmade bed. Now what the hell was she supposed to do? She had the whole day to fill. She'd been sure there would at least be a market full of tacky tea cosies and patchwork quilts to rummage through.

She couldn't even indulge in a good old-fashioned chocolate or chip binge; wouldn't have believed the supermarket wasn't open if she hadn't seen it for herself.

She'd ventured out after breakfast, sceptical about Tiffany's assurances that shops weren't open on a Sunday – what was leisure if it wasn't wandering the shops?

Even worse than Tiffany being right was the window-shopping – a bloody disaster, to put it mildly. Nicola had marched boldly up the two shopping strips on the map – the main street and then around the corner. She was resigned to a purely reconnaissance mission, but buoyed at the hopeful prospect of never-before-seen one-offs from designers yet to burn under the bright lights of the city.

She'd found the window of the only boutique – which catered for both women and children – even less interesting than the strategically arranged boxes of spare parts and seat covers back at the auto shop.

Apparently the General Trader made up any shortfall in the town; the window was a mishmash of faded boxes of toys, outdated electrical products, sporting apparel and country music CDs.

Judging by the varying depths of fine red brick-coloured dust, the display had been added to over years, possibly decades.

'Quaint.' Nicola scanned the precarious piles for any sign of vinyl record sleeves to indicate just how far back this collection went.

Walking the strip had taken a grand total of twenty-three minutes – and only that long because of her legs' leaden reaction to her growing disappointment.

Wandering back to the motel, Nicola imagined a town meeting where representatives of all the stores went through their inventories to make sure no one was doubling up.

Damn not having an internet connection. At least then she could have gone shopping – online – and the day wouldn't be a complete waste. Which reminded her: she hadn't checked her email or Facebook since leaving Adelaide.

Nicola could kill hours checking the online news, instant messaging, and trawling through the lives of friends and acquaintances – and often did. Whole days could pass unnoticed, especially on weekends. And now, when she had a whole heap of time that needed passing, what did she have? No bloody internet connection. Oh, to be connected to the outside world once again.

Sighing, Nicola rolled onto her side and found herself staring at the phone.

'Sandy, it's me, Nicola.'

'And how's our pampered little puss today?'

'Um, it's…'

'Taking a moment between facial and manicure, are we?'

'Not exactly.'

'Day spa not as grand as we were expecting, eh?'

'Actually there isn't one,' Nicola said sheepishly.

'Well, chin up, the weather here is positively awful. We're at Cibo and having to sit inside – can you imagine? And the eggs are rock hard.'

'Um…Sandy?'

'Yes sweetie, what is it? Hang on a sec. Bob, can you tell that awful little man I'm still waiting for my OJ. Now, Nicola, you were saying?'

Nicola bit her bottom lip hard, her eyes awash with unshed tears.

'Sandy, it's just horrible,' she gushed.

'What is? Has Scott upset you? Needs a kick up the arse if he has.'

'No. Well, not really. This place is a dump and I want to go home,' Nicola whined.

'It's just the body releasing tension. You'll be fine after a good cry. Then pop along and get a shiatsu.'

'Can't,' Nicola groaned.

'Oh well, a standard massage will be better than nothing.'

'Nothing, there *is* nothing here: no day spa, no shops, no B&B, nothing!'

'Well you're obviously staying somewhere,' Sandy said indignantly. 'Now let's just calm down. It can't be all that bad.'

'Believe me, it is,' Nicola groaned.

'Must be all the excitement catching up on you − a sign you need a break. Enjoy it while you can… Oh, I've got another call coming in. Can you hold? Back in a tick.'

Nicola's ear was filled with the tinny pinging of synthesised classical music. She brought her knees up to her chest and laid her head in the crook of her elbow.

'Sorry to keep you.' Sandy's voice was a roar after the gently soothing music. 'That was Joanna − since you're away thought I'd keep an eye on her. Apparently Versace is having a one day sale. So I really have to run. My advice? Retail therapy, darling. Works every time.'

'Okay, bye. Have fun,' Nicola said, forcing herself to sound bright. Sandy was probably right − she always was.

She put the phone back in its cradle and wiped her nose. She knew it was ridiculous to be jealous of Sandy spending time with Joanna, but it didn't help.

What was even worse was that she couldn't call Joanna for a whine; Joanna who had been on the phone in tears every day of the past few months seeking Nicola's advice and sympathy. Nicola pouted and slammed her fists into the bed.

Get a grip – you are an independent, successful, attractive woman.

'Right, getting a grip, getting a grip,' she mumbled as she straightened the bed. She checked her watch. It was only eleven; too early for lunch. Not that she needed yet another steak and chips. If only the bakery was open.

But it wasn't, nothing was. She slammed her fists into her thighs again, then gasped at the pain and fought back a new rush of tears.

Looking back at the phone, she desperately wanted to ring Bill and give him a piece of her mind, then beg him to let her come home.

She'd had her teeth firmly on the wrong end of the stick when she agreed to this. Come to think of it, Bill had looked a little surprised that she'd been so keen.

Nicola allowed herself a smile. Quite funny when you thought about it, but there was no way she was going to give herself up to Bill – the office would roar with laughter for weeks.

Walkley or not, deep down she knew that if she complained it would be detrimental to her career. Bill didn't have *all* the power; even he wouldn't be able to explain away the airfares.

She'd seen it numerous times – presenters given the flick the instant they got too feisty. There was no shortage of wannabes waiting in the wings, desperate for the glamour jobs.

Yep, one false move and she would be sweating under a bear suit on some kids' program.

Chapter Fifteen

Checking street numbers wasn't necessary; Beryl Roberts' gleaming periwinkle blue picket fence stood out brightly against dark green rose foliage and the predominantly brick and plain white fences in the street.

Hardly 'lilac', Nicola mused. *Couldn't men get anything right?*

The blooms of white, yellow and pink poking out between the slats were breathtaking, like something out of *Better Homes and Gardens*.

'This must be it. And I've been spotted,' she muttered, noticing the edge of a curtain ripple slightly and a shadow move across one of the windows of the double-fronted stone home.

A grumbling stomach reminded Nicola that she was starving – she'd chosen to avoid the motel breakfast. She hoped the myth about country hospitality was true – that she'd be served cream cakes and scones. Though given it was the twenty-first century and not nineteen-sixty-four, there was little likelihood.

Nonetheless, an image planted itself in her mind – piles of home-made sweet and savoury delicacies like the photos in Ruth's old *Women's Weekly* entertaining books; the apron-clad lady of the house standing proudly behind.

'Can't blame a girl for dreaming,' she groaned, getting out of the vehicle.

Nicola crossed her fingers and hoped Beryl Roberts would turn out to be her first decent lead. She really didn't relish having her ear chewed for hours over the price of eggs during the nineteen-thirties depression.

Not that there is much else to do around here, she thought, as she strode up the herringbone red brick path.

She was way off the mark: the woman who answered the door was, yes, in a nice floral dress, delicate pink cardigan, and broad-brimmed cream hat with a row of silk roses. Under the hat was a round face – tanned and weathered but not overly lined. On the pudgy cheeks sat a pair of large old-fashioned spectacles, magnifying bright blue, slightly watery eyes. A chain draped from their thin, pale plastic arms and went around her neck.

Nicola tried to pick her age and came up with anywhere from sixty to ninety. But instincts told her there was something a little odd about Beryl Roberts.

'Welcome. Come on in,' Beryl gushed, without even asking her name or what her business was.

In the hall she peered around Nicola as if looking for something.

'Don't you need sound people, cameras and things?' She poked at her hair.

'Sorry?'

'Cameras – for the TV program.'

'Oh…well no, I…'

Just what had Richard told her? Nicola fought the urge to laugh when she realised why Beryl was in her Sunday best.

'That'll come later. I'm still in the research phase,' she explained.

'Oh. Right. May as well get rid of this ridiculous hat then,' Beryl said, throwing the floral arrangement onto the nearby hallstand. 'Thought if I was going to be on the television I'd better at least look half-decent,' she chuckled, giving Nicola's arm a hearty slap and leading the way down the hall.

In the kitchen Nicola stood awkwardly while Beryl shouted at a man in a checked flannel shirt, apparently her husband, to get up and be sociable.

The man leapt to attention, mumbled some sort of apology – Nicola wasn't sure to whom – and shook her hand.

'Stanley, Nicola's a *journalist*, here to do some *research*,' Beryl said proudly. 'Just excuse me for a sec,' she said, and left the room.

Stan was nearly a whole foot shorter than his wife, but Nicola suspected years of stooping to dodge Beryl's words rather than genes.

'So, Mister Roberts, are you a retired farmer?' Nicola asked, trying to ease the awkward silence.

'Call me Stan. Just what exactly are you researching? And what program did you say you were from?'

'*Life and Times* – current affairs. I'm here to do a story on the drought.'

'Oh, so why are you talking to us – er, Beryl?'

'Background really. Richard from the paper said she knows most people around here.'

'Don't we all – it's that kind of place.'

'So you're not from around here?'

'Well that depends. I've lived here going on forty years, but that doesn't qualify you to say you're *from* here. For that you need to be at least third generation, or else be handy with a football or cricket bat,' he said with a laugh.

'But you've come to the right place; Beryl does indeed know most of what goes on around here.'

'Great. So what did you do before you retired?'

'I used to run the local fuel depot until ten years ago.'

'Stanley, don't badger,' Beryl crowed from the doorway.

Nicola turned. Beryl had changed into navy slacks, a burgundy and white striped polo, and navy canvas shoes. Yep, Nicola thought, the woman looked a lot more comfortable in pants.

'Well I'll leave you ladies to it then,' Stan shrugged, and made to leave.

'You can at least be sociable for two minutes and have a cuppa – it's not often we have a celebrity in our midst, Stan.'

'Right then.' Stan sat back in his chair like a scolded child.

'The kettle, Stan. We'll need the kettle on if we're to have a cuppa.'

'Right you are then.' Stan again leapt up.

'Now you just sit yourself down while I find us some cake and bikkies,' she said, touching Nicola's arm.

'There's really no need to go to any trouble,' Nicola offered.

'No trouble. You just sit.'

Nicola sat on the edge of a chair, wary of making any false moves. How would Scott react to such treatment? Maybe she should try it.

She watched open-mouthed as Beryl strode back and forth from another room, bringing a large platter of steaming savoury pastries, an oblong plate of dainty ribbon sandwiches, a cloth-lined basket of dusty scones, a tray with butter, jam and cream, and finally a tiered trio of plates with an assortment of sweet, cream-filled delicacies.

Stan looked on with relative disinterest.

'Wow, this is amazing – are you inviting the rest of the town?' Nicola chuckled nervously.

'Well, I thought since you're staying at the pub you might enjoy some old fashioned fare – they're lovely people but, really, it's hardly like home cooking.'

And this is? Nicola thought, staring in awe at the spread before her. 'This is wonderful, Beryl, thank you,' she said, tucking into a sausage roll.

★★★

They passed a pleasant morning talking about the weather and who'd won what at the recent local show; Beryl had taken first prize for her apricot jam and chutney, and Stan for his tomatoes and zucchinis.

Nicola thought the judges would be hard pressed to find a better cream puff than the one she'd just finished, and was about to say so when Beryl changed the topic to her job. She was very apologetic about never having seen *Life and Times* – they watched the ABC news instead – and promised to watch it that evening.

'What is it exactly you wanted to know?' she asked suddenly.

'Oh,' Nicola started, reminded she was actually there for a reason other than consuming cups of tea and devouring a mountain of food.

'Well, Richard at the *Echo* suggested the McCardle brothers' feud might make an interesting story to show the human side of the drought. Apart from…'

'Human all right, but nothing to do with drought,' Beryl snorted.

'I beg your pardon?' Nicola frowned.

The old lady put a finger to her lip and looked thoughtfully at the ceiling.

'Well,' she began after a few moments' silence. 'I reckon it all started back in… No, it must have been during the war… Sorry, I'm just trying to remember.

'People round here seem to think it all began when Bert came back – from Vietnam that was – but I know different.' Beryl tapped her nose conspiringly.

'It was sixty-nine – March. I remember because…' Beryl paused, lost in her memories.

Nicola smiled back patiently, and resigned herself to spending the rest of the afternoon.

'…Right, sorry, um, Bert McCardle. Well, he was off doing his duty and Graeme was home with his old man, Arthur, running the farm. He tried to enlist but they found something wrong; weak heart, flat feet, or something, can't remember what.

'There'd always been this rivalry between them – from Graeme's side. For some reason he always seemed to have to prove he was better than Bert, like having the prettier girlfriend, better car – usual stuff.

'If Bert somehow managed, in Graeme's eye, to be getting the upper hand, he'd do his level best to even the score. Half the time I don't think Bert even noticed. He doesn't much care what anyone thinks – never has, never will.'

Nicola shifted in her chair, hoping to prompt Beryl back to the point.

'Bert left just after he'd married Janet Avery – only daughter of local Catholic aristocracy.

'Things sure would have been different if Vietnam, Graeme and her need for *entertainment* in the interim hadn't got in the way, if you know what I mean.' Beryl's eyebrows were raised with disapproval.

'I know she was young and all, but being married to one brother and seeing another on the side while he was away fighting in a war is not what I would call acting like a lady. And Graeme had been their best man, for goodness sake. But it was free love and all that nonsense back then.'

Nicola wondered if Beryl was miffed because she'd missed out on a bit of free loving herself. Was there any point to all this?

'Poor Bert, he was a changed man when he got back. He was never quick but after Vietnam…

'The whole town knew the truth except Bert. But do you think anyone spoke up? Oh no.'

Nicola wanted to ask Beryl why she didn't speak out, but from what she was hearing, it wouldn't be worth getting her off-side.

Another thing troubled her: how much of this was being said out of spite? The woman had to have a vested interest, but what? Nicola realised she'd have to be careful where she let her loyalties lie.

'…Waste of time that marriage – only lasted about six years – after all the catering we bowls ladies did. She had the best spread money could buy, did little Miss Avery.'

Six years sounds like a decent marriage by today's standards, Nicola thought ruefully. Surely she's not bitter over a few rock buns.

'Sure, Bert was suffering the odd nightmare, but when you say "I do" to "in sickness and in health", that's what you do. Not leave the poor man.

'So what if he wasn't quite right in the head? Not a nasty bone in his body. But what did she do? Just ups and disappears.'

'Oh,' Nicola cut in, unable to hide her surprise. 'She didn't leave him for Graeme then?'

'No. Graeme eventually married Dorothy Jacobs. As I said, Janet just upped and left town. Don't know where she went.

'Her parents were so ashamed – probably disowned her – they even stopped going to church. Some say the hall project was scrapped because of Paul's withdrawal. Bloody Catholics. Bunch of hypocritical…'

'Beryl, this young lass probably isn't interested in your religious views,' Stan interrupted. 'She wants to know…'

'Well it's true, Stanley. They're the first to bellyache about people's lost faith, but where do you find the soul of some poor violated choirboy who's…'

'Beryl!' Stan fairly shouted.

'Um, Beryl,' Nicola said, trying to prevent a row. 'You were saying Janet left. Didn't Graeme and Bert then patch things up? And why didn't Bert go after her?' *Why didn't Graeme*, she wondered.

'Reckon he thought she was too spoilt to get in and help on the farm. Also, it was around the time Arthur split up the holding. Since the boys weren't getting along I guess he figured it was the only way.

'Well, that's all I know,' Beryl stated suddenly. 'Janet left – hasn't set foot in town since, far as I know – and Bert still refuses to give Graeme access to his water. Fair enough too!'

Nicola stared at Beryl, wondering what the hell any of this had to do with the drought. Hadn't Richard briefed her? She was back at square one.

Bill had given her free rein, but she knew he wouldn't see an ancient love triangle as relevant.

★★★

Back in the four-wheel-drive, Nicola heaved an exhausted sigh. She wondered what, if anything, of what Beryl told her would be useful for a story on the drought.

On the seat next to her was a silver foil package that Beryl had insistently pressed into her hands at the door. Well, at least she would be spared another greasy pub meal.

'Small mercies, Nicola, small mercies,' she groaned, and turned the key.

Chapter Sixteen

Nicola let the vehicle idle at the old fridge mailbox while she gathered her thoughts. She wasn't sure she was doing the right thing visiting Bert McCardle unannounced – hopefully Beryl was right about him being a 'gentle soul'.

Releasing the handbrake, she followed the well-worn track to a crooked weathered grey picket fence that gave only a hint it was once painted white. Behind it were the skeletons of long-dead garden plants.

Beyond the fence, a path of large square concrete pavers ended at a small porch covering three steps with railing. Where the steps ended was a plain brown door that was powdery with age.

Nicola turned off the ignition and the diesel engine shuddered as it died.

The house itself was a plain, square dwelling rendered in grey concrete except at the edges and around the door and windows. Nineteen thirties or forties, she surmised.

The addition of verandahs might make it considerably more attractive; the bald facings would make it a hot box in summer. Maybe the front and sides she couldn't see were more attractive.

It was obvious that money was tight, and that whatever Bert had, he didn't spend it on his house. Everything she saw was in stark contrast to his brother Graeme's. Was it the lack of a woman's presence that made the difference? Perhaps out here.

At home it wouldn't matter if she was sharing the house with Scott or not; there was no way he'd ever let standards slip. She shook the thoughts aside – she'd try to call him when she got back – and got out of the vehicle.

Next to the house was an open car shed in matching concrete render. It was empty. Fifty metres away was another shed, larger, made of dark corrugated iron. It had four sliding iron doors – two were open.

Nicola turned to take in the wider view, and continued to look for signs of activity.

In a nearby paddock, a flock of sheep attacked a pile of hay in a frenzy of bleating and frolicking. Otherwise the place was eerily quiet. She pulled her coat closer, telling herself it was the cold making her shiver.

She really should have rung ahead.

★★★

She turned quickly, too quickly, towards the crunch of heavy foot-steps on gravel. A stocky man, dressed in overalls over a faded navy shirt and wearing a floppy towelling hat, sauntered towards her.

'Can I help you?'

'No. Oh…I'm sorry, I…'

'Sorry, didn't mean to startle you.'

Nicola felt caught out. She should have knocked on his door, but here she was, nosing about. Suddenly she had no idea what to say.

'Ah, you're Nicola Harvey, aren't you? The journalist from TV,' he said, pointing at her with a wavering finger.

'Yes, I…' Nicola didn't like how close he was standing.

'Bert McCardle,' the man said, grinning broadly and offering his hand.

Nicola found herself nodding, more a reaction to the pumping he was giving her arm than anything else.

'Damn cold out here; that wind's icy. Come in and have a cuppa.' Bert strode off toward the house without waiting. He turned at the concrete step. 'Come on. I won't bite, you know.'

He slipped his boots off and put them on the step, and Nicola was impressed at how agile he seemed. Was she expected to do the same? She hoped not; it would take forever to squish her jeans back down into her boots again, and she wasn't about to do that with a complete stranger looking on. Anyway, she hadn't been wandering around in sheep poo or grass, or grease, or whatever farmers wandered around in.

Nicola hesitated before pressing the remote to lock the vehicle and following him.

The wooden screen door slapped shut and Nicola jumped. As she did, the odour of years of burnt tobacco assaulted her nose. Bert was a smoker. Heavy, Nicola realised, as her eyes began to water. God she hoped she wouldn't start sneezing. She hadn't taken an antihistamine tablet.

Actually, she hadn't needed one since she'd been here. That was weird. Here she was in all this dust and pollen, and she hadn't so much as had a sniffle or a puffy eye.

Inside was dark. All she could make out was the shadowy bulk of a hallstand draped with layers of coats and hats.

Even the stale air wasn't enough to conceal the sour earthiness of rising damp.

They passed a closed door to the right, and then a few strides more up a hall, they turned right into the kitchen. It was a simple square space lined with avocado green cupboards. An upright oven, fridge – barely more modern than the mailbox – and a wooden pedestal table and six matching red vinyl and chrome chairs helped break up the expanse of brown and beige geometric lino.

Nicola watched the blue-grey haze of tobacco smoke sweep in around them while pretending not to notice Bert remove a scattering of chipped crockery, then crumbs, to the sink.

She shivered and pulled her coat tighter. It wasn't much warmer in here than outside.

'Sorry about the cold; I've been out all day. I'll put the heater on,' he said, and reached under a chair. Instantly there was a whirring and Nicola could feel warm air beginning to swirl around her. While Bert filled the kettle and got fresh cups out of the cupboard near the sink, she was drawn to the blue heeler snoozing in the old fireplace at the far side of the kitchen.

'Isn't he lovely?' she cooed, bending down. 'Mind if I give him a pat?'

'Not if he doesn't. Too damn lazy to bite. Aren't you, mate?' Bert knelt down next to Nicola and ruffled the dog's ears. 'Name's Jerry – only arrived last week. Certainly made himself at home, hasn't he? Never had a dog inside before; it's not the done thing. But this bloke sort of insisted.'

'Hello there,' Nicola said, patting the dog. Its tail slapped hard against the lino.

'Lost the old bloke the other week,' Bert continued. 'When you get to my age you like a bit of company, but not the energy of a pup. This one belonged to the neighbours. With no sheep to work he's just another mouth they can't afford to feed. Not that I can really. But we muddle along, don't we Jerry?' Bert smiled down at the dog.

Nicola ran her fingers through Jerry's thick short fur. She'd always loved dogs, but with her lifestyle had thought it selfish to own one. But she could definitely get used to the adoring expression beaming back at her. Unconditional love; now that'd be nice.

An image of her sleek home with its non-existent backyard formed in her mind, a glimpse of herself in the park, and then, oh-my-God no! Nicola could see herself, nose wrinkled, right hand outstretched with little black plastic bag attached, reaching for a warm, steaming pile of newly dumped dog poo.

Perhaps when I'm on a couple of acres, she thought. *Where did that come from?* She hated the country.

The screaming of the kettle brought her back to reality and she withdrew her hand and stood up, much to Jerry's apparent dismay.

'Yeah, the last one hung himself on a fence and broke a leg. Poor old bugger. Hardest time I've ever had getting the gun out.'

What? He shot his dog! Nicola actually had to force herself to shut her mouth. He had just told her, regretfully yes, but quite casually, that he'd shot his own dog. She couldn't believe it.

'If he hadn't looked away at the last minute…' Bert shook his head sadly. 'I'll never forget him; one of the best dogs I ever had. Poor old Timmy.'

Nicola looked away when she noticed a couple of glistening spots on his cheeks. Her own heart was clamping. Out of the corner of her eye she saw Bert swiping roughly at his face.

'No offence, Jerry; you're a good dog too,' he said, bending down and ruffling the dog at the hearth. 'We'll be all right, won't we mate?' The dog lifted its head and gave Bert's hand a couple of licks. 'Good boy,' he added, gave the dog a hefty pat, and stood back up straight again.

Looking at Nicola he said, 'I don't think you ever get used to seeing death, no matter how much of it you've seen over the years. And I've seen more than my fair share, I reckon.'

'I'm sure,' was all Nicola could manage. She didn't mean to

sound so dismissive. But what else was there to say; she was still coming to terms with what she'd just heard.

'Have a seat,' Bert said, waving an arm at the table. 'Tea or coffee? Milk, sugar?'

'Tea would be lovely – just as it comes, thanks.'

Nicola noticed how Bert's hands shook when he put the cup and mismatched saucer down in front of her. When he sat down she got her first really good look at him. He seemed at ease yet there was a certain intensity about his expression and movement.

Nicola sipped the tea – the stale smoke had permeated it – and regretted not asking for sugar.

Bert reached behind him to the bench and in one fluid, well-practiced motion brought an old sardine can, pouch of tobacco, wad of papers, and box of matches to the table.

There was no sign of unsteadiness while he nimbly rolled a cigarette between gnarled, stained fingers. Nicola felt her back tighten in annoyance.

Job done, Bert leaned back in his chair and lit up. A look of sheer contentment washed across the tight creases of his face as he expelled the smoke.

Nicola concentrated on breathing through her nose so at least some of the toxins would be filtered before making their way into her lungs. She was sure she could feel them already filling with tar. She coughed in response.

'Sorry, bad habit I know – picked it up in 'Nam. Want me to put it out?'

Damn right I do, she wanted to say, but instead forced a smile and said, 'It's your house, go right ahead, but thanks anyway.' Boy did Bill owe her big time.

'My brother rang and told me about the other day – that's how I knew who you were. Sorry if he was a bit gruff. He's under a lot of pressure. I guess we all are really, what with the drought and all.'

Bert said, tapping the skinny cigarette on the side of the sardine tin.

'Oh.' Hadn't Richard said they weren't on speaking terms?

'So, you're a journalist; what did you want to discuss?' he asked.

Nicola realised she hadn't brought her notebook and recorder in – she'd been too rattled. Damn. She began fiddling with the handle of her cup.

'Um, I'm doing a story on the drought. I thought perhaps your dispute over water would show the desperation such a phenomenon induces in ordinary people.' Nicola immediately reddened when she saw the look on Bert's face; she hadn't meant to be so blunt.

'Water? Oh right, yes, the feud over water, of course.'

The hesitation told Nicola that Beryl's theory held considerable weight.

She wanted to change tack, start all over and let Bert reveal all himself. But she'd gone in too hard. Now she just hoped he wouldn't clam up. She crossed the fingers of her left hand under the table.

'Well, the long and short of it is that Graeme's run out of water. He wants access to my spring, but the Water Board is monitoring consumption. Water is water out here, no matter where it comes from – mains, rainwater tanks, bores or springs. We're under really tight restrictions, and rightly so.'

Nicola wondered if Bert was just being stubborn, and made a mental note to check out government restrictions.

'But he *is* your brother.'

'Doesn't come into it – it's about whose name is on the property deed. I'm the rightful owner of the water. End of story. Anyway, it serves him right.'

Nicola could sense Bert getting ready to tell all and again cursed herself for not having her recorder. She certainly couldn't interrupt him now.

'Why's that,' she prompted.

'I suppose someone in town will tell you anyway,' he sighed. 'May as well hear it from the horse's mouth.'

Nicola held her breath, not wanting to distract him. He'd obviously not spoken to Beryl, and she was interested to see how their versions compared.

***

Nicola glanced at her watch and was surprised to find she'd been listening to Bert for over an hour, mesmerised by his words and the constant rolling, smoking and butting out of cigarettes.

It seemed that Bert, unlike his brother, loved the chance to tell a story. Nicola couldn't have got a question in if she'd wanted to.

Again it was a case of information overload. He'd flitted in and out of decades without drawing breath, leaving Nicola wondering a number of times if he was talking about Vietnam or last week.

Her head swam with the stifling smoke and the strain of trying to keep up.

One thing was for sure; Bert McCardle was content with his life and harboured no further ambition, unlike his aggressive brother.

Finally she was outside, saying goodbye and taking large gulps of fresh, cold air.

She cursed the twice-stale odour that wafted into the four-wheel-drive behind her.

With all the windows down and air-conditioner blasting on full heat, Nicola retreated to the end of the rugged driveway, and parked, hopefully out of Bert's sight.

She pulled her notebook from the backpack on the passenger seat and began furiously writing.

Nicola liked that Bert seemed honest and down to earth. But the chain smoking and nervous fidgeting had made her uneasy. Was it simply nerves – not being used to having a woman in his house – or symptoms of something else?

There was so much evidence linking Vietnam vets and emotional instability. But then your wife having an affair with your brother while you were away was sure to have a major lasting effect.

And the feud; fighting with Graeme could send him completely over the edge, if it hadn't already.

Nicola was frustrated – he appeared to be on the level but she couldn't be sure. She made a note to look into it, would start with asking Richard.

And what of the situation with Janet leaving? Time had a wonderful way of healing pain, but it could also foster resentment and anger. No, she decided, pen between her teeth. Bert had definitely come to terms with his wife's sudden departure all those years ago.

Unlike Beryl Roberts, who didn't seem to have forgiven the poor woman at all.

Nicola tried to remember the words he'd used to describe her: 'free spirit'. It wasn't like he hadn't cared – he still did, she'd seen that; had looked away quickly at seeing his brimming eyelids.

'Yes,' Nicola said aloud, 'that's what he said: "It was her choice. No point keeping her here like a bird with its wings clipped."'

Nicola had a lump forming in her throat and wasn't sure why. She felt for both Bert – more than likely screwed up by Vietnam – and Janet, unprepared for the change in her husband. For all she knew, he might have become violent, and no one should have to live in fear.

Suddenly Nicola remembered a flicker of information fighting to escape. It had happened in a fleeting moment between butting and rolling. She had been concentrating on breathing and willing him not to light up again, but now she vaguely recalled something about a pregnancy, or was it a baby? Shit, what was it? Nicola nibbled on her bottom lip for a few moments before giving up.

She returned to her notes about what she *could* remember: not competitive with his brother (Graeme was but it wasn't reciprocated); content to keep business small; no women since Janet; felt sorry for Janet because of strict parents...

Ahh. Nicola sat up. That was it. Bert had mentioned her parents would have had a fit. And he hadn't meant their splitting up because he said they'd never approved of him in the first place.

Nicola's instincts told her she was on the right track.

She made a note: *Janet pregnant when left Bert?* It would explain her sudden disappearance from the district. Bert had been so flippant with his comment – hell, she'd almost missed it.

Now she remembered what he'd said: 'Janet might have told me she was pregnant but I was on so many drugs for the nightmares that nothing was clear – life was rather foggy at that time.'

Nicola's head swum. She could see this story becoming huge – and having nothing to do with drought. Bill would kill her. She had to get some focus; snag an angle.

Chapter Seventeen

At dinner that night, Nicola wondered whether her relationship with Scott was slipping away or if it was only her imagination. Surely she was just being paranoid about his lack of support. He hadn't even rung to see how she'd survived her first weekend; how she was full stop.

Scott's voicemail had probably recorded her curse of 'bastard' when she'd phoned earlier. He bloody well deserved a wake-up call. But he'd probably just think she was hormonal; his reason for any ripple of disquiet.

Nicola thought she'd cry if she allowed herself.

But no, she was not going to feel sorry for herself; she was a woman of the world. And anyway, Nowhere Else was bad enough without being depressed.

★★★

'Sorry, Nicola, lounge bar's closed now. You'll have to head down to the front bar if you want another drink,' Tiffany said, picking up Nicola's empty glass.

Nicola looked up at Tiffany while she tried to work out if she'd had three or four drinks.

'I'm really sorry, but rules are rules,' Tiffany added, clearly misreading her expression.

'No worries. I think I do fancy another,' she said, getting up and using the table for support. Definitely four drinks. Drinking really wouldn't do her mood any good, but she wasn't ready to return to that dreary room. Just one more, she told herself, and moved towards the glass door that led onto the street.

Nicola was relieved the cool breeze didn't affect her further, and her legs were pretty steady. All good, she thought, opening the door to the front bar.

A thick cloud of smoke, beer breath and body odour hit her. There was a strong, sweet, earthy smell she couldn't identify, and she pinched her nose in disgust.

The pub was packed with men in filthy work wear, a row of stained, battered Akubras on pegs along the back wall.

Tiffany materialised at the other side of the bar to take her order.

'Sheep sale today. Bit whiffy, eh?' she offered, grinning at Nicola.

'Hmm,' Nicola agreed. 'I'll have another Bundy and Coke, thanks Tiff.' She looked around for a familiar face, hoping Richard would be there but knowing it was unlikely on a school night, what with his wife and two kids at home. She took her drink to a stool at an empty table in the corner and gradually became lost in her thoughts.

Before long, Nicola was a little horrified to realise she'd not only got used to the smell, but was actually finding it oddly comforting.

Even – heaven forbid – a little alluring. It made a change from Scott and his Gucci Envy cologne.

Bloody Scott. Why hadn't he called? Was he missing her like she was him? *Was* she actually missing *him*, or just having someone's attention? She looked at the engagement ring on her finger and a sense of dread settled in her stomach.

No, it's not over; it's me; I'm just being needy. Distance always makes things difficult. She took a long sip of her drink.

When she got home she'd ravish him like never before, suggest they get married, maybe even discuss having kids…

She knew he wanted children; he said so casually every so often – more as if it would be his next achievement than from any paternal emotional yearning.

Everything Scott did was logical and well-ordered: great career, fantastic home, nice car, good looking partner, two-point-one kids. The goal was to have all this before he hit forty, which was approaching fast. They didn't have long in which to make it happen.

Nicola had managed to sidestep the topic until now. She thought she might like children, one day. Yes, her biological clock was probably ticking, but she couldn't hear it.

And she certainly wasn't ready to kiss her career goodbye, especially when things were starting to go so well.

Who wanted to be ripped apart or sliced open, whichever way it went, anyway? Not to mention the stretch marks, saggy tits, ruination of her perfect television figure, possible incontinence et cetera. She'd done enough post-baby makeover stories for *Life and Times*. Yuck. It was a wonder babies were born at all. Maybe they could adopt – it hadn't done her any harm, had it?

Nope, Scott wanted two perfect little fruits of his loins to hold up to the world. Fair enough, she supposed. Well he'd have to start showing some interest if that was ever going to happen. She frowned into her drink.

'We must stop meeting like this – fancy a game of pool?'

Nicola turned, an alcoholic grin plastered across her face. She blushed. Standing next to her was probably the only clean, well-dressed male specimen in the place – Alex from the other night and, groan, the plane. She really wished her memory would wipe that.

Tall, dark, and handsome were the words that instantly popped into Nicola's head. The journalist in her knew it was the ultimate cliché, but the description fit him, and the type of guy she was attracted to, perfectly.

'Hi Alex. Yeah, great, thanks,' she said, and followed him. Alex who, anyway? Had Tiffany said?

A couple of wolf-whistles and cheers from the group around the table, deep blushes and the odd hiccup from her, and the game was on.

At the pool table, Alex stood close, to offer her suggestions of what ball to go for. So intent was she on trying not to embarrass herself with her poor play that it took her a few minutes to realise that he was flirting.

It started just after she potted her second ball. The first time, he offered his palm for a high-five. The second time, he put his arm around her shoulder and pulled her to him in a quick hug. After that, every time they handed the pool cue back and forth their hands had seemed to touch.

She was trying to ignore it, pretending she hadn't noticed. She really should make it clear that she wasn't interested. But the attention was nice. It was a long time since she'd enjoyed this sort of attention from a man. What was the harm in a little innocent flirting?

The only words spoken between them during the game were general; 'oh bad luck', 'robbed', 'better luck next time', 'oh well done,' and the like. Totally benign.

They lost the game by a country mile – whatever that was. Alex didn't seem to mind though, and the distraction had stopped Nicola drinking. Her head was starting to ache.

'Can I get you another drink?' Alex asked, leading her away from the table.

'I think I need some fresh air,' she said, suddenly feeling wrecked. She looked around for the nearest exit.

'This way.' He grabbed her hand and led her through the thinning crowd and out the side door.

Outside, Nicola took deep gulping breaths, still feeling the heat from inside blanketing her.

'Ah, that's better,' she said, suddenly feeling awkward.

She shuddered involuntarily as the cool air started penetrating her thin top.

Alex put his arm around her, sending warmth of a different kind flowing through her. She was enjoying his scent – Brut – an aroma that reminded her of an era before life got complicated. A twinge of guilt in the pit of her stomach brought her back.

'I have a jacket in the car if you want.'

'Thanks, but I really should be going,' she said, fighting the urge to snuggle into his strong arms

'Are you sure? I'd really like to get to know you better.'

'Well, coffee and a chat somewhere quiet would be nice, but as we both know…'

'…there's nowhere else.' They both laughed.

'I'd better go,' she said, rubbing her arms.

'Guess I'll just walk you home then,' Alex said heavily.

'I'm only going over there,' she chuckled and pointed.

'I know, but rule number one – always walk a pretty girl home.'

Chapter Eighteen

Despite having the key in her grasp from the outset, Nicola spent an age looking in her handbag while justifying what she was about to do. Slipping the key into the lock, she turned at the door, instantly feeling like she was in a corny movie. She didn't care. Suddenly she wasn't tired anymore – it wasn't even nine-thirty.

'Would you like a coffee?'

'Yeah, that would be great.'

'You can tell me all about this drought.'

'Deal.'

'Only instant, I'm afraid,' Nicola said, throwing the door open and ushering Alex in. 'Make yourself at home.'

Nicola turned from filling and putting on the jug to find Alex had taken her words to heart. He'd kicked off his shoes and was sprawled across the bed. Nicola felt a stirring in her groin, and at the same moment, guilt began to gnaw at her.

In the years she'd been with Scott she hadn't so much as looked

136

lustily at another man. Now here she was with one lying on her bed.

Jesus. Shit, shit, shit. 'Sorry, just need the bathroom,' she spluttered, and nearly sprinted into the adjoining room.

Closing the door, she picked up the phone and dialled home. This time the answering machine wasn't even on. That's odd, she thought, and dialled his mobile, despite knowing he'd be annoyed if disturbed.

Scott was like that, a bit precious about taking calls while out and about. But, damn it; she needed to hear his voice, and now! Bloody voicemail. She was not leaving another message. She hung up.

Nicola stood for a few moments, leaning over the basin and looking into the mirror, before washing her face and leaving her sanctuary.

Alex was at the bench, taking control of the coffee-making and waiting to turn off the almost bubbling jug.

Nicola paused to take in his profile – even yummier from behind.

'Okay, do you take milk and sugar?' he asked, turning around.

'Both. Actually, two of everything. Milk, sugar, and coffee,' she said, snapping back to sensibility. 'One sachet of coffee and it's disgusting, two and it's almost drinkable.'

'Here you go.'

'Thanks.' Nicola accepted the cup and perched herself on the edge of the saggy bed. Alex sat next to her, leaving a modest gap between them.

Both sipped in silence, trying to ignore the awkwardness. Damn not having a table to put between us, Nicola thought, noticing a warmth flooding through her that was definitely beyond that of instant coffee.

★★★

Nicola leaned forward to put her empty cup on the bench. But Alex leapt up and saved her the trouble. His hand lightly brushed her fingers and sent ripples of electricity down her arm.

They were like two teenagers at the movies; pretending to ignore the tension but not knowing how else to behave.

'You have really nice hands,' he said quietly, and sat back down on the bed next to her – closer this time – and gently lifted her left hand from her lap. The diamond ring was unmistakable. What was he doing? What was she doing?

'Office hands,' she shrugged, retrieving it.

Nicola was proud of her hands – long, lean and smooth – she'd always been careful to look after them. Well, ever since an eccentric aunt had told her they were the window to the soul.

She knew it was *eyes* that were supposed to be the window to the soul; decided Mabel was losing her marbles.

Nonetheless, Nicola did have the hands of a sixteen year old.

'So do you,' she said, nodding at Alex's. The nails were clean and short, not bitten, attached to strong, fleshy digits. Apparently he knew how to look after them.

'Don't tell anyone,' he started shyly, 'but I use hand cream every night.'

'Really?'

'Yeah.' Alex blushed slightly. 'I once knew this old Italian lady who told me girls like men with smooth hands.'

'Wise lady.' Nicola beamed at him.

'Yeah, she was,' he said, grinning and visibly relaxing. 'Said you can't go wrong with the fairer sex if you have a good heart and can give a decent massage,' he added, obviously mimicking.

'And has it worked?' Nicola couldn't help herself.

'Never really put it to the test.'

'Never?' She raised a questioning eyebrow.

'Well,' he started, obviously embarrassed. 'Not never, just not seriously.'

'I'd have thought women would be falling over themselves to have those hands rub away their woes,' Nicola said, then suddenly stopped, dipping her head.

She really hadn't meant to be so obvious. Flirt, yes, but no more than that. There was something about Alex – beyond his rugged looks and charm – that made her want to know more. He was intriguing – and, dare she say it, alluring.

'Well, let's just say there isn't an abundance of eligible women around here,' he said wistfully. 'Sure, there are your usual slags, like in any place but… Oh shit, what an awful thing to say. Sorry.'

'I like your honesty,' Nicola said, genuinely flattered he was comfortable enough to be himself.

Most men she met were usually too busy trying to cover up their insecurities about being around a good-looking woman who was also intelligent. That's what her friends said, anyway.

It's also what she'd first liked about Scott; that he wasn't in awe of her. Perhaps it had been the vulnerable state she'd been in when they'd met.

Suddenly she saw what had happened with Scott. She'd let him take total control of the relationship, and now look where they were – far too comfortable.

Eight years in, they were like a pair of sixty year olds who merely happened to share the same house. It was as if it was easier, less traumatic, and of course cheaper, to just carry on rather than split everything and go their separate ways.

Sure they loved each other on some level, but this just wasn't like she'd expected love and homemaking to be. Shouldn't there be more?

She was thinking through the implications when Alex gently pushed her back onto the bed and lay beside her, easing the unruly tendrils back from her face, staring into her eyes through his long dark lashes, testing her mouth with his.

Disregarding the nag of guilt, Nicola responded with a tentative kiss, and found his lips just like his hands, strong and smooth – in control but not controlling. Where did a country boy learn to kiss like that?

But unable to ignore the burning shame, she pulled away with a groan of reluctance.

Alex sat up, a frown clouding his dark features.

'What's wrong?'

'I can't. I'm sorry.'

'Okay,' he shrugged.

Nicola's stomach was churning. He was so close, his leg draped over her thighs, his arousal obvious even through two layers of clothes.

She thought how nice it was just to feel the closeness of another body when he laid his head in the crook of her neck.

Was he, like her, just wanting to savour the closeness, the electricity of desire, without the guilt and complication that would follow? Or was there something else? Did she dare use him like that?

'Um…' Nicola inspected the buttons on his chambray shirt, buying time, then held up her left hand.

Alex broke in. 'I have a confession. I recognised you on the plane – I saw on the news how you'd won the Walkleys. Congratulations. I know why you were scared to fly that night. And I know about Scott.'

Nicola felt a shiver rush up her spine, signalling danger. He knew so much about her it was a little scary. But then there had been so much publicity, the fact she had a fiancé wasn't exactly a secret.

'Anyway, it's not like I could miss that ring,' he said with a grimace. 'It's beautiful.'

He looked back up at her, peered deeply into her eyes. 'I know this is really awful, but I still want to.'

'Hmm, me too,' Nicola said, surprised at her own admission.

'We wouldn't have to actually…well, you know.'

Nicola found herself thinking that the sex side of a relationship should have a use-it-or-lose-it clause – like the bonus minutes on her mobile phone account. Scott was forever cutting her off at the pass, so to speak, so, why should she go unfulfilled?

But Alex, yet again, had read her mind and was easing his gorgeous hands under her shirt and beginning to cautiously explore her curves.

It was going to be up to her to put a stop to proceedings. But Nicola desperately wanted to rip her clothes off and take full advantage of those hands.

And she also wanted to do something for him – not just lie back and luxuriate. She pushed a hand under his shirt and ran it down his ribs, tracing the smooth curve of his hips with a long manicured nail.

He groaned, edged closer to her.

Nicola could now feel the bulge in his pants and inched her hand down. Alex moved away slightly, and not wanting to appear aggressive, Nicola removed her hand. But she needn't have feared, he was only getting in a position where he could undo the buttons on her shirt – slowly, carefully, all the time gazing at her through those beautiful lashes and deep brown eyes.

Shirt bunched up under her, Nicola shuddered with a mixture of tingling pleasure and chilly air on bare skin.

'Shall we get in?' Alex asked tentatively, nodding at the bed.

Nicola was relieved that this seemed as foreign to him as it felt to her.

Silently they got off the bed, pulled the covers down, and stepped out of their clothes with their backs turned.

Nicola was back in bed first, still in her knickers and bra. She pulled the sheets up to her chin, suddenly self-conscious and wishing she'd turned the light out.

Alex's muscular back rippled as he bent to take off his socks – he kept his trunk-style underpants on. The man took care of himself, but it was a body sculpted by farm work – not the gym.

As he wrapped his almost naked body around her, she again felt the twang of guilt. It was nice to be held, but she wasn't sure she wanted anything else just yet.

'Really, we don't have to do anything. I won't mind,' he said, reading her mind for about the third time that evening.

Mmm, how lovely was this man?

She pressed her finger to his closed lips, said, 'Hang on a sec,' got out of bed, and went to the bathroom. She made no attempt to cover up despite noticing in the wardrobe mirror Alex watching her intently.

She found a lone condom in the side pocket of her toiletry bag. She stared at the expiry date – it wasn't *that* far out; surely it couldn't matter *that* much – and acknowledged each of the feelings surging through her.

Back in bed, she put the small square packet on the bedside table, saying, 'I know, it's just in case,' as if he'd only just made the comment.

Snuggling back into his arms, Nicola wondered if this was love. What a ridiculously juvenile thought!

And then they were kissing and becoming entwined again, Alex pushing into her, she not resisting.

'Condom,' she murmured, her body on fire.

'Sure?' he asked, already dragging his underwear off with one hand while the other continued to hold her.

'Mmm,' she mumbled, instead wanting to scream, 'yes, yes, yes, get on with it you're killing me.'

Nicola gasped with pleasure at feeling herself totally filled — it was as if they were made for each other.

★★★

Nicola murmured dreamily, her head fuzzy from too little sleep and too much rum. Alex was wrapped around her, his partially open lips puffing warm, sweet breath on her cheek. He had every right to be exhausted after the incredible few hours they'd spent.

Even the dull ache of guilt deep inside did little to erase the soft contentedness in her features. Yes, he was definitely heaven sent. And wasn't she the cat who'd got the cream?

Even if it was a one-off, which it has to be.

But her instinct was telling her she wanted more — a whole lot more. Once more couldn't hurt. After all, dawn hadn't yet broken.

Nicola eased herself back, and Alex responded by snuggling her neck and pulling her towards him. She felt him harden again.

She rolled away before turning back to face him, and then shuffling closer. Alex, now awake, was smiling dreamily at her through those to-die-for lashes.

Nicola edged into prime position, her heart pounding in anticipation.

Then he had her face in his hands, kissing her passionately.

'Condom?' Alex mumbled into her mouth.

She'd only had the one. Nicola pulled away slightly. 'Oh no,' she groaned. Tonight she'd been reckless but there was no way she'd ever be *that* reckless. She rolled away.

'And I am so bloody horny.' Nicola was surprised at her words; she'd never admitted such feelings to a man before. She'd always been particularly shy and reserved about intimacy.

'Well, we'd better solve that then hadn't we?'

'I can't, not without protection.'

'Shh,' he said, putting a finger to her lips.

Nicola was tense – what could he mean?

'Enjoy,' he murmured, running his tongue around just inside her ear, then her neck, while his hands teased her breasts. She closed her eyes as he continued downwards.

Nicola had never had someone take so much time and genuinely enjoy lavishing her with pleasure.

★★★

'Wow', Nicola breathed.

'My pleasure,' he said, beaming.

He had every right to be pleased with himself. 'Can I return the favour?' she whispered.

'No, I want to be able to see your pretty face.'

'Are you sure?' Scott never missed an opportunity, especially when it came around so rarely. She felt self-doubt niggle. Wasn't that what all men craved?

'I'm serious. Not that I won't take you up on that on another occasion,' he added, grinning cheekily, and then kissing her tenderly on the forehead.

Oh shit, Nicola thought, *there can't be another occasion.* But how could she give him up now? After the most perfect love-making of her entire life? She snuggled into him. Could she be in love? No; after an orgasm like that, it could only be lust.

'I'd like to see you again,' Alex announced. 'Do you think we could just be friends?'

Just friends; after last night and just now? You've got to be to be joking.

'Sorry, I'm being too pushy. It's just…'

'I know, but I can't afford a scandal,' Nicola said, shaking her head.

'No, I understand.'

He bent and stretched to get dressed, and Nicola moaned quietly as she again admired his muscular back. Then he pecked her on the cheek and was gone, leaving her to be savaged by her emotions.

Chapter Nineteen

What the hell had she been thinking? God, forget public scandal; what about Scott? Should she just tell him?

And say what exactly? 'I got drunk, it just happened'? Since when did she get drunk enough to be unfaithful, anyway? She didn't even feel hung-over – unlike the other morning. What the hell was happening to her? It was this place; the isolation, being away from home.

If only Scott had shown her more attention, more affection... Why couldn't he be more like Alex? From day one, Scott hadn't got anywhere near that passionate and tender.

Perhaps that was the problem; they were too comfortable. And they couldn't claim that the passion had waned over time; they'd been that way from the start. She'd thought it nice; now she could see it might have been a mistake. Perfunctory was the best way to describe their love-making – pretty much the same every time. And really, she was as much to blame as Scott; it did, after all, take two.

But there hadn't been any sex whatsoever lately. And she certainly couldn't be blamed for that. Other than tying him up and feeding him Viagra there really wasn't any more she could have done. She'd tried.

How long had it been? Nicola bit her lip in concentration. Over two months. He clearly wasn't interested in her any more.

Was it any wonder she'd sought the affection of another man? She rolled over and pushed her face into the pillow that still bore the imprint of Alex's head. She breathed in his woody, musky scent.

She had to stop thinking about him. Alex. Shit! She eased herself upright. Alex who, anyway? She didn't even know his last name. Why hadn't she asked?

Nicola burnt with further shame; she had to find out. But how? It wasn't like she could risk complete embarrassment by asking Tiffany.

Did it really matter now anyway? No, all that mattered was what she was going to do about this mess. Should she fess up to Scott? Would he dump her? Of course he would; *she* would if the situation were reversed. The trust had been broken, and there was no way back from that.

They got on so well together, generally made a pretty good team; it would be a real pity to split up.

But really, did she love him? Was she *in* love with him? With a deep sigh Nicola admitted to herself that no; she wasn't *in* love with Scott. She did care for him very much and she did love him – just not madly, passionately, deeply.

She looked at her engagement ring – she'd be disappointed to give that back. And they'd have to sort everything out – all the finances. What a mess. It was all her fault; there was no one to blame but herself. Nicola's heart ached. Tears filled her eyes. And then she began to sob. She felt so alone. Why had she agreed to come out here?

Slowly Nicola's tears slowed and her mind began to clear. No, she would not tell Scott while he was away at a conference. This was not a conversation to have over the phone. It would wait until she got back. She felt a glimmer of relief. Good; a decision.

She got up, went into the bathroom, and turned on the shower. Soaping herself all over, she wondered if Sandy would agree with her telling Scott – in person or otherwise. Should she ask her advice?

No, she decided, now rubbing shampoo through her hair. As much as she loved Sandy, she couldn't risk her telling Bob.

What would her friend say? Probably that it had happened because it was meant to happen. That it served Scott right for not keeping her satisfied. And what would Sandy suggest she do? Nicola sighed again. She'd tell her to leave Scott and not fess up; there was no point – if she was lured into another man's arms then clearly the relationship had run its course.

And she'd finish by saying something funny, Nicola thought, as she put conditioner through her hair. 'And darling, take those hideously expensive pots and pans with you and find yourself a man who can damn well use them'. Sandy had a knack of lightening dark moods.

Nicola found herself smiling sadly at how she came to own the 'hideously expensive pots and pans' Sandy so often made fun of.

They'd only recently moved in together. The occasion was Scott's next big promotion. He'd wanted to go off to a trendy bar and graze on tapas, but no, she'd naively wanted to prove herself the great woman behind the man. She remembered how insecure she'd been, with her career being slow to take off while he climbed the corporate ladder two rungs at a time.

There was no way she was doing a common Sunday roast – really the most elaborate thing in her repertoire. So she'd gone all out: bought an exquisitely illustrated cookbook by one of the designer chefs of the day – Hugh somebody-or-other.

Looking back, she realised that the woman at the hospitality supplies store had sold her the offending tome with tongue firmly in cheek – adhering to the tenet 'give the customer what she wants'.

In addition to the cookbook, Nicola also spent a small fortune filling her cupboards with cherry red Le Creuset cookware because, according to Hugh, cooking with anything other than the very best cast-iron pots and pans would almost certainly end in disaster. He must have had a lucrative endorsement deal.

Nicola now knew she should have taken 'disaster' literally and stepped away, her hands raised in surrender, and got out the Yellow Pages. But no, she'd blindly forged ahead.

Dainty individual rolled pork loins looked fabulous drizzled with jus – really just a posh name for thin gravy. She'd been careful not to overcook them, so the meat was lovely and pink in the middle, just like on TV and in restaurants.

It wasn't until someone mentioned a disease one could get from eating rare pork that she remembered only lamb and beef were served that way. Scott had bolted around the table whisking plates away from startled guests.

Sure enough, rereading Hugh's instructions, Nicola found it clearly stated in bold, highlighted with red stars, that there was to be 'no hint of blood'.

The individual cheesecakes were also looking remarkably good until she tipped the first out of its mould – *dariole* to those in the know. It instantly let go like thighs released from control underwear. How was she to know how long 'refrigerate until set' took?

Always the lateral thinker, Nicola shoved the biscuit base back in, spooned the creamy mixture on top and shoved all eight cheesecakes into the freezer. If frozen cheesecake was good enough for Sara Lee, it was damn well good enough for her – bugger Hugh, smug prick.

Coffee from her new two-thousand-dollar Gaggia machine might have redeemed the night – had she remembered to offer it.

The whole thing had been a disaster, but Nicola received charming letters from Scott's bosses thanking her for a 'refreshing evening'. Apparently it had been a 'pleasant change' from the stuffiness of five-star restaurants. She was mortified.

The cookware and assorted paraphernalia – with its lifetime guarantee – was relegated to a bottom cupboard where friends who cooked couldn't ooh and ahh over it. Meanwhile the cookbook became a fashionable doorstop.

After that, she learnt that the thing to do for dinner parties was to employ a caterer; ovens were only for the heating up of canapés, and sprawling granite benches merely for arranging silver platters.

It had taken Sandy quite some time to wear out the story. Over time Nicola had come to see the funny side of it, but still didn't like it mentioned in public. Nor did Scott.

And now she thought about it, not once had he ever given her a hard time about it. He was a genuinely kind and gentle man; they'd had a good life together. And here she'd gone and done this to him. Nicola felt her heart clamp again.

No, she'd been through this; if she was going to tell him, it would be in person. Now she had to get outside, clear her head and forget about Alex. Yeah, like that was possible.

Nicola dried her hair, and then put on jeans, t-shirt and ultra-warm microfibre top. As she was sitting on the bed pulling on her short boots with barely a heel, she wondered if she should or could confide in Bill. In the aftermath of her parents' death and the subsequent investigation he'd become almost like a surrogate uncle.

No, it would be pushing the boundaries way too far. Anyway, she'd made her decision. She pulled her black padded waterproof jacket from the back of the chair, grabbed the key and her handbag from the desk.

Nicola was just turning out the light when she heard her mobile phone start to ring. Yay! Finally! She fossicked in her Louis Cardini handbag and retrieved it from its special leather pocket in the side.

'Bill. Hi.'

'Nicola, how are you this fine morning?'

'Oh Bill it's so good to hear your voice – on my mobile!'

'Well, thank you very much,' he said with a chuckle.'

'You know what I mean,' Nicola said, rolling her eyes.

'So you're sounding chirpy.'

'You have no idea how much I've missed my phone, email, and Facebook.'

'I think I do. So, how are things?'

'Just peachy.'

'Wow, are you starting to like the place?' Bill said, missing her wry tone.

'Not exactly.'

'Just as well you're there to work and not for socialising then, eh?'

'Hmm, yeah.'

'Well, just wanted to check on you – and that your phone's working again. I'd better be off – powwow with the bigwigs in half an hour. Oh, oops, I nearly forgot; some mail came for you – I'll forward it on.'

Nicola stiffened slightly. Could it be? She'd know soon enough. 'Great, thanks. And thanks for the call – and for sorting out the phone; you've no idea how much…'

'I know – just find me a damn good story.'

'I'll do my best, boss.'

'That's my girl. See ya.'

'Bye Bill.'

Nicola cuddled her iPhone to her chest for a few moments

after hanging up. It really was a huge relief to feel connected to the outside world again. Though she'd have a shitload of emails and Facebook posts to trawl through. Oh, well, at least it would give her something to do. But right now she needed some fresh air.

Chapter Twenty

Nicola approached a group of five old men standing huddled together outside the newsagency. They were engrossed in animated discussion, with puffs of white wafting from their mouths. Feet were tapping and shuffling; trying to keep warm, she supposed, wrapping her arms around herself. Watches were being checked every few moments.

'Good morning,' she said, joining the group and peering at the sign in the window that said the shop opened at 8:30 a.m. Nicola checked her own watch; 8:40.

There was no way patrons in the city would wait for a store to open ten minutes late, Nicola mused. But, as she was quickly learning, there was nowhere else. She smiled at still finding amusement in the quip.

'Bit chilly this morning,' she ventured, trying to ease the silent, awkward atmosphere that had descended. The men nodded and mumbled their agreement before lapsing into silence again. *Hmm, a real warm, country welcome*, she thought sardonically.

Nicola wished the damn shop would just hurry up and open. She couldn't care less if it took two generations to become fully accepted; she only wanted the latest *Cosmo*. She really hoped it'd have some advice to help her through her predicament.

She stepped away from the group of men, got her iPhone out, logged into Facebook, and started scrolling through all the activity she'd missed.

Suddenly she was jolted by what felt like an elbow to her arm. She looked up in surprise to find Beryl Roberts standing very close to her. She wanted to step back and reclaim some personal space, but to do so would mean getting squashed up against the window.

'You looked a million miles away,' Beryl said.

'Um, yes, sorry.' *Why am I apologising for being busy on my phone?*

'Newsagent's open now,' Beryl said, nodding towards the door.

'Yes, so it is.' Nicola reddened when she realised she and Beryl were alone on the street corner.

'Now, I've taken the liberty of teeing up the young McCardle lad to give you a good look around.'

'Oh, right, thanks very much.' *I think.*

McCardle lad? Son of Graeme or Bert? Or was there another family? She made a mental note to ask Tiff; she was bound to know.

'Thought it would make a change from us oldies – hope you don't mind. And,' Beryl leaned into Nicola, 'he's single.'

'But I'm not, Beryl. I'm engaged,' she said, holding up her left hand and wiggling it.

Though, that wasn't the way she'd behaved last night. Ah, Alex. She sighed. She felt a new mix of guilt, bliss, regret, and yearning surging through her all at once.

What she needed was to focus on work. And driving around the dreary, barren countryside learning more about farming would be as good a way as any.

'...And quite a catch, I might add.' Beryl continued, ignoring her.

Nicola was surprised to receive an overly familiar dig in the ribs. *This town is just too much.* If she didn't need information, she'd have told the old busybody to mind her own business.

'Really?' Nicola said, raising her eyebrows, pretending to play along. 'Thanks for the tip.' She smiled sweetly while desperately looking for an exit without seeming too rude. Nicola was always wary of burning bridges – one never knew who would prove useful down the track.

'You'll be thanking me when you see how gorgeous Alex is – you'd make a handsome couple.'

'Beryl, as I said, I'm...' Oh, what was the point? *Hang on.* Alex? How many Alexs could there be in a population of under a thousand? *Oh no, it couldn't be,* she thought, feeling her face become warm.

'He'll be around to see you shortly, so you'd better get along, dear,' Beryl said, giving Nicola a gentle shove.

'Yes, right, well, thanks. See you then.' Nicola was half turned, looking for the opportunity to bolt, when Beryl put a gentle hand on her arm.

'Don't forget your paper, dear. Otherwise you won't know what's happening.'

'Yes, thanks, of course.' Nicola's teeth were clenched into a fake grin.

★★★

She was most of the way across the car park and about to step onto the concrete path that went past the motel rooms when she heard a voice.

'Ah, there you are.'

Startled, Nicola looked up from the sealed section on 'Sex tips – how to get him out of the office and back into bed' to find Alex turning from her door. His clenched fist was paused from knocking. *Ah, no need to ask Tiffany who the McCardle lad is.* She couldn't prevent her face from lighting up. But it quickly fell as she reminded herself she should be feeling guilty, not be pleased to see him.

'Hey there,' she said, trying not to look him in the eye.

They both stood in silence staring at their feet for a couple of beats until Alex cleared his throat and spoke in a quiet businesslike tone.

'Right, well, Auntie Beryl told me you'd be needing a tour – gories of the drought and all that.'

She's his aunt? Is there anyone around here who's not related?

'Beryl's your aunt?'

'Well, not really – second cousin once removed or something of Dad's.'

'Oh, right.'

'Bossy as hell but she's not a bad old stick. Anyway, it's usually worth my while to do as I'm told when it comes to Auntie Beryl. So, here I am. If you're not interested, just say and I'll…'

'Don't go…' Damn, too eager. '…I mean…it's actually a pretty good idea.'

'Well I'm free now unless it's too short notice.'

'I haven't any other plans.'

'Cool, we'll take my ute,' he said, leading the way back to the car park where a white Toyota Landcruiser traytop vehicle was parked beside her maroon four-wheel-drive wagon.

'Now I've gotta warn you that you're about to see the drought in all its gruesome glory – I make no apologies.' He started the vehicle and backed out.

'Thanks for the warning.'

Nicola thought he sounded more like a journo himself than a farmer, and then pulled herself up. What right did she have to think less of him because he was from the country?

For all she knew he'd gone off and got a PhD in astrophysics before coming back on the land. She actually didn't know anything about him. At least she had his last name now: Alex McCardle.

He turned left at the corner beside the newsagent's and exited town the same way Nicola had that first day – the day she'd come across Graeme McCardle waving his pitchfork.

★★★

'So are you Bert's or Graeme's son – or are there more McCardles?' She mentally crossed her fingers.

'Graeme's. And no, there's no more of us.'

'Oh,' she said, unable to hide her disappointment.

'Yeah, though you could say we're as different as chalk and cheese. Sometimes I wonder if we're even related at all,' he said with a laugh.

He didn't look like Graeme – his features were definitely darker, and less elongated. And he certainly seemed a whole lot friend-lier, she thought, letting her mind wander for a moment before bringing herself back. Oh well, at least she'd be more welcome on Graeme's farm this time around. She assumed that's where they were going.

'So have you always been a farmer?' she asked.

'Pretty much. It's something you're born and bred into,' he said with a shrug.

Nicola thought 'pretty much' was a bit vague. Had he tried something else first? If he had, and wanted to talk about it, he would have. She looked out the window and noticed they were passing the milk churn where she'd previously turned to drive into Graeme McCardle's. Where was he taking her? She wrapped her hand around the camera in her pocket, ready to get it out when they came across something worth capturing.

'Drought's heartbreaking, but if the land's in your blood it's pretty near impossible to walk away. Unless of course a bank forces you to.'

'Hmm,' Nicola said, not wanting to interrupt him.

'It's the death that I find so hard to deal with. Not being able to put a crop in and not being able to pay the bills is one thing, but seeing animals suffering is what really gets to me.' The dark eyes under the slightly floppy, ruffled fringe looked genuinely sad.

What a nice guy, Nicola thought, looking over at him for a moment before reminding herself he was off limits.

Five minutes later they turned off the main dirt road, crossed a corrugated steel ramp, and began making their way across a paddock.

Nicola thought it interesting that he could drive all over someone's farm. But then he was a local – no pitchforks would be waved at him.

Alex was silent as they drove towards a large mound rising from the bare earth. After skirting what she realised was a dam, he pulled up on a rise, sighing deeply. Nicola gasped.

'This is what happens when the water level gets low. The sheep have to wade in. They get stuck in the mud, eventually fall over, and drown. Once their wool gets wet, they've had it – it's damn near impossible to get them out without a tractor or loader.'

Nicola's hand released the camera and went to her mouth in response to her churning stomach. She couldn't smell anything, could only imagine the stench from the three corpses so bloated their legs were like toothpicks in a rockmelon. Black pools spread into the cracked mud drying in the sun.

A flock of black crows were fighting over the eyes and nasal secretions. Bile erupted in her throat, the sour acid overcoming the morning's mouthwash.

Nicola could almost hear the buzz of blowflies collecting the beginnings of disease, and the quiet squelching of millions of maggots crawling through the slops.

Thank goodness for the heating recycling the mix of spicy masculine scents and synthesised fresh lemons throughout the cabin.

Alex released the handbrake and they moved on.

'Does the farmer know?' Nicola asked, shooting a final glance at the devastation.

Alex sighed. 'Yeah – they're mine.'

'Oh.' She knew it was hardly adequate, but didn't know what else to say. She urged her mind back to why she was there. Where to start the story? She really wanted some kind of optimistic ending.

Nicola wondered what the wool of dead sheep in stagnant muddy water smelt like – nothing like her childhood memory of Martha Gardener Wool Mix and lanolin permeating the laundry while hand-washed jumpers lay drying on racks.

No, judging by the blowflies she'd seen, it would be gut-wrenching – literally.

Nicola knew it made a good story great to be able to describe in detail all the senses, but this was about the effect of drought on people. If only she could come up with a concrete angle.

'Prime wether hoggets. Worth nearly a hundred and fifty each at the moment.'

'Right.' Again Nicola wished she had a better response.

But then something clicked. It was the loss of equity that she'd seen in his face, not the loss of life.

Now it made sense. She hadn't understood him being so cut up about the death of livestock when he would have lived with it his entire life. Yet the expression had been the same as Bert's when talking about the old work dog he'd lost. Perhaps loss was loss.

'I hear you met my dad the other day,' Alex said after quite a few moments' silence. 'Crazy old bugger,' he chortled.

'Hmm. Yes – he wasn't exactly pleased to see me.'

'You know he didn't mean to scare you with the pitchfork – he just had it in his hand. Can be a bit of an old grump but he isn't a bad bloke. Drought's wearing him down though. It didn't used to be this bad.

'I'm assuming you know about the fight – it's why you're interested in us, right?'

'Oh. Well, it has been mentioned. I haven't really settled on an angle yet. I am curious about the effects the drought has on humans – and a feud between two brothers over water would be a pretty good example, I think.'

'Well, I'm not so sure it is about water.'

'Really? Why not?'

'Well, it doesn't make sense to me. Dad could truck in water like the rest of us – and the stand pipe is closer and easier to get to than Uncle Bert's spring anyway.'

'Oh.' Nicola could see her only angle slipping away.

'Dad reckons Uncle Bert's just being spiteful. But why would he? He's one of the most generous people I know.'

'So why won't he give your father access to the spring?' She got out her camera, wound down the window, and took some shots of the endless barren landscape before winding it back up.

'He says he's just following the rules – water restrictions. And he doesn't want trucks driving back and forth across his paddocks.'

'That sounds fair enough, doesn't it?'

'I suppose so. But you know that feeling you get when you're not being told everything?'

'Yep. I certainly do.'

'Well, I've got it. Anyway, it's nothing to do with me. There's probably nothing more to it than two men being childish and stubborn.'

Nicola felt her heart sink. She was back at square one.

'So you and your father don't work together then?' she asked.

'Help each other out every now and then, but no, I went out on my own five years ago. We've got such different ideas; it's easier than fighting all the time.

'Bit of advice when it comes to dealing with Dad: It pretty much comes down to money these days – oh, and apparently water. Make him think you're here to do a story on lobbying the government for funding and he'll probably clamour to be interviewed.

'He's a proud man, but at the moment he's also a desperate one. Trying to hold onto the last of his ewes – breeds fat cross-bred lambs. Irrigates lucerne to feed them – well, he used to.

'Most around here just coast along – have for generations. Not Dad – ambitious to the core,' he added proudly. 'That's the trouble. Higher up the ladder you are, the further you have to fall. He's mortgaged to the hilt; bank won't even give him five grand for more hay – even though he's been one of their best customers for thirty years.

'That's what happens when they shut down the local branches and run everything from the city – all the fat cats can see are figures in red or black. They've got real antsy in the past couple of years.'

She wondered how Graeme would like his son discussing his finances with strangers – a journalist no less. Where had the seemingly sophisticated and well-spoken Alex of last night gone? He was sounding as ocker as anyone out here.

They drove on. She was becoming bored of the drab browns, tired-looking trees, and generally desolate scenery; it all looked the same. She stared out the window, trying to stay awake, but the gentle shake of the vehicle beneath her and the sun shining in through the window meant she struggled to keep her eyes open.

'Seen enough do you think? It's all pretty much the same from here on.' Alex asked, jolting her. Thank goodness; she'd almost fallen asleep. She sat up straighter.

'Okay, thanks, it's been great.'

★★★

Heading back towards town, they had to wait for the road to clear of sheep coming towards them. Nicola marvelled at the serenity. The farmer had his feet up on the front of his quad bike, Akubra pulled low over his eyes, reading a paperback. A black dog, coat glistening like treacle in the sun, was stretched across the cargo rack behind, long white legs dangling over the edges. She snapped away with her camera.

Sheep systematically scanned the roadsides, bumping and pushing each other in the fight for anything edible. The image would be great for the opening or closing credits.

Alex waited patiently for the farmer to look up and realise they were waiting to pass.

Nicola longed to reach across and honk the horn. 'Shouldn't we let him know we're here?'

'He'll figure it out soon enough. Don't want to stress the sheep; they won't eat.'

'Isn't it a bit dangerous having them just roaming all over the place?'

'We all know to be careful. You need a permit but the council refuses to issue them because of public liability. But since the councillors are all farmers, they turn a blind eye.' Alex winked at Nicola and she wondered if he was being affectionate or teasing her for her impatience.

She didn't care either way; she was in no mood to sit around waiting for some bloke to finish his chapter and move his bloody sheep. She had things to do.

Sighing, she folded her arms tightly across her chest, then, realising how childish she was being, unfolded them again.

'Anyway, everyone's doing it so it's impossible to police.'

Nicola felt like asking why they'd even need police when everyone knew what everyone else was up to – you couldn't even scratch yourself without Auntie Beryl or some other busybody knowing about it.

'Don't worry, won't be long now,' he offered.

How would you know, Nicola wanted to snap, trying to hate him so she wouldn't want him so badly. But the more she tried, the worse it was.

Finally the farmer looked up, gave a big wave and a wide grin, and turned on his seat. The dog slowly stood up, stretched, glanced at the sheep, back to the farmer, and reluctantly clambered from the bike. In a matter of seconds, it moved the mob aside.

A little way along the road they came across another farmer and his flock. This time Nicola was resigned to waiting; being annoyed was pointless.

'How come they don't all get mixed up?' she asked.

'Well, most farmers only graze their boundaries, so they let each other know where they are by UHF radio. Also, having a decent dog helps. These dogs are used to working mobs ten times the size, so this is a walk in the park.'

'Bert told me heaps of farmers are getting rid of their dogs,' Nicola offered.

'Yeah. It's tough on the kids. You'd be amazed how young they are when they get introduced to the harsh realities of life. I was nine when I buried my first dog, Smokey.

'Dad had accidently run over him – only the best get taken to the vet, even now. I'll never forget it as long as I live; Smokey writhing and howling in pain while I struggled to dig the hole and Dad got the gun.' Alex stared straight ahead with both hands wrapped tightly around the steering wheel.

Nicola stared at him. She wanted to reach over and hug him, or at least squeeze his hand; let him know she understood.

'I tried so hard not to cry. Dad put his hand on my shoulder and then left me to fill in the hole; for closure I guess.

'Mum found me still sitting there a couple of hours later. I'd covered up Smokey, but I was so exhausted I could barely hold up the spade. I knew boys weren't supposed to cry, but once I started I just couldn't stop,' he said, looking at her and smiling sadly. 'Maybe that's why Dad left me there; so I wouldn't be embarrassed.'

Nicola could almost feel the tears and sweat burning furrows down his cheeks and his little boy chest heaving uncontrollably while sitting out there alone. She felt her own throat constrict, and swallowed the lump back down.

Staring across a barren paddock, she wondered how long it had taken Alex to forgive his father for the loss, and if he ever really had.

At nine she'd been busy playing dress-ups, treating her dolls to elaborate tea parties, and fantasising about meeting a tall, dark and handsome prince who would cart her off to some faraway land to be queen.

Chapter Twenty-one

Alex pulled into the hotel's car park next to Nicola's hire vehicle and sat with the ute idling.

'Stay and have some lunch with me,' Nicola said. She didn't want her day with Alex to end. 'Bill's shout – least he can do for you driving me around.'

'Who's Bill?'

'My boss,' Nicola laughed.

'Well, okay, thanks.'

'Great.' Nicola said, beaming at him. 'Come on then.'

Alex turned the vehicle off. They made their way around to the main entrance and into the lounge bar, where they stood at the counter and perused the menu. Nicola's stomach grumbled.

'Anything you recommend?' Nicola asked.

'I reckon you'd be in a better position to know than me – I don't eat in here very often. Not 'cos the food's bad or anything; just not in town all that much.'

164

'Oh?'

He reddened slightly. 'You just happened to see me the only two nights I've been here in the last month. Anyway, I usually eat in the bar. The burger's pretty good though, and I bet it's the same one they serve in here.'

'Indeed it is,' Tiffany said, appearing behind the counter. 'Hi Alex.'

'Hi Tiff.'

'Okay, great. I'll have the burger, thanks, Tiff.'

'Make that two.'

'Righteo then. Two burgers. Any drinks? Alex, Bundy and Coke?'

'Yes, thanks.'

'Nicola?'

'Yep, me too, thanks. When in Rome!'

'Would you like a jug?' Tiffany asked.

'Um, okay,' Nicola said, despite knowing it was a bad idea.

Alex followed her over to what was now her usual table. They sat around one corner of the six-seater and remained silent as Tiffany put out crockery, cutlery, and bread rolls.

'So, what's this story all about? Really?' Alex said.

'I told you – the drought. I don't have a clear vision for it yet.' She sounded a little snippy. 'Sorry, I'm just finding it frustrating. The drought is so big; it seems to touch everyone and everything – I'm struggling to find a thread.'

'I'm sure you'll find it when it's ready to be found,' he said, shrugging his shoulders.

'Well I hope it shows up soon or else I'll be stuffed,' she said, reaching for the jug of dark, carbonated liquid and the two glasses that had appeared on the table without her noticing.

She poured one and pushed it across the table to Alex, then picked up the second glass. She stared at it for a few moments before telling herself not to worry; the answer would come eventually. *Hmm, and hopefully to my other problem as well*, she thought, filling it up.

Nicola watched the way Alex deftly peeled open the small foil-covered pat of butter, tore a piece of bread from his roll, and began buttering it with surprising delicacy. It was exactly how Ruth had taught her to do it. She always said that the way someone buttered a roll was a good sign of their upbringing. Apparently those who ripped it in half and buttered both sides weren't as well brought up as those who tore off a small morsel, buttered it, and then put it into their mouth.

For years Nicola had been watching how people buttered their bread rolls. More because she found it a fascinating phenomenon than anything else. For as long as she could remember, Nicola had loved to watch people. It was part of the reason she'd become a journalist in the first place – she'd liked the idea of being paid to be nosy.

Where did he learn to butter a roll like that?

'Nice bread,' Alex said, obviously trying to make conversation.

'Hmm, good,' Nicola said, nodding furiously.

It was suddenly all a little uncomfortable. Part of her wished she had just said goodbye, gone back to her room, and settled into checking her emails and Facebook.

'So, how long are you staying for?' Alex said, trying again.

'Not sure. Two weeks, month tops,' she said, focussing on her own bread roll.

Moments later their burgers arrived. 'Thanks Tiff,' they said in unison.

'Yum,' Nicola said, with her mouth half full of her first bite.

'Mmm' Alex agreed, nodding, his mouth full.

★★★

They'd finally pushed aside their empty plates and moved their chairs away from the table a little when Tiffany appeared beside Nicola looking agitated. 'Tiff, what's wrong?'

'Nicola, I've got a message for you,' Tiffany said. 'It came in yesterday and I forgot to give it to you,' she said, blushing. 'I'm really sorry.'

Nicola took the folded scrap of paper and tried to decipher the messy scrawl.

'Alex, can you excuse me for a couple of minutes?' she said, reaching for her mobile.

'Sure, no worries.'

'Back in a bit,' she said brightly. She left Alex at the table sipping his drink and Tiffany collecting their plates, and went outside into the courtyard to make her call.

She shivered; it was cold and windy, but she was also a little afraid. She took a deep breath, pressed his number, and held her breath while it connected.

★★★

'Hi Scott, it's me – sorry, I've just got your message.'

'How's it going? I was getting a little sick of playing phone tag,' he added, with a laugh.

'Well I've finally got mobile coverage again. I feel almost human.'

'That's great.'

'How about you?'

'Flat out with meetings. Off to Canberra tomorrow to try and stop a major client jumping ship.'

'Oh right. So how was your little powwow away?'

'Good. Great fun, actually.'

The hair on Nicola's neck tingled with foreboding. 'You usually hate those things, what was so special?'

'You would have loved it. The room, the food, everything was amazing.'

'Stuffy dinners, pep talks to rally the troops – I doubt it.'

'No, this year was different. They made a special effort for partners.'

'You could have told me.'

'I did, months ago. You weren't interested,' he said wearily.

Remorse stabbed below her ribs as she remembered. She leant against the corner post of the courtyard's pergola. 'Sorry, maybe next time.'

'Nicola, I really miss you,' Scott sighed.

'Well, you could come up here for a weekend.'

'Okay.'

'Really?'

'Yeah, why not?'

'Well, I didn't think you'd be interested; it's probably not even three stars.'

'I'm sure I can slum it for one weekend. I'll check my schedule and give it some thought.'

Nicola knew she should be pleased and excited, but felt sick to the pit of her stomach.

'I warn you, it's miles from anywhere.' She laughed tensely. 'You have to catch a tiny plane.'

'Sounds like you don't want me to visit.'

'Of course I do.'

There were a few moments of silence on the line. 'Is everything okay?'

Nicola's heart became frantic and she was sweating, despite the cold. She began to pace back and forth. Through the window she could see Alex waiting for her.

'Yeah, great, it's just not a very exciting place as it turns out.'

'We'll just have to find other ways to entertain ourselves then, won't we?'

Nicola was riddled with shame and guilt at the prospect. Tears threatened to overcome her.

'Sorry, Scott, I really have to go – my steak has probably arrived,' she lied.

'Yeah, me too. I'm waiting for Chantelle to call back with my travel details.'

'Okay then, have a good trip.'

'Nicola?'

'Yes?'

'I love you.'

It was like a kick to her solar plexus; the last thing she'd expected him to say – she could probably count the number of times he'd uttered the words since their engagement.

'Okay, you take care.'

Why now, when Alex was waiting on the other side of the glass? How could she look him in the eye now – look herself in the mirror for that matter?

Nicola wanted to retreat to her room. But her handbag with her key in it was still inside.

She slipped the phone into her pocket and pulled her coat tightly around her. After what she'd done, she deserved to suffer. Standing there, leaning against the post with her arms wrapped around her and her head bent, Nicola felt a pang of total loneliness so strong that her throat contracted and her eyes began to burn.

What am I going to do?

★★★

A few moments later the nearby door opened, startling her. 'Are you coming back in or should I go?' Alex asked. He had a big grin spread across his gorgeous face, and Nicola found herself smiling tightly back.

'No, I'm coming,' she said, relieved her tears had remained unshed. Thank goodness she wasn't all red-eyed and puffy. The last thing she needed was him putting his arm around her and asking what was wrong.

'Thanks,' she said, sitting down and picking up her refilled glass. Buoyed by the warm smile that greeted her, Nicola wondered if she and Alex could just be friends after all.

'Scott coming to rescue you from Camp Grenada?'

'What? Oh, no, actually, it was my friend Louise – couldn't remember the shade of lipstick we bought together the other week. Lost hers, needs a replacement.'

Even as the lie burst from her lips, Nicola was wondering why; why she couldn't just laugh it off, why she didn't want Alex to know it had been Scott she'd been speaking to.

Desperate to escape reality, she skulled her drink, screwing up her face as the fumes assaulted her tastebuds then burnt her throat. Almost immediately she felt the comforting wooziness of teetering on the edge of sobriety and drunkenness.

Nicola threw back half the next glass and tried to stifle a burp with her hand. 'Bloody Coke,' she giggled, and Alex joined in.

'Another jug?' Tiffany asked, collecting their empty.

'No thanks,' they both said at the same time, and erupted in uproarious laughter.

'Good, because I don't want to have to refuse to serve you later or kick you out for being drunk and disorderly,' Tiffany said, waggling a warning finger at them and chuckling.

'Actually, I'll have a glass of beer. How 'bout you Alex? Not going to let a girl drink alone, I hope?'

'Never,' he grinned. 'Make that two, thanks Tiff.'

They watched her walk away before turning back to each other and finishing their drinks.

'Here you go,' Tiffany said a few minutes later, thumping the two glasses down on the table. Nicola thought she lingered a little too long, glancing back and forth between her and Alex, as if wanting to say something but thinking better of it.

They ran out of conversation and suddenly Nicola felt exhausted.

'Reckon I might catch a bit of telly – have an early night,' she said, well aware of the each way bet she was placing. It was like being a teenager all over again – torn between wanting and wanting to be blameless.

'Anything special on?'

'Not sure.'

'I wouldn't mind seeing *Australian Story* tonight – it's about the artist Tom Roberts' descendants.' He blushed slightly and dipped his head.

'Really?'

'Yeah. I love art.'

'Wow, would never have thought.'

'Actually, I went over to the opening of the Art Gallery's renovation – that's where I was coming back from the night we met on the plane.'

'Well, it's almost eight – you'll miss it by the time you drive home.' Nicola frowned at her watch, wondering where the last few hours had got to.

★★★

'So are you into art at all?' Alex asked as they made their way across the courtyard.

'Um, not really. I used to quite enjoy going to galleries, but Scott likes the walls bare,' she said with a shrug.

She'd been allowed the two pieces from Sandy and Bob's shop, but that was all. And they hadn't been to a gallery in years. She supposed she'd stopped seeing the point if she wasn't actually allowed to take anything home. Though she now remembered that before Scott had come on the scene she'd quite enjoyed just appreciating the talent of the artists. She'd often seen works she could understand the merit in but wouldn't necessarily want to own.

Alex seemed to take her answer as a rebuff, not the sign that she'd lapsed into deep thought. He followed her in silence.

We're only watching TV, Nicola told herself as she turned the key and let them inside.

★★★

'We can't sleep together again,' Nicola blurted.

They were sitting side by side on the bed, propped up by pillows, the closing credits of *Australian Story* rolling up the screen.

'I know – Scott,' Alex said.

'But I really like you.'

'I really like you too,' he said, turning to face her.

Nicola thought her heart would melt. There was so much warmth and regret in his eyes.

'Could I just hold you?' he said, shuffling closer. 'I know it sounds weird, but it's nice.'

After accepting his embrace and burying her face in his smooth strong chest, Nicola felt the overwhelming desire to cry. She stifled it by breathing deeply into his collar.

'This is too hard,' he whispered into her hair, and gently pushed her away.

Nicola knew it was for the best, but still the rejection hit her like a slap across the face. She so badly needed to be held. A single tear broke free and trickled down her cheek. She hoped Alex hadn't noticed.

'Want to talk about it?' he said, giving her shoulder a squeeze.

'No, it's okay.' She swallowed and pushed the lump back down her throat. The last thing she needed was to come across as pathetic and needy. She was Nicola Harvey, woman of the world, presenter of *Life and Times*, and recent Gold Walkley winner.

'He doesn't understand you, does he?'

'You watch too many movies,' she said. *Plenty of people have long-term affairs*, she thought, then instantly wanted to put her head in a bucket of ice water. As if she could have an affair undetected.

Nicola pulled away and sat upright.

'No, he does not understand me, and I don't understand him. We take each other for granted but there's too much at stake to…'

'Why? If you're not happy you get out – simple. Nothing's worth being unhappy.'

How out of touch were these people? And she'd been thinking he was different – somehow more sophisticated.

'Simple!' She stared at him in disbelief, 'It's not bloody simple! Anyway, what would you know, you're…'

'I'm what, just some country hick? Just because I don't have a hotshot job, massive *warehouse conversion*, Mercedes in the garage, doesn't mean I'm stupid.'

'I didn't say…'

'You didn't have to.'

'But…'

'I might not have much but I've got enough, enough to know who I am and what I want. But you? You're a fraud, Nicola Harvey. *Life and* bloody *Times* – you don't have a clue. You're nothing but a snob. And to think I…'

Alex shook his head, gave her a long sorrowful look, threw his legs over the side of the bed and grabbed for his boots.

Watching him leave, Nicola was too stunned to say anything. What hurt most were not his words but the look in his eye and the fact he closed the door carefully, sadly; didn't slam it to make his point.

Tears streamed down her face as she stared at the faded fire evacuation instructions on the back of the door, wondering why she felt so bad. It had only been the one time. He was nothing; *they* were nothing.

'So why do I feel so fucking awful?' she asked the empty room.

What right did he have to call her a snob anyway? Hadn't he seen all the heartfelt stories she'd done helping fat shoppers get justice in a skinny shopper's world; the family reunion with the group of wards of the state? Jesus, where did he get off? He didn't know her at all.

Nicola paced the room. Stopping at the desk, she pounded her fists in frustration. She wanted to give him a piece of her mind. But, damn it, she'd be over the limit. No one was worth losing her licence over.

Fuck him!

She pulled on her boots, grabbed her room key and jacket, and ripped the door open, almost colliding with Alex's fist that was raised, ready to knock.

'Um, er. Well, I suppose you think I'm going to beg you not to go; profess my undying love or something,' she hissed, aware that a number of lights were still burning behind nearby curtains. Her cheeks flamed, eyes wild and searching.

'Well are you?'

Was he smirking? She couldn't tell. Sexy bastard – but a prick like every other man.

'No, I wanted to stop you driving. You're over the limit,' she snapped, aware she was crumbling.

'How touching.'

'Didn't want your death on my conscience.' She scowled like a sulky child and folded her arms across her chest.

'Well, you can offer me a coffee to sober me up then,' he sneered, pushing past her into the room.

The nerve, she thought, still unable to read his mood.

'You might want to shut the door.'

Nicola snapped back to reality, shut the door, and leant against it, unsure what to do next. She and Scott didn't have rows; according to him they were adults and thus there was no need for raised voices – ever. Now she didn't know how to react; it had been so long she had even forgotten how to fight.

'I think you should go,' she said, her voice unsteady. 'Get a coffee at the pub.'

'Sure.' Alex shrugged, put down the cups and coffee sachets, and walked towards her.

Nicola was shaking all over. She hoped he wouldn't get too close, feel the heat of her desire, her fear.

But her feet were welded to the floor; her knees bound to buckle if she moved. Her arms were tense at her sides, sweating palms burning holes in her thighs, and her stomach a sick molten well of churning emotion.

She blinked away the beginning of tears and when she opened her eyes his face was inches from hers. His cold hands clasped her hot face, tilting it up.

And then his mouth was on hers, roughly grinding their lips together. And he was rescuing her from her buckling knees, laying her on the bed.

Hands fumbled hungrily at clothes and bodies melted into each other.

Chapter Twenty-two

It had been in the early hours of the morning when they'd finally untangled their limbs and Alex had reluctantly left. Nicola had tried to sleep, but given up. She now sat up in bed with her phone in hand, making her way through her email, deleting the obvious spam and junk. She'd deal with the important ones later when her head was clearer.

How could she go to bed with him again after hearing Scott say he loved her – those three little words she'd been longing to hear for so long? Was it really too late for them? What if she'd gone to his conference with him – could they have rekindled? Possibly. But they hadn't. Sandy would say that was a sign.

Yeah, a sign that I'm a two-timing tramp.

How could she have been so stupid? Once while drunk and senseless was one thing, a second time was entirely different. Yes they'd been a bit tipsy, but certainly not drunk enough not to know what they were doing or the consequences.

Perhaps if Scott never knew? But she'd know. She couldn't go back and live with that for the next forty years. She looked at her ring twinkling in the light from her bedside lamp. And she certainly couldn't stand up in front of their friends and his family and declare she'd be faithful et cetera et cetera.

But she was throwing away eight years with a man she cared very deeply for. And they had a great life together. What was Alex to her anyway? Her pressure valve, her release? She hated the thought of using him, hurting him; he seemed like such a nice guy.

But she certainly couldn't hop out of one serious relationship and straight into another. Anyway, what was she thinking; she'd slept with him twice – technically it was just a fling, right?

They knew barely anything about each other – except that their bodies seemed to fit together so well – better than Nicola had ever known before. She sighed.

Was that any basis for a lasting relationship? They were born into completely different worlds; what could they ever have in common? She was a city girl and he a country guy. He'd never live in a city; he belonged out here. And she'd never live in a place as isolated as this.

We're too different, she told herself again more forcefully. It wouldn't work. *But love can conquer all,* a little voice inside whispered. Could it? Really? *Did* she love Alex? No! What a ridiculous thought after knowing him less than a week! But to feel those arms around her; those lips upon hers. To feel totally adored, even for just a few hours…

Exactly; it wouldn't last forever. At some point they'd become like most other couples; taking each other for granted, no longer bothering with the nice little gestures and words. Just like she and Scott.

But not like Sandy and Bob, Nicola thought, biting her lip in concentration. She'd often felt a little envious watching them across the café table over breakfast – the little touches they gave each other, the winks, the tender smiles, the 'dear this' and 'darling that'. After so many years the high school sweethearts were still in love. She wanted that.

She wanted to be put ahead of emails, current clients, potential clients, and phone calls. Yes, Nicola realised, she'd been put on hold far too often – and for far too long.

And it was her own fault. She'd taught Scott how to treat her by not speaking up, not putting her foot down. She thought she was being a good supporting partner. And maybe she was, but in doing so she'd been letting herself down. And it was too late to change the rules now. How could she go back and tell Scott that things had to change? Especially when she was so blatantly in the wrong.

Of course she wouldn't have to tell him about Alex, but he'd need some sort of explanation for her change in attitude. She couldn't get away with saying that the time away had just made her think she wanted, needed more. It was the truth, but not the whole truth.

And anyway, she wasn't sure she could give up Alex and go back to faking orgasms again. What a mess! Nicola clutched her gnawing stomach; she actually felt sick – like she was being physically torn in two, not just emotionally and mentally. Her heart and head ached.

Thank goodness Alex had teed up for her to visit Graeme again today. She'd have something to distract her. He'd phoned him while they were waiting for *Australian Story* to start. Nicola wished she wasn't spending the day with someone so closely related to Alex, but at least she would be getting on with the story. And that was, after all, why she was here.

If only Bill hadn't asked her to come out here. If only she hadn't agreed. But then she wouldn't have met Alex. And if nothing ever happened between them again, she'd still have those two nights.

'Oh God, here we go again,' she said, shaking her head. She

really had to get herself together. Otherwise she'd end up losing everything. The way it stood, no matter what happened with her and Scott and did or didn't happen between her and Alex, she'd still have her job. But if she wasn't careful she'd be putting that on the line as well. What she had to do was get her story done, and then she could get out of here and get her life back in order.

Nicola returned to her emails. She checked the time. It was nearly dawn. She'd skip breakfast at the hotel and get something at the bakery – the last thing she needed from Tiffany were comments or silent knowing glances. The girl was young, but she wasn't blind, and she certainly wasn't stupid.

★★★

At eight-thirty Nicola pushed open the glass door to the bakery and joined a throng of people; mainly young men in tradesmen's gear and high visibility attire. They all seemed to be chattering about severe wind and the damage it had done.

Wind? She hadn't heard a thing while she'd been tucked up with Alex. Though, now she thought about it, there had been twigs and fresh, green leaves scattered across the courtyard.

Her mouth watered at the smell of fresh bread. She ducked and weaved a little, trying to get a look at the display case before her turn came, but there were too many people. Slowly she shuffled forward with the group as one by one the customers got their orders and left. She checked her watch.

Damn! She was due at Graeme and Dorothy McCardle's in twenty minutes and there was still a fifteen minute drive ahead of her. She couldn't eat and drive, especially if she got a pie, which she was leaning towards – she'd end up with gravy all over her front. Should she just give up on breakfast? She was almost at the counter; just a few minutes more. But she hated lateness; it was rude.

Nicola sighed and turned around. She was about to walk to the door when she was interrupted by a lean woman almost her height, dressed in tailored khaki slacks and a navy and white rugby-style jumper.

'You're Nicola, aren't you? Nicola Harvey?'

'Yes, hello.'

'I'm Dorothy, Dorothy McCardle. You're visiting us this morning,' she said, holding out her hand.

'Yes, yes I am,' she said, shaking Dorothy's hand and taking in her wavy shoulder-length auburn locks, carefully shaped eyebrows and smooth skin.

So this was Alex's mother? She didn't look old enough. She had to be mid to late fifties, but she could have passed for a decade younger.

And it wasn't just because she was fully made-up; there was barely a wrinkle in the fair, freckled skin of her oval face. Lucky thing. Large steel grey eyes were framed by long lashes highlighted with dark mascara. Not classically beautiful, but certainly a striking woman, Nicola concluded, as she let her hand go.

'I'm just getting us something for morning tea,' she said, waving a perfectly manicured nail. A couple of people made their way past them mumbling, 'Excuse me'.

'Oh, that's really not necessary,' Nicola said. 'I was going to get something for breakfast, but I realised I'd be late if I waited any longer.'

'Well there's no need – we'll be having morning tea soon. Unless of course you'd rather something more substantial – I'm getting something sweet.'

'Dorothy, what can I get you?' a voice said, and Nicola suddenly realised they were standing well back from the counter with a crush of people waiting patiently behind. She moved forward to get a good look at the cabinet. She couldn't get a pie now. But, oh, they looked so good. Her mouth was watering as she took in the dozen different types of pies with little labels in front of them.

'Anything in particular you like the look of, Nicola?' Dorothy asked.

'It all looks very good,' she said. And it did. She cast her eye across the shelves of sweet delicacies, many oozing with red jam, cream or custard.

'Just one of the elephant's feet then, thanks Trude,' Dorothy said.

What had she said? Elephant's feet? Nicola looked across the rows of the display cabinet and saw the shop assistant drag out a large, flat, elongated bun covered in white icing and coconut, and put it into a paper bag.

'Anything else?' She asked, putting it on the counter and holding up her tongs.

'No, that'll be all. Did you want anything, Nicola?'

'Can I bring anything?'

'No, this will be more than enough.'

'No, thanks,' she said, smiling at the woman behind the counter, 'I'm fine.' She still fancied something savoury, but was having trouble deciding between the steak and mushroom pie and the pepper steak version. She hadn't had a pie in years. Not since the day she'd last followed Scott around the golf course, she realised. That must have been six years ago.

Nicola felt uncomfortable waiting and watching while Dorothy paid – she should have been taking something herself. Anyway, she thought she was going for another farm tour, not morning tea.

And here I am, following Alex's mother out of the Nowhere Else Bakery and Deli. Well, he certainly got her long, lean legs. Not that she'd had much chance to take in Graeme's physique when she thought she was being threatened with a pitchfork. The ludicrousness of her melodrama now struck her as funny. As if!

'Well this is me,' Dorothy said, standing on the sidewalk in front of a silver four-wheel-drive that looked just like her hire one except for the colour. 'Are you right to find your own way again or would you like me to wait for you to follow?'

'Thanks; that would be good. But there's no need to wait, I'm parked right here,' she said with a smile, pointing to the vehicle parked next door.

'Great, see you there then. Just watch out around the bends for the council truck – it's out picking up branches that came down in the wind last night.'

'Okay, will do, thanks.'

'Bye,' Dorothy said, opening her door and getting in.

Nicola waited for the silver four-wheel-drive to reverse out of its forty-five degree angle park before doing the same and following it. As she did, she acknowledged she was indeed getting used to the cumbersome vehicle. She was even beginning to like the high driving position and the extended view it gave her. It would be quite a shock to get back into her little road-hugging Mercedes sports coupe again. She'd be back to feeling overshadowed, though parking would be a lot easier.

Nicola was right behind Dorothy until she turned onto the dirt and Nicola hung back to keep out of the thick cloud of dust. Giving herself space and driving much slower than Dorothy meant that by the time Nicola turned into the driveway at the old milk churn, Dorothy was nowhere to be seen. She parked near the large tree as she had a few days ago and got out.

Graeme was on the verandah to greet her – but with no pitch-fork in hand this time. She thought he looked like the lord of the manor standing like that above her. As she made her way up the steps, Nicola realised she felt a little nervous at meeting Alex's father – well, meeting him properly.

'Nicola, Graeme McCardle. So lovely to meet you – er, properly,' he said, gripping her hand in both of his, and giving it a good pumping.

'Hi Graeme, thanks very much for seeing me.'

'Pleasure, pleasure, come in,' he said, standing aside. He wasn't nearly as tall and imposing now as she'd thought the other day. Actually, he was only just her height. And now she noticed, he was quite stocky.

'Straight down the end and to the left,' he said.

Nicola would have loved to take in the décor properly, but was very aware of being ushered forward by Graeme two steps behind her.

'I'm very sorry about being so rude the other day – the drought has us all on edge around here.'

Nicola made her way down the red Persian hall runner on honey-coloured polished floorboards. The day that had been cold but sunny was now cloudy, and when darkness suddenly descended in the previously well-lit hall, she looked up briefly and noted the skylights.

They turned into a large kitchen with the kind of proportions lauded by interior design magazines. Dorothy was at the sink with the bun in front of her on a chopping board. Through the window she saw a house yard surrounded by a traditional corrugated iron fence with a variety of shrubs growing against it. Beyond that was a rubble area like the driveway and then two large silver sheds side by side.

Dorothy turned and waved her knife in their general direction. 'Hi Nicola, welcome. Have a seat. Won't be a minute.' She turned back to the bench.

'Thanks Dorothy.'

'Oh, you know each other?' Graeme said, looking perplexed and a little uncomfortable.

'We bumped into each other at the bakery,' Dorothy said to Graeme without looking around.

'Oh.'

'Yes,' Nicola said. 'Dorothy saved me from eating a pie for break-fast.' She grinned.

'Would you like some toast? It'd be no trouble?' Graeme said, hanging his hat on a hook on the back of the door.

'Thank you. I'm fine,' Nicola said, sitting in front of one of the three plates, each with a paper serviette and knife laid across it. Without his hat, Graeme had a head of slightly receding lightish grey hair. The skin on his long face was tanned, weathered, dry, and deeply lined, as were his hands. Nicola was surprised to notice that the deep crows' feet wrinkles ended at blue eyes – kind-looking blue eyes. Hmm, she had got him so wrong the other day. But where had Alex's dark, Mediterranean looks come from? They must have skipped a generation or two.

'Can I get you a tea or coffee? I've just boiled the kettle,' Dorothy said, bringing Nicola back.

'Tea would be lovely.' She was about to say 'milk and a dash of sugar' when she noticed the small bowl of sugar and jug of milk in the middle of the table along with a dish of butter.

Within seconds a white porcelain mug appeared in front of her.

As Dorothy put Graeme's mug in front of him, Nicola thought she detected tension between the husband and wife. Had she walked in on a fight or something? She put the thought aside. As Graeme said, they were all on edge because of the drought.

'You have a lovely home here.' Nicola said, looking around her. The kitchen was well appointed. The timber cabinetry and stone-look glossy Laminex bench tops were a little dated, but the room was light and airy. And tidy; not a thing was out of place.

'Thank you.' If Nicola hadn't been looking at Dorothy, she would have missed the icy look she gave Graeme as she put the bun on the table.

There was definitely tension in the air, Nicola thought, beginning to feel a little uncomfortable.

'I can't wait to try this bun. What did they call it? Elephant's something?'

'Elephant's foot,' Dorothy said. 'I think it's because of its shape,' she added, offering the plate to Nicola.

Nicola took a piece and scrutinised it as she put it on her plate. It was a traditional-looking plain iced finger bun, except for its size and shape, and the thick jam – that looked like apricot – running through its centre.

'I've never seen anything like it before,' she commented as she carefully buttered around the jam.

'I think the bakery makes everything on premises,' Graeme said.

'Yum,' Nicola said, taking a bite. She was conscious of being watched, and wished they would tuck in themselves. Finally they did.

They spoke about the wild weather the night before and the damage it had done. Ten minutes later Graeme was shifting in his chair and sneaking glances at his watch. Nicola took the cue, drained the rest of her tea, and pushed her plate away from her.

'Shall we go? Take you for a look around?' Graeme asked, as he pushed his chair back from the table. It was more a statement than a question.

Chapter Twenty-three

Graeme led her out the back door near the kitchen, out under a verandah and across to an iron gate in the back fence. They went to where a large weeping native pepper tree grew beside the far shed, encircled by a high steel mesh fence. Two huge black and white dogs stood up on their hind legs with their front claws hooked into the mesh, whining and wriggling, obviously thrilled at the thought they were being let out. The closer Graeme and Nicola walked, the louder they whined and the more furiously their tails wagged behind them.

'Come on then,' Graeme said, going over and opening the gate. 'Stay down!' he yelled, as they clambered around her. She tried to push them away from her crotch and laughed off their attentions.

'Not bad lads,' Graeme said, ruffling their ears once they'd settled down and were standing calmly beside them.

Nicola followed Graeme to a white ute parked in the shed, and got in.

'Come on then, up,' he called. The two dogs leapt effortlessly onto the back. They clambered onto the bales of hay covering the tray. 'Come here.' She watched as he clipped them onto short lengths of chain behind the cabin. 'To keep them safe,' he said, noticing Nicola watching. 'So they can't fall off the back. Was there anything in particular you wanted to see?'

'No, I just want to get a bit of an idea of farm life, really,' she said, with a shrug. 'Thanks so much for this – I really appreciate it.'

'No worries.'

They drove out into the paddock, where Graeme unloaded the hay as hundreds of sheep ran towards them from all directions. Nicola was pleased she was safe in the cabin – did sheep bite? They weren't at all skinny like the ones she'd seen the other day.

Back in the cabin, Graeme explained that they were the important ones. 'I'll keep hold of these ewes as long as possible. The rams are in another paddock – I fed them earlier. You can't do anything without good breeding stock. And the drought has to end eventually, right?' he added with a lopsided grin. Nicola smiled back.

'So you plough all you have into feeding the buggers. Hence the tension back there,' he said, tossing thumb back towards the house.'

'Sorry?'

'You have to be born on a farm to really understand...'

Understand what? Nicola wondered.

'The townies come out here thinking we only work five months of the year and the rest of the time we're off fishing or available to do work around the house. Dorothy's been a farmer's wife for thirty-odd years and still doesn't like the sheep and everything else on this place coming first. I did the house up in the early days to keep her happy – an expense I really could have done without. You do your best, but it's rarely good enough,' he shrugged.

Nicola was beginning to feel decidedly uncomfortable. What did his private life have to do with her?

'I suppose you're wondering why I'm telling you. You might think it's not relevant to the drought. But it is; it's crucial to understanding the people involved. Townies and true farmers' daughters are a completely different kettle of fish. One understands that the proceeds need to go back into the farm first and foremost, and the other doesn't. All the old-timers will tell you; but do you think we young whippersnappers listen?

'If only I could afford to get the damn house renovated, or take her on a long overseas trip, we'd be fine,' he said with a laugh.

'Now take my brother Bert; he married a lass from good, tough farm stock who knew how it all worked...' he said wistfully. 'It wasn't her fault Bert ended up in Vietnam... Oh, listen to me. Going on like a sentimental old fool.'

'I met Bert the other day – seemed like a nice man,' Nicola ventured.

'Well I don't blame him; he's pretty angry at me. And he has every right to be.'

'Because of the water?'

'No, it goes a lot further back than that.'

'Oh?'

'Yeah, a very long way back.'

Nicola wanted to say she had all day to listen, but it seemed Graeme McCardle was done talking about his brother. They drove on in silence, out of the paddock and onto a rubble road.

'Now you're about to see the damage last night's wind did,' he said. In front of them dirt was strewn across the road. 'I warn you, the going's about to get a little rough.'

They moved forward slowly, the mounds of powdery brown dirt becoming higher and stretching further across their path. The four-wheel-drive heaved and grunted in protest as it climbed up and over corrugated piles that reached almost halfway up the wire fences on either side.

'What we're driving over is topsoil — farmers' livelihood for the past two hundred years or so. The winds we've had in the last twelve months have been unheard of — last night was just the icing on the cake.'

Nicola got out her camera and started snapping away. She wondered how sand could stay put for two hundred years but not last night, but didn't want to look like an idiot so kept silent.

'Heaps of us took a punt on rain coming this year and sowed with the ground almost dry. Before the crop could come up and hold the soil, we got a couple of really blustery days and this is the result.' Graeme swept an arm around dramatically, but looking at his grim expression told of the true devastation he felt.

'Another problem it caused was contamination of the bay. When we sow we spray to keep weeds down and give the seed a chance to germinate. They reckon the chemicals got into the fish farm. I'm not sure how badly they were affected — a bloke was talking in the pub. So you see it's not just the dirt farmers who are affected by the drought and bad weather. It permeates every part of the district.

'One of the worst hit is old Kevin Young who's going for his organic certification. They reckon he won't get it now because of the contaminated dirt that drifted through his fence from his neighbours.

'You'd be forgiven for thinking they should be all banned,' Graeme continued, shooting Nicola a knowing grin. 'Most city people do.'

Mind reader, she thought.

'But chemicals have their place — we need them. Otherwise the weeds and bugs take over. A lot of us are experimenting with direct drilling, which means you don't work the land as hard. But you still need to spray.' He shrugged.

By the time they got back to the house, Nicola's head was spinning from all the information. A few times she'd wanted to stop

Graeme, turn her recorder on and have him say something again, but she hadn't wanted to break the flow. She'd have to make notes that night; she only hoped what she'd seen and heard had seeped well into her. At least she had plenty of photos as reminders.

They enjoyed a thick homemade lamb and vegetable soup that was more like a stew, accompanied with steaming grainy bread that Nicola watched Dorothy take out of the bread maker.

Nicola had thought many times of getting a bread maker – the idea of fresh bread awaiting her on a Sunday morning was very alluring. But Sandy had warned her against it; she and Bob bought one and then put on a couple of stones each by consuming twice as much bread as they had before. Nicola had decided the threat to her television physique was far too risky. But now her mouth watered.

She watched Dorothy buzzing about and then sitting at the table eating. She wouldn't have thought it if Graeme hadn't said anything, but now she could see that Dorothy did seem a little out of place – the manicured nails, the well-dyed hair; not a grey hair or root in sight. She couldn't imagine Dorothy setting foot outside the house and risking getting anything dirty. She certainly hadn't shown the slightest interest in joining them for their drive, or entering into any of their farming-related discussions at the table.

After lunch, Nicola thanked them profusely, shook their hands, and made her way to her vehicle under the tree. The sun was shining brightly, but there was a bitterly cold breeze.

As she drove off, waving to them standing stiffly side by side on the verandah, an image of her parents flashed by – they had been happy, loving, and almost sickeningly affectionate to the end.

She thought of Alex. Hopefully they made more of an effort for him. Perhaps it hadn't always been like this. She couldn't imagine what it must have been like to grow up in this atmosphere.

★★★

Nicola had parked the four-wheel-drive and was absently and slowly making her way to her room when Tiffany popped her head out of the door marked Cleaner.

'Eh Nicola, hang on,' she called, waving a pink fuzzy duster on a wooden stick.

Nicola grinned. 'Nice look,' she said, nodding at the rubber boots, pink gloves and the red and white checked scarf covering her hair. The garb made her look at least double her age.

'Thanks,' Tiffany said, wrinkling her nose. 'Roxanne's crook. Anyway, just wanted to tell you some mail came – I put it on the desk in your room.'

'Thanks,' Nicola said, 'From my boss no doubt. I've obviously been here far too long if I'm getting mail delivered, huh?' she said with a laugh.

'Yeah,' Tiffany said, grinning back. 'So, get anything good from Graeme?'

'Not sure yet; lots to take in.'

'Meet Dorothy? Odd couple eh? Him so nice; her with all her airs and graces.'

'Hmm.'

'Occasionally they'll have a meal in here. It's like she's punishing him for something – and I don't mean by having tea here,' she chuckled self-consciously.

'I know what you meant.'

There was a moment's silence before Tiffany spoke again. 'Anyway, I'd better get on,' she said.

'Right, thanks, see you later.'

'Yeah, see you.'

Nicola wandered the last few steps to her room, thinking about what Tiffany had said. Fascinating. But it really didn't seem relevant to the drought so she couldn't waste time on it. Bill was sure to be getting antsy if she didn't present him with a reasonable synopsis sometime soon.

Chapter Twenty-four

Nicola stared at the envelope with the government stamp in the corner. Her heart was thumping hard against her ribs as she opened it and pulled the contents out. As she read the information on Department for Families and Communities letterhead, her mouth dropped open.

What!? No. It couldn't be. Bert and Janet McCardle? Impossible.

Had Bill known all along? Was that why he'd sent her here? No, there was no way he could have; it was just one almighty coincidence. Jesus, what were the odds?

Nicola searched her mind for the first person to tell; she needed to tell someone. With shaking fingers she brought up the number and called.

'Scott. Hi, it's me. You're never going to believe this.'

'What?'

'I've found my parents, well, my father anyway. I've met him, been to his house…'

'What are you on about?'

'My parents are from here…'

'Where?'

'Nowhere Else.'

Scott laughed.

'Why are you laughing?'

'Sorry, I couldn't resist – too funny.'

'Scott, this is serious. I've found my biological father. I've met him.'

'How?'

'My information from the Department of Families and Communities arrived.'

'Nicola, we discussed that and…'

'I changed my mind.'

'Are you sure this is wise?'

'You don't know what it's like not to know.'

'No, I don't.'

'There's this yearning inside – like a question mark; on everything you do, everywhere you go.'

'Nicola, you're being melodramatic.'

'No. It's how I feel.' She put a hand to her aching heart for reinforcement, to try and stop the tears she could feel building in her chest.

'I just don't think there's anything to be achieved looking back into the past.'

'At least I'll know,' she said quietly as two big, fat tears started rolling down her cheeks.

'Well, as you said, I don't know what it's like. Look, I'm sorry, but I've got another call coming through. I've got to go.'

'Wait!' She was about to say, 'Don't you want to know what I found out?' But he'd already hung up.

Nicola stared at her phone for a few moments before putting it down.

Scanning the room, she fought the lump in her throat and tried to ignore the phone book beckoning from the shelf beside the bed.

Tears blurred her vision as she thumbed the pages and found the listing for McCardle, A.

Still struggling with her conscience, she picked up her phone and started to dial.

The click of connection collided with Nicola's realisation like a bolt of lightning. She dropped the handset and leapt back. The phone book slid from her lap onto the floor. She stared at it, her head tightening as the room began to revolve around her, gathering speed.

Blood surged in her eardrums, the truth hammering at her with every pulse. *Oh my God.* Nicola continued staring at the crumpled phone book, dumbfounded.

Reluctantly she accepted it was not a nightmare she would wake from. *Should I tell him?* Tell him what exactly? 'Oh, you know that fantastic sex we had? Well, surprise! I'm actually your cousin. Sorry old chap.'

Tears streamed down her face.

What she needed was to get away and find someone to talk to – someone who would understand and wouldn't judge. But how could anyone understand *this*?

Nicola wanted her mum with an ache that reached the depths of her soul.

The last time she'd seen her parents was when she'd had to identify their waterlogged bodies. She had fled the room after barely thirty seconds. Most distressing had been the huge technicolour bruises to Ruth's thighs, and the humiliation for her modest mother at being found by rescuers in her underwear.

Nicola had cringed at the deep gashes to her father's forehead. She hadn't been able to ask the doctor about the sections of flesh peeling snake-like from Paul's chest. The inquest report explained that it was the reaction skin had after coming into contact with aviation fuel.

Paul and Ruth's eerily peaceful grey expressions had haunted her day and night for weeks before Nicola managed to get herself back into research mode and focus on finding answers.

Nicola felt totally alone. She didn't want to bother Sandy – who was bound to be out shopping; she couldn't bear a flippant comment from her if she was half-undressed in a change room and not concentrating. This was important. And none of her other friends would understand, would even attempt to understand.

Why did she even consider them friends at all? They were too shallow, too worried about hair, nails and shoes to give a damn. They'd tell her all she needed was a bit of retail therapy – their answer to all life's dramas. Nicola sighed.

And Scott. Hadn't he shown his true colours?

Nicola realised there was only one person she could speak to – she just had to summon the courage.

★★★

After knocking for what seemed an eternity, Nicola slumped onto the concrete step, defeated. How could Bert not be at home, today of all days?

The sun warmed the top of her head as she drew stick figure houses and families in the hard, compacted dirt between her feet; she would wait all day if she had to.

Nicola was brushing her canvas clear and starting over when she stopped and cocked her head. What was that noise?

She stood up. There it was again. The sound was coming from the nearest shed. She moved slowly, pausing with every step to listen.

Nicola stepped through the partially open door.

'Hello?' she called into the darkness, willing her eyes to adjust. She stared, trying to make sense of what she was seeing. A ute was parked in the shed, nothing wrong with that.

'Help.'

Nicola looked towards the floor beside the ute. Bert was lying on his side on the concrete, clutching his chest. She ran over to him and squatted down.

'I think it's my heart,' he whispered between gasping breaths.

'My phone's in the car. I'll get help.' She bolted, feet pounding to the rhythm of her heart and her silent chant of hope that Bert could hang on.

The remote snagged in her pocket and she struggled to pull it free. She was frantically pushing buttons, but nothing was happening. Why had she locked it anyway?

Finally she found her mobile in the bottom of her handbag on the floor. Her fingers were shaking so much she could barely dial triple zero as she ran back to the shed. She waited for it to connect, hoping she was being directed to the local station and not somewhere interstate.

'Ambulance service, what is your emergency?'

'There's a man here – I think he's had a stroke, or a heart attack, or something. I found him on the floor. I'm not sure how long he's been here. He's conscious, but...'

'Do you have a grid reference?'

'No I...I don't know. About ten kilometres from the town of Nowhere Else – west. Bert McCardle's farm. Just off...um...Karkarook Road – mailbox is an old fridge.'

'It's okay, we know it.'

'It's the shed just past the house.'

'They're approximately seven minutes away. If he's still conscious, try and keep him talking.'

Nicola hung up, blessing the small town way of life; at least there was one good thing about knowing everyone and where they lived.

Back at the shed she paused, swallowed deeply, and summoned her strength and composure.

'Bert! Wake up, talk to me. The ambulance is on its way.'

Bert groaned.

'I need you to stay awake. Stay with me.'

He was a terrible shade of ash-grey. She leant forward and gripped his limp hand, wanting to scream that he couldn't die because he was her father and she needed him.

After what seemed hours Nicola heard a siren approaching. She heard a slight sigh escape his lips.

'It's not over yet – you need to stay strong.'

Suddenly the sliding doors were being hauled wide open, sunlight was streaming in, and Nicola was nudged aside. Two men in blue, carrying backpacks, rushed to Bert's side.

'How long has he been like this?'

'He was on the floor when I arrived – I was just visiting.'

'Does he have a history of heart problems?'

'I don't know,' she said wringing her hands. Should she tell them she was his daughter? No, she couldn't; she'd be expected to know at least some of his medical history. And there was no time to explain the truth.

'I'm a journalist; I came to interview him,' she added. Telling Bert she was his daughter would have to be handled very carefully, especially now.

God, what if he didn't make it? What if she never got the chance? She couldn't think about that.

Their voices were mumbled and earnest. Nicola knew there was nothing more she could do. She should leave, but couldn't bring herself to. She sat on an oil drum out of the way and watched the ordered chaos, which faded to a distant blur as the adrenaline began to subside.

Nicola felt a squeeze to her shoulder and looked up. One of the ambulance men was standing beside her. The other was standing by the stretcher where Bert now lay covered in blankets.

'We have him stabilised now.'

'Will he be okay?'

'We won't know until they do some tests at the hospital – he'll go to Port Lincoln via the air ambulance. The police will let his family know what's happened.'

'Oh, right.'

'Well, we'd better get going. Are you okay to drive? We could send for another ambulance.'

'Thanks, but I'll be fine,' she said, getting up slowly. 'Please take good care of him.'

'We certainly will. You drive safely now.'

She waited until they had loaded him and shut the doors before making her way on unsteady legs to the four-wheel-drive.

She caught up with the ambulance at the end of Bert's driveway, and followed it to the outskirts of town and then around to the gate marked Aerodrome. She bumped along the winding dirt road and parked behind a chain link fence. There she watched the white mounded stretcher being transferred to a small plane humming on the tarmac.

The ambulance left, closing the Trespassers Prosecuted gate behind. The plane taxied, took off, and within seconds was out of sight.

Chapter Twenty-five

Nicola was alone. The diesel four-wheel-drive was idling throatily. Her temples throbbed with the beginning of a headache. Nearby birds began heralding the change from day to evening.

She had to let Graeme or Alex know. She pulled out her phone, then realised she didn't have their numbers programmed into it. She'd left her notebook and all the details back at her room; it hadn't been a visit for work.

She reversed and made her way back to town. About to turn towards the motel, she glanced back at the *Nowhere Else Echo* office. She hesitated, slowed to a crawl, stopped in the middle of the street, and drummed her fingers on the wheel.

No, he wouldn't understand.

She sighed, turned away.

'Changed your mind?'

She turned around. Richard was standing on the other side of the vehicle, looking in at her through the window.

'Tough day?'

'Yeah.'

'Cuppa?' Nicola silently accepted his invitation by nodding.

★★★

'Sit,' Richard said, pulling out a chair for her.

'Thanks.'

'You look like you're carrying the weight of the world.'

'Actually, can I borrow your White Pages?'

'Sure,' he said, reaching into a drawer. 'Anything I can help you with?' He asked, handing her a slim, soft volume.

'Bert McCardle has collapsed. I was there; had to call the ambulance. I should let Graeme know before the police do…' Her eyes filled.

'What, worried your story's kaput?'

Nicola glared icily, any sign of tears disappearing.

'Sorry, that wasn't fair. Don't worry. He's a tough old bugger. And Graeme will already know.'

'Sorry?'

'It's all over the radio.'

'Already?'

'Emergency channel.' Richard tapped a nearby metal box with microphone attached. 'Heard the ambulance chatter this afternoon. Lucky you turned up when you did. Otherwise he could have been lying out there on his farm alone for days. So, what can I get you? Tea, coffee, Milo?' He got up.

'Milo thanks – two spoons…'

'…Lots of milk. I remember. Back in a sec.'

Nicola sat fiddling with the edge of her jacket.

★★★

'So, talk to me. What's really bothering you?'

'I'm fine.'

'No you're not. I know you Nicola, remember.'

'No, really. I'm just a bit freaked by the whole Bert thing – being there and all.'

'Why though?'

'Why what?'

'Why so freaked?'

'What do you think? I've just seen my…a bloke laying on a concrete floor, fighting for his life. Have you lost all your compassion, writing nothing but footy scores and police reports?'

'I'll ignore that. "My"?'

'Your what?'

'No, you said, "I've just seen my…" Your what, Nicola?'

'Nothing.' Nicola drained her cup quickly and moved to get up. 'I'd better go, thanks for the chat.'

As she stood Richard grabbed her hand.

'What are you running away from?'

'Don't be melodramatic, Richard. I'm not running away from anything; I'm just going back to my motel room.'

'I'm not letting you drive any further in this state.'

'I told you, I'm fine. Anyway, I'm only going up the street.'

'Nicola, you're not fine – you're all over the place.'

'Okay, you win. I'm not all right. Happy?' She sat heavily.

'No. Don't get all defensive. I care about you – I'd like to help if I can.'

Nicola fought to keep her guard up. She studied the floor, hoping to blink the tears away. When she looked back, Richard had pulled his chair closer and was sitting with his knees almost touching hers, reaching for both her hands.

Nicola pulled her hands away, linked them in her lap, and took a deep breath.

'You remember I'm adopted, right?'

Richard nodded.

'Well, I finally got the guts to start looking for…'

'Wow, that's great. Good on you,' Richard said, reaching for her hand again before stopping himself.

Nicola examined her hands in her lap.

'I take it you've found something then – otherwise you wouldn't be mentioning it.

She nodded.

'Oh come on, you're killing me. What? Your parents were child molesters or murderers or something?'

Nicola shook her head. Her lips were pursed.

'What then; they're the mega-rich owners of some huge corporation?'

Nicola frowned and shook her head again.

'Just bloody tell me!'

'They're here in Nowhere Else – well, one of them is.'

'No! Are you serious?'

'Yup.'

'So you've met them – one of them, both?'

'Yes and no.'

'Huh?'

'Richard, Bert's my biological father.'

'Oh.' Richard took a moment to respond. 'So that's why you're so upset.'

'Uh huh.'

'Does he know? Have you spoken to him about it?'

'That's why I was at the farm. I didn't get the chance to say anything. And now…'

'Nic, he's strong – he'll pull through.'

'But what if he doesn't?'

'Worry about that if and when it happens.'

'So, does he even know he has a daughter out there somewhere?'

'No idea. All I have is a birth certificate with my parents' names on it – Bert and Janet McCardle.'

'Fancy you going out and speaking to Bert when he was your father all along. Wow, Nic, that's mind-blowing.'

'Yeah, hell of a coincidence. But there's more. I slept with Alex...'

'Alex, as in Alex McCardle?'

Nicola nodded as she watched Richard's eyebrows shoot up and his eyes bug again.

'But he's your... Oh my God, he's your cousin!'

Nicola winced. 'Uh huh.'

'But you're engaged; you're the most loyal person I know.'

'Thanks. I feel so much better.'

'Sorry. So does Alex know – about you being related?'

'I haven't had a chance to tell him. I only found this out myself a few hours ago. But I'm going to have to, aren't I? How bloody embarrassing.'

'Well, it's not like you knew.'

'But still, it's disgusting,' Nicola said, screwing up her face in distaste.

'And it was only a one off, right?'

'Um.' Nicola looked away.

'Right?'

Nicola dropped her head further.

'Twice.'

'Oh God. Please don't tell me you think you're in love with him.'

Nicola nibbled on her lip. 'I can't be if I hardly know him, can I?' she asked, sounding like a little girl.

'I'm a man; what would I know?' he said, throwing his hands in the air. 'Well you certainly can't sleep with him again; that would be just icky.'

'Should I be revolted?'

'Yes, you most certainly should. You're not?'

'Well, I am at the thought of, you know… But when I think about how good it was with…'

Richard held up silencing hands. 'I don't want to know.'

'But Richard, I still have feelings for him. How could I now, knowing this?'

'You're sick?' he said with a shrug. 'Should I be phoning *The Jerry Springer Show*?'

'Richard!'

'Surely even you can see the funny side.'

'No, I can't actually. This is me, my life, we're talking about – not some story I'm doing.'

'Maybe you should.'

'Richard, I thought you were my friend.' Nicola got up to go.

'I am. I'm sorry. Look, don't go. It's all so unbelievable; I'm just having trouble taking it all in.'

'Well how do you think I feel?' Nicola sat back down heavily.

'What can I do?'

'I don't know,' Nicola said with a deep sigh. 'Stop laughing for a start. My life's a bloody mess,' she said, burying her head in her hands.

'I'm not laughing,' he said, smiling kindly at her.

There were a few moments of silence.

'Okay, let's see. Firstly, Scott – do you love him?'

Nicola shrugged.

'Has something happened?'

'I think we've been drifting apart for ages – years if I'm being honest.'

'Well could you, or would you *want* to, spend the rest of your life – say, the next fifty years or so – with him? Forget anyone else. Infatuations or flings are not reasonable grounds.'

'I don't think so.'

'Easy. You have to end it then.'

'It's not easy.'

'No, it won't be easy, but it's what you have to do. The longer you leave it, the harder it will be.'

'But financially, it's all so…'

'Not a good enough reason to stay. Deep down you know that, Nicola. You have to be true to yourself – follow your heart. Which brings us to Alex. Your cousin.'

'Don't remind me,' Nicola groaned.

'Hey, it's not that bad. You weren't to know. Question is, what are you going to do about it now?'

'Nothing. Well, obviously I can't ever sleep with him again.'

'Well, that's solved then.'

Yeah, real easy. How was it men could turn their feelings on and off like a tap? Stupid question – of course she knew how.

'So that leaves us with Bert. Are you going to tell him he's your father?'

'I don't know. What do you think?'

'I think only you know the answer to that.'

'Thanks a lot, Yoda.'

'Well, for what it's worth, I think you should at least go and see him. Get to know him. You'll know if and when the time's right. And as for your story – just give it time. You'll discover the angle if you don't force it. Bill trusts you – you're a Gold Walkley winner now.'

'Jealousy's a curse, Richard.'

'No, you're not listening. What I mean is, you've proven yourself.'

'But I had a plane crash – something big to work with.'

'And now you have the drought – something even bigger. You'll come up with something great; might just take a little more time.

You know it and Bill knows it. Lighten up on yourself, Nicola. You're a young, beautiful and incredibly talented woman.'

Nicola flinched slightly as Richard tenderly brushed aside the few strands of hair that had stuck to her earlier tears.

They leapt apart at the shrill of the phone.

As Richard talked with his wife about the dinner arrangements, Nicola tried not to listen. Feeling a pang of envy, she got up, collected the cups and wandered down the hall to the kitchenette.

After a few moments, Richard materialised in the doorway and put his hand on her shoulder. 'Sorry, but I've got to get going. Will you be okay?'

Nicola nodded.

'Yep.'

He carefully turned her towards him.

'Sure?'

Nicola returned his gaze, relieved at having spoken her problems aloud.

'I'll be fine, really. Thanks for listening.'

'No worries. Anytime.'

Chapter Twenty-six

Nicola drove the hour and a half to Port Lincoln with a queasy mix of apprehension, fear and excitement in her stomach. The scenery was quite lovely in the daytime, but she was too distracted by everything else going on in her head to totally appreciate it. By the time she arrived at the hospital, her jeans were damp from the constant wiping of her palms on her thighs.

She'd gone over her speech until it sounded too contrived – and then scrapped it. Deep down she knew this was one of those occasions that could only be played out ad lib. Here she was, the queen of preparation, at the most important interview of her life, with absolutely no idea what to say.

She got out of the vehicle and glanced around, half expecting some sort of recognition to kick in. According to the photo, and confirmed by her birth certificate, this was where she'd been born. Her legs were weak, temples pounding, and she was pleased to have the gentle cool breeze drying her damp shirt.

Just a few minutes, she told herself, and sat on the nearby raised concrete planter, leaning forward and resting her head in her hands.

But she had driven all this way and she couldn't put it off forever.

Nicola walked stiffly toward the hospital's main entrance, making every effort to commit the experience to memory but hampered by the other thoughts whirling through her mind.

The glass doors slid open and she was greeted by the odours of new paint and carpet. She looked around, imagined how it had looked thirty-four years ago.

In fact the reception area was nothing like it would have been back then. Skylights sprayed light onto soothing mauve walls. Large silk floral arrangements splashed strategic colour. Piped classical tunes were a far cry from the snap of feet on hard shiny linoleum halls of old.

'Can I help you?' A receptionist in crisp pink and white stripes beamed at her from behind a counter.

'Bert McCardle's room, please.'

'Let me see…'

Her perfect hot pink nails flashed across the keyboard.

'Ah yes. Go down the hall to the nurses' station – first on your left. He's in ICU; they'll let you know if he's allowed visitors.'

'Thank you.'

'Pleasure.'

The last time Nicola had walked down a hospital corridor was when she'd left the morgue after identifying her parents.

Now, just as then, she felt weak, nervous, and sick to the stomach. Part of her hoped Bert wouldn't be allowed visitors, another part hoped otherwise.

Quivering, unsteady legs barely got her to the next reception desk.

'Yes?' The voice was stern, not particularly friendly. The name badge said Rose, but Nicola thought that with her large, masculine frame and short hair, she couldn't be less rose-like if she tried.

'May I see Bert McCardle? He was brought in last night from…'

'Family?'

'Um, yes.'

Nurse Rose looked sceptical.

'Daughter,' Nicola added.

'Right then, through here – you have five minutes. He's still critical, but he's sleeping now. He was awake earlier; should be again soon. Talk to him though, he can probably still hear.'

Nicola sat down in the blue vinyl armchair by the bed. She wanted to examine Bert's features for similarities with her own but the tubes and him lying down made it almost impossible.

His dark, sandy grey hair was wiry and sticking out all over the place. Had it been blonde, soft, and wavy like hers when he'd been younger? She looked at his forehead, closed eyes and bridge of his nose, frowning, unable to remember the shape of her own for comparison. She needed a mirror.

Nicola's gaze paused at his chin. Again, no remarkable similarities stood out. She looked down to his dark, stained and weathered left hand lying on top of the tightly tucked bedclothes. His fingers were a lot shorter and fleshier than her own.

She stroked his wrist, had no idea what else to do. Talk to him, the nurse had said. And say what? Why was she even here?

'Bert,' she whispered. 'It's Nicola, Nicola Harvey. The journalist. I found you yesterday. You gave me quite a scare.'

Now what? Just tell him? No, she couldn't do it, not with him in this state. But she wanted him to know – it had been too long. She didn't want to waste another minute, now that she knew the truth.

It had seemed only seconds had passed before the nurse was by her side saying her time was up, that Bert had another visitor. Nicola got up.

At the doorway Graeme grabbed both her hands.

'Thank God you were there. Thank you, you saved his life.' Dried tears were dull lines down his unusually shiny face. 'Thanks for coming.'

Nicola nodded, thankful his uneasy rambling negated the need for any words from her. And then he was silent and frowning, looking from her to the floor, indecisive, as if he wanted to ask her something, but wasn't sure how to go about it, or didn't want to offend her and seem ungrateful.

She knew exactly what he wanted to ask: why was she there yesterday? Why had she driven all the way to Port Lincoln for a relative stranger? And why was she still here? They were the questions she would have asked in his position. But now was not the time or this the place for the lid to be peeled back on that particular can of worms.

'I'll leave you to it,' she said, and turned away, making her way down to the visitors' lounge she'd noticed on her way in.

As she made herself a cup of coffee, she wondered how long she should hang about; how long before questions started being asked? Thank goodness Alex hadn't arrived with his father. How would she ever look him in the eye? And how confused would he be, after the other night, with her suddenly running cold without any explanation? That wouldn't be fair.

She paced the room before stopping at the glass sliding door onto a small balcony. With her hands wrapped around her mug, Nicola took in the magnificent view stretching out and down below her for miles. It was quite breathtaking, but would be soon just be a sea of twinkling streetlights when the setting sun finished its journey. Beyond the multi-coloured rooftops and dark green trees was the brilliant blue bay. In the darkening volcanic sunset she could just make out a large, flat ship moored alongside the cluster of white grain silos. A few amber streetlights came on.

Nicola turned away. How long should she stay? Should she stay the night; check into a hotel? She sat down on the hard couch and instantly felt exhausted. No, she wouldn't risk driving back; she'd find somewhere to stay – wasn't there a swanky new waterfront hotel that some footballer was part-owner of? She'd find that one.

Nicola knew she should leave the hospital. Bert had his brother here now. But she couldn't make herself get up; she didn't want to leave now she'd finally found her father. She needed to speak to him, to be there when he woke up. But she couldn't ask to stay by his bedside like other family members without explaining why. And she wasn't ready to do that.

No, if she left this room, the hospital, she really couldn't come back without it looking weird. They knew her as a journalist; soon they might start to think she was just there for a sensationalist story.

She finished her coffee, got up, rinsed her cup and teaspoon at the sink, and dried them per the instructions on the laminated page on the wall above. *Right*, she thought, hanging the tea towel back over the rail. *I'll go say goodbye – that wouldn't be out of place – and then I'll leave, find somewhere to stay the night.* She hadn't decided if she'd visit again on her way back to Nowhere Else in the morning; there was plenty of time to decide.

Nicola made her way back down the hall towards Bert's room, rehearsing her goodbye speech and excuse for still being there as she went; 'I needed a cuppa to wake me up – it's been quite a day. Just wanted to look in and wish you all the best before I left.' That would work, she decided as she approached the ICU nurses' station again.

It suddenly struck her that it would seem odd to Rose, whom she'd told earlier that she was Bert's daughter. *Oh well, let the nurse think what she likes; there's nothing I can do about that now.*

Oh no! Rose wouldn't tell Graeme that she was Bert's daughter, would she? God, she hoped not. She hadn't looked like she'd believed her anyway.

'Oh hello; you're still here,' Rose said.

'Yes, but I'm afraid I have to leave. Can you please let Bert know? I don't want to disturb him with his brother…'

'Oh he's not in there; went for some fresh air or a cuppa, or something. You can go in again if you like. Just for a minute or two,' she said.

Back in the chair beside the bed, Nicola slid her hand under Bert's. She felt the gentlest of pressures – was it her imagination? She squeezed back, tears building from her throat.

Wake up, Bert, I need to talk to you, she silently pleaded, eyes shut tight. The nurse said he'd been awake earlier, which was a good sign.

Nicola looked back to find Bert's eyes open, recognition clear on his ashen, strained features.

'Hi there,' she said.

'Hmm. Sorry about the fright,' he mumbled. Or that's what Nicola thought he said.

His eyes fluttered shut, then opened again, glazed and wandering. Nicola willed him to stay awake.

'I think I might be your daughter,' she whispered desperately.

Bert's eyes opened slightly wider before closing again.

Chapter Twenty-seven

Nicola was exhausted, but she knew she'd never sleep. She'd driven back from Port Lincoln after all, feeling a burst of second wind as she pulled out of the hospital car park. She'd also felt a strange yearning to return to her motel in Nowhere Else; the need to get back to familiarity.

Now she turned the battered baby photo over while thinking about Bert in hospital over a hundred kilometres away. Were their noses similar? Their eyes? Smiles? She couldn't wait for the chance to study him, compare their features properly. There was so much to learn. And she had a whole new family to meet and get to know. Who else was there other than Graeme, Dorothy, and Alex? Beryl wasn't quite related, was she?

What about Janet, her mother; where was she now? Would she ever get to meet her? She had to think positive; Janet was out there somewhere, just like Bert had been.

Could she be here too, right under her nose this past week? No, Beryl had said she'd left years ago.

I could check the local phone book, Nicola thought, leaping off the bed. But she'd most likely have remarried and changed her name – it had been thirty-four years.

She sighed, returned to the bed, crossed her legs back under her, and picked up the photo again.

'She'll turn up if and when she's meant to,' she said, stroking the picture. That's what Sandy would say. And she had to believe it; there was nothing else she could do.

She really should call Sandy; tell her what she'd found out – it would blow her mind. But it was too late for phone calls. Sandy was old school; you didn't phone after 9 p.m. unless it was a life and death emergency.

Well this is *life*, Nicola thought, feeling a little cunning. But not an emergency, she conceded in the next breath. An image of Alex flashed through her mind. Oh God, she had that to face up to as well. She shook the thought aside; she wouldn't let it overshadow her excitement.

Wow, she'd found her father. And it had been so easy. Why hadn't she done it years ago? Because she wasn't meant to, Sandy would say. And she'd be right.

But what a bloody coincidence. Bless Bill for sending her here. She chuckled. *Wait till I tell him!*

So how long would Bert be in hospital? Would he be transferred back to Nowhere Else's smaller hospital or discharged? She could offer to look after him. Bill would understand. Of course she'd have to tell Graeme and everyone the full story first.

Hmm, how would she go about that? Organise a family picnic, tea at the pub to celebrate? No, they might prefer the privacy of their own home. She'd take something from the bakery for morning or afternoon tea. She could picture them sitting around the table firing questions at each other, trying to fill in the last thirty-four years as quickly as possible. She hugged the photo to her and rocked back and forth. It was so exciting she felt like she could leap out of her own skin.

Suddenly Nicola stopped and sat upright. What if they weren't pleased with the news at all? Here she was, becoming all excited, looking forward to getting to know her new family, but what if they didn't want a bar of it – of her?

She'd been given up for adoption; sent away – not kidnapped or gone missing. And for something as serious as giving a baby away there had to be trauma, secrecy, all sorts of negativity attached. She wasn't returning as the long lost child who'd been missed, cried over for years.

No Nicola realised, sighing heavily, she'd have to tread very carefully or this could go very badly. God, she hoped she hadn't already blown it by telling Bert at the hospital. She really shouldn't have done that. Perhaps he was too out of it to have taken it in.

Nicola was startled by a knock at the door – it was well after ten.

'Coming,' she called, getting up and putting the photo on the bench.

'Oh. Um, hi there.'

Richard stood on her step. He looked pale. Perhaps it was just the cold night air. 'Are you okay?' He asked.

'Yes, I'm fine…' Nicola frowned slightly.

'Can I come in?'

'Er, yeah, sure.' Nicola stepped aside.

'I thought you might need some company,' he said, stepping around her.

Why hadn't he offered to go on the three-hour round trip to Port Lincoln with her?

'I'm fine, but thanks.' The timing was a little odd, but she supposed it was a nice gesture.

'You don't know, do you?'

'Know what? Tea, coffee?'

'No, look I...' Richard rubbed at the palm of his left hand with his right thumb and stood shifting from one foot to the other.

'At least take a seat. You're making me nervous,' Nicola laughed.

'Um.'

'Are you all right?'

'It's not me.'

'Well, who is it? What's happened?'

'I don't know how to tell you,' he muttered, rubbing his face with his hands. 'Actually, I would like a cup of tea, thanks.'

'Okay.' Nicola took the kettle to the bathroom and filled it up. Richard was still standing just inside the closed door when she returned. He was looking very edgy.

'Now you really are making me nervous. Would you just sit down,' she said, pointing to the bed.

Richard sat on the bed, but remained bolt upright. As she opened the little bulbs of UHT milk and sachets of tea bags and sugar, she wondered what could be wrong. *Has he had an argument with his wife? Is one of his kids sick? Has he been fired?* A million different possibilities ran through her head. She dumped an extra sugar in his tea.

She handed him the mug, noticing that his hand was shaking. Shit, Nicola thought, it *was* bad news – real bad for Richard to be losing it like this. He'd said, 'You don't know, do you?' *What am I meant to know? What has it got to do with me?*

'Jesus, Richard, come on. You sure you're all right?'

'Yes, it's not about me.'

'Well who, or what, is it about?'

Richard rubbed his face again.

'Look, come *on*, it can't be *that* bad. Just spit it out. Is it your wife? One of your kids?'

Richard swallowed and shook his head. He inspected the hands in his lap, still rubbing them together.

Nicola put an arm around his shoulders.

'Come on, maybe I can help.'

'Bert's dead. Massive stroke.'

Nicola slowly swivelled to face him, her mouth dropping open.

'There must be some mistake.'

Richard shook his head.

'But he was awake; was getting better. He can't be dead!'

'I'm so sorry, Nic.'

'But I only saw him a few hours ago. They said he was stable.'

'It must have been worse than they first thought. Or his body just gave up.'

Nicola stared at him, and she started to grasp what had really happened. It wasn't Bert McCardle, the farmer, her interviewee, who had died; Bert McCardle, her *father* had died. Fat tears began rolling down her cheeks. She hadn't got the chance to tell him anything. They hadn't even met properly.

'Why now? I didn't even get to… It's not fair…' She leaned into Richard's shoulder and began sobbing. He put both arms around her and held her heaving, shuddering body tightly to him. Her tears came from the core as she sobbed for all the losses in her life.

Slowly Nicola eased herself out of Richard's embrace and took a handful of tissues from the box he handed her. He smiled sympathetically. She dabbed at her cheeks and blew her nose loudly.

They sat together in silence until his mobile phone began to vibrate and then ring. He fished in his pocket, pulled it out, and checked the display.

'It's Karen.'

Nicola nodded.

While Richard spoke in hushed tones, Nicola wondered why he didn't have a more modern phone. Jesus, as if it mattered. Bert was dead. For all Nicola knew, she was now an orphan. The thought almost made her laugh. Imagine the headline: Girl Orphaned at Thirty-four.

Why was it said that losing your parents as a child was so much worse?

Grief was grief; sad, debilitating, devastating. But you never stopped needing love and nurturing, no matter how old and worldly-wise you became – no matter how much you told yourself you didn't.

A psychic had once told Nicola that she needed love and affection like other people needed air. At the time she'd protested; hadn't wanted to acknowledge a weakness. Now it was gone she knew the psychic was right.

Call ended, Richard was back by her side. He was fidgety.

Nicola let him off the hook. 'You'd better get going.'

'I can't leave you like this.'

'I don't think you can die from crying,' she said, smiling weakly, her chin starting to quiver again.

'But…'

'I really appreciate your concern, but there's nothing you can do; I'll just go to bed.'

'If you're sure…'

Nicola nodded, on the verge of tears again. She went to the door and opened it.

Richard hesitated.

'Seriously, I'll be fine.' She wished he'd just go; she was having trouble holding the tears off, and her legs were starting to feel weak.

They stood awkwardly in the doorway. Richard seeming to want to hug her, Nicola wanting him to but both knowing how hard it would be to let go.

'I'll call and check on you tomorrow,' he said, gave her the briefest of kisses on the cheek, and bolted.

Alone again, Nicola felt the overwhelming need for company; to be held, to curl up next to someone. Alex.

She should at least phone him and give her condolences. But it was too late to do it now. And what if he too needed someone to hold? She wasn't ready to explain, to give him up completely.

Chapter Twenty-eight

Nicola woke feeling tired and washed out. She still felt a great sense of loss, but at least she'd slept; she hadn't thought she'd ever get to sleep.

She climbed out of bed, went to the window, and threw aside the heavy brown velour curtains. Sunlight streamed through the outer net layer, bathing the room in a filtered glow.

After showering, dressing, and applying makeup to hide her puffy, red eyes, Nicola felt ready to face the town and get back to her story. She couldn't stay cooped up in the dreary, chilly motel room when it was so lovely outside. And the vitamin D would do her good.

As she walked across the courtyard, the sun penetrated her thick clothes, warming her to her bones. She paused for a moment with her eyes closed, luxuriating in the feeling.

Here it was, the middle of winter, and there wasn't a dark cloud or sign of rain to be seen. Goody. She instantly felt a twinge of contrition; clear skies were the last thing the farmers wanted. But she was allowed to enjoy the fine weather, wasn't she?

Graeme had said that a farmer's second worst enemy, after no rain, was wind. Well, it was fine and still; she was going to enjoy the sunshine and not feel guilty about it.

Nicola's tread was slow as she made her way up the street towards the newsagent, nodding and mumbling vague greetings to all she passed. It was obvious that most of the town knew about Bert's death, and her involvement. More than once she was offered grim nods of understanding, gentle pats to the back, and encouragement to keep her chin up.

Such a simple phrase, she thought, yet so damn real. That was the thing with clichés, wasn't it? They became ingrained for a reason – because they were dead right. 'Keep your chin up.' Well, she was finding that damn hard.

Nicola walked past the newsagent. The group of old men, who seemed to be there every time she passed, paused in their conversation to raise their hats and nod acknowledgment. She found herself appreciating their simple gestures, nearly felt part of their world.

There was that feeling again. What was it? Comfort? Familiarity?

Nicola bit her lip in contemplation as she made her way up the hill to the quaint limestone and red brick Anglican church. As much as she wasn't one for religion, a church minister was bound to have a good, but different, perspective on the effects of the drought on the town – beyond the farming community.

After walking up the stone steps, she hesitated just inside the door at the edge of the carpet.

Nicola wasn't sure what she was, really. She believed there was something out there; a higher power making sure the cogs of existence meshed; and that everyone's life was predetermined before birth. She just wasn't convinced that power was a person.

Though whenever she was asked what religion she belonged to, she always answered 'Anglican'. It was the safe option.

Saying 'Catholic' opened you up to the question of whether you were lapsed or practicing, which in turn could result in attempts to trot you off for communion or confession, depending on your answer.

Anyway, she was sort of Anglican – she'd attended Sunday school, snacked on wafers and giggled at being allowed to sip wine at twelve – enough to stop her drinking until she was fifteen. Now *that* was something the authorities should consider introducing as a mandatory program of social welfare.

Nicola was standing inside the vestibule, taking in the stonework of the old building when a rotund man wearing a short sleeved black shirt with stiff white dog collar came out of a small room just beyond. He peered up at her through wire-framed spectacles with small round lenses. Nicola took the hand that was offered. She noted its softness.

'Welcome.'

Ah, that was the feeling she'd been trying to place – welcome. She belonged here.

The minister urged her forward with an arm gently in her back.

'Would you like your solace or to talk it over?' The man was gazing patiently at her, his lids almost fluttering with kindness.

'Actually, I'm hoping you might be able to help me.'

'Of course. You seek guidance.'

'Sorry?'

'Bert McCardle – a tragedy after all you did. But you're not to blame.'

'What? Oh, no, I…'

'It's okay. He's in a better place now. He was a good man.'

Nicola looked.

'I think you misunderstood. I'm a journalist researching a story on the drought and its effects on a community. I was wondering if I could interview you – get your perspective.'

'Of course.' He was obviously chuffed at the thought. 'Ordinarily it would be my pleasure. However, today is a little frantic, what with Bert's funeral arrangements.'

'I'm sorry, I didn't think.'

'Next week perhaps?'

'I'll try Gary Hodgson of Hodgson Transport then,' Nicola said, thinking aloud.

He shook his head.

'No luck there either, I'm afraid. You probably won't find anyone of note.'

'Sorry?'

'I've been here twenty years and it never ceases to amaze me how the town drops everything and pulls together in a crisis. You'd be best to just sit back and observe – could make a story in itself.'

Nicola felt a pang of annoyance. Who was he to tell her what to take note of, what would make a good story? She was pleased the man who had been her father had been popular, but his death was hardly a 'crisis'. Surely family would take over. Graeme would sort things out. What did the town have to do with it?

'Right. Well, thank you for your time.' She shook his hand roughly, turned on her heel, and marched out.

★★★

Much to Nicola's annoyance, Reverend Lawrie turned out to be right – the whole town seemed to be running on a skeleton staff. And she'd been counting on the diversion.

Back at the motel, Nicola slumped onto the bed. She'd been putting off the call for long enough. It was time to offer Alex her condolences. She got up, picked up her iPhone, and started pacing back and forth across in front of the desk.

She brought up Alex's number, but hesitated before calling. She pressed the home button and returned to pacing.

After a few moments she stopped. She was being ridiculous. She found the number again and pressed it before she had a chance for second thoughts.

Her heart thudded heavily while she waited; one ring, two rings, three rings, four, five… An answering machine kicked in. Nicola waited until the end of the message, opened her mouth, and then closed it again without saying a word. She hung up, put the phone on the desk, and lay back down onto the bed.

Staring up at the ceiling that was yellowed from the days before the non-smoking policy, Nicola wondered if her mother would attend the funeral.

Janet. Would she know her if she saw her? What would she say? Would they hug, the mother-daughter bond just instantly repaired despite their years apart? Perhaps she wouldn't want a reunion; perhaps there would be no bond to repair. Nicola shook it all aside; she couldn't think that. Anyway, she was getting way ahead of herself.

Nicola rearranged her underwear drawer and wondered how else to fill in her day. Her emails were up to date, she'd checked all the latest online news, and it seemed Facebook was down. Sandy would be too busy at the shop to chat on the phone.

It suddenly struck Nicola that perhaps it was time to think about popping back to Adelaide after the funeral, touching base with Bill. Was it worth trying to sort things out with Scott? Or was it time to cut their losses? Either way there was a serious discussion to be had.

There was a knock at the door and Nicola opened it to find Alex standing there with his hands in his pockets. His hair was all over the place, his face drawn and his eyes red. Was it from tears or lack of sleep, or both?

'Oh Alex. I heard about Bert. I'm so sorry.' She felt tears well up, but forced them back.

'Can I come in?'

'Um, I'm sort of in the middle of something.'

Her heart ached at the memory of their last meeting. She so badly wanted him close to her, but if she didn't let him in, she wouldn't have to deal with it. But his confused, crestfallen expression was too much.

'Oh right, okay,' he said, looking down and starting to turn away.

'Nothing that can't wait,' she said, standing aside.

'Thanks.'

Nicola remained standing near the door, running a hand through her hair while Alex sat down heavily on the end of her bed.

'You okay?' he asked, looking up at her. 'You can't blame yourself.'

'Sorry? Oh, Bert, right. I know.'

'What else is wrong?'

'Nothing, I'm fine.' Nicola remained standing.

'Have I done something wrong, or upset you somehow?'

'No, why would you say that?'

'Well, last time I was here we, you know…'

'Sorry, I'm really not in the mood.'

'Me neither, but I could do with a hug.'

Nicola stayed put, avoided looking him in the eye.

'Has someone said something?'

Nicola shook her head.

'Well, what's wrong then?'

Nicola cringed at the hurt clouding his gorgeous dark features, but knew she couldn't do anything to soothe it. How could she still be yearning for this man?

After a few more moments she sat on the bed, not too close, and fiddled with her hands in her lap. Her stomach churned with inevitability.

'Well, it's a bit embarrassing really,' she started.

'Oh, I get it,' he said, sitting up a little straighter. 'Woman's stuff – that time of the month.'

Nicola sighed, wished she'd thought of it herself. She shrugged.

'You're being silly. It doesn't matter. Come here, give me a hug. It's all I want anyway.'

Nicola allowed herself to be pulled to him, her nose to his neck, drinking in his wonderful scent. But the shame was overwhelming and reluctantly she extracted herself and pushed him away.

She swallowed deeply and gnawed at her lip.

'Alex, we can't do this anymore.'

'I know,' he murmured, reaching for her.

Nicola pushed him away, hard.

'I mean it, Alex. We really can't.' She paused, looking into his eyes. There wasn't any easy way to say it. 'We're cousins.'

'Don't be ridiculous.'

'It's true.'

'We're what?' Alex leapt off the bed as if burnt, then wiped the back of his hand across his puckered lips. He leant on the desk and slowly shook his drooping head.

'I only found out the other day.'

'I don't understand. How?'

'Remember the story I won the Walkleys for, about the plane crash my parents died in? They were my *adopted* parents. I finally got the guts to apply for my adoption details from the Department for Families and Communities. The information just arrived – I've been waiting months. What are the odds of my parents being from here of all places? I always knew I was born in Port Lincoln, but that's all.'

Alex stared at her.

'My birth certificate has Janet McCardle named as my mother and Bert as my father. I went out to see him straight away – that's how I was there when he…' She got up and started pacing, leaving the bed between them.

She rubbed her face with her hands. 'It's all such a bloody mess. And you. Of all people to fall…sleep with…'

Even with his back to her, Nicola could tell he wasn't listening. She stopped speaking and sat back down on the edge of the bed.

After a few moments Alex turned slowly to face her. He swallowed. She searched his face, her breath catching when she saw tears pooling in the corners of his eyes.

'I was falling in love with you, Nicola. How could I if…?'

Her heart skipped a beat. She bit back her own rising tears, nodded, but continued staring into her lap.

'Me too.' She knew it was ridiculous. They hardly knew each other. But she couldn't help how she felt.

'What are we going to do?'

'Nothing. There's nothing to do.'

She jumped a little as his fist thumped hard onto the laminex.

'Finally, I find someone…'

'Alex, don't,' she pleaded, more at the tears running down his cheek than his words.

He bit hard on his lip.

Her heart ached. Big fat tears dropped from her chin. They remained silent, avoided looking at each other.

'I've heard of cousins getting married – back in the old days,' Alex finally said, shrugging and offering Nicola a tense smile.

'Alex,' she said, groaning.

'Sorry, just trying to lighten the situation. Well, there's nothing we can do to change what's happened. We just can't let it happen again.'

'No.'

They sighed in unison.

Alex pulled the chair out from the desk, sat heavily, and let out a deep breath.

'So your mum is Janet?

'Do you know her?' Nicola's eyes widened with anticipation.

He shook his head. 'No. Never met her. She left before I was born.' He glanced down at his watch. 'Oh shit, is that the time? Sorry, I've gotta go. Town meeting. See ya…um…cuz.' He paused, looking at her, and then gave her shoulders a quick squeeze before turning for the door.

'Hold on. What meeting?'

'This one will be more of an early wake. We're getting together to discuss what needs to be done to keep Uncle Bert's place running.

'If it was late spring or summer there'd be heaps to do – we'd have to sort out a roster for harvest and shearing. As it is, there'll just be a few weeds to spray and the sheep to feed and check on.

'I can handle most of it, but we're meeting anyway. I guess more out of tradition than anything else,' he said with a shrug. 'Sort of collective grieving, I suppose.'

'So if someone dies the whole town pitches in?'

'Yeah. With Bert it'll just be till we know what's going on with the will.' He stopped, and then added thoughtfully, 'Be you, I guess.'

'He didn't know about me.'

'I'm no lawyer, but who knows? You might be able to prove a claim.'

'Oh, I wouldn't do that.' She hesitated. 'Hey Alex?'

'Yeah.'

'Don't tell anyone, okay?'

'Course. Not a word. Anyway, I'd be tarred and feathered.'

'Just until I know more. It's all a bit of a blur at the moment.'

'Why don't you come with me? Might be good for your story. See the inner workings of a small town and all that.'

'Okay.' She grabbed her bag from the desk, then stopped. 'Actually, on second thoughts.'

'What's wrong?'

'Nothing really, it just feels weird. I guess I just need time to get my head around everything.'

'Fair enough. Lot to be said for gut instinct.'

Nicola nodded. 'Can we catch up afterwards?'

'Righto. In that case, front bar, five o'clock.'

'Okay, five o'clock.'

Chapter Twenty-nine

Nicola waited until a quarter past five before heading into the front bar. She wanted to make sure Alex would be there when she walked in.

Even though she would be greeted with g'days and friendly nods, she was still uncomfortable about walking in alone and having everyone turn towards her.

She took a deep breath and pushed the heavy door open. The place was packed elbow to elbow.

'Hey, there you are,' Alex said, appearing beside her at the bar and shuffling aside to give her space.

He leaned in slightly as if about to kiss her, then appeared to think better of it, and instead gave a friendly nudge to her shoulder. She allowed herself to briefly enjoy his scent and warmth before catching herself and regaining focus.

'How was it?' Nicola strained to be heard over the noise.

'Okay. As I said earlier, I'm not sure why we were even meeting

– Dad and I are going to sort out everything. One bloke's going to donate some hay and another is going to cart it. Other than that it's just an excuse for a booze-up and a chin wag. Group therapy, I guess you could call it,' Alex added with a shrug. 'Beer or Bundy?'

'Beer thanks.'

'Two schooners, thanks, Tiff.'

'Hey Alex, need a quick word if you don't mind,' someone called.

'Be right with you, Harry.' He grimaced. 'Sorry, excuse me a sec. Duty calls.' He wandered off.

Nicola wished she hadn't asked Alex to keep her relationship with Bert a secret. She raised her glass to toast him at every opportunity, hoping for a wildcard into conversation. But all she got were polite nods and mumbles as the individuals shuffled their way past. They'd obviously decided an out-of-towner couldn't possibly understand the intricacies of country life and allegiance.

She couldn't remember ever feeling so alienated. She wanted to scream that she had every right to be involved, that Bert was her father.

They probably wouldn't believe her anyway.

She wished Alex would come back, but he was engrossed in arm-waving conversation by the far wall.

Suddenly she felt cheated – realised she'd missed a major part of life. All these people had come together to collectively mourn. She should be a part of it.

Nicola wondered how comfortable she'd be with everyone knowing her business, but decided it was possibly a small price to pay to be part of a community like this.

'Sorry about that,' Alex said, appearing again beside her. 'Harry couldn't get to the meeting but was keen to donate some hay. You know he hardly has two cents to rub together himself, yet there he is…' Alex said, shaking his head. 'Bet you wouldn't get that in the city, huh?' he added, before draining his beer.

It was nice that people cared; Bert must have been a well-liked member of the community. She really wished she'd had the chance to get to know him.

Before the sadness had a chance to overwhelm her, she told Alex she was going. There was an awkward moment while he shifted on his feet as if trying to make up his mind about something.

Every other time, he'd insisted on walking her to her room. And every time he had they'd… It couldn't happen again. They both knew that.

'Right, see you,' Nicola said, giving him a quick peck on the cheek and bolting for the side door.

★★★

Later that night, Nicola realised there had been one noticeable absence – Graeme. Perhaps he was still sorting things out at Port Lincoln hospital, or speaking to an undertaker, or something.

It was important that she talked to him before he learned from someone else who she really was. She had to tell him soon. It wasn't fair for Alex to keep that big a secret from his own father.

But the thought of going out there and dropping the bombshell sent a shiver of fear through her. No, she couldn't. Not when he was dealing with his brother's death. It would be too much, too soon.

But when would be the right time? The information on the government adoption website said it should be taken slowly. But Graeme was her uncle; surely that wasn't quite the same as a birth parent? If she left it too long, it wouldn't seem right either. The 'why now' question would be there.

Oh God, she suddenly thought, bringing her hands to her face. He might think she was coming forward now to claim something from Bert's estate. What if he thought she'd known all along? That the interview was merely a ruse to find out more about them?

That's how it might seem to *her* if the situation were reversed. But if that's what he really thought, time wouldn't make any difference; he'd feel the same whether she told him tomorrow or next week.

No, she'd go out and offer her condolences, end of story, and see how it went from there. She had to be patient.

After waiting thirty-four years, she could wait another few days.

★★★

Next morning, Nicola was on her way to visit Graeme when a thought struck her. She slowed the four-wheel-drive down.

Bert's dog, Jerry; had someone picked him up, at least made sure he'd been fed? Alex hadn't mentioned him. God, he hadn't been stuck in the house all this time, had he? She pulled the vehicle off the road when she noticed another car in her rear vision mirror. Idling, she wondered if she should go back to town and buy some food just in case. No, surely someone had thought of the dog.

She pulled her mobile out of her handbag and rang Alex. It eventually went to voicemail. She didn't leave a message; she'd go straight to Bert's, make sure Jerry was okay and leave him a message when she knew more.

If she had to bring the dog back to the motel, she would, regardless of the no pets allowed rule. Tiffany would have a fit, but that would be too bad. It was one thing she could potentially do for Bert, a small chance to pitch in like everyone else in the community.

Nicola checked her mirrors, pulled back on to the road, and then took the left turn onto a road she knew eventually fed into the cross-road near Bert's driveway.

As she drove slowly up to the house, she scanned the area for any sign of the dog. Nothing. She turned the car off and, feeling nervous and reluctant, went up to the back door. She took a few deep breaths. God, what would she find?

She was just about to try the handle when she heard the crunch of car tyres on the dirt behind her. She turned to see a white ute pull up beside her vehicle. Thank goodness. Graeme got out and stayed standing beside the ute. Nicola let out a deep breath she didn't realise she was keeping. And then nerves took over; she started quivering all over.

'Hello there,' Graeme said. He seemed to be eyeing her a little suspiciously.

'Hi. Um. I just wanted to check on the dog, Jerry. Have you seen him? Has someone fed him?' Nicola's words tumbled out in a guilty-sounding torrent.

'Yep. He's here with me,' Graeme said, tossing his head and thumb towards the back of the ute.

On the tray were the two large black and white dogs she'd seen the other day at Graeme's, and also the stocky little blue heeler that had been snoozing in Bert's old hearth. All three had their tongues out and were wagging their tails so much their whole bodies wiggled.

'Oh, that's great. I had this sudden thought that he might have been missed – stuck inside the house or something...' Shut up Nicola, she told herself.

'No, he's fine, aren't you mate?' he said, reaching in and patting the smaller of the dogs.

'I was actually on my way to see you. Before I got distracted by Jerry here,' Nicola said. 'I wanted to say how sorry I was about Bert.' At her words, Graeme turned back.

'Thank you. I really appreciate it – and you being here, calling the ambulance, and going to the hospital.'

Nicola shrugged. 'It was nothing.'

'Well it meant a lot to me – and to Bert.'

He held out his hand to her and Nicola took it. He then covered hers with his other hand.

'If it wasn't for you, I wouldn't have had my last conversation with my brother. I will be forever grateful to you for that. Other than my wife and son, he was the only family I had. It hasn't been an easy relationship, but we were still brothers.'

Nicola noticed his eyes had filled with tears. He let go of her hand and turned back to the dogs. Tears welled up in her own eyes. She wanted to grab his hand again; tell him he had her, that she was family too. She nibbled her bottom lip.

'There's some…' she began in a barely audible whisper, then stopped herself.

'Yes?'

Graeme peered at her as if waiting for her to continue.

'I think it's great the way everyone is pitching in and helping.'

'It's one of the good things about being part of a small community. Must be quite revealing to you as an outsider.'

'Hmm.'

Nicola wondered what Bert would think if he knew his brother was on his property. She felt a surge of annoyance towards Graeme, and loyalty towards her father.

'So did you manage to patch things up?' she asked.

'Not quite.'

'That's a pity.'

'Yes, it is,' Graeme said, looking down at the ground.

Suddenly she noticed that the ute was towing a trailer and that on the trailer was what looked like a tank. God, Bert wasn't even buried, and here Graeme was helping himself to his water. Or was it for fuel, or chemicals, or something else? Didn't Alex say they use trucks for carting water? That tank wouldn't hold much.

They seemed to be having an unspoken standoff; neither wanting to leave before the other. They stood there in silence for a few moments.

Nicola sighed to herself; there was nothing she could do about it. As far as Graeme was concerned, she was just a journalist who had come to check on the dog and had ended up paying her respects. She couldn't stay there any longer without it looking odd.

'Well, I'd better be off. I'm glad Jerry's okay. And again, my sincere condolences,' she said, offering her hand.

As she turned to get back into her vehicle, Nicola wished she could take the dog with her; he had been important to Bert. She really didn't think he'd like him to be with Graeme. Maybe she could talk to Alex about it. She got into her four-wheel-drive, leaving Graeme standing where he was.

She was saddened by the thought that Graeme could now take all the water he wanted from the spring Bert had apparently been so protective of. It had meant a lot to Bert, even if no one really knew why.

She drove back down the driveway, checking in her rear vision mirror every few seconds, willing Graeme to follow. But really, what did it matter? He could come and go now as he pleased; Bert couldn't do anything about it now, and she certainly couldn't.

Nicola wondered if Bert had a will. It was a fact that many people who lived on their own never got around to drawing one up. She hoped Bert had been an exception. If he had, would he have left the property to Graeme, given their feuding? Graeme had mentioned their rift was down to him, hadn't he?

If that was true, Bert would surely have cut him out. The next logical beneficiary would be Alex. Unless of course he'd left everything to a lost dogs' home or something – just to stick it up everyone. Nicola smiled at the idea.

If there wasn't a will, she'd have to at least step forward and admit her relationship, wouldn't she? God, she could really do without having to do that. She was glad Alex already knew the truth; somehow it lessened the burden.

As she drove, she couldn't shrug off the feeling that Graeme had seemed to have a sense of entitlement standing there. Would he be happy if Alex inherited the farm, or would he be bitter it wasn't to be his? There was the potential to cause another family rift.

Hopefully it won't become my problem, she thought, and actually crossed her fingers on top of the steering wheel.

★★★

'Richard? Nicola. You at the office? Got a few minutes to spare? Great, be there in a sec. Thanks, bye.'

'That was quick,' Richard said, as Nicola threw herself into the empty chair by his desk.

'Yeah, I was right outside,' she said with a mischievous grin.

'Thought your mobile didn't…'

'Does now – my boss got my carrier changed. Yay,' she said, waggling her iPhone in front of him.

Richard rolled his eyes in mock consternation.

'Don't be too proud. We out in this "backwater", as you so eloquently put it, have had the technology for quite some time now.'

'Gotta burst a girl's bubble, don't you? You really don't under-stand the two joys in a woman's life – retail therapy and chatter.'

'Something I can help you with, or did you just want to show off your return to the twenty-first century?'

'What do you know about law – wills, legal rights upon death, that sort of thing?'

'I take it we're talking about Bert McCardle. This isn't just some general knowledge quiz, is it?'

'No. Do you reckon he would have been the sort to have a will?'

'Nicola Harvey, I wouldn't have picked you for the gold-digging type.'

'Richard!'

'Well, you should see how it looks from here. Convince me otherwise.'

'I've just been to see Graeme. You know he's still trying to get his hands on the water.'

'He said that?'

'No, but he was towing a tanker type thing.'

'Carry on.' Richard's raised eyebrow went by unnoticed.

'He wasn't at the meeting, was he?'

'Ah, well spotted, Miss Marple. No he wasn't.'

'Richard, what aren't you telling me?'

'No need; seems you've figured it out all on your own.'

'So it's not just coincidence, or my imagination?'

'Nope. Town's fighting Bert's side for him.'

'Why?'

'Because we, they, think he got a rough deal.'

'It *was* just a stroke, wasn't it?' Nicola asked slowly.

'Listen to you, little miss conspiracy theory. What, you reckon Graeme bumped him off for his water?'

'Of course not! But they could have argued.'

'Well then, Graeme would have been there to call the ambulance...'

'Not if...'

'Oh come on; you're being way too melodramatic.'

'Wouldn't you love to know for sure?'

'Yup. But it wouldn't bring Bert back. There are other ways to help him now.'

'Hmm.' Nicola thought about the community rallying around. 'I'm starting to see why you like this place so much.'

'Has its moments.'

'So, how do I find out if he had a will?'

'Legally?'

'Yes, legally!'

'Not sure. But I think that if there was one naming Graeme as sole beneficiary he would have presented it by now. But there's no solicitor in town, so there's no way of knowing.'

'Oh.' Nicola let her shoulders slump.

'There's always the illegal to consider.'

'Which is?'

'Search his house.' He shrugged.

'Richard! We can't do that!'

'Well you did ask. And I don't know where you got "we" from.'

'Well, I *do* have information naming him as my biological father. I could say he gave me permission – before he died.'

'We'll turn you into a real criminal yet.'

'Richard, this is hard enough,' Nicola groaned.

'Sorry.'

'But how would I get in?'

Richard raised his eyebrows.

'No way. I'm not breaking in.' Nicola was wide-eyed.

'I'm suggesting nothing of the sort.'

'What then?'

'Turn the handle, silly. Most people still don't lock their doors around here. I'll put money on Bert being one of them.'

Nicola's phone vibrated on the desk. Her face clouded as she stabbed the phone then threw it into her handbag.

★★★

Back in her room, Nicola held her breath as she put the phone to her ear and waited.

'Scott, it's me.'

'How's it going?'

'Okay. Sorry about before, I was in an interview. Forgot to turn it off.'

'No worries. I'm pretty busy myself.'

'Bad time?' Nicola rolled her eyes.

'Got a few minutes. What's been happening?'

'Well... you know how I told you I had finally found my biological father?' Nicola blurted. 'I went out to see him, and found him on the floor of his shed. He'd collapsed. So I had to call the ambulance.

'They flew him down to Port Lincoln, so I drove down there – not to tell him or anything, well maybe to tell him, but I didn't get the chance because...' Suddenly it all overwhelmed her again. '...he died. Oh Scott, I'd just found him, and now he's gone,' she wailed. Nicola expected tears, but none came. Instead she was just breathless.

'And... Doesn't matter,' she said, stopping herself. She was about to tell him about the town's rallying, but realised he wouldn't understand, just like she hadn't only days before.

'Sounds pretty full on.' Was he being sarcastic? Probably.

'Actually I'm seeing the place in a whole new light.' Was she being defensive? Absolutely. 'I want you to come up for the weekend, check it out. Please.'

Scott sighed. 'Sorry, but I'm snowed under here – I've got a big report due from my Canberra trip.'

'Come on, it'll be fun.'

'Why don't you come home instead?'

'I asked first. Come on, give me five good reasons why not,' she teased.

'All right,' he said. 'One; I'm way too busy.'

'Surely you can have one weekend off. Anyway, you can work from here if you have to – I'll even let you use my iPhone if yours doesn't work.'

'Two; it's over five hundred kilometres away.'

'Forty minutes by plane then one hour and fifteen by car. I'll pick you up.'

'Three; it's full of country hicks.'

'They're not that bad,' she said quietly.

'…There's nowhere decent to stay, eat, or get a cup of coffee…'

'Okay, that's your five. You can stop there,' she said.

'And it's dusty and freezing cold,' he added triumphantly.

There was a painful, hollow gnawing deep in Nicola's stomach. Tears sprang into her eyes. *And there's me*, she wanted to say, but the lump in her throat wouldn't let her.

'Damn, I've gotta go,' she said, and hung up without waiting for his reply. Let him think she'd been hit by a bus or something.

Nicola collapsed on her bed and let the tears flow.

Chapter Thirty

It was late, but Nicola rang anyway, and kept her fingers crossed while the number connected. She had no idea what she would say, but if she was going to seek reliable advice, this was the only number to call.

'Bill Truman.'

'Hi Bill, Nicola.'

'Hey, what are you doing calling so late?'

'Well what are you doing working so late?'

'Touché. So how's my favourite gun reporter this fine evening?'

'Pretty good.'

'Got me a decent lead? Another potential Walkley winner?'

'Working on it.'

'So, getting used to being in exile then?'

'Actually I am. The people are great, weather's great...'

'Tell me to back off anytime you like, but something tells me you haven't called to discuss work or the weather – not after nine at night.' He paused.

Nicola sighed deeply. 'Well, it's a bit complicated.'

'Come on, tell Uncle Bill. Three ex-wives makes me the king of complicated.'

She'd done the right thing by calling Bill. The burden was lifting already.

'Okay.' Nicola took a deep breath, and then opened her mouth and let it all spill forth. Listening to herself speak, she found it hard to believe it was her own life she was talking about.

But Bill was like one of those strange uncles some families had – the one the grown-ups never understood because he never married or had kids; the one the younger generation loved because he was cool enough to sort things without getting the other oldies involved.

He didn't interrupt once; just let her get it all off her chest. He soothed her through the tears, reminded her to keep breathing, and never said, 'There, there, it can't be *that* bad'.

Finally there was silence. Bill waited a few moments more then cleared his throat.

'Right. Well, you certainly don't do things by halves, do you?'

To others his remark may have seemed flippant, but Nicola knew he was buying time while he gave it all some thought. Bill was real, and for that she was grateful. She stayed silent, the tears now drying on her flaming cheeks, her breathing becoming easier.

'I reckon you're the one we should be doing the story on.'

Nicola smiled sympathetically. Two token comments; she must really have him stumped.

'Bear with me a sec.'

'No worries, take your time. If you can sort out my life, I'll be grateful.'

'How grateful?'

'Very.' Nicola could hear him scratching notes while he spoke.

'Enough to let us do a story on you?'

'What? "Walkley Winner Woes"? No thanks.'

'Successful search for identity – self-discovery – there *is* no better story, Nicola. You could at least think about it.' More scribbling.

'Okay.' She paused. 'Never in a million years. Anyway, it's not looking very successful from where I'm sitting.'

'You'll get there. You're just at a crossroads; you need to choose a direction. It'll all work out, you'll see.'

'Bill, do you have anything other than philosophy to offer?' Nicola heard a deep metallic thud as he carefully put down his heavy Waterman fountain pen.

'Right, I'm seeing four choices. One; come back here and work on things with Scott. Two; come back here and tell the prick it's over – he doesn't deserve a girl like you.'

'Thanks Bill.' Nicola was close to tears again.

'Three; stay out there and get to know your roots. And four; stay out there and find someone else to shag yourself stupid with.'

'Bill!'

'Sorry, scrap that last one – that's what *I'd* do. At my age you take what's offered, no questions asked.'

'I'm sure I didn't need to know that.'

'No, probably not. Okay, your other option would be to take time out, escape overseas or somewhere. And about Alex, I really don't know how you deal with that. Hearts are funny things, but rarely wrong. Maybe there's a piece to the puzzle missing. Just sit tight on that one.'

'Bill, I'm impressed; you're sounding like a life coach or something.'

'Enough of that rubbish, right there. But seriously, whatever way you decide to go, you have my support.'

'Thanks, it means a lot.'

Nicola went through the options again in her mind. Bill knew to remain silent.

Taking time out was not her style. Maybe when it was all over, but certainly not as a solution.

But Scott. What to do?

Well, they'd have to split; it was never going to work, she could see that now. But she wasn't just going to walk away, hide out here in the bush until it was all over. No, she'd confront it head on – owed it to her personal growth.

They'd been silent for a few minutes when Bill spoke.

'Nicola; I think you know what you have to do. Just gather the courage and go for it. I have full faith you'll do the right thing. Just listen to your gut.

'Now, if you want to look into your legal situation with Bert or get advice on de facto settlement – if that's the way you go – ring Tony Mophett. Tell him you're practically family and he'll see you right.'

'Bill, you're the best.'

'Got a pen; I'll give you his number.'

'Fire away.'

When she finished recording the numbers, Nicola glanced at her watch and was shocked to find they'd been on the phone close to an hour.

'It's after ten. I'd better let you go.'

'Only if you're okay.'

'Thanks, you've been a real help.'

'Anytime.'

There was that lump in her throat again.

'I'll let you know.'

'If you need to come back, sort things out, let me know. It might be a good idea to touch base here. We don't want everyone forgetting you.'

He was right.

'Actually, you have a point. Can you get a flight organised for the end of the week?'

'Consider it done. I'll let you know details in the next day or so.'

'Thanks Bill, you're a legend.'

'No drama. Nicola, ring Tony – even if it's just for future reference. He's a good bloke, and a vault of discretion.'

'Will do.'

'See ya kiddo.'

'See you Bill. Thanks – for everything.'

Nicola hung up and felt a strange concoction of emotions surging through her. On the one hand she felt liberated, buoyed; on the other fearful, apprehensive – the tough times were yet to begin.

She wasn't so much at a crossroads as at the start of a maze. There was only one objective, but any number of potentially blind twists and turns to get there.

Chapter Thirty-one

Small groups of people in shades of black and grey milled around chatting in the sunshine, their cardigans and jackets pulled tight around them to keep out the icy wind while they waited to be ushered into the small limestone and red brick church.

Nicola stood back by herself under a tree and observed the crowd making its way towards her and the church. People greeted each other on the grass with handshakes, hugs, pecks on the cheek, before continuing into the building. She recognised quite a few faces, and greeted them with a nod, a smile, or 'hello'.

Nicola turned at hearing her name. Dorothy McCardle was coming towards her, having apparently come from inside the church. She walked quickly, her sleek black leather handbag swinging by her side.

'Nicola. Hi. Graeme wondered if you would like to come in – there's room in the pew behind us.'

'Oh, thank you, but I really couldn't,' Nicola said, despite every part of her yearning to be included, to be welcomed into the family. But it wouldn't be right when they didn't know the truth. As it was, they were probably only being polite. And it was bound to cause a stir; a rippling of whispers throughout the little building. No, she couldn't do that to Bert; she'd stay outside.

'Okay, if you're sure,' Dorothy said, and returned the way she'd come.

Nicola pulled her thick belted cardigan more closely to her, as much to comfort her from feeling self-conscious and out of place as to protect her from the cold. It was a lovely sunny day. She must stop thinking that; these people were praying for rain. There was a brisk chilly breeze, but it was quite warm with the sun beating on her back. She inspected the ants clambering for a vantage point atop her shoes, then attempted to remove them. This was the first funeral she'd attended since her parents'.

'Hi. Are you coming in?' Tiffany asked, appearing beside her.

'Thanks, but I think I'll stay out here.' Nicola thought there couldn't possibly be any more room in the church anyway.

'Bloody nerve.' The acidic voice was very close to her ear.

Nicola spun around and found herself face to face with an elderly woman dressed in a plain brown long-sleeved crepe dress. She couldn't remember seeing the woman before.

'I'm sorry?' she said, successfully retaining her composure, more shocked than upset.

'You've got a nerve coming here.'

'So you said. Would you care to explain why?'

'Piranhas – bloody journalists. I feel sorry for you if you have to prey on grieving people to get a story,' she said.

'Come on Ida,' Beryl said, suddenly appearing and grabbing the woman by the elbow. She rolled her eyes at Nicola and then winked at her as she dragged Ida towards the church. Nicola offered a grateful smile back.

Finally the church seemed to be full and people were beginning to sit on the stackable plastic chairs set out for those it was unable to accommodate. Nicola settled in one, pleased to be off her feet. As she did, she spied Richard on the far side. Next to him was a woman. Ah, the elusive wife, Karen, she thought, craning her neck. But other than seeing that the woman was wearing a long black skirt, she wasn't any the wiser. She willed Richard to look across and acknowledge her, but he was busy studying the photocopied and folded sheet of paper being handed out at the gate by the two middle-aged funeral directors.

Her heavy heart ached with grief and loneliness. She longed to be next to Alex, Graeme and Dorothy, her new family, inside the church. She knew she'd done the right thing declining their offer, but it didn't make her feel any better. She studied her copy of the order of service.

She'd once heard a guest psychologist on the radio say that grief compounded. It would explain why she felt so sad. Saying goodbye to Bert was more frustrating than sad; she hadn't known him well enough. Yes, she sighed, she did indeed feel like she was saying goodbye to Ruth and Paul all over again. Nicola's chin began to quiver. She pulled a wad of tissues out of her handbag and dabbed at her tears as they fell.

★★★

The service passed quickly; Reverend Lawrie's sermon and a brief eulogy delivered by Graeme in stilted, formal tones. She sat numbly through *The Lord is my Shepherd* and *Amazing Grace*, and then the pallbearers – with Alex leading them – carried the coffin into the sunlight and down to the hearse.

Nicola exchanged a weak, sympathetic smile with Alex as he passed slowly by.

She was watching the glum, tear streaked faces as the church emptied past her. When she realised that very few people remained seated on their plastic chairs, she stood up. Soon the churchyard was almost clear.

A woman was standing next to her. Nicola turned her head a little and took in the tall lean frame and grey bob of her only companion. She was dressed simply in black slacks and a black and white striped shirt. She looked a little familiar, but Nicola couldn't place her.

She thought she noticed a look pass between Graeme and the woman as he passed. Having enjoyed watching people and their expressions for so many years, Nicola recognised it as a fond but covert greeting.

Maybe they'd been in love many years ago; high school sweet-hearts or something. Perhaps their lives had taken different paths and they'd recently reconnected again through chance.

If there was something going on, Graeme would want to hope Dorothy didn't find out – she looked like she could be a little scary. She watched as Dorothy put her arm around her husband and steered him on – a little forcefully, she thought.

No, she was being way too melodramatic. And the look between Graeme and the woman had been so fleeting she could have imagined it – yes, her imagination was running away with her.

Nicola sighed. She missed sitting in a café with Sandy, sipping lattes and people-watching for hours, constructing the lives of complete strangers.

She missed lattes. And she missed Sandy. Where the hell was she, anyway; she hadn't returned Nicola's voicemail when she'd tried to phone her on her way back from the hospital the other night.

Probably off in Asia somewhere on a buying trip, she concluded. She smiled to herself. *With no global roaming.* Bob was careful to ensure global roaming was turned off on Sandy's phone whenever they went away – ever since they'd returned from their first trip to

find a two-thousand-dollar bill Sandy had racked up because she
didn't consider the extra charges involved with being overseas.

Now only Bob's phone worked overseas – being as he was the
responsible one, he told everyone. Sandy was one intelligent woman,
but boy she could be dippy at times, Nicola thought fondly.

She could always call Bob if she got desperate. But of course
the thing with global roaming was that the other person paid the
overseas portion when receiving a call. It was way too complicated.
Nicola turned to the woman beside her as she spoke.

'Are you heading out to the cemetery?' the woman asked.

'I hadn't quite decided. Are you?'

'Wouldn't feel right not to. You can come with me if you like.
Car's a bit of an old bomb but it's just around the corner.'

'Thanks, that would be nice.' Nicola breathed a sigh of relief at
having the company.

'Couldn't help overhearing that comment earlier – don't take
it too much to heart. They don't cope well with outsiders. I don't
mean to be rude, but you're not from around here, are you?'

'No, I'm not – and you?'

'No.'

Both women were thoughtful while they got into the old white
Toyota Corolla and put on their seatbelts, wondering what and
how much they'd tell a complete stranger.

'So, what do you do?' the driver asked Nicola, as the funeral
procession snaked towards the cemetery at walking pace.

'Journalist. I'm surprised you didn't hear.'

'Ah, no wonder,' she said, nodding.

'We're not *all* bad,' Nicola said defensively.

'Everyone's allowed to know everyone's business, but only if
you're one of them.'

'Third generation, you mean,' Nicola groaned.

'Sometimes not even then.'

Nicola thought the woman sounded wistful, but didn't want to risk ruining whatever it was they had going.

'So, what do you do?'

'Nurse.'

'Ah, so you must be at the hospital Bert was in – I thought I'd seen you somewhere before. I think I might have passed you in the hall as I was leaving.'

The driver nodded, keeping her eyes on the road ahead.

'Port Lincoln. That's a long way to come for a patient's funeral.'

Nicola thought the woman's jaw tightened.

'So how did you know him?'

'I was interviewing him for a story I'm doing on the drought. I was actually the one who found him and called the ambulance.'

'Oh. Right. Hence your visit to the hospital and you being here today.'

'Mmm,' Nicola said, nodding.

They stayed silent a full minute.

'Any idea why they walk with the casket?' Nicola asked, merely to make conversation.

'No – tradition I guess.' The woman shrugged.

'God I hate these things. Funerals I mean.'

'Me too.'

'Always so damn morbid.'

'Not sure how else they could be.'

'Yeah, stupid thing to say really.'

'Doesn't matter.' The driver turned the radio on. 'Think we need something a little more up-beat.'

Nicola was relieved to be excused from further conversation with… What was her name? Had they even introduced themselves? She couldn't ask now; they'd got to that point where it would be too awkward.

★★★

They stood back from the throng, Nicola grateful to have someone to share the feeling of being on the outer. Unless she was imagining it, her chauffeur seemed to be receiving scowls and dirty looks. Before she had the chance to ask what her crime was, the undertaker spoke and the service began.

Both stole glances at the other's tears while they dabbed at their own. Nicola hoped the woman wouldn't probe her further about being there. And what was a nurse doing there anyway? Though, she wasn't just a nurse, was she, Nicola thought, remembering the look she'd seen from Graeme earlier. And the townsfolk seemed to know this woman. Otherwise, why the hostility? She was certainly not imagining *that*.

Finally the sand had been sprinkled, the basket of single blooms emptied by the line of mourners, and the casket lowered into the ground.

They had started to wander back to the car when it was announced that afternoon tea would be served at the hall – all were welcome.

'I'm game if you are,' Nicola's companion said, turning to her.

Although her eyes were hidden behind dark glasses, Nicola thought she detected a mischievous twinkle.

'I'm not sure.' Nicola realised her feet were burning. And she was starting to feel a little weary. She longed to get back to her room and have a hot shower.

'Well, think about it. You've got about five minutes to decide.'

Nicola smiled; she liked this woman's style.

'Okay. I'll come with you, thanks.'

'I don't reckon Bert would mind. He never did go in for all this political rubbish.'

So her new friend had known Bert too, really known him –

before the hospital. And she'd known Graeme – really known him. Nicola was now sure she hadn't imagined the look that had passed between them.

★★★

'One of the few really good things about this place is the cooking – so make the most of it,' the woman said, handing Nicola a plate and paper serviette.

They were still receiving icy glares from around the room; Nicola couldn't believe her acquaintance was so unaffected. Pleased to have her attention diverted, she piled her plate with homemade sausage rolls, scones, brandy snaps, lamingtons, and cupcakes.

After devouring their platefuls and savouring every delicious morsel, they gravitated towards where tea and coffee was being served.

Nicola looked up from pouring milk into her cup of tea to find Beryl Roberts standing alongside.

'Hi Beryl,' she said brightly, pleased to finally see a friendly, not just familiar, face.

Beryl fixed a tight-lipped smile on her face as she turned to Nicola's partner. 'Good of you to come.' Was she being curt?

The woman looked to Beryl, then turned to Nicola. 'I'd better go; I'll leave you to it – lovely to meet you.'

But we didn't.

'Goodbye,' said Beryl.

Definitely curt, even menacing, Nicola decided. What was it with these people? What had the woman done?

'I see you've met Janet.'

Nicola turned in slow motion, her mouth falling open. She'd wondered if Bert's ex-wife might have been there, but thought she would have recognised her mother. No, it must be a coincidence, wishful thinking, clutching at straws – all of that. The woman was already out of sight.

'Got a nerve showing her face around here.'

Nicola couldn't help herself. 'Why, who is she?'

'Only Bert's ex-wife – tramp,' Beryl snorted, and slowly lifted the cup to her lips.

'Oh.' Nicola almost dropped hers, and spun back around to search for the woman again. She felt like she'd been punched, had to fight to keep herself doubling over. So it was her. How come she hadn't recognised her own daughter?

'Word to the wise. Steer clear of her if you want any respect around here.'

'Well I'd better be off myself,' Nicola said. Her hand was shaking as she set her cup down. 'It was a nice service.' *Is that what one is expected to say?*

Nicola tried to catch Alex's eye to say goodbye, but he was at the far side of the room with a large group around him. Dorothy and Graeme were nearby but looked to be deep in conversation with Reverend Lawrie. She didn't like to interrupt.

She hurried back to the motel, trying to conjure up the features of the woman who she'd sat next to for half an hour, shared a car with, and a cup of tea. A complete stranger who just happened to be her long-lost biological mother. Why couldn't she have taken more notice? Did they share the same nose, chin, forehead, hands, ears, anything?

She couldn't remember anything specific – all that came to her was that she'd been tall and lean, and had been wearing black pants and a black and white striped shirt.

Why couldn't I have damn well been more observant? The one time it really matters? I'm a journalist, for God's sake!

Chapter Thirty-two

Nicola kicked her shoes off and threw herself onto the bed on her back. She stared up at the ceiling. She felt the need to vent, rant and rave; at least talk to someone about this. But who? Sandy would have called if she was back, and anyway, just the thought of having to relay the whole sordid story again was exhausting. Should she phone Bill? No, she couldn't keep running to him with every little problem. And anyway, this would just give him more ammunition to push her to do a story on the search for her biological parents.

God, so close, yet so far – again, she thought, thumping her head on the pillow a couple of times.

Why is this happening to me? One step forward, two steps back!

She was just about to get undressed to have a shower when her phone started ringing. Seeing Sandy's name on the display caused her to feel a strange sense of both relief and disappointment. She really didn't have the energy for this.

'Hi Sandy. Have you been away?'

'Now Nicola, what's this I hear about you finding your biological father? Out there of all places. Why didn't you tell me?'

'I tried – left a message...'

'Yeah, sorry about that – Bob and his tiresome ban on my global roaming. Scott told Bob you found your father and had to call an ambulance because he'd had a stroke or something. Wow! Is he okay?'

'No, he died.'

'Oh God, you poor thing.'

'Yeah, I've just come back from the funeral actually,' Nicola said wearily.

'Ghastly events we're obliged to attend.'

'Quite.' It was so good to hear her friend's chirpy voice after so long. But what she really needed was a hug.

'So, any other long-lost relatives there then? A bunch of cousins, maybe?'

'Actually, my mother was there.'

'Your what? God, what did she say? Did you instantly recognise her, did you hug? Nicola, this is huge. Tell me, tell me! What happened?!'

'Um.' All Sandy's questions were spinning around in her head. 'Well, I didn't actually get to meet her.'

'Oh.'

'Well not properly. I spoke to her, but without knowing who she really was.'

'So does she look like you? Same nice straight little nose, neat, flat ears?'

'No idea. Oh Sandy, I didn't take enough notice of her. Why couldn't I have been more...'

'Because you weren't meant to, darling. Stop being so hard on yourself.'

'Thanks Sandy.'

'What are friends for? I'm sorry I've been a bit AWOL lately.'

'That's okay, but I'm so glad you're back now.'

'So what are you going to do now – about your mother?'

'Well you're probably right; if I was meant to meet her properly, I would have. And anyway, the adoption website says to take things very slowly and carefully.'

'Bugger that! I'd say go for it. And anyway, since when does Nicola Harvey – Gold Walkley winner – not go after a decent lead? Is she still there in town; can you go visit her?'

'Are you serious? You think I should just knock on the door and introduce myself?'

'Hmm. Now that I've said it, I'm not sure. Only you can know if it's the right thing to do – follow your heart.'

'Thanks Sandy, real helpful – *not.*'

'I know, sorry.'

'Anyway, I don't even know if she's still in town, or if she is, where she's staying.'

'Wouldn't one of the contacts you've made know – like that guy from the paper, or the girl from the hotel you were telling me about?'

'Hmm. Not sure. Anyway, as much as it's going to drive me mad, it'll have to wait. I'm flying back tomorrow morning – need to check in with work.'

'Couldn't you put it off a few days? Bill would understand; aren't you always saying what a great boss he is?'

'Well, I don't want to muck him around; he's been so good about everything. Anyway, what happened to "if it's meant to be, it'll be"?'

'Hmm, good point. Yep. This is a sign,' Sandy said thoughtfully. Nicola rolled her eyes. 'If you were meant to meet her today, you would have. So obviously the universe thinks you need more time, or a different place, or something.'

'Right, so you think I should just let it unfold in its own time?'

'Yeah, I reckon.'

'But how the hell am I just going to just sit back and pretend I didn't meet my mother today for the first time in my thirty-four years? I'm already a nervous wreck about it – I'll be certifiable by the time I get back!'

'Well, maybe you need to focus on your relationship with Scott a bit more anyway.'

Nicola detected the change of tone. 'Has he said something?'

She heard Sandy sigh. 'He doesn't need to, Nicola. You haven't mentioned his name once. And you said you're coming back to check in with work. What about checking in with your fiancé?'

'Well, he's been dead against me looking for my parents, so forgive me if he's not my favourite person at the moment,' she said indignantly.

'There's something you're not telling me. Come on, what have you done? Spill.'

How the hell does she do that? Nicola wondered. There was no point being evasive; Sandy would get the truth out eventually. And she couldn't lie; she was dreadful at lying.

'Um… I slept with someone else.' There, she'd said it.

'You what?'

'I…'

'Yes, I heard you, I just don't believe it. You're one of the most faithful people I've ever met. What's going on with you?'

'It just happened.'

'Just the once?'

'No.'

'Oh Nicola.'

'Sandy don't – I feel bad enough.'

'So was it just a fling, or are you and Scott over?'

'Both probably.'

'Sorry?'

Nicola toyed with telling her that Alex was her cousin, but was already feeling judged. Which, of course, Sandy had every right to do.

'It was just a fling. It won't happen again. And I think it's over with Scott. We're like ships passing in the night – there's no passion anymore; we're more like two people sharing a house.'

'You're just saying that because you've had a brief moment of passion – but trust me, it doesn't last. You can't throw you and Scott away because of that. You get on so well.'

'I know we do. And I know what you mean about passion, but it's like we've always just been friends – mates.'

'But companionship is important.'

'I'm thirty-four, Sandy, I want more.'

'Fair enough. So what are you going to do?'

'Well, I figured I'd cook dinner and see if it sparks anything. And then take it from there – whichever way that turns out to be.'

'Well it would be a shame if you broke up.'

'I know. Sandy, I'm not taking this lightly. It's been a long time coming. Just took me a while to realise.'

'I know you're not, Nicola. You don't take anything lightly. Just remember what a nightmare sorting out the finances will be.'

'I don't think that's a good enough reason to stay,' she said, remembering Richard saying the same thing.

'I know. But…'

'So will we get a chance to catch up while you're back – to either commiserate or celebrate?'

'Of course. What about Saturday at three at Cibo on King William Road. Just the two of us?'

'Sure. Now, regarding your dinner…'

'Yes?'

'Do you need me to scan and email you any recipes?'

'No, I think I'll be right, thanks.'

'Well, leave Hugh what's-his-name right where he is. You're trying to impress, remember, not poison the man!'

'That was seven years ago, Sandy. When are you going to let me off the hook?' Nicola said with a laugh.

'Never, darling; it was way too funny.'

'Maybe to you,' Nicola said with a groan. But she found herself smiling at the memory.

'Well, I'd better go. You know where I am if you need me – now I'm back in the land of communication. Bloody Bob and his global warming. Oops, I mean global *roaming*,' she added, erupting into laughter.

'Thanks. See ya.' Nicola hung up, chuckling at her friend's game.

She was feeling much more chirpy as she got undressed. It was probably best that she wouldn't be able to contact Janet for a few more days; just the thought of it was terrifying enough. Yes, some breathing space would be good.

Meanwhile she'd focus on gathering the information she'd collected about her non-story story on the drought for her meeting with Bill. And she'd think about what to cook Scott for dinner. Yes, she would make one last ditch effort; give it all she'd got and see what they had left to work with. She owed them that. Her heart pinged. It would be nice to feel his strong arms around her again. He really did give a nice hug.

As did Alex. God, why did he keep plaguing her thoughts like this? No, she had to think about something else. Like how good it would be to get back to civilisation again.

Ah, shopping; here I come, Nicola thought, almost salivating at the thought of being able to cruise her favourite shopping strip again. It had been less than two weeks, but it felt like forever.

Her mouth began to water at the thought of wrapping her lips around a nice rich, creamy latte. Hmm, she thought, stepping into the shower. And I might even treat myself to a slice of mud cake.

Chapter Thirty-three

Nicola gripped the armrests, closed her eyes and tried to hold her breath while the plane taxied and then took off. Only once the engine was a steady drone did she allow herself to relax slightly and let her mind wander.

During the drive down the coast she had thought again about meeting with Janet, and again told herself it wasn't meant to be right now. If Janet was gone when she got back she'd try and track her down at the hospital in Port Lincoln.

Meanwhile, there was unfinished business to deal with in Adelaide.

She'd organise a lovely dinner for the two of them – candles, bottle or two of good red. Scott had replied to her SMS, promising he'd be home for dinner, and Nicola was a little nervous and excited.

They'd been apart so long; it would be nice to be enfolded in familiar arms, have the comfort of nakedness to curl up to in the middle of the night. If she was lucky he might even consent to a few hours lazing about in bed, making love and just being together. Yes, she thought, absence does make the heart grow fonder.

Her mind went back to Richard. The poor fellow had seemed quite unhappy when she'd set eyes on him at the funeral and wake afterwards. How could he keep doing it day in day out – living in a relationship that had so obviously run its course?

He obviously loved Karen on some level, but Nicola thought it was probably more the mother-of-my-children kind of affection. Richard was no longer *in* love. What had he said now? Nicola tapped her lips with her index finger, trying to remember the conversation they'd had.

Ah, that's right: 'We didn't know each other well enough,' he'd said. 'If she hadn't got pregnant it probably would have petered out. Not really enough in common.' And then he'd shrugged like it didn't matter.

That's what had floored her; that he'd seemed to be okay about spending the next fifty-odd years with someone he knew he shouldn't be with; someone he wouldn't be with if he'd had his choice.

He should have been stronger. There was no real reason to get married; this was the twenty-first century. Hell, they hadn't even needed to stay together. Richard could have kept up with his responsibilities with a healthy support payment – which was likely before he took a massive pay cut to live out in the sticks.

He could have had regular visits – plenty of kids lived like that and did quite well.

But her daddy had intervened and Richard had done the right thing. 'That's the price you pay for sleeping with local aristocracy,' he'd said.

But life was too short; there was more to happiness than money and possessions. If he wasn't happy, he should just get out. Isn't that what he'd told her? That staying together because it was easier than splitting up and dividing the assets wasn't a good enough reason? She didn't have children to consider; that could make all the difference.

Either way, she had tough decisions of her own to deal with; Richard's choices were nothing to do with her.

★★★

Warmth and comfort flooded Nicola as she stepped into the tiled vestibule and clicked the door closed behind her.

She left her bag and bounded up the stairs, and was almost disappointed to find everything exactly as when she'd left, except the rack of clothes drying in the spare room. She didn't know what else she'd been expecting – Scott was the tidy one. But if there'd been dishes in the sink or a pile of dirty clothes on the floor, at least she'd feel a bit needed.

Unless she'd been replaced. Nicola's heart started racing. She carefully checked every drawer and ran her eye around the surface of each room, looking for any indication.

Exhausted, she finally sat down on the top step of the stairs. It was ridiculous; the only affair Scott was having was with his job. Of that she was certain. So why was she acting like a neurotic housewife?

Nicola checked the pantry, fridge, and freezer. Since when had he taken a liking to pizza? She found herself feeling better; pizza was a sure sign of bachelorhood, even if it *was* gourmet.

She pictured him with a thickened waist, love handles and the beginnings of a flabby gut, and smiled. She'd have him back on salad and in the gym in no time.

Nicola took her bag upstairs, emptied it, put a load of washing on, and took a quick shower. It was so nice to be in her luxurious bright white bathroom again after all the browns and beiges of the motel.

Back in the bedroom, she tore the sheets from the bed, stuffed them in the wash basket and got a fresh set from the hall linen press.

Fresh, clean linen was one of Nicola's favourite smells, and one of the things she loved best about staying away from home. Ordinarily. The Nowhere Else Hotel Motel had been a considerable let down in that department. The sheets were clean, but seemed to always have a slightly burnt, oily odour about them. And they'd only been changed every three days, thanks to the water restrictions.

'Ahh, heaven,' she said, burying her nose in the bundle of linen in her arms.

But she didn't have time to linger. First she had to email all her notes and photos to Bill – thank God for finally having high speed broadband again – and then she had a romantic meal to plan, shop for, and cook. She quickly made the bed, anticipating how nice it would be to slide between those lovely thick, yummy-smelling sheets again, before bounding back downstairs with her laptop.

★★★

Her eye caught the cookbook acting as a doorstop and she almost picked it up. No, Sandy was right; now was not the time for another culinary disaster. She stood at the sink waiting for the Gaggia to work its magic, while trying to think of what to cook.

Roast rolled leg of lamb with all the traditional trimmings was always nice. She'd get one already rolled and stuffed – the butcher down the road was sure to have a selection; fetta, pine nuts and spinach, or something. Nicola got out a pen and paper from the drawer and wrote down 'Rolled leg of lamb – stuffed (?)' She'd also need potatoes, carrots, pumpkin, garlic and some greens – perhaps cabbage with cream and seed mustard like Sandy did it. Yum.

She tucked her pad under her arm, stuck her pen behind her ear, retrieved her mug of freshly brewed coffee, and went to sit in the lounge. God, it felt like forever since she'd enjoyed a decent cup of coffee. Surely the hotel motel could afford five grand for a decent small machine?

She revelled in her first few sips, and then returned to planning her menu and making her shopping list. She looked over what she had so far, and felt content with her decision and the level of difficulty. Now the hard part; dessert. Of course she could always put together a cheese platter. But she really wanted to make an effort; the cheese platter was their 'Get out of jail free' card whenever they had to take something to a friend's place.

No, as much as they both loved cheese, it didn't show enough initiative for tonight. Hmm, she tapped the pen against her lips. What did Scott like? What did he order for dessert on the rare occasion he wanted it? She thought back over where they'd eaten. Uh huh. Sticky date pudding.

And didn't someone bake one on *MasterChef* the other week? Nicola got her laptop out, turned it on, and sipped on her coffee while she was waiting for it to fire up. She found the site and the recipe. It looked a damn sight easier than anything Hugh whatever-his-name-was had in his book. Nicola wrote down all the ingredients. Bloody hell, it was an absolute sugar and fat fest. Oh well. The way back to a man's heart was through his stomach – shaping up could wait a couple of days.

She raced upstairs, dragged the washing from the machine into the dryer, grabbed her handbag, ran back down the stairs, locked the front door, and stepped through into the garage where her Mercedes convertible sat. It looked tiny after the four-wheel-drive she'd been travelling in.

She pressed the remote for the car and the garage, opened the car door, sat down, and slid her long legs down under the steering wheel. Golly, she could see why everyone drove such big vehicles; they were so much easier to get into. Her own car felt totally foreign.

Nicola gunned the engine, remembering what she'd loved about it – apart from the ease of parking. She'd love to have taken it up the freeway or the winding Gorge Road, but she didn't have time; she was on a mission.

She greeted the butcher with a broad grin, and didn't even flinch when he said he had rolled legs of lamb, but none that were stuffed – traditionally or with anything gourmet. Oh well, obviously stuffing was no longer in, she decided with a shrug.

The last thing she wanted was to be considered old-fashioned. And Scott would know; he ate out all the time. She stuffed the lamb into her eco-friendly calico carry bag, said goodbye and moved on to the greengrocer next door.

Nicola's final stop was the supermarket, which was jam-packed, thanks to it now being late Friday afternoon. Never having bought most of the ingredients for the sticky date pudding, she was slow making her way through the final items on her list. This necessitated her going down almost every aisle, and of course seeing all the items she needed but hadn't thought about in her quest for the perfect romantic meal. There'd been no milk in the fridge, no fresh bread, and they were low on fabric softener and washing liquid.

She finally made it to the express checkout with her hand basket brimming and her shoulders burning. She really needed to get back to a gym and build her muscles up again, she thought, ignoring the glares of the shoppers and pointed looks between her and the nearby Ten Items or Less sign.

She was weary by the time she got back to her car, and exhausted and dishevelled when she walked back into the house and dumped everything on the counter top. She set the coffee machine into action again, and bustled about, unpacking everything and putting it away.

Upstairs she paused to pull her clothes from the dryer into the basket, dumped it on the bed on her way past, and bounded back down the stairs.

All these stairs she had to get used to again, she thought, feeling the muscles tightening in her thighs, buttocks, and down the backs of her legs. She was even starting to feel a little breathless. *Just how unfit am I?* She didn't think she'd looked *that* bad in the mirror earlier. God, she hoped Scott would still find her attractive. But she didn't have time to dwell; she could hear the Gaggia calling.

Adorned in apron and headscarf, Nicola hummed, sang and whistled her way through the recipes. Ruth would be proud. Surprised, but proud, she thought with a grin. She remembered the time Ruth had thrown her tea towel on the bench and said, 'I give up, Nicola. You and cooking are not friends.'

To her teenage insecurities, the unspoken words 'You are no daughter of mine' had also stung. She'd tried, but just couldn't seem to concentrate enough. And so what if there was a dash of this here or an extra pinch of that there? Why did it have to be so damn precise? Did it really matter that much?

She smiled at remembering Ruth's hands-on-hips I-told-you-so smirk, the day after the now infamous dinner party. When she'd tried to blame Hugh whatever-his-name-was, Ruth had calmly pointed out that if it was published in a cookbook – especially one by someone so famous – it would have been tested, probably hundreds of times.

'Perhaps we can put it down to operator error,' she'd suggested with a grin, before dragging out of the oven the apple tea cake Nicola had watched her whip up – without a recipe.

Nicola suddenly wondered what sort of cook Janet was. Was it in the genes? It must be; Ruth hadn't succeeded in 'nurturing' it in her, so it had to be a 'nature' thing. Was she a one-off crap cook, or was there a whole line of them out there?

Nicola worked out the schedule for what she had to do and when to put things on to cook, writing everything down. She was determined to get this right. And, as she'd learnt the hard way, timing was everything when it came to cooking.

She checked her watch every few minutes as she worked; cooking the lamb, preparing the vegetables and staggering their entry into the oven, all the while keeping an eye on the dates simmering in one pot and the gravy in another. 'I'm the multi-tasking cooking queen,' she said, wiggling her bum and twirling the two whisks at once.

Finally it was time to take the meat out and rest it. There was only one ingredient missing: Scott.

She admired her crispy potatoes and the caramelised carrots and pumpkin. It all looked so perfect. She checked her watch. He should have been here by now; she'd told him seven. He'd agreed. It was now ten to. Scott was never late.

She thought about ringing him, but decided against it. If he could remember all the meetings with clients and all the other stuff he did, she shouldn't need to remind him about dinner – it was one night for goodness sake. For a fleeting moment she wondered if he'd had an accident or if something else bad had happened, but she pushed the thought aside.

No, she had a very strong, sick feeling in the pit of her stomach; he'd forgotten.

At seven she carved the meat. It was perfect – pink and juicy, just like in a restaurant. She went ahead and served up two plates, stuck Scott's in the oven, and took hers to the dining room table. She opened the bottle of red and poured herself a glass. She ate in silence, hardly tasting her meal, her eyes fixed on the flicker of the candles as she alternated between mouthfuls of food and sips of wine. It was probably a good drop – Scott's wine inventory told her it was prime drinking – but it could have been château cardboard for all the enjoyment she was getting out of it.

She shook her head at her perfect sticky date pudding still cooling in its cake tin, and the pot of sauce with whisk sitting on the stove – she felt sick; couldn't face anything sweet and rich now.

She scraped her plate clean, rinsed it, and stuck it in the dishwasher. Then she turned off the oven and shoved the baking dish covered in foil back into it. Let him deal with it.

She looked around the kitchen. A couple of tears dripped onto the marble bench top.

It was nine o'clock when she stumbled back into the dining room and blew out the candles. Really, what had she expected? Their life together had always been about grabbing a bite on the run, snatching a few minutes of conversation here and there.

She'd been gone too long; long enough to paint a fantastical rosy picture in her mind. Thinking they could fix things; now *that* was the fantasy.

Nicola hauled her large suitcase out from under the stairs and lugged it up to the bedroom. Her head was clear and her pulse steady while she systematically chose what to pack and what to leave.

She hesitated when the phone rang, checked her watch – ninethirty – and continued packing while listening to Scott's breathless message about how he'd got caught up and not to wait up for him.

He had obviously forgotten about dinner, but he'd sure as hell remember when he found the dried up meal in the oven, the wax spilt and hardened on the good tablecloth.

Bastard. Let him see the effort she'd made and be consumed with guilt. It was his mess. Let him clean it up.

Back in the kitchen, Nicola wrote a note saying she'd gone back to Nowhere Else; no reason, no explanation, no anger in her hand or words. She flicked through her key ring, paused at her Mercedes key, and then placed the whole lot on her note.

She took a deep breath at the open door, did a quick inventory in her head, and then pulled it closed behind her.

Chapter Thirty-four

Standing at the curb, Nicola hung up from calling the taxi, offered a silent prayer for an efficient service, and dialled Bill's number. She knew Sandy would be disappointed she didn't come to her for help, but hopefully she would understand that she couldn't; not with her and Bob's connection to Scott.

And anyway, she thought, biting her lip as she waited for Bill to pick up, she was doing them a favour by not getting them involved. As much as she would have loved Sandy's support right now, she just couldn't have it. Finally the phones connected.

'Nicola? Is everything okay?' Bill said.

Nicola sighed. 'Not really. Could I borrow your spare room?'

'Sure, come on over.'

'Thanks. See you soon.'

Nicola hung up feeling a weight had been lifted. If only the taxi would turn up. She paced back and forth while trying to think if there was anything she'd need but hadn't packed.

Taxi, hurry up!

If Scott arrived home first she'd look a right fool. And the time for pleading and trying to change her mind had passed. If he cared that much about her – them – he would have been there for dinner three hours ago. Dread and anxiety filled her.

She looked back at the warehouse conversion; she wouldn't miss much about the place – maybe the bathtub and the coffee machine. But the stark walls and cold minimalism were definitely more Scott's thing than hers. If only she'd stood up for herself more, not let him dominate her so much. In some ways, she'd been just as weak as Richard, she realised with slight shock.

Feeling exposed, she leant against the side wall of the porch, careful not to trigger the sensor light. That way she'd be hidden from view if Scott arrived home.

Nicola checked her watch every few seconds. It had only been five minutes since she'd called the cab, but it seemed like an hour. Her heart beat steadily but hard against her ribs. She took a few deep breaths. She stared out into the orange glow from the street-light. A few raindrops darkened the concrete.

Nicola watched, mesmerised, as the drops slowly started to join up, and found herself wondering if they were getting rain in Nowhere Else. Not that a few drops made any difference; Alex had said they needed two solid days and nights of gentle, soaking rain to save their season.

The rain was falling steadily by the time the taxi arrived. Nicola thanked the driver profusely as he loaded her two heavy cases in the boot. She gave Bill's address and leapt into the back seat gratefully.

As they pulled away from the curb, she turned and looked back at the warehouse through the side window, which was streaked with clear shining droplets. She caught sight of her face in the reflection and smiled sadly at the irony; this was the classic break-up scene from almost every romantic movie.

She was exhausted; too tired to think about the magnitude of what she'd done, or what she was going to do next. She'd just get through the night. And her catch-up with Sandy tomorrow, she thought wearily.

It would probably be the last thing she'd feel like, but it had to be done. Sandy was her friend; had been too good a friend for too long to be shut out, even with her connection to Scott. The sooner she faced up, the better. Small steps, Nicola told herself, closing her eyes and trying to think of calm tropical island scenes; difficult with the squelch and hiss of water under the car and the beat of rain on the roof.

Nicola opened her eyes when she felt the car pull over and stop. She fished her wallet from her handbag, paid the man and got out. At the back of the car she waited for the driver to assist her. The porch light was on in front of Bill's stunning double-fronted sand-stone villa. The taxi driver put her cases on the end of the path. He nodded in reply to her thanks and got in his car.

Nicola turned back to find Bill standing on the porch, bathed in light. She smiled at his brown velour robe and matching slippers, before a wave of sadness washed over her; seeing him standing there like that reminded her of her father, Paul. She tried to swallow back the lump in her throat and took two deep breaths as she pulled the handles of her two cases up. She dragged them up to the porch where Bill took over; he clearly hadn't wanted to get his feet wet.

They went inside, with neither saying a word, and Bill closed the door behind them.

'Good to see you kiddo,' Bill said. He put an arm around Nicola's shoulder, pulled her roughly to him for a moment before patting her arm firmly and saying, 'You'll be right.' He let her go.

'Thanks so much for this, Bill,' Nicola croaked.

'It's quite all right. Now, let's get you settled. This way,' Bill said. Nicola looked around the spare room, which was left off the wide central hall. It was tastefully decorated with an ornate old timber wardrobe, a matching chest of drawers, a plush armchair upholstered in pink floral, and a cast-iron bed covered in a cream damask quilt.

Next to the bed was a freestanding wooden towel rack with a fluffy pale lavender towel folded over it. It was much more friendly than the spare room back at the warehouse, with its low-line bed and base adorned in black leather.

She'd been in Bill's home before, but never past the kitchen, main living areas, and bathroom. She'd expected Bill's bachelor pad to be dark minimalism too. But then he had been married three times; some of the feminine touches were bound to rub off over time.

Standing there looking at the inviting bed, Nicola suddenly felt exhausted.

'Ensuite is just through here,' Bill said, going over to the door on the wall beside the bed and opening it to reveal a bright shiny room done in heritage cream and burgundy.

'I love the sound of rain on an iron roof,' Nicola said, nodding towards the ceiling.

'Best sound in the world.'

'It sounds quite heavy. I hope they're getting it over at Nowhere Else,' Nicola said thoughtfully.

'Listen to you, suddenly all concerned about rain,' Bill said, pushing at her shoulder. 'Next you'll be telling me you're throwing in your job to become a farmer,' he said with a hearty laugh.

'Oh ha ha, you're hilarious,' she said, rolling her eyes. They stood there in silence.

'Anyway,' Bill said, thoughtfully, 'it'd better still look like drought over there when we bring in the camera guys, or else we'll be buggered.'

They listened to the rain on the roof for a few moments more.

'Right,' Bill suddenly said, clapping his hands together. 'Now, there's a bottle of red open if you'd like to drown your sorrows. Or I can get you nice warm cup of cocoa if you'd prefer.'

'You don't need to wait on me, Bill,' Nicola said, smiling warmly at him.

'I know.'

'Actually, would you mind if I just went to bed?' Nicola asked quietly, hoping he wouldn't be offended.

'Of course not. You've had a big day, what with flying back this morning and everything else… You just make yourself at home and I'll see you in the morning. Though no sleeping in – I'm taking you out for breakfast at ten.'

'Oh. Right, okay,' Nicola said tentatively.

'We don't do moping in this house, do we, Oscar,' he said, bending down and picking up the sleek black cat that had wandered in looking like it had just woken up.

'I didn't know you had a cat,' Nicola said, rubbing the cat's ears. He began to purr loudly.

'Legacy of wife number three. She took him with her but he kept running back here. Figured out what a nut case she was too, didn't you mate?' He put the cat down. It rubbed against Nicola's leg.

'He likes you; you should feel very honoured,' he said.

'Will he let me pick him up?'

'You'd better ask him.'

Nicola bent and picked the cat up. He held no objection to her holding him tightly to her. She could feel the comforting vibration of his purr against her chest.

'Well, I'll leave you to it then.'

'Does he need to be put out or anything?'

'No. If he decides to keep you company, just leave your door ajar or else he'll wake you up to get out later.'

'Thanks so much for this, Bill.'

'Pleasure, Nicola. And it will be all right. You'll see,' he said, gave Oscar a final stroke and left.

Nicola put the cat down, opened the smaller of her suitcases, retrieved her toiletries bag, and used the bathroom. When she got back she found the cat washing himself in the middle of the quilt. Obviously preparing himself for bed too, she thought, smiling.

The cat paused mid-lick and watched while she carefully pulled back the covers and squeezed into bed.

'You could at least shove over a bit,' she told the cat. But he ignored her and returned to his ablutions.

What was that saying: 'Dogs have owners, cats have staff'? Too true, she thought, giving the cat a pat before turning out the light and snuggling down. Nicola closed her eyes and revelled in the softness of the feather pillow and its sweet floral scent. Oscar's purr seemed extra-loud in the darkness. She liked the feel of his warmth and gentle vibration against her leg.

I should seriously consider getting a pet, she thought, yawning. An image of Jerry flashed into her mind. She hoped he was happy with Graeme. And she hoped it was raining this hard in Nowhere Else.

★★★

When she woke, it took Nicola a few moments to remember where she was. There was a gentle glow in the room. Oscar was still on the bed, but further across; she must have forced him over. In the early days, Scott had often ribbed her about how much room she took up in bed. *Ah, Scott,* she thought sadly.

She checked her watch; nine o'clock. She hadn't thought she'd ever sleep, let alone for ten hours or so. And yet she didn't feel too bad. Thank goodness she hadn't sat up drinking with Bill. She should get up; they were heading out at ten. But staying like this meant she didn't have to face things.

She rolled over and stroked Oscar's back. The cat responded by presenting his belly for attention. *Cheeky bugger*, she thought, smiling and doing as she was bid. The rain was still sounding quite heavy on the roof – had it been raining all night?

She mentally crossed her fingers for Nowhere Else. Moments later there was a tap on the door.

'Come on sleepy head, time to get up,' Bill said. 'You've got forty minutes before we leave.'

Gosh, Nicola thought with a start, that could have been Paul on a school morning all those years ago. Really, she was so lucky to have a friend like Bill. It was a little weird that he was her boss as well, but that couldn't be helped. If he wasn't her boss, they would never have met, and they wouldn't be friends.

'Righto, thanks,' Nicola called. She climbed out of bed, had a quick shower and dressed in jeans, and was in the kitchen twenty minutes later. Oscar rubbed at Bill's leg while he spooned food from a tin onto a plate.

'I see you've turned my cat into a traitor,' he said, grinning at her as he put the plate down on the tiles and gave the cat a pat.

'Yeah, sorry about that,' Nicola said. 'But in my defence, I don't think I had a choice,' she added with a shrug.

'Probably right,' he said nonchalantly. 'How are you feeling this morning? Sleep okay?'

'Not bad, and yes, thanks, good.'

'Well, shall we head off now since we're ready?'

'Good idea,' Nicola said, relieved to be spared a bit longer from the inevitable discussion that had to be had. 'Before I forget, I'm meant to be catching up with my friend Sandy at three. But I can cancel if...'

'You will do no such thing. It'll be good for you – save me having to listen to you bellyaching about emotions and feelings and crap,' he said, flapping an arm.

Nicola laughed at him. He really was just what she needed. He'd keep her distracted. And so would work, which she suspected was the reason for breakfast.

★★★

At the café, Nicola savoured her first sip of 'real' coffee, running it around in her mouth for as long as was polite.

'Bill, you have no idea how good that tastes. I thought my machine at home was good, but this…'

'The look on your face is priceless.'

'Ah, the joy.'

'And not available out in Nowhere Else, I take it?'

'Got it in one. That and many of life's other small luxuries.'

'Trying to make me feel guilty?'

But Nicola didn't bite. She was staring thoughtfully into her cup.

'Now don't get all mopey on me. Scott does not deserve you, and the sooner you realise that, the better.'

'Look, Bill. Thanks, for everything. You're being amazing. Putting me up, and putting up with me.'

'I said, don't go getting all mopey on me. Now I'm making an executive decision to change the subject: work.'

'Can't I finish my coffee first?'

'Don't fret, it's all good.'

'That's what I need to hear.'

'Firstly, I've had a chance to look over what you've already got from out bush.'

'And?'

'And I think it's great. Now I know this sounds a little odd, but I don't think we need to find a tight angle. Leave it as a mix of thoughts, opinions, and segments: the fracturing of dreams, livelihoods, people's lives. Drought is such a big thing, we'd be wrong to try and oversimplify it. What do you think?'

'I think you've got a point. It would explain why I couldn't focus. Maybe I'm not meant to.'

'Exactly.'

'Not too arty?'

'No. I think when we've reworked the order it'll be great.'

'I haven't done much. Most of it is just notes and pictures from roaming around getting a sense of the place. I've just been putting words to sights and sounds – and not many of them even.'

'Right, that's that settled then. I'll talk with editing and we'll arrange a camera to go out and shoot some footage. Now, there's something else I want to discuss.'

'Sounds ominous.' Nicola's heart started fluttering. 'What is it?'

'Well, I'm not sure how you're going to take this, but I want you to hear me out then think it through before answering.'

Oh shit.

'I want you to reconsider doing your reunion story. There's still time. We can film you meeting Janet, when you do.'

Nicola was so relieved she was angry.

'Great. And turn it into the same beat-up shit the other stations spit out nightly. This isn't current affairs, Bill. It's my life.'

'Listen to me. You're going off half-cocked. I'm talking about show-ing an extraordinary woman dealing with an ordinary situation.'

'Gee, thanks a lot.'

'Just calm down. Look at it from a journalistic perspective. Here's someone who seems untouchable, leads a perfect life but, wow, she's just like you and me. Started life as an abandoned baby and look at her now, sort of thing. Nicola, you could give thousands of people of all ages hope.'

'All right, but why me?'

'Because you have the gift to give. Come on, what do you say? You can have John for sound and Andrew for film. You're going to want to find out anyway. Why not do it on my budget?'

'Oh well, when you put it like that, how can I possibly resist?'

'There's no need for sarcasm. Come on, just say you'll do it.'

'On one condition.'

'Name it.'

'The budget stretches to a decent coffee machine.'

'Looks like someone's going shopping.' Bill stuck out a hand and waited for her to shake. 'I can almost smell another Walkley,' he said, slipping his thumbs into an imaginary pair of braces.

Chapter Thirty-five

Nicola wished she had her Mercedes so she wouldn't have to impose on Bill any further, but not so much that she was prepared to go back to the warehouse and pick it up. Anyway, she was back off to Nowhere Else soon and wouldn't be needing it; best that it stayed safely locked up in the garage.

Sandy had just arrived at Cibo when Nicola got out of Bill's navy blue BMW. He waved to Sandy, who was standing under an umbrella. Nicola wondered for a moment how they knew each other, until she remembered she'd taken Sandy to last year's Christmas party – Scott had been too busy to make it. She rolled her eyes at the thought of how often he had been 'too busy to make it'.

Bill lowered the passenger side window. 'Hi Sandy,' he called.

'Hi Bill.' She waved in at him.

'You take care of her. And you, missy,' he said, pointing a finger at Nicola, who was now on the curb beside her friend. 'No more than three grand.'

'Okay. Thanks Bill.'

'See you later. Dinner's at six.'

'Anything I can pick up?' Nicola asked, peering into the car.

'No thanks, it's all under control. You just concentrate on having some fun.' He waved as he pulled away from the curb and drove out into a gap in the traffic.

Nicola would much rather have been going back with him, curling up on the couch with a glass of red in front of the TV or maybe a book. The last thing she felt like doing was putting on a happy face and being good company. For a moment she wished she was back in Nowhere Else. Who would have thought! She shook her head at herself.

'So, I take it last night didn't go so well,' Sandy said.

Nicola spun around. God, she'd almost forgotten her friend standing there on the sidewalk.

'It's so good to see you,' she said, sounding a lot more effusive than she felt. She pulled Sandy into an embrace. If only she could shake this empty, sad feeling. Sandy hugged her back.

'Come on. Let's sit, and you can tell me all about it,' Sandy said, tugging gently at Nicola's elbow.

Nicola followed slowly. She wasn't tired, but her body felt like a dead weight. They sat at their favourite table in the corner of the front window. People strolled back and forth and they watched in silence for a few moments.

'So what was that Bill was saying about three grand?' Sandy asked.

'For a coffee machine – it's my price for going back to Nowhere Else,' Nicola said, smiling weakly. She pulled a sachet of sugar from the pot in front of them and began fiddling with it.

'So we've got a mission then. Goody,' Sandy said, clapping her hands together. 'Shopping's always so much better when you're actually shopping for something,' she said.

'Hmm.' Nicola knew she should be trying harder, but couldn't seem to make herself. The waitress materialised and took their order, buying her some time. After she left, Sandy was the first to break the silence that was stretching on into awkwardness.

'So, Scott rang us last night looking for you,' Sandy said, now fiddling with her own tube of sugar.

Nicola sighed but remained silent and focussed on her packet of sugar.

'Why didn't you call me – come to us?' Sandy pleaded, putting her hand on Nicola's arm.

'Sandy, you know why,' Nicola said quietly, looking at her friend. She sighed. 'It's over; the last thing I need is an intervention. It's too late for any of that.'

'So what happened? Scott didn't say; he just wanted to know if we'd seen you.'

'I cooked a nice, romantic dinner. He didn't turn up. I left,' Nicola said with a shrug.

'What; just didn't show?'

'Yup. Forgot. And just when I finally conquered that damn oven too,' she said, smiling weakly.

'So what are you going to do? Where are you going to live? I take it you're staying with Bill.'

'I haven't given it any thought. I'm going back to Nowhere Else on Monday. That's as far as I've got.' Monday couldn't come soon enough, Nicola thought, again surprised at just how keen she was to return to the tiny, remote place.

She was itching to phone Alex and see if they'd had any rain – it was still falling steadily there in the city. She was starting to feel strangely connected; almost like she had a stake herself. *Well, I kind of do*, she thought, *though not in farming*.

'Well, if there's anything we can do to help, you only have to ask. You know we both think the world of you. Bob's often said Scott takes you too much for granted.'

'Really? He said that?' She glanced at her friend. Maybe she'd misjudged them; their loyalty. She felt a little guilty for not leaning on her.

Sandy nodded.

'Well I guess that's my fault for letting him,' she said. They both looked up and thanked the waitress who delivered their hot chocolates.

'So, what sort of coffee machine are we shopping for?' Sandy asked.

'I'm not sure what the options are these days,' Nicola said with a shrug, as she picked up her cup and took a sip. She wished she could muster some excitement, or at least some energy.

They sipped in silence.

'You don't really feel like shopping at all, do you?' Sandy asked when they'd almost finished their drinks.

'Not really,' Nicola said. 'It must be pretty bad when I don't feel like shopping, huh,' she said with a wan smile.

'Well, this weather's probably not helping. Look, why don't we go and see a movie? That new Jennifer Aniston movie is meant to be hilarious. And the cinema is the one public place you can emerge from puffy eyed without getting any weird looks. What do you say?' Sandy said, laying a hand on Nicola's arm.

Nicola looked at her friend's warm, sympathetic expression. She couldn't say no. 'Okay,' she said with a shrug.

Nicola got out her iPhone. She ignored the list of missed calls from Scott and the text messages telling her she had voicemail messages, and went to the website for the nearest cinema. She read the information and checked her watch.

'It's on in Norwood in twenty-five minutes,' she announced. They gathered their handbags, paid at the counter, and made their way up the street to Sandy's white Peugeot hatch.

While they drove, Nicola sent a text to Bill, telling him she might be a bit later for dinner because she was going to see a movie that wouldn't finish until six. She told him not to wait for her. She didn't want him ruining his meal on her account.

She got a simple 'Okay – enjoy' back from him.

***

As Nicola watched the advertisements up on the big screen, her mind drifted back to her breakfast conversation with Bill.

What was I thinking?! She sat up straighter in her chair. How dare she agree to film her reunion with Janet without even discussing it with her? She had no right to do that. Just because she was in the media and comfortable with it, didn't mean everyone else was.

Not only that; this was way too private to film. Maybe after the fact, but certainly not during. Hadn't the government adoption site urged caution; consideration of the other people involved. No, this was not just about her.

Besides, Janet might not even be looking for her; might not have even given her a second thought in all these years.

God, just who did she think she was? And there was no way she wanted a camera crew going back with her on Monday. What if Janet was still in town and she got the chance to meet her? She couldn't have John and Andrew tagging along. If it was accidently filmed, there'd be no going back. No, she ran the risk of ruining things completely with her mother if she did finally get to meet her. She had to tread carefully.

Bill will kill me, she thought, instantly wishing she had stayed with Sandy and Bob after all. Oh well, he'd just have to get over it. It was her life; her story.

'Are you okay?' Sandy whispered.

'Yep,' Nicola said, and tried to focus on the opening shots of their movie.

★★★

Nicola emerged from the cinema feeling a little cheerier. She hadn't found it as funny as she should have, or laughed as much as Sandy, but she probably couldn't blame the movie for that. Sandy insisted on driving her back to Bill's.

'Thanks so much for today, Sandy,' she said, giving her friend a hug. 'Sorry I was such bad company.'

'That's all right; you're allowed. Now you just remember, we're here for you – both Bob and me. We choose you when it comes to divvying the friends up,' she said, smiling warmly.

'Thanks Sandy. Love to Bob,' she said, getting out of the car. As she waved her friend off, she wondered how Bob would feel about his wife's assertion. It would mean giving up his weekly golf session; he wouldn't like that too much.

She knocked on the door and Bill opened it, adorned with a navy and white striped apron that accentuated his ample gut. Though she wasn't about to tell him that.

'What, no coffee machine?' he said, stepping aside to let her in.

'Um, about that...'

'Ah, this sounds ominous.'

Touché, Nicola thought.

'Something smells good,' she said, walking into the kitchen. She slapped her forehead when she saw the open bottle of red wine on the bench. 'Damn, I was going to get a bottle. Sorry, I completely forgot,' she said.

'Don't worry about that; there's a whole cellar full of the stuff,' Bill said. 'And anyway, I'm not sure I'd trust your taste,' he added with a laugh. 'So, what's this about the coffee machine?'

'You'd better sit down,' Nicola said with a sigh, and led the way through to the lounge room.

'Jesus,' he said, following her. He sat down.

'I'm really sorry, but I can't go through with filming our reunion,' Nicola blurted. 'I'm happy to do a piece on it – if it ever happens – just not the initial meeting. We could re-enact if Janet agreed. It's just that… Hell, Bill, I don't even know yet if she wants to meet me.'

'Fair enough,' Bill said, with a shrug.

'That's all? I thought you'd be ropable,' Nicola said, staring at him in disbelief.

'It's your story, Nicola, so it's your choice to make.'

'So you're okay, really okay about it?'

'Yep.'

'I'd also rather John and Andrew didn't come back with me,' she said quietly. 'It's just that…'

'It's okay, Nicola. I get it,' Bill said, holding up a silencing hand. 'I'll send them a bit later on. It was probably a stretch to get them there on Monday as it was. Right, so was that all then?' Bill asked, putting his hands down ready to launch himself off the couch.

'Yep.'

'And here I was, thinking you were going to tell me something bad. Getting me to sit down,' he muttered, shaking his head as he made his way back into the kitchen.

Chapter Thirty-six

During the flight, Nicola kept her mind on the possibility of a reunion with Janet; it was easier than thinking about Scott, who had left at least a dozen messages on her phone in the past two days.

His first message had begged her to come back; the second to stop being so silly. Gradually his emotion had petered out and the last message just wearily asked her to call him. She had, four times, refusing to leave a message. If he was that upset, he could damn well pick up when her number displayed.

Not that it would make any difference. Nicola's mind was made up – he'd kept her on hold for too long, chosen one too many clients over her. And now it had cost him his relationship. She hoped the commission had been worth it.

★★★

More comfortable with the drive from the airport now, Nicola was able to take note of her surroundings. She still didn't know how much rain there had been; the news had reported good falls right across the growing regions of the Eyre Peninsula, but no more detail than that. When Alex had driven her around, he'd made it clear how patchy the rain coverage could be. Some farmers could have plenty while their next door neighbours received nothing. Yep, the weather was a fickle thing.

There were plenty of puddles by the side of the road, but the closer she got to Nowhere Else, the dryer it seemed to get. Nicola's heart slowly sank in sympathy for the farmers.

She smiled at the Welcome To Nowhere Else sign; she did feel welcome. And she had a strange sense of coming home. She was even looking forward to her motel room; not its shabby décor, but the familiarity of it.

Yesterday afternoon at Bill's, the feeling of not belonging – not having a home – had struck her hard. She was sure Bill had noticed her change in mood, but thankfully he hadn't said anything; she would have crumbled for sure.

And she was doing so well at appearing strong. On the inside, she was a nervous, empty, sick mess, but on the outside she was calm and composed. Only those who knew her would see how much more subdued and quieter she was than usual. Nicola was relieved to be going back to Nowhere Else, where people didn't know her so well, rather than into the office.

She smiled as she pictured being greeted by Tiffany's big grin and bubbling personality. It would also be nice to walk down the street and receive friendly nods from the locals again. And then she had a strange thought; could she imagine herself living here – permanently? She tried to laugh it off, but as she drove, the question stayed with her.

She pulled into the car park, turned off the four-wheel-drive, and made her way to room eight, thinking that she should have handed in her key and saved Bill three nights of accommodation. Oh well, too late now.

Having dropped off her bag, Nicola headed across the courtyard to the hotel, with her fingers crossed that Tiffany would be there.

'Nic!' Tiffany rushed over and gave Nicola a hug. 'Good to see you back.'

'Good to be back, Tiff,' Nicola said, and meant it. She beamed at Tiff.

'How was the big smoke? I *so* can't wait to move over there. When – if – I get into uni,' Tiffany said, pulling out a chair and plopping herself down.

'So you haven't heard yet?' Nicola asked, dragging out a chair of her own and sitting down.

'Nope. But should be any day now.'

'I've got my fingers crossed for you. So, what did I miss?' Nicola asked, keen to keep the conversation away from herself.

'Well, it rained all weekend.'

'That's great – is it enough?'

'Not enough to declare the drought broken, but apparently enough for the farmers who took the risk and sowed to breathe a big sigh of relief.'

'Oh, Tiff, that's brilliant.'

'Yep; it's nice to see everyone cheery again. The front bar was packed on Saturday night.'

The hotel's phone started ringing. 'Bugger,' Tiffany said, leaping up. 'I'll see you later.'

Nicola got out her mobile and was scrolling through her Facebook wall when it started to ring. She was pleased to see Alex's name.

'Hi Alex, what's up?'

'Are you back, yet? I was in town Saturday night and Tiff said you'd gone to Adelaide.'

'Just got back a few minutes ago. Hey, great about the rain – did you get enough?'

'It's never enough. Come on, you should know that about us farmers by now,' he said with a laugh. 'But yeah, I did pretty well out of it.'

'That's great.'

'Yeah. Hey, Bert's wife Janet stayed after the funeral. Thought you should know because of…well…you know.'

'Really? Any idea where she's staying?'

'Bert's, actually.'

'Oh. Did she inherit it?'

'I don't know where things stand there; no will has turned up yet as far as I know. Dad said she could stay. Not sure why.' Nicola wondered what right Graeme had to make such a decision.

'Well, thanks for letting me know.'

'No worries. I'd better go. I'll catch you around.'

'Thanks for the call.'

Nicola sat staring at the phone for a few moments.

★★★

Nicola felt uneasy parking out the front of Bert's again. So much seemed the same, yet the presence of the old white Corolla reminded her how much had changed. Why was Janet still in town after the iciness people had shown her at Bert's funeral?

She glanced at the shed and shuddered as she climbed out of the four-wheel-drive. Tears threatened but she set her chin and swallowed them back. Now was definitely not the time.

Jerry greeted her with a gentle slap of his tail. Why was he here again?

His brown eyes were watery and pleading; if a dog could be depressed, this was what it would look like. Nicola almost lost control of her emotions. She bent and rubbed the dog's ears and received a sympathetic lick in return.

She suddenly felt the urge to cradle the large, hairy beast in her arms, tell him everything would be okay. The poor thing was something of a lost soul. And didn't she know how that felt – well, metaphorically speaking, anyway.

Still bent over, ruffling the dog and talking to him in soothing tones, Nicola felt another presence. She looked up to find the woman from the funeral – Janet, her mother – standing on the top step, arms folded defensively.

'We meet again,' Janet said, unfolding her arms and extending her hand with a smile.

Nicola had rehearsed what she would say until it was a clear, bold statement but now her palms and underarms were suddenly moist, her mind blank, and her voice a mere croak.

'Um, hi,' she managed, straightening and moving forward with her hand extended.

They stood, neither knowing how to break the silence. Finally, Janet spoke again.

'Come in. Would you like a cuppa?'

'Yes, thanks.'

Janet held the door open for Nicola but pushed the dog back roughly with her foot.

'You. Out,' she scolded.

'He lived inside,' Nicola said, returning the beast's sad, imploring gaze.

'Not while I'm here it's not.'

Nicola's heart sank a little for Jerry, who slunk off and lay at the bottom of the steps. She entered the house while avoiding his eye.

Inside, the kitchen was almost as it had been the day she'd sat with Bert. Different was the absent haze of smoke, the tidy sink, the jar of bright yellow sour sobs in the centre of the table. Jerry's bedding was still in the old hearth.

Nicola sat while Janet went to the sink to fill the kettle.

'Nice bit of rain we've had,' Janet called over her shoulder.

'Yes, huge relief for the farmers.'

'Though not enough to break the drought.'

'No, apparently not.'

'So, tea or coffee?'

'Tea, thanks. Drop of milk, no sugar, thanks.'

'I didn't see you around town over the weekend.'

'No, I had to go back to Adelaide.'

They fell into silence.

Nicola wondered why Janet seemed nervous. Had she guessed the truth? Had someone told her? But the only people who knew around here were Richard. Oh, and Alex, sort of. Nicola knew she could count on both of them to keep it to themselves. She decided Janet must think she was about to be interviewed – enough to make most people uneasy.

'Here we are,' Janet said, putting two mugs on the table before sitting down.

'So, what can I do for you? Or is this just a social call?' Janet finally asked, when each had a cup of tea in hand. Both seemed to be gripped by the awkwardness of being held at arm's length by history, but together by DNA.

Nicola searched for the right words, her speech entirely forgotten. Here she was, an award-winning journalist, as tongue-tied as a teenager.

'I think you're my mother,' she whispered, instantly ashamed at her lack of composure. She forced herself to meet Janet's shocked and bewildered gaze.

Nicola silently fished the battered photo and birth certificate from her handbag on the chair beside her, and slid them across the table, no longer trusting herself to speak.

Janet pushed her chair back and staggered from the room.

Nicola put her head in her hands and waited for the tears. Her only chance and she'd ruined it. She'd wanted her mother to embrace her, say she knew, that she'd felt it at the funeral. Say anything, do anything, except run from the room in fright, denial. Should she leave?

Nicola was quietly sobbing when an object slid across the table came into her distorted vision. Her tears stopped abruptly and she looked up, blinking. Janet's face was tearstained and flushed, but held a tight smile.

Nicola looked back to the table where the two old polaroids, almost identical, lay side by side. With shaking hands she picked up both photos and examined them.

'I never thought I'd find you,' Janet whispered, the table still between them.

Nicola nodded.

'Nicola – they kept your name.'

Nicola nodded, the tears streaming again.

Then Janet was at her side, reaching for her.

Nicola melted into her mother's arms and buried her head in her shoulder. Both women embraced and wept for what seemed hours until they finally broke apart, spent.

They sat down on the same side of the table, as close as the two chairs would allow.

'But why, when you had a husband?' Nicola finally quietly asked.

Janet shrugged. 'It was a long time ago. Things were different...'

'I need to know.'

'I don't know what to tell you.'

'Everything.'

'I'm sorry.'

'Please, you have to.'

'I…I can't.'

'Can't or won't?' Nicola couldn't stand it any longer. She'd come this far but had got nowhere.

Back in the four-wheel-drive, her vision blurred with tears, Nicola's heart lurched again as she caught sight of the dog staring after her, bewildered, as if begging to be leaving too.

How could her own mother do that to her? Hadn't she done enough by abandoning her all those years ago?

By the time she was halfway back to town, Nicola was furious with herself for her overreaction – more so for leaving her treasured photo and birth certificate behind. But she wasn't going back; she'd made the first move and look where that had got her. And she was not going to be bitten twice.

Chapter Thirty-seven

Nicola stumbled into her motel room after being barely aware of her drive back and parking the vehicle. She threw herself on the bed. She'd call Sandy, but only when she'd calmed down. She pushed the button on the remote to turn the television on – anything to distract her. She found nothing but daytime infomercials, soap operas and old movies, so turned it off again. She lay back on the bed, staring up at the ceiling.

Nicola was startled slightly by the vibration of her mobile on the laminex desk in the otherwise silent room. She got up and retrieved it, silently praying it wouldn't be Scott. She knew the time when they'd finally stop playing phone tag and have to speak was getting close, but she couldn't deal with that as well at the moment. Bill's name was lit up on the display.

'Hi Bill,' she said, trying to force a cheery tone.

'Everything okay?'

'Yep, fine,' Nicola lied. 'Hey, you'd better get Andrew over here to film before there's a green tinge everywhere – there was a heap of rain over the weekend. Not enough to break the drought, but enough to make everyone cheery and change the look of the place.' She was rambling, but didn't want Bill to detect her mood and start asking personal questions.

'About that.'

'Yes?'

'I've got some bad news, I'm afraid. The drought story has been canned.'

'What?! Why? When?'

'As of about half an hour ago. It's out of my hands, but someone higher up has decided to do a huge thing on the live export trade. And they don't want two big rural stories too close together.'

'So, do you need me to come back and work on that then?' Half of Nicola hoped he'd say yes, but the other half wasn't ready to leave. She didn't want to put her career in jeopardy by refusing.

'No, Jarred Bailey is insisting on doing it himself; being the owner of a huge cattle station up north, he's…'

'Jarred? But he's a TV exec, not a journalist! And don't you think he'll be just a *little* biased?'

'Tell me about it,' Bill said with a groan.

'So what about my reunion story – do you want me to can that as well?' *Not that I'm leaving*, Nicola thought. She'd do whatever it took to buy a few more days or weeks here. She wasn't sure she'd quit her job – she wasn't that stupid – but she'd certainly take leave without pay if she had to.

'Well, I still want to do it, but it might be taken out of my hands.' Nicola noticed the heaviness in his voice.

'Bill, what's going on? What aren't you telling me?'

There was a moment's silence, a deep sigh, and then the sound of a breath being taken. 'You'd better sit down.'

Nicola sat down, and as she did her heart rate became a slow, heavy, hollow thud in her chest. She wanted to make some quip about Bill being way too melodramatic, but found that she couldn't speak. And she suspected he wasn't. That wasn't Bill; Bill was real, told it like it was, in all its gruesome reality. What now? What more could possibly happen in her life?

'Now, this is the last thing you need to hear right now, and I don't want you to worry – and it might never happen, but you need to be prepared for the worst in case it does…'

'Bill, just tell me.'

Another sigh. 'It looks like the network is being taken over by an overseas consortium after all.'

'After all? When did this happen? How long have you known?'

'There's been discussions back and forth for a few months.'

'God, why didn't you tell me?'

'I didn't want to bother you with it unnecessarily if it wasn't going to happen – and I honestly didn't think it would.'

'Hang on, won't things just continue as normal, just with a different owner?'

'Apparently not. They're going through the place like a dose of salts. They're talking about canning *Life and Times* in favour of some renovation or cooking show.'

'Jesus, so that means me. I'm going to lose my job,' she said, thinking aloud. 'But I'm…' She was about to say, 'But I'm a Gold Walkley winner.' But there wasn't any point. Bill knew that; he didn't need convincing.

'Look, it might not happen. And it goes without saying that I'll do all I can to look after you. I'm sorry to have to put this on you, especially now, but I thought you should know.'

'Is it common knowledge?'

'No, so keep it to yourself for now. I'll keep you in the loop. I'd better go, I've got another meeting in half an hour.'

Nicola's heart went out to him; she knew how hard it must have been for him to tell her. He'd probably agonised over it for days. Poor bloke, having to look her in the eye all weekend, knowing.

'Thanks Bill; I do appreciate the heads-up.'

'Just remember, it might not happen. And if it does, you'll be fine. So for now, sit tight. Forget the drought, but you may as well find out what you can about your family on the network's budget. I think we can get away with it for a few more days.'

'Okay, thanks. See ya.'

Nicola sat staring and blinking at the phone in her hand. Christ, her whole life was crumbling around her. She searched her contacts, found Sandy's number and pressed it. It had barely rung once on the other end when it was answered.

'Hey Nic, I was *literally* about to call you – was just about to press send. How about that; spooky huh?' Sandy said.

'Hmm.'

'What's up, other than the obvious of course? Have you spoken to he-who-shall-not-be-named yet?

'No. We're still playing phone tag.'

'Oh well, probably for the best. You know Bob played golf with him yesterday and said he doesn't seem at all affected. Bob says it's the last time he's playing with him – he was so disgusted with his attitude. Maybe he's just in denial.'

'Hmm, maybe.'

'God, you sound terrible – and you didn't bite – what's happened?'

'Where do I start?' Nicola said with a groan.

'How about at the beginning? Come on, I've got all day if you need it.'

'Oh Sandy, my whole life is falling apart around me.'

'What's happened? I'm sure it can't be that bad.'

'Well I've met my mother again – my biological mother – and spoken to her.'

'But that's great, isn't it?'

'No; she didn't even want to know me.'

'Are you sure? What happened?'

'Oh Sandy, I stuffed it up so badly. I turned up with this whole spiel prepared and then I just went and blurted out that I was her daughter. I totally blew it.'

'I'm sure you didn't. Maybe she just got a shock and needs time to process it.'

'Hmm.'

'Just give her some space and see what happens. I'm sure she'll come around. At least you know she exists. That's a good thing, right?'

'Yeah, I suppose you're right.'

'So what else is wrong with your life? Apart from the obvious, that is.'

'My drought story has been canned and I'm about to lose my job.'

'Why? You're an award-winning journalist, for goodness sake!'

'Well, you'd think that would count for something, wouldn't you?'

'It doesn't?'

'Not when some overseas consortium buys the station and starts throwing their weight around. They probably don't even know what a Walkley *is*.'

'When did this happen?'

'Bill just rang. You know they're talking about taking *Life and Times* off the air in favour of another bloody reality show.'

'Oh, I love those shows. Oops, sorry.'

'Sandy, you're not helping.'

'But it hasn't actually happened yet; they're *talking* about it, you said, right?'

'Yeah, but…'

'Well, it might be okay. Anyway, losing your job isn't life and death; it's not the worst thing that can happen, Nicola – there are other jobs. And sometimes it's actually a good thing.'

'Oh God, this is where you tell me that maybe the universe is trying to send me a message. Give me a break.'

'Maybe it is a sign; a sign that you need a change of direction, different focus or something. I think you need to calm down and see what happens.'

'Jesus Sandy. I'm homeless, I'm about to lose my job, my biological mother that I've just found doesn't want to know me, and now you're telling me it's not that bad, to just sit back and wait and see?'

'That's exactly what I'm saying, Nicola. All this stuff happens for a reason. The universe sends opportunities and options; if you're too stressed you won't see them. Just take each day at a time and deal with each thing as it happens. It will work itself out, I promise.'

'Oh really?'

'Yep. In time you'll see I'm right. In the meantime, just focus on the good things. At least you're no longer cursing the place.'

Nicola knew from her friend's voice that she was smirking. 'Yeah, it's not so bad. It's actually nice to be back. There, I've admitted it; happy?'

'Very. Now on that note, I'll let you go. I'll speak to you soon. And Nicola?'

'Yes?'

'You will be okay. It will all work itself out.'

'Thanks Sandy.'

'You're welcome. Chin up.'

Again Nicola found herself staring at her silent phone with her head in a spin. Was Sandy right? Could all this really sort itself out?

Would she be okay if she lost her job? Jesus, she was orphaned, single, homeless, and nearly jobless.

At least nothing else can go wrong, she thought with a sigh.

★★★

Minutes later there was a gentle knock on the door. Nicola ignored it. The last thing she felt like was being friendly and chatty with Tiffany, or whoever else it might be – Richard, Alex.

There was another knock – louder this time. Again she tried to ignore it.

'Nicola, I know you're in there,' a voice called. 'It's Janet. Can you open the door please?' Nicola couldn't ignore that. She got up and opened the door.

Janet stood on the doorstep with her head hung, looking as distraught as Nicola felt.

'I hope you don't mind – I insisted Tiffany tell me which room you were in. Please don't be mad with her. I lied and told her it was about your drought story.' She held out the birth certificate and battered photo Nicola had left behind. Nicola accepted the items with a mumble of thanks, but continued to stand there with the open door between them.

'Could I come in?' Janet asked.

Nicola silently stood aside. She pulled the chair out from the desk for Janet, indicated for her to sit down, and sat down herself on the end of the bed.

'I'm sorry,' Janet said. 'I'm so sorry. It's just a lot to suddenly face up to after so long.'

'And I'm sorry for ambushing you like that. But I need to know.'

'I know,' Janet said with a deep sigh. She was silent for a few moments, as if trying to assemble her thoughts.

'I gave you up because I couldn't have you as a reminder…
or bear the gossip. You don't know what it's like, living in a small
country town where everyone watches, discusses.'

Nicola resisted interrupting her, but what she said didn't make
sense. If she was married, what did it matter, and why would people
talk?

'Graeme is your father, not Bert,' she said quietly.

It suddenly felt like all the oxygen had been sucked out of the
room. Nicola's eyes bugged, but still she stayed silent.

'I had an affair. Bert wasn't able to…so it wasn't fair to make him
pretend… And I wouldn't have dared; not with his temperament.
It was bloody Vietnam; that bloody war. If that hadn't happened
everything would have been different…'

Nicola sat dumbfounded, the words spinning around and around
in her head: 'Graeme is your father, not Bert'.

'But the birth certificate says…'

'I know. There was a mistake. I'm sorry.'

'But how?'

Janet stared down at the floor. 'It was a traumatic time. You were
quite a difficult birth. I was weak from blood loss, delirious for a
few days. I was worried about where I'd live when I left hospital…
I don't even remember giving the details,' she added, shaking her
head. 'It was all a blur, and a very long time ago…'

Janet continued to speak, her words becoming a torrent, but
Nicola was stuck on the thought that it wasn't fair. Graeme? The
man who had, by all accounts, made his brother's life a living hell?
Just when she'd been getting used to the idea of her father being
Bert, Nicola felt as if she'd lost her family all over again.

She wanted to say it didn't matter – that no words on a piece of
paper could change biology, but her throat was too dry, her head
too crowded. *How do I know Janet is telling the truth? But why would
she lie about something like this?*

★★★

At some point, Nicola looked up to find her mother had left and she was again alone.

Nicola tried to remove the facts from the rest of the sludge swimming around in her mind. What else had Janet said?

That she and Graeme's wife Dorothy had been best friends since kindergarten. That she and Graeme had fallen in love while Bert was fighting in Vietnam and Dorothy was at boarding school. Nicola couldn't cast stones at her for that, given her own recent behaviour. But six years!

The affair with Graeme had ceased when she'd left the town – left to have their baby. Graeme had eventually married Dorothy.

Nicola wondered if Dorothy knew she'd been his second choice; that Graeme and Janet had been an item. Nowhere Else was too small for such a secret. Imagine living with that all these years – it would make anyone bitter. And no wonder Janet rarely visited. Why was she back now? Had they started their affair again? Poor Alex; was he about to lose his family as well?

So, Graeme was her father. How could she ever like such a man, make herself love him like she should?

Nicola began experiencing her very own tsunami. First a slow rumble of impending doom, and then the devastating crash of comprehension. If Graeme was her father, that meant… Oh my God. Alex was her brother. She'd slept with her brother!

Now she was being dragged back out to sea, slowly and painfully through the reality – her period was over a week late. What if she was pregnant?

Nicola only had time to get to the rubbish bin under the desk before she threw up, and continued dry retching until her stomach was contracted and aching.

Nicola heaved again, harder than she thought possible, the spasm starting somewhere in her groin and rising up as far as her throat, making her gag over and over without relief.

Through her pain and tears Nicola thought of Richard, then Sandy, and then Bill, but decided she couldn't bear the shame of anyone knowing the horrible, disgusting truth.

What a mess. Her whole life was a fucking mess!

The thought of pills flashed through her mind – but she didn't have anything serious enough for the job. There weren't any late night chemists in town and probably no doctor.

Anyway, what was she thinking? Rival journalists would have a field day feeding off her pathetic demise. And the truth would come out: it always did in the end.

And that was what brought Nicola out of her foetal curl around the bin on the floor of her dingy motel room in Nowhere Else.

Hysteria gripped her, and she giggled. If it wasn't true – if it wasn't her – it would be hilarious.

Bill really had bitten off more than he could chew by sending her out here. He'd have a fit when he found out his Walkley-winning presenter was a candidate for *The Jerry Springer Show*.

This was little old Nowhere Else, total population nine hundred and ninety-three, whose only notoriety was the odd mention in the state Tidy Town awards.

Wasn't incest supposed to be an urban myth? Something you only saw in sensational headlines in trashy magazines? Something that happened to other people – *elsewhere*? Well, here she was, living proof. She hadn't done it on purpose, but she had done it.

Bloody hell, what if she *was* pregnant?

Chapter Thirty-eight

Nicola woke still fully dressed, but underneath the covers. She couldn't remember getting in. Two headache tablets with codeine did that. Her mouth tasted stale and sour; she'd forgotten to clean her teeth.

Slowly the revelations of the day before came back to her. She pulled the pillow over her head. If only she could have woken to find it had all been a horrible nightmare. But it hadn't. She had slept with her brother.

Nicola's stomach growled. God, she was starving. She tried to calculate when she'd last eaten – nothing since the two sweet biscuits they'd handed out on the plane. She looked around, trying to think of how to ease her hunger without setting foot outside her room. There was tea, instant coffee, and sugar. Coffee usually held stomach pains at bay for a few hours. But not this time; she was way past that level of hunger. No, she sighed, she would either have to go over to the hotel for breakfast or venture further to the bakery down the street.

What was she so worried about anyway? It wasn't like anyone except Janet knew the dreadful truth – and Janet only half of it. God, how long would it take to get around town?

Would Janet say anything to anyone? She didn't know Alex and Nicola had slept together. Oh God, she thought, rubbing her hands over her face. If only she'd told her and made her promise not to tell anyone. But it wasn't something you told a complete stranger, was it? And, really, they didn't know each other at all – they only shared DNA. There was nothing emotional between them yet.

How would Alex react? Should she be the one to tell him? Probably. Definitely. Especially if... But first she needed something to eat. Not that the idea of food was at all appealing. But she'd have to force herself; she'd need her strength. The last thing she needed was to catch a cold or something.

If only I'd never come here.

You wouldn't have found your family, she found herself answering. And no matter what happened, that was important. Wasn't it?

Nicola dragged herself out of bed, took a quick shower, put on clothes, and went across to the hotel for breakfast.

'God, you look terrible,' Tiffany said, turning from setting out the breakfast things and seeing Nicola walk through the door.

'Thanks.'

'Sorry, but you do. Did you just have a bad night or are you coming down with something? If so, stay away from me; I can't afford to get sick.'

If only it was, Nicola thought. 'Just not enough sleep.'

'What did you get up to last night? I didn't see you in here.'

'Just couldn't sleep; lots on my mind.'

'Oh,' Tiffany said. She seemed to want to say something else, but decided against it. 'I'll get you a coffee. Help yourself as usual; everything is here. Unless you'd rather a cooked breakfast?'

'No thanks.' Just the thought of bacon, which ordinarily Nicola loved, made her decidedly queasy. Even toast and vegemite, her when-all-else-fails breakfast, didn't appeal. But she had to eat; starving herself wouldn't help matters.

She went over to the breakfast things, put two slices of bread into the toaster and stood staring at the brightly glowing elements. Tearing herself away, she poured a glass of orange juice, regretting it when she felt the cold acid biting on its way down. She put the half full glass on the table with her phone and went back to wait for her toast.

At least I've found my family, she told herself. *And I've still got my job. Things could be worse. Focus on the positives.*

'There you go,' Tiffany said, beaming at her.

'Thanks,' Nicola said, smiling weakly back. Friendly faces; there was another positive. She wasn't alone; there were people who cared. And she had Sandy and Bob. And Bill – he'd come through for her.

By the time her toast popped up, Nicola had conjured enough of an appetite to spread it with butter and marmalade from the little packets, and was actually looking forward to eating it. Even the coffee was starting to taste better. Tiffany seemed to be putting more milk in it these days.

Nicola munched her way through four pieces of toast and drank two cups of coffee. She was starting to feel restored when her phone rang beside her. The display said it was Bill calling. Nicola felt her heart skip a beat and her nerves kick in. She checked her watch. Seven-thirty. This couldn't be good.

'Hi Bill, what's up?'

'Bad news I'm afraid. There's no easy way to say it. We're both officially jobless.'

'What?' Nicola felt the blood drain from her face.

'We've been fired. I tried my best, Nicola, but unfortunately it wasn't enough.'

'But we get a payout, right?'

'No. We've been fired, not made redundant.'

'Can they do that – like, legally?'

'Apparently so – I've run it past Tony. It's all above board. Your paperwork is in the mail; I just wanted you to know straight away.'

'Oh God, Bill, I'm sorry. What are you going to do?'

'No idea. Worry about it another day. I'm more worried about you – with all the other crap you're going through at the moment.'

'I'll be all right. I'm sure something will turn up,' Nicola said, not believing her own words for a second. But the last thing she needed was Bill worrying about her when he had his own problems.

'So, I'm afraid your room is cancelled. If you want to stay on after tonight you'll have to pay for it yourself. Same with the four-wheel-drive. Don't forget, it needs to end up back in Port Lincoln when you're done. Oh and you'll have to get the phone put in your name – you've got until the end of the month.'

Oh God, Nicola thought, her head starting to cloud again.

'Sorry about the short notice,' Bill added.

'That's okay; it's not your fault. I'll sort it out.'

'Well, I'd better go. I'm being escorted out by security in ten minutes. Still have to pack up my coffee machine.'

'Oh Bill, I'm sorry.'

'I know. But I'm a big boy. I'll be in touch. You take care of yourself.'

'You too. See ya.'

Nicola hung up just as Tiffany arrived to clear the table.

'Are you sure you're not sick? You're as pale as a ghost.'

Nicola nodded and stared up at her.

'Jesus, what's happened? Who died?'

'My career,' Nicola said, frowning. A couple of tears started making their way slowly down her cheeks.

'Sorry?'

'That was my boss. I've been fired.'

'Bastard! What did he do that for? Being here too long?'

'No, he's been fired too.'

'Oh.'

'Foreign invasion. The station's been taken over.'

'But you're hot property – you're a Gold Walkley winner.'

'Apparently not hot enough.'

Nicola's phone vibrated and started ringing again. Oh God, now what? She saw it was Richard calling. She thought about ignoring it, but found herself putting it to her ear.

'Hi Richard,' she said blandly. 'What's up?'

'Good morning,' he said jovially. 'Just wondering if you'd consider doing a stint as editor of a country newspaper?'

'Bill's put you up to this, hasn't he?'

'Sorry? Who's Bill?'

'You know damn well. Well I don't need your charity; I'll be just fine.'

'But I...'

'Stop playing dumb. Goodbye Richard,' she said, hung up, and slammed the phone down on the table.

'Oh God.' She picked up a folded napkin and blew her nose loudly, not caring who heard.

'Can I get you anything?' Tiffany asked tentatively.

'A new life,' Nicola ventured with a weak smile.

'You'll be okay.' Tiffany laid a hand on her arm. 'There'll be other jobs.'

If only that was the sum of my problems, Nicola thought, nodding at Tiffany. But she wasn't about to tell her the worst of it.

'I think I'll go back to my room,' she said with a sniff, got up, and left.

As she crossed the courtyard, she seemed to run out of tears and her racing heart slowed. Well, it certainly couldn't get any worse now. That was the good thing.

She paused with her key in the door and took a quick inventory. No, she concluded; things could only get better from here. The thought buoyed her ever so slightly. She went inside, washed her face, reapplied moisturiser, and turned on the TV. She was officially unemployed – morning and then daytime television was in order. She considered putting her pyjamas back on and climbing under the covers. Maybe later.

Her phone rang and she ignored it – let them leave a message. Probably well-wishers from work who'd heard the news. She wasn't ready to face that yet. But she couldn't resist checking the voicemail message as soon as she got the SMS notification. It was Richard.

'Hi Nicola, I obviously caught you at a bad time just before. I honestly don't know what you meant by charity. Or why you were angry with me. And I really don't know a Bill. I need to talk to you about filling in for me. Um, well, call me back – please. Thanks.'

Nicola had just put the phone down when there was a knock at the door. Oh God, now what! She practically ripped it off its hinges in her annoyance. There stood Graeme with Alex slightly behind him, both looking awkward, both staring at their feet.

'Oh. Hello,' she stammered.

'Er, Janet told me she spoke to you yesterday,' Graeme said. Nicola nodded.

'I understand you know my son, Alex,' he said, indicating Alex.

'Yes, hi Alex.' Alex was having as much trouble looking her in the eye as she was him. Did he know? He must do.

'Do you think we could come in for a minute?'

'Oh. Of course, sorry,' Nicola said, stepping aside. *Why not? There's nothing you can say to shock me now.* 'Sorry, but I only have the one chair,' she said, indicating it.

Graeme took his Akubra off, pulled out the chair and sat down. Nicola sat down on the end of the bed. Alex remained standing.

'I understand you're my daughter,' Graeme said.

'So I believe.' How awkward was this?

'It's true that Janet and I had an affair – for a number of years, many years ago. I had no knowledge of your existence. You have to understand that,' he said, bashing his knees with his hat.

Nicola looked across at Alex, who was staring at his father, his face suddenly devoid of colour. So he *hadn't* known. Suddenly he was sitting on the corner of the bed, rubbing his hands across his face. They were less than a metre apart, but didn't look at each other.

'Well, I look forward to getting to know you,' Graeme said. 'In the meantime… Oh hell, this is awkward. I'd really appreciate it if you didn't tell Dorothy, my wife, Alex's mother, for the time being. Although it was before we were married, it will still have to be handled delicately.

'Well…' He got up and stood fiddling with his hat. 'It's all come as a bit of a shock. We'll leave you to it. There's a lot to take in.' Nicola walked them to the door, Alex still struggling to look her in the eye.

'Oh,' Graeme said, turning back, 'and if there's anything we can do to help with your drought story, please don't hesitate to ask,' he said, clearly more comfortable with this topic.

'Thank you, but there isn't going to be a story on the drought after all,' Nicola said quietly.

'Oh,' Graeme said, clearly disappointed.

'Why?' Alex asked.

'It's a long story,' Nicola said with a sigh. 'Now if that was all…' she added, desperate to be alone.

'Of course. I look forward to catching up again soon when things, uh, settle down a bit. Unless you're heading straight back to the city – since…'

Nicola noticed Alex had looked up. 'No, I'll stay for a couple of days. It would be nice to get to know you all a little – depending on Dorothy that is. I don't want to cause any problems.'

'Thank you. I appreciate that,' Graeme said, with obvious relief. 'I'll be in touch. Bye for now,' he said, grasping her hand in both of his.

'See you,' Alex said, with a wave of his hand.

Nicola closed the door and sat back down on the bed. Well, that couldn't have been more awkward, she thought, allowing herself a wry smile. Poor Alex. The look on his beautiful face; the anguish… God, why was she still finding him attractive?

She pressed Richard's number and waited for him to answer.

'Hi Richard. I got your message. I'm so sorry about earlier. A bit of a misunderstanding. I'd just found out I'd been fired and…'

'Fired! Are you serious?'

'Yes.'

'Oh, and you thought I had heard and was offering you a job out of pity…'

'Exactly. Sorry for biting your head off. My life is falling apart all around me, so I'm a little snippy,' she said, forcing a tight laugh.

'Oh well, I was actually hoping you'd consider doing a stint for me in a month or so – I wanted to give you plenty of warning to get some leave approved if you were interested. But now you won't need to…'

'What's going on, Richard?'

'Nothing much. Karen wants us to go on a decent family holiday. It was her idea to ask you, actually. My excuse has always been there just isn't anyone suitably qualified. And there wasn't until you turned up.'

'Richard, what do I know about the newspaper game? Let alone single-handedly running a country paper.'

'There are a couple of good staff here who know the ropes, so it would be more a matter of supervising and doing a few articles. You can still write, can't you?'

'Of course I can write, Richard.'

'Well, you'll have plenty of time to get up to speed now you're unemployed.'

'Richard, that's not funny.'

'Hey, I'm not laughing. I can't say I'm not secretly thrilled at the prospect of having some time off, but I am certainly not laughing at your expense. Honestly.'

'You may as well. My life has become laughable in a really sad sense. You could say I've pretty much hit rock bottom.'

'Oh come on, it can't be that bad. Have you split up with Scott or something?'

'Yeah, but it's the "or something" that's bothering me.'

'What? What's going on?'

'I've spoken to Janet – my mother…'

'Wow, that's great.'

'…who told me that while Bert's name is on my birth certificate, my actual father is his brother Graeme.'

There was silence.

'So that means that…'

'Yup; that Alex McCardle is my brother. Cool huh?'

'Oh, God, Nicola.'

'Yeah, doesn't get much worse than that, does it?'

'Well, I hope you were careful. Is there anything I can do?'

'How about turn back time?'

'I would if I could. Oh God, you poor thing.'

Nicola was suddenly exhausted. 'Richard, I've got to go. I can feel a migraine coming on. I'll call you in a few days. I'll think about helping you out, but I've got to get my head around all this other stuff first.'

'I totally understand. No pressure. Call me if there's anything I can do.'

'Just please don't tell anyone.'

'As if, Nicola. You take care.'

'Thanks. Speak to you soon.' Nicola hung up, feeling that she was indeed getting a migraine.

Chapter Thirty-nine

Nicola spent the day snoozing in front of the television and trying not to think about her life. Late in the afternoon she was jolted awake by another knock at the door.

'Who now?' she wondered as she untangled her crossed legs and launched herself off the bed. Surely there wasn't anyone left; she'd spoken to Janet yesterday, Graeme and Alex had visited that morning, she'd told Richard she'd get back to him... Perhaps Tiffany was checking on her. She opened the door.

'Janet. Uh, hi.'

Janet rushed into the open doorway and embraced Nicola tightly, sending her stumbling backwards.

'Sorry, but I've wanted to do that for years,' Janet said in response to Nicola eyeing her warily. 'Hope you don't mind.

Nicola dropped her guard. 'Not at all.' She paused, and dipped her head shyly. 'May I?' she asked, holding out her arms.

It felt like a *Brady Bunch* moment, but she didn't care; there was no one around to watch and, anyway, this was her *mum* she was hugging – after thirty-four years.

Both women's shoulders were stained with tears when they finally eased apart. They wiped their eyes with the backs of their hands. Both noticed the similarity of the movement but neither commented.

'I was going through Bert's things, making some space, and I found this.' Janet thrust an envelope at Nicola.

Nicola accepted it, and stared at the typed Last Will and Testament of Bertrand Arthur McCardle, lost in the formality of his full name. Then she was confused.

'He wasn't my father. Why are you giving me his will?' *You haven't been his wife for over thirty years. And when you were, you were unfaithful.*

Nicola didn't like thinking ill of Janet, but that was the truth. What right did she have to be going through his things?

'Go on, open it.'

'But I'm not...'

'I know, but you'll see.' Janet looked ready to rip the contents from the already opened envelope herself.

Nicola's hands were shaking and fingers unusually dry as she struggled to extract the flat pages. It felt wrong to be doing this. It was private; none of her business. None of Janet's business. But what could she do?

After reading every word twice she looked back to Janet, blinking with bewilderment.

Janet smiled back.

'I couldn't believe it either.'

Nicola sat down on the bed, took a deep breath and reread, convinced they both must have got it wrong. But it clearly stated '...hereby leave the contents of my estate to be equally divided between any nieces and nephews that exist at the time of my passing...'

'Alex and I,' Nicola said, thinking aloud. She still felt very uneasy; even having read the document.

Janet nodded and sat down next to her.

'What about Graeme?' Nicola asked quietly. Suspicion crept into her mind. Why was he letting Janet go through his brother's things? Were they having an affair again?

'He doesn't know. I've only just found it – I came straight here.'

Nicola wished she hadn't; this would make her life a whole lot more complicated. She didn't want to know. But perhaps there was another, later, will naming Graeme. That would be better; right?

'He'll be furious.'

'He'll be okay. Your father, Graeme, he's a fair man. Anyway, law's law.'

Oh God. I don't like the feel of this.

Nicola's shoulders slumped. On the one hand it was amazing, but on the other she was already sensing the potential burden of the document. Then she brightened slightly; she wasn't alone in this, had Alex to share the load. He had known Bert better than she did.

But she still couldn't shake the feeling that Janet really shouldn't even be in Bert's house. And then something dawned on her. Could Janet have spoken to Bert at the hospital – before he died? Perhaps he'd told her to sort things out if he didn't make it; to make sure Graeme didn't get his hands on his property.

She glanced back at the paper and noticed the date – five years before. Why *then*, if the feud had started more than a quarter of a century earlier? Did Alex know; had they discussed it?

'So, when are you moving in?' Janet asked.

'Sorry?'

'Bert's place. When are you moving in?'

'I'm only here temporarily.'

'Anything's better than this.'

'Well, if this is right – and I'll need to get a lawyer to check – then it's half Alex's.'

'He's already got a home.'

'So do I – in Adelaide…'

But it suddenly struck Nicola that she didn't actually have a home in Adelaide – or anywhere else for that matter.

Janet noticed her indecision. 'I can be out by tomorrow if that's the problem. I'm due back at work next week anyway.'

'It's not that. It's…' Nicola stopped and sighed deeply. The true realisation of her situation came crashing down around her and she burst into tears.

★★★

Nicola's heart thudded steadily against her ribs while she waited for the phone line to connect, and then leapt into her mouth at Alex's deep throaty greeting.

'Alex, hi. It's Nicola.'

'Hi there.' He definitely didn't sound over the moon to be hearing from her.

'Um, Alex, there's something I need to talk to you about.'

'Yes?'

Nicola took a deep breath. He wasn't making it easy.

Alex sighed. 'Sorry, I don't mean to be cold, I'm still getting used to the idea of…'

'Yeah, me too.'

'You know, after…everything.'

Nicola still couldn't shake the impure thoughts and emotions. Despite trying to retrain her brain, her heart was racing at the mere sound of his voice. It would be easier if she could avoid him altogether – go cold turkey. But that was impossible.

She swallowed deeply. 'Look, Alex, there's something I need to discuss with you.'

'There's more?'

'Yes. But don't worry, this is good news.'

'Give me a hint.'

'No, meet me for dinner – seven o'clock.'

'I'm sufficiently intrigued. It's a date.'

Nicola groaned inwardly. She was really going to have to get over this.

★★★

'You're kidding!' Alex was wide-eyed.

Nicola grinned back.

'Nope – see for yourself.' She pushed the paper across the table.

Alex stayed silent while he read. He then looked up at her open-mouthed, and then back down to the table.

'Dad's going to freak,' he groaned.

'Uh huh,' Nicola agreed.

'But you know, we can be partners – run the place together. What do you say, sis?'

Nicola was chuffed by his instant acceptance of her, but it wasn't that simple.

'You already have a full-time job with your own property…'

'Well, you'll just have to pull your weight then, won't you?' he said, winking.

Nicola was relieved the awkwardness had finally subsided between them. Maybe there was hope for platonic friendship after all. Not that there was any other option.

'…and I don't know the first thing about farming. I'm city through and through.'

'You'll learn. I bet you're a natural – you've got blood on your side, remember? The McCardle family motto means "high valour," you know.'

'Really?'

'Yup. So, when do you move in?'

She shrugged. Why did everyone assume she was going to move in to Bert's? Didn't they realise she lived in Adelaide; that she wasn't actually from around here?

'Come on, you've been here at the motel long enough. And what's the deal about you no longer doing a story on the drought – and don't give me that line about it being a long story; I've got all night.'

'God, where do I start,' Nicola said, more to herself. She rubbed her hand across her forehead.

'From the beginning,' Alex offered. 'What's been going on?'

'Well…' Nicola began, and proceeded to tell him about her past few days.

'Why didn't you tell me, especially about Scott – it must have been terrible for you.'

'Sorry, but I didn't think…'

'I know, it's been weird for me too. But I'm your half-brother. And your friend.'

'I'm really sorry. I guess I'm not really used to having one – a brother that is.'

'Well, you do now, so make the most of it.'

Nicola grinned back, warmth surging through her.

'Hope there aren't any more we don't know about.'

'Sorry?' Nicola frowned.

'Other kids or nieces or nephews out there.'

'Alex!'

'Well, they say it's the quiet ones you have to watch. Anyway, I think we'll make a great team – just you and me.'

Chapter Forty

Nicola slowed the four-wheel-drive to an idle at Bert's mailbox and took a couple of deep breaths while she surveyed the property she now co-owned. There was a tinge of green on all the paddocks, along the roadsides, and around the house. Fresh and fertile, Nicola thought.

How much brighter and cheerier everything seemed. She took special note of the view of the front of the house, which she'd never done before; the main drive ended behind it. It was a stone cottage, not nearly as grand in its proportions or general appearance as Graeme's, but its stonework and bullnosed verandah showed definite character. It might be quite lovely with some TLC.

They were right – why not move in? At least until she sorted out the split with Scott. It was as good a place as any.

'Who would have thought?' she said with a sigh. She was jobless, homeless, separated from her partner, and about to move into a run-down farmhouse in a remote rural area. She shook her head.

How had it come to this? She'd found her family, and she was really starting to feel a sense of connection. Perhaps farming did run in the blood after all.

She frowned. Could she ever live out here permanently, or would she miss the pace of the city; the shops, the cafes, the hustle and bustle?

All these questions would have to wait – she had to catch Janet before she left. She put the vehicle in gear and made her way up the driveway to the back of the house.

It was weird to now be knocking on her own door. Living here sure would take some getting used to. But she needed somewhere to stay and here was somewhere.

As she waited, Nicola found herself making mental notes to replace the rusting hinges, repaint the woodwork and add a shiny welcoming brass knocker. The house was crying out for a woman's touch.

Janet, flustered and red-faced, threw the door open and stood back for Nicola to enter.

'Hello.'

'Hi,' Nicola said, giving her a hug. 'Oh, you really didn't have to do all this,' she said, looking around. Her mouth gaped at the changed kitchen.

The windows had been cleaned and curtains taken down. Sunlight streamed in over the sink, across the floor, up and onto the table. She could smell the fresh scents of orange and lavender. On the sink was a spray bottle of orange cleaner. In the window, hanging from a piece of green baling twine, was a bunch of fresh lavender.

Janet saw her looking at the lavender. 'Sorry about the twine – it's the only string I could find. Farmers – if it can't be fixed with baling twine or wire, it can't be fixed. I'd forgotten how much I liked country life,' she said wistfully.

'It's so lovely and fresh in here. Thank you,' Nicola said, and hugged her mother again.

As she turned around, Nicola noticed the dog's bedding was still in the hearth. Even more surprising was the blue heeler snoozing on it. She smiled. So Janet was a softy after all. Jerry didn't look up, but flapped his tail gently as if to acknowledge her presence.

'Gave it a bit of a spruce. Don't want to speak ill of the dead or anything, but the place was putrid. And the damn dog will howl all night if you leave it outside,' she said, rolling her eyes. 'Actually he's not bad company, but don't tell him that.' She grinned.

'And you'll need new curtains. I've washed them but they're barely hanging together.'

'How did you know I was staying, anyway? Ah, Alex. I still can't get used to how fast word gets around,' Nicola laughed.

'Yes, well, I'm not sure that's something you ever get used to,' Janet replied.

'Actually, I have a favour to ask. Feel free to say no if it's a pain or...'

'Ask away.'

'I just thought about it this morning, but would you mind taking my hire four-wheel-drive back to Port Lincoln? I don't need it now and it's costing a fortune. Alex said he'd come down and pick me up, but he's busy spraying or something for the next week or so.'

'Not at all. That's no problem.'

'We'll run your Corolla down when he gets some time. Maybe we could visit you.'

'Absolutely. And I can catch the bus back if it all gets too hard.'

'Oh. Well, hopefully it won't come to that, but thanks. I'll give you some money for taxis for work and getting around,' Nicola said, fishing in her handbag.

'You certainly will not. I'm happy to be able to do something for you after all these years. And anyway, I hardly use my car – I'm only a five minute walk away from the hospital and all the shops I need.'

They moved back outside, where Nicola unloaded her bags from the four-wheel-drive and Janet put hers in.

'Thanks so much for doing this for me,' Nicola said.

'Much better than paying unnecessarily. And it'll give us an excuse to see each other again.'

'Great,' Nicola said, beaming.

'If you want to use the Corolla, two pumps on the accelerator before you turn the key and you'll be right – starts every time.'

'Right,' Nicola said tentatively, not sure she would be.

'Okay, I'd better get cracking. I'll speak to you soon.'

'Thanks again.'

Nicola hugged her mother and watched her depart, feeling a slight sense of loss. She waited until she was out of sight before going into the house.

★★★

Nicola unpacked her carry-on and matching suitcase into the old wooden cupboard in the spare room.

Janet had taken the trouble to put a patchwork quilt and vase of dried purple statice from the garden into Bert's room. But Nicola had decided on the small room across the hall.

Nicola wished she had more to unpack, to keep her mind off where she was and how she'd arrived there. She sat down on the end of the nearest twin beds and stared at all the brown timber furniture and dark polished floorboards.

The room was barely more than a broom cupboard – would only be described as a study in the city. Two single beds separated by the one bedside cupboard were draped in pale blue candlewick. A small gentleman's wardrobe in oak veneer crouched behind the door.

Nicola wondered if Alex used to sleep where she sat; if Bert had been a favourite uncle who'd welcomed sleepovers. There had to be a pretty good relationship for him to leave the farm to him. She couldn't believe Bert would be the type to so consciously think of giving the final blow of the feud – he just hadn't seemed that calculating, that bitter.

A shuffling sound disturbed her reverie and she looked up. A forlorn-looking Jerry was standing in the doorway. His glossy head was cocked like an old man's whose only concern was when his next meal would be.

Nicola had completely forgotten about him. She hoped Janet had left some dog food; otherwise he'd be sharing the casserole in the fridge.

Jerry lifted his kinked ears slightly and ran a tongue around his lips as if reading her mind. She laughed and got up to investigate the dinner situation.

'Hang on a tick,' Nicola said to the dog. She paused at the threshold to Bert's room, and then entered. The click of claws followed and Jerry positioned himself under her hand.

Nicola ran her fingers through his fur while taking in the room. Her throat thickened, just as it had when she'd entered her parents' room the first time after their passing.

It had been so unnerving to find everything the same when everything had changed. The clothes they would never use again were still hung and folded in the same meticulous order with the scents of man, woman, and proud domesticity clinging to them.

But Nicola felt a strange sense of calm; a good energy in Bert's space. Her heart eased.

Chapter Forty-one

Nicola had just finished moving her belongings into Bert's old room, and was sitting on the end of the bed when she heard the crunch of tyres on gravel. She padded down the hall behind Jerry, excited at welcoming her first visitors.

'Thought we should celebrate your new lodgings,' Alex beamed, waving a bottle of champagne and two flutes.

Nicola's heart skipped.

'Wonderful, come in.'

'Couldn't remember if there were champagne glasses here,' he said, brushing her cheek with a kiss on his way past. 'Let me just put these down – more goodies in the car.'

'Can I give you a hand?' she called as he disappeared into the kitchen.

'How about you get plates and cutlery ready. I'll be two secs,' he said, reappearing. She watched him bound back down the steps and reach into the back of the ute.

'This looks impressive,' Nicola said, nodding at the large wicker basket he held.

'Couldn't have you starving on your first night – or being all alone.'

Nicola blushed slightly despite her best efforts.

'So,' Alex said, settling into his chair. 'Interested in becoming a farmer?'

'I wouldn't know where to start.'

'Ah, it's a piece of cake.'

'Yeah, right.'

'Seriously. Uncle Bert's always run a pretty tight ship – small but tight.'

'Um, this might be a really dumb question, but exactly what sort of *ship* is this that I've inherited?'

'We, big sister – *we've* inherited.'

'Right.' Nicola giggled, her head full of bubbles and anticipation. As long as she thought about the farm, she wouldn't have to worry about Scott, the life she'd left behind, or the job she'd lost.

Can I completely change careers and become a farmer? She doubted it. It was way too unpredictable and insecure for her liking.

But only a few weeks ago she'd thought she had her life and career all sorted. And look how things had changed. She'd have to deal with all that later, but right now, the farm was as good a distraction as any.

'Don't leave me in suspense. What are we growing here?'

'Wool – and hay for feed.'

Nicola rubbed a hand through her hair.

'Right.'

'Don't worry, there's only sheep to be fed and checked, which I've got under control. And thanks to donations, there's still a month or so worth of hay in the shed. I'm doing the spraying next week, and lambing doesn't start till September – you have that long to

swot up. Anyway, don't forget we're in this together. But meanwhile, we have champagne to drink and dessert to enjoy.'

Nicola looked at him with raised eyebrows.

'Hope you like mud cake.'

'Mmm, chocolate,' Nicola murmured.

'Jaffa actually – orange *and* chocolate.' He grinned, reached
into the basket and brought out two large wedges of glistening
darkness.

'Did you make it?' Nicola asked, thinking he couldn't possibly
have. Lasagne and salad, yes, salmon pinwheels maybe, but jaffa mud
cake? Beryl must be involved.

'Of course.'

Nicola stared him down.

'What's so hard to believe?'

'Well, aren't you full of surprises?'

'So it seems.' He dropped his gaze, and Nicola blushed slightly at
recognising the slightly seductive tone. 'Life's just one big surprise
– thought you'd have figured that out by now,' he added, a little
harshly.

'Yeah,' Nicola said, letting it go. She pushed her fork into the
dense cake.

So he was experiencing strange feelings too. She rolled the thick
earthy mound around in her mouth and watched Alex do the same,
relieved she wasn't going mad after all.

It certainly wasn't going to be easy working side by side – she'd
have to find a way to think differently about him. But the man
could produce delicacies like this with his own hands – he was
impossible not to totally adore.

'This is amazing,' she groaned, trying to scrape every smear of
chocolate from the plate with her fork.

'I'll give you the recipe if you like.'

'No use,' she said, still scraping, 'I'm a pathetic cook.'

'Ah, hail the modern woman,' he said, capturing another forkful.

'But there is no need when we have the modern man,' she teased, waving her fork. 'Seriously, though. Where did you learn to be such a good cook?'

'Finishing school.' He simultaneously met her gaze and stabbed at the cake.

'As in Switzerland? I thought they were for girls.' Her eyes were out on stalks.

'Italy actually, for *gentlemen*, thank you very much.' His accent was suddenly clipped, which Nicola found very sexy. She looked at the floor and realised his R.M.s had been replaced with loafers. Looking back she noticed his heavy gold dress watch for the first time.

'You're seriously telling me you went to Italy to learn to be suave and sophisticated?'

Alex set his fork down, picked up the linen napkin and delicately dabbed at his lips.

'I was sent, actually.'

Nicola, suddenly feeling like *she* was the unrefined country hick, reached for her napkin and copied his movement.

Alex offered the sigh of one about to embark on a story he'd rather leave unsaid. But the journalist in Nicola remained silent, insisting he continue.

'When I finished high school, Mum thought I should experience the world – not just come back on the farm. Only after she'd tried her best to get me to lose interest completely, bless her. But if you're born a farmer, you can only hide from it for so long.

'Anyway, somehow she knew these people in Tuscany. I spent about eight months with them – went to day classes, helped with their olive grove and vineyard in my spare time in return for board.'

'Alex, that's so cool. When I was ten I wanted to go to finishing school to catch myself a handsome prince.'

'It was mainly cooking and service – butler school really,' Alex said, blushing slightly.

Nicola gave in to the champagne and giggled before regaining her composure.

'Did you enjoy it?'

'By the end. But it was a lot harder than I thought it would be. Farming's a breeze after spending six hours a day walking around with a book on your head, carrying a load of drinks on a slippery silver tray.'

Nicola pictured him and giggled again.

'I didn't know mud cake was Italian.'

'It's not – I learnt that here. We were only really taught emergency dishes – pasta, risotto, pizza, that sort of thing. I realised cooking was something I liked. Considered doing a chef's apprenticeship, but I hate being yelled at.' He laughed.

'Me too.'

'I do the odd dinner party, and occasionally I'll enter something in the show to help out numbers.'

'I've always wanted to go to Italy – I know how clichéd that sounds, since apparently *everyone* wants to go to Italy,' Nicola added with a shrug. 'I actually went into journalism thinking I'd travel the world.

'But of course I end up on an Australia-only show and haven't even been sent to Tasmania. I did Bali and a cruise, but they're so full of Aussies they don't really count.'

'Well, I got really homesick – came home four months early. I'm glad I went, but I didn't exactly get bitten by the travel bug. The passport's been in the filing cabinet ever since.'

'So then you came back to the farm?'

'Yep – and started an arts degree, by correspondence.'

'Why?'

'Why not?'

'Sorry, I didn't mean why study, why arts?'

'Psychology and philosophy actually – to keep me sane. You've been here long enough to see,' he laughed.

'Yes,' she said knowingly. 'Did you finish it?'

'No, I realised I wanted to do more than analyse and summarise what had already been recorded. Decided it was more important to study myself and my place in society – the curriculum just seemed a bit outdated to me.'

Nicola stared at her chocolate-streaked plate.

'And there you were, thinking I was just a country hick.'

Nicola blushed at being caught out.

'I never said…'

'I'm kidding, big sister – lighten up.' He gave her shoulder a gentle shove.

Nicola smarted at being patronised.

'I'd better get going. Dad wanted me to call in and I have to shut up the chooks before dark. He and Mum went to Port Lincoln for the day.'

It's a pity she hadn't known about Graeme and Dorothy's trip – she could have asked them to take her hire vehicle back, rather than muck Janet around. Oh well, it was done now. She returned her attention to Alex.

'Why don't I pick you up for a tour of the place first thing – give you a bit of context?'

'Good idea. At the moment I don't have a clue what's what.'

'How's seven?'

'Seven?'

'Come on, I'm being generous. I could have said six.'

Nicola watched his muscles rippling under his linen shirt as he strategically packed everything back into the basket. She couldn't believe he was still single – he wouldn't last three minutes in the city.

'All right, seven it is.'

★★★

Nicola looked up from her laptop and was surprised to find it was almost eleven o'clock. She rubbed her burning eyes, shut everything down, and closed the lid. As usual she'd spent hours going around in circles.

She'd learned that merino sheep were the most popular breed for wool production; that they were white all over; and that any black wool was considered contamination – even the smallest spot. Made sense, Nicola decided, considering the 'black sheep of the family' saying.

'Night Jerry,' she said, leaning down to ruffle his ears before leaving the kitchen.

Climbing into bed, she noticed the dog at attention in the doorway, as if waiting for a command.

'If you think you're sleeping up here with me you've got another think coming.'

But the dog had only registered 'up' and with a wag of his tail was on the bed and grinning broadly.

'Oi, I said…' But Nicola couldn't finish. The beast's soppy eyes gazed at her lovingly over his paws, daring her to tell off such a perfectly behaved pooch. *Well, he is grieving.*

'All right – just don't snore. And you'd better not have fleas,' she said, clicking off the bedside lamp.

Jerry gave a deep victorious sigh.

Chapter Forty-two

A bluish tinge was just peeking through the gap in the curtains when Nicola was eased from sleep. She spent a few moments trying to remember the dream she'd been having. It had been so real and so detailed that she felt a little changed. Just how she wasn't sure.

It had been about Bert; understandable given that she was in his house, on his farm. But he hadn't actually been in the dream, had he? Nicola frowned. What had it been about?

His spring? She frowned harder, trying to grasp the strand of memory that was hanging just out of reach.

Ah, that's right. A couple of snippets came back to her. She'd been looking over the farm, investigating the spring that Bert had kept Graeme from gaining access to. In a paddock right next to it, she had found a small mob of black sheep.

Some kind of metaphor? Bert being the black sheep of the family? Maybe, but there was something else there – she couldn't shake it.

There's no way Bert would have bred black sheep. He would have been ridiculed, and neighbouring farmers would have been worried about his rams getting in with their white ewes and potentially contaminating their flocks. Perhaps that's what had prompted her dream; she'd been reading about it right before going to sleep.

Okay, so white wool was popular, but wasn't there a thriving spinning and weaving culture that used naturally black, grey, brown, and charcoal coloured wool? She'd seen it at the markets a few years ago. Nicola had thought the lambs even cuter than their white relatives; probably because of their outcast status.

Perhaps it was just the seed of an idea for a story, but the more she tried to tell herself that, the less she believed it.

So, Bert wouldn't have done it, but what's stopping me? And not just wool for spinners, what about superfine; like for high fashion or something? If it can be done with white sheep, why not black? Why not dream big?

Was this something she should investigate? As a newcomer it was unthinkable – she'd be run out of town for sure. But Nicola couldn't shake the feeling there was something to her dream; something worth holding onto, pursuing. Was this some kind of channelling from Bert; his spirit here in this room while she'd been sleeping?

Excitement surged through her. It did indeed feel like an epiphany; like some monumental piece of the jigsaw of her life had just fallen into place. God, and she couldn't wait to tell someone.

Alex. But he was a farmer; would he make fun of her? He'd shown her last night that there was more to Alex than met the eye. Well, if he did, she'd just have to make him understand. Nicola had the strongest feeling this was a sign of what she was meant to do.

Jerry occupied half her pillow, his nose inches away from hers, breathing warm sour puffs on her face. Nicola hoped he hadn't licked her while she slept – she knew where that tongue had been.

She made a lemon face at the thought. Then, deciding that nothing could ruin her day, leapt out of bed.

In the kitchen Nicola glanced at the clock, surprised to find she was actually up at six and not the slightest bit cranky about it.

She stared out the window while filling the kettle at the sink, marvelling at the peace and beauty.

The sheep were white balls of cotton wool on the bare earth. As far as she could see, the canvas of the sky was tie-dyed satin; shimmering gold at the horizon, shades of peach and salmon. She stood, mesmerised.

Snapped back to reality by the kettle's whistle, Nicola realised she'd actually seen the sun rise.

'This is the start of the first day of the rest of my life,' she announced to the bewildered dog, who was waiting patiently to be fed.

She shuddered slightly at remembering the forecast of fourteen with a brisk south-easterly for the area — at least the motel had had reverse-cycle air-conditioning. She turned on the little blower heater under the table.

★★★

'And here I was expecting to have to drag you out of bed,' Alex said when Nicola bounded into the ute beside him.

'Nope, today is a great day — worthy of an early start.'

'Are you okay?'

'Fabulous — why?'

'Sound like you're on drugs or something — far too cheery.'

'Just the drug of life,' she cried theatrically.

'Stop it, you're scaring me.'

Nicola lapsed into silence while she thought about when and how to bring up her idea; she couldn't bear it if he just dismissed her like Scott would.

Lost in her thoughts, it took her a moment to realise he'd spoken.

'Sorry?'

'You haven't heard a word I've said, have you?' Alex demanded.

'Just thinking about something.'

'Care to share?'

'Um. Well…'

'Come on; there's clearly something on your mind.'

'You'll probably think I'm mad.'

'Try me.' He brought the vehicle to a halt and turned to face her.

Nicola was breathless as she relayed the dream and her interpretation of its meaning – her grand plan.

Alex remained silent, staring at her.

'Well?'

'I can't believe it,' he muttered, shaking his head.

'I knew you'd think it ridiculous.' Nicola folded her arms defensively.

'I don't.'

'Well you just said you can't believe it,' she snapped.

'Did Bert ever show you his sheep?'

'I can see plenty of sheep from the kitchen window.'

'Not those. Did Bert show you any others?'

'No, why?'

Alex had a white-knuckled grip on the steering wheel, and was staring out the windscreen.

'You're sure?'

'Alex, as if I'd forget. Stop patronising me.' Nicola turned to the window, anger and disappointment stinging.

'Nicola calm down, it's not that…'

'I thought you were different – a free thinker.'

'I am.'

'Not from where I'm sitting.'

'Just let me explain.'

'I can hardly wait,' she sneered.

Alex opened his mouth then shut it again without speaking.

'Well?'

He responded by slowly driving the vehicle to the top of the rise, then turning to her with raised eyebrows.

Nicola's mouth dropped open and her eyes bugged. She stared at the scene spread out before her. It was the scene from her dream, *exactly*. It came flooding back: in a small gully was a paddock, totally surrounded by medium sized gum and mallee trees. In the far left corner was a lush area abundant with thick grasses and reeds – the spring. Behind it, only just visible through the trees, was a small creek. There was a trough in the fence, fed by a windmill next to the spring.

In the paddock to the right was an open corrugated iron lean-to. A flock of sheep with filthy once-white rugs on were standing at the closest fence looking at them. From their heads, necks and legs poking out, they were obviously not white. Wow! A flock of black sheep! She looked across at Alex, her eyes wide with disbelief.

'Sorry you didn't have the idea first,' Alex said.

'But black wool's supposed to be a curse to farmers.'

'Not to Uncle Bert.'

'What about his neighbours?'

'They don't know. He's always kept this flock out of sight. I believe I'm the only one who knew.'

'What's he doing with them?'

'Not just black wool – *superfine* black wool.' Alex grinned.

'Superfine black wool. Are you serious?'

'Uncle Bert was. He'd been selling it to spinners and weavers interstate for a few years now.'

'Oh,' Nicola said, suddenly aware her plan had already been accomplished.

'Don't worry, there's still a way to go – these are only at eighteen micron.'

'And we want less than thirteen,' Nicola said, thinking aloud.

'Exactly. There's only one known flock of black sheep in the world – owned by a woman in New Zealand. She decided to save the outcast sheep from other farmers, and now makes an absolute fortune selling black wool. A Milan fashion design house discovered her on a buying trip, and now they use her wool for expensive black-tie suits and overcoats.'

'Wow.'

'Bert heard her interviewed once and decided he wanted to create the second flock of fine black wool – the first in Australia. And here we have it.'

'Are you finding this really spooky?'

'Little bit – but you can't mess with fate.'

Chapter Forty-three

Nicola whistled, hummed and danced around the kitchen. From his bed in the hearth, a bemused Jerry watched her throw together a dish of pasta with pesto and blue cheese for dinner.

She'd done the sums. With what she had tucked away, she could get the rams and ewes needed to complete Bert's project. When Scott bought her out of the apartment she'd be able to up the scale of production. Hopefully then it wouldn't take long before they were talking in terms of bales rather than kilos.

Was this really what she wanted; to become a farmer? By all accounts it was one of the riskier occupations out there. She should be saving up to buy her own apartment. But would she be going back to the city? Could she really stay out here indefinitely?

Nicola knew she didn't have any other choice. It was there burning in her soul. Yes, she had to give this a damn good go, not just for Bert and Alex, but for herself.

Shit, she had to let Richard know she wouldn't be helping him out at the paper. That wasn't going to be a pleasant call; he'd been counting on her.

Perhaps the bush telegraph had done its usual magic and he already knew, she thought wryly.

It was time she stopped worrying so much about everyone else. Richard's job was his problem, her life was hers. She wouldn't burn a bridge – you never knew when you might need it again – but she had to begin putting herself first. If she'd done that earlier, perhaps she wouldn't have wasted eight years with Scott. And it was a waste; they'd been wrong for each other from the start, she'd just refused to see it. She'd been too busy needing *somebody*.

Nicola's diamond engagement ring gleamed at the edge of her vision. She brought her hand up for closer inspection. It had become such a part of her she hadn't even thought to take it off.

Had she been hoping, somewhere deep within, that Scott would beg her to come back, acknowledge his faults and the desire to remedy them, propose properly? Maybe. She sighed. If it hadn't happened by now, it never would.

They'd finally had one curt phone call the day before. She'd wanted to talk, discuss things calmly and rationally. He'd taken the 'I've spoken to my lawyer' path instead.

With a heavy heart, Nicola prised Scott's two months salary (minus tax, superannuation, and car payments) from her finger, and laid it on the table. Even if its meaning had been lost, there was no denying it was beautiful. She sighed. She'd post it to him tomorrow via registered, insured mail.

Looking back at the notes of scribbled figures she'd pushed aside, Nicola marvelled at simple old Bert being the keeper of the best kept secret in town. Probably the only secret, she mused.

Had he ever stopped to consider the irony in what he was doing? She laughed aloud at her next thought: the town has really had the wool pulled over its eyes.

'Clever man was your boss, Jerry.' She ruffled the dog's ears.

Nicola glowed with wonder at Bert's ingenuity. Of course he couldn't have had Graeme wandering in to get water from the spring. As much as she only wanted to think good of her father, she knew Graeme would have been the first to ridicule Bert.

Enlightenment buzzed; she had to ring Alex. She picked up the heavy old beige handset in the hall, but replaced it again. At least let him feed his chooks and have some dinner.

Returning to the kitchen, Nicola heard the muffled tone of her mobile coming from inside her handbag on the bench. Sandy? She hoped so; she hadn't spoken to her friend since she'd moved in. What would she say about the sudden turn of events? Nicola smiled. Sandy would say that everything had happened for the best, and that it was high time Nicola stopped fighting the world and her place in it. This was where she was meant to be.

But God, becoming a farmer – of fine black wool of all things – Sandy would have a field day with that. Shit, she hadn't even had a chance to tell her about being fired. Boy, was she in for a surprise.

Nicola dragged the phone out and brought it to her ear without checking caller ID.

'Hello, Nicola speaking.'

'Nicola. We need to discuss this settlement.'

'Scott!' A hand reached into her chest and began squeezing and twisting her heart.

In the back of her mind she could hear her lawyer cautioning against saying anything 'that could be used in evidence against her in court'. She became light-headed and imagined being charged with idiocy; the fool who'd thought love could conquer all.

Nicola was vaguely aware of Scott ranting about it not being fair, that he'd earned more, something about the ring. Blood rose into her ears, drowning out his voice and her confusing thought.

Clenching her fist, she took a deep breath and then swallowed.

'Scott, I have nothing to say to you.'

Still the ranting continued.

'Have your lawyer call my lawyer.'

'Bitch.'

'Goodbye Scott,' she sighed and disconnected the call.

Gradually the pressure eased and her heart slowed, but instead of feeling better, Nicola was gripped with a concoction of sadness, fear, and foreboding. It was as if she'd stepped into quicksand.

Her decision and future seemed difficult enough without him getting nasty. What about the good times, the love they'd once shared? She wiped away a few tears burning their way down her cheeks but they were instantly replaced. Putting her head in her hands she let herself weep openly. Jerry's paw scratched earnestly at her knee, and her sobbing became a wail.

Nicola was startled from her self-pity by the ringing of the landline in the hall.

Fingers crossed it's Alex, she said to herself, as she left the cosy kitchen and went out in to the icy hall. She picked up the handset.

'Hello.'

'Nicola.'

'Alex?' She sighed and offered thanks to the ceiling.

'Um, Nicola?'

'Yes.' Something wasn't right. 'Alex, what's wrong?'

'Um...'

She brought a worried hand to her forehead. Something was definitely wrong.

'Is it Graeme? What's happened?'

'I...' The word was a croak.

'Don't move – I'll be there soon.'

'We're at...'

'Where are you?'

'The hospital – Nowhere Else.'

'Right. I'm leaving now.'

'Thanks.' Nicola noted the defeat in his voice.

Her head swam with the possibilities of what could have happened, as she drove into the town exceeding every speed limit.

'Hold on, Dad. I'm coming.'

★★★

Nicola found Alex sitting, head bowed, in the waiting room. *Australia's Funniest Home Videos* was playing on the television screen mounted high in the far corner. She sat and put an arm around him.

'What's happened?'

'Mum; she's had some kind of turn.'

Nicola sighed with relief at learning it wasn't her father in trouble, then chided herself for her insensitivity.

Alex leant into her as much as the moulded plastic arm of the chair would allow, his sobbing easing. Nicola's heart lurched and her throat tightened. She squeezed the top of his arm firmly and laid her head on his shoulder and waited.

Moments later the quiet was shattered by Beryl bustling into the room, accompanied by the aroma of homemade soup. Nicola sat up and instinctively smoothed her clothes like a teenager caught snogging.

'I've just heard the terrible news – came as quickly as I could.'

In different circumstances it would have made a funny scene; Beryl in slippers and pink hair rollers, clutching a large saucepan of soup with faded red potholders.

Stanley was three paces behind, a wicker basket overflowing with aluminium-wrapped parcels swinging from the crook of his arm.

Beryl plonked the pot down on the nearest flat surface – the reception desk, much to its occupant's bewilderment – and sat down next to Alex and kissed the top of his head.

'How is she?'

'They're still doing tests. Not sure where they're at. Dad's just gone to get coffee.'

'What happened?'

Alex shrugged.

'Dad rang, just said she was having chest pains.'

'So why didn't she go to the Port Lincoln hospital like Bert?'

'Because Dad brought her in – they didn't call the ambulance. The ambulance would have most likely taken her down there.'

'Oh, right.'

'So it's a heart attack then?' Beryl said.

'Don't know.'

'Right, well, who's for soup? Hearty beef,' Beryl said, leaping up again. Turning to take orders, she noticed Nicola's bewildered look.

'Well, there's nothing we can do but wait. May as well have some sustenance – it could be a long night.'

No doubt about it, Nicola thought, *the woman was a godsend in a crisis.*

Once again she remembered the day of the crash; how she had sat waiting for news, living on nothing but coffee for over twelve hours, the toxicity and diminishing hope of finding her parents alive eating away at her insides. She stood up to get one of the steaming mugs lined up on the counter.

'Any news?' Graeme called from the doorway.

'Not as yet,' Beryl replied.

'Right.' Nicola noticed Graeme's tight, ashen face relax slightly. He joined the group, nodding in silent greeting.

'Here, this will do you good,' Beryl said, handing him a mug of soup and accepting his polystyrene cup in return.

'Thanks.'

They sat with heads bent, focussed on the ritual of the soup, each appreciative of the distraction.

Nicola examined the steaming contents and savoured the aroma before bringing the mug to her lips. The thick concoction was heaven; at least six different vegetables, masses of stringy beef chunks, and spirals of pasta.

'Ahem.'

Everyone looked up a little guiltily to find an elderly gentleman in jeans, rugby top, and sneakers standing in front of the semi-circle.

Graeme leapt up and extended his arm.

'John, how is she?'

Gradually they each stood and greeted the man. Nicola noticed that he gave nothing away with his expression, and she remained back to observe while the small group milled about earnestly asking the same question. He wrung his hands.

'Look, it's not good, I'm afraid. The next twenty-four hours will be crucial. She's had a heart attack. There's not a lot else we can do but monitor and keep her comfortable at this stage; I don't want to transport her. But where there's life there's hope,' he said, smiling warmly, 'and Dorothy is a fighter.'

The small group nodded grimly in unison.

'Can we see her?' Graeme asked.

'Yes, she is conscious. But she's weak, so keep it short. Room one; this way,' the doctor said, moving off.

Graeme and Alex followed, and slowly Nicola, Beryl, and Stanley returned to their seats. Nicola finished her soup and began fidgeting with a four-year-old magazine, flicking the pages back and forth and trying to lock her attention onto an article, but failing. God, the waiting was excruciating. She checked her watch for the umpteenth time; they'd only been gone a few minutes, but it seemed like hours.

Suddenly she detected a presence nearby and saw Alex coming towards her. He was very pale and drawn.

'She wants to talk to Dad on his own,' he said, with a shrug, then sat down heavily and buried his head in his hands.

Nicola put her arm around him and rubbed his shoulder. 'Did you get to see her?'

Alex nodded. 'It's not good, Nic. She's so weak, just lying there – she's this dreadful grey green colour.' He leaned into her, and she began stroking his hair.

A few minutes later, Graeme reappeared looking even more grim than before. He was looking about him as if he'd lost something. Nicola's heart clenched.

The doctor came up behind Graeme, rubbing his hand across his forehead. Nicola recognised the action. Slowly they all stood up again and remained where they were.

'I'm really sorry,' the doctor said, shaking his head. 'She's gone.'

There was stunned silence punctuated by a couple of quiet gasps. Nicola glanced around. Everything seemed to lapse into slow motion; mouths gaped, hands were rubbed across faces, eyes bulged and then filled with tears.

Slowly Beryl sat, followed by Graeme, then Stanley. Alex continued to stand, looking around in bewilderment, as if searching for the answers in the pale pink walls. He accepted Nicola's embrace, clung to her and sobbed quietly into her hair.

Nicola allowed herself again to cry for all her losses and the knowledge of what Alex was yet to face.

'She was a great lady,' the doctor muttered, and gave a sympathetic pat to each shoulder as he left.

Nicola raised her head slightly to offer her unspoken sympathy and noticed the unshed tears in his eyes. For the first time she was struck by the extra burden on country doctors.

Chapter Forty-four

'Right Jerry, if they don't need us to help, the least we can do is some cooking.' Nicola licked her lips at remembering the trestle tables piled high for the afternoon tea after Bert's funeral.

The dog cocked his head at hearing his name, untangled his legs and went and stood next to Nicola at the old kitchen dresser where she was pulling out a pile of dusty, faded cookbooks.

'These ought to be in a museum,' she moaned, turning up her nose at the out-of-date covers as she sorted through them at the table.

'Oh well. When in Rome!' she cried, clutching four paperbound Country Women's Association cookbooks and pushing the others aside.

The dog went back to his bed and re-settled with a groan and a deep sigh. Nicola looked over and smiled. She was starting to enjoy having her own sheepdog – it was oh so country; quaint but necessary.

Nicola discarded *Calendar of Puddings* without a second glance. She almost gagged at the first page of *Meat and Fish Recipes* – Ham and Tongue Mould – and quickly shut it. After cautiously opening *Fingers and Forks*, Nicola stared horrified at the page she'd randomly selected: Sheep's Head Soup, Kidney Soup, Kangaroo Tail Soup.

'Ugh,' she cried, slamming the book shut and tossing it aside. 'Anyway, since when do you eat soup with either fingers or forks?'

'Something easy yet impressive,' she muttered, picking up *Calendar of Cakes*. 'No bloody pictures! How will I know if it's good enough to serve? I could be the laughing stock.'

She scanned the contents page.

'Weird,' she mused, pausing briefly at Chocolate Potato Cake, Sour Milk Ginger Cake, and Beer Cake.

'Uh huh.' Nicola's attention was on Foolproof Scones. Not that she was concerned with failure – she was in the country now.

'Scones; that's what one does in the country,' she announced, wrapping a tea towel around her head as a scarf then rifling through the drawer for an apron.

★★★

Nicola was proudly extracting her nicely risen and browned scones from the oven when there was a knock on the door.

'Bit nineteen-fifties housewife isn't it,' Janet grinned, jabbing a finger at Nicola.

'I wanted to cook something for the funeral – it's what everyone does, right?'

'Guess so.'

'Need a hand with your bags?'

'Wouldn't mind – there's just one more in the boot.'

'You're in Bert's room,' Nicola called as she skipped down the steps.

★★★

'Mmm, there's nothing quite like the smell of fresh home baking,' Janet said, entering the kitchen and taking a deep whiff. 'Are we sampling?'

'Well I…'

'You do realise these scones have the ability to haunt you for the rest of your time here,' she warned.

Nicola's eyes widened in fear and disbelief.

'Believe me; the smallest things can make the biggest difference in a place like this.'

'Now you're scaring me,' Nicola said, grabbing a plate from the drainer and two scones from the dusty tray.

Nicola filled the kettle and got out mugs while Janet attended to the scones.

'How are they?'

'Um, well…'

'What? What's wrong?'

'I'm afraid they're a little on the…um…tough side,' Janet winced.

'You sure?'

'Well, take a look.'

Nicola poked at the dense, hard texture, frowning. 'They're supposed to be foolproof.'

'How much rolling did you do?'

'I don't know.'

'More than just the once?'

'Considerably,' Nicola sighed.

'Well, plenty of time to make another batch.'

'I'm bored with this cooking thing.' Nicola pouted, folding her arms.

'Thought living in the country would naturally make you a good cook, eh?' Janet said, dunking her teabag.

'As if,' Nicola snorted.

Janet looked over her cup knowingly.

'Weeeellll,' Nicola whined, her expression softening.

The women looked at each other and erupted into laughter.

★★★

'So, how long are you staying?'

'Trying to get rid of me already?'

'No, just wondering,' Nicola stammered, colouring.

'I'm thinking of moving back – there are a few jobs going at the hospital.'

'What about the town?'

'Thirty-four years is long enough in exile. Anyway, now I've got Graeme's support.'

'What about Dorothy's parents?'

'Nursing home in Adelaide. Don't get me wrong, Nicola. I feel bad about everything, I really do. But it was a very long time ago – people need to forgive and forget.'

'Fair enough, I guess.'

'I reckon I've been given a second chance – I'm damn well gonna take it. I'm hoping Graeme and I might be able to make a real go of it,' she added quietly.

'What, so soon?'

'No, I want us to take things slowly. Would it be okay to stay here with you for a while? I'll be coming and going a bit while I sort things out, but I need somewhere to base myself.'

'Of course, but what about Alex?'

'What about him?'

'He'll be devastated. He's just lost his mother.'

'We'll talk to him when things settle down a bit. He's already gone through the worst – learning about you and his dad and me.'

'I suppose so.'

'Nicola, please don't think bad of me. Things happen for a reason. People fall in and out of love. It's just the way it is.'

'But…'

'You can't be worrying about things you can't control. Even Dorothy didn't know her heart was a time bomb.

'If it had been my time I would have gone happily, having met you. But it wasn't, so I have to use what's left wisely.

'Nicola, Alex will be fine, of that I'm sure.'

'I just worry about him, that's all.'

'He's lucky to have you as a sister.'

Chapter Forty-five

Graeme and Janet were to have their talk with Alex, and while Nicola knew they needed their space, she couldn't help feeling left out. Not only was she family, Nicola wanted to be there for Alex when the blow came.

After three weeks, life was settling into a new kind of normality; no longer was she the celebrated oddity – the city television presenter who had chucked it all in for country life. While it had been inconvenient to be the centre of gossip and attention, right now Nicola yearned to be included, not going home to her empty little house to be alone – Janet was rarely there these days.

She could almost hear Ruth's wise words:'The grass is not always greener my dear' and 'life itself is a compromise' – dear old Mum.

Nicola paused Bert's old white ute at his mailbox, sighed, and began making a list of pros and cons. City life won hands down in the categories of decadence and entertainment. But the peace, tranquillity and slow pace of the country were things to behold.

'Ah, but no decent shops…' The voice in her head was Sandy's.

'You obviously haven't discovered Mitre 10 or Landmark Rural Supplies,' she'd sarcastically rebutted.

Bless her; her friend had spent ages quizzing her about her decision when she'd finally got around to updating her. Sandy hadn't tried to talk her out of it, or criticised; she was just checking that Nicola had really thought everything though. It had been good for Nicola too, because the discussion served to dismiss any lingering apprehensions.

Sandy had wished her well and promised to visit soon. Nicola vowed to hold her to it. Though she'd have to do some serious painting and tidying up around the place before then, or else risk Sandy trying to drag her back to civilization. Nicola smiled at the image that had formed itself in her mind. She had a great friend in Sandy; life was good.

So why do I feel like crap? This is supposed to be exciting, liberating. I've got an exciting new career ahead, plenty of money…

'Money,' Nicola sighed. What she was feeling had nothing to do with money. The yearning went a lot deeper than that. It was in her womb; a deep, dull spasm; the desire to be nurtured, to nurture.

'You made your choice,' she said aloud.

Nicola ignored the inner voice telling her it wasn't too late to change her mind, got out of the vehicle, and pulled the few letters from the old fridge.

Her heart leapt then landed with a thud when she recognised the handwriting on one of the envelopes.

Back in the ute, she threw the other mail on the floor and stared at Scott's rough scrawl. She wound the window down to let the brisk air in to ease her fluster, and with shaking fingers slowly and gently prised the envelope open. A single blue sheet of paper was attached with a paper clip to a few sheets of white behind.

Tears sprang into her eyes and a large lump wedged itself at the base of her throat as she read.

Dear Nicola,

It is with great sadness that I write this and enclose your cheque and papers for final settlement.

I understand now why you've done what you have, and I hold myself responsible. If I had been more supportive, more sympathetic of your past, I believe we'd still be together.

But we are who we are and we make choices when called to. Twenty-twenty hindsight and regret are things we must all learn to live with.

I don't wish to fight over the settlement as the money is nothing compared to losing you – use it wisely eh? (Let me know if you want some share advice!)

All the best of luck in finding what you're looking for – I hope you're happy with what you find.
All my love,
Scott.

P.S. If you change your mind, I'll have you back in a heartbeat.

Tears streamed down Nicola's face as she held the paper to her aching throat, going over and over the last sentence in her mind.

Was this the wakeup call he needed? Could he have changed?

With blurred vision, Nicola looked up the long driveway stretching out before her, then back to the letter, and tried to swallow the painful lump.

She knew she should be happy the financials weren't going to get messy. But he'd given up – given up on *them* – so easily. Nicola's whole being ached with the reality.

She wiped her eyes, tossed the letter on top of the pile on the floor and continued up the dusty, corrugated track to her new home.

Chapter Forty-six

Nicola woke with a jolt, rubbed her prickling eyes, and looked about trying to get her bearings. What had she heard? Jerry was at attention – something must have been worthy of arousal. It couldn't be Janet coming back – he knew her car. Anyway, she'd rung to say she was staying over at Graeme's.

Sound and vision became clearer. Mary Poppins was still doing her thing on the wood-grained box in the corner.

That's right; she'd closed her eyes during that awful beer ad where the bloke's tongue leaves his mouth and wanders off. Yuck! She ran her own around her dry mouth.

She must have only dropped off for a few minutes; just long enough to get past the refreshed and into the groggy state where you felt worse.

There it was again, an animalistic wail of pain or ecstasy – she couldn't tell which. Suddenly she was at attention like Jerry, who was looking nervously from her to the window. Nicola shuddered from the goose bumps all over her body.

'What is it, Jerry?' The dog whined, leapt onto the dirty cream vinyl armchair and peered out the window. The dog's hackles were up and his whole body quivered. Was it fear or the expectant thrill of the chase? Should she let him out to scare whatever it was away?

Jerry turned to her, as if reading her mind, then back to the window and began scratching at the glass. Nicola found the click and scrape of his claws oddly reassuring.

She went over, hysteria lurking near the edge of her consciousness, and peered out at the eerie blue glow of the clear half-moonlit night.

'Come on, nothing to see,' she said, patting the dog's head and willing the fear to subside. 'We're being silly, just a silly noise. Come on, bedtime.' She slapped her leg.

Lying in bed, the dog snoozing at her feet, Nicola couldn't get it out of her head. It sounded like a cry that could have been just outside or miles away – one of those sounds that pierced the soul and reminded her what animals were capable of.

★★★

Light was filtering into the room when Nicola awoke. Her jaw ached to her temples. She rolled over, willing herself back to sleep, but her investigative spirit and the security of daylight pushed her from bed and helped drag her clothes on.

Jerry was on her heels, ambling along behind as she tramped over the rise, looking for what she didn't know.

She stopped so suddenly the dog's snuffling nose bumped her leg. It might have been amusing if she hadn't been busy staring at something odd a little way off.

Her hand instinctively went to her mouth as she got close, her brain struggling to decode what she was seeing.

From the front, the large woolly mass of a fully-grown sheep was almost perfect. Nicola needed the full three-hundred-and-sixty degrees to piece the scene together, but when she did, she was too stunned to even dry retch.

Blood pooled behind the sheep, black as treacle. And the sight of a small mound nearby brought tears to her eyes, tearing at her heart.

Finally she knew what she was really seeing; the death of a mother and her baby, slaughtered by goodness only knew what. Mother Nature could be so cruel.

'No Jerry, come away,' she croaked to the dog, which was sniffing hungrily at the carnage. He looked up, questioning.

Her hands fell to her sides and she shook her head wearily.

A flock of squawking crows, circling overhead finally brought Nicola back. Revulsion at their scavenging and fury at their good fortune catapulted her into action. She strode down towards the house, barely paused at the pile of implements leaning in the corner of the shed and went back.

Nicola was so engrossed in her task she didn't hear Alex's vehicle, and only saw him watching her, arms folded, tight expression, when she straightened to give her back a well-earned stretch.

'What are you doing?'

'It's been mauled.'

Alex looked on in thoughtful silence.

'Are you just going to stand there and watch?' Nicola snapped, suddenly exhausted by the effort she'd put in and the enormity of what she saw ahead.

'Help a damsel in distress, you mean?'

'Fine,' she scowled, and dug the shovel hard into the ground. It barely made a chip.

Alex put his hand on her shoulder. Nicola tingled all over from his touch but shook him off. She knew he was the one needing the gentle hand, but she was too full of the mix of emotions surging through her. She couldn't have explained how she felt if she were lying on a shrink's couch and paying two hundred dollars an hour for the privilege.

'We don't bury them,' Alex said quietly.

Nicola turned, lifted a hand skyward.

'But the birds...'

'It's what they do – part of the cycle.'

'But it'll stink.'

'Without a doubt,' Alex nodded. 'You'll get used to all this.

But Nicola wasn't giving up. Standing there, clutching her shovel in a two-handed, white-knuckled clench – her wide don't-fuck-with-me stance, steely gaze and grim expression – she was the epitome of McCardle defiance.

Alex sighed, pushed his own heaviness away, and smiled kindly.

'Come on then, there are easier ways.' He returned to the ute without waiting to see if she'd follow.

Nicola climbed into the idling vehicle, trying to hide her relief – she would never admit to biting off than she could chew.

'What are we doing?'

'You'll see.'

★★★

'Oh, of course,' she breathed, colouring, as Alex pulled Bert's large shed door back to reveal an old rusty tractor with front-end loader.

Alex grinned and winked back at her. 'Don't feel bad. You weren't to know.'

Nicola's ears flamed. But she should have known; she'd wandered through all the sheds the other afternoon.

'Anyway, I'm guessing you've never driven one.'

'No.'

'Right. Well, up you get.'

Nicola frowned. 'I...um...don't think...'

'You want to be a farmer, right?'

'Yes, but...'

'Well, this is all part of it. Come on.'

Nicola swallowed, and with numb shaking limbs, sweating hands and all the elegance of a jellyfish, climbed onto the split blue vinyl tractor seat.

'You'll need these,' Alex said, handing her a pair of bulbous orange earmuffs. She put them on and peered at him expectantly.

'In a minute,' he said, carefully pulling the headset down to around her neck. 'This old girl's like driving a car,' he explained. 'You've driven a manual before, right?'

★★★

Back at the carnage, Nicola carefully followed Alex's instructions, picking up the mess and depositing it behind the scrub, out of sight – and hopefully smell range – of the house.

Driving back, she allowed herself to enjoy a little of the liberation of her new skill. But the thought of the poor slaughtered ewe and her cruelly aborted lamb kept her face tight.

She sighed with a mixture of relief and satisfaction when she'd turned the key off.

'Pretty cool, huh?' Alex said, reading her mind.

'Yeah.'

'Congratulations, Nicola Harvey. You have just graduated from tractor and front-end loader driving one-oh-one,' he said solemnly, and patted her shoulder.

'Thanks,' she beamed, glowing to her core.

★★★

Nicola sighed. She'd been in denial long enough, really had to check the calendar.

She circled the days as she counted back, then paused and pursed her lips. Her cycle had always been a couple of days out either side, but never this long.

Only a matter of weeks ago she'd half-craved this moment of anticipation. *Am I scared? No, just a vague concern — for my health*, she told herself.

'Just all the stress,' she said, shutting the desk diary with a sigh. That's right; the breakup with Scott, being officially homeless, finding a new family, losing her job — all bound to upset the system.

Any day now she'd be again cursing the inconvenience, bloating and discomfort of her period.

She spent the day checking for signs and trying to convince herself she was not petrified, just a little niggled by her body's lack of appropriate scheduling. Nicola Harvey prided herself on being impeccably organised — wouldn't have got where she had in her career otherwise. It wasn't her fault some overseas company had taken over the station and got her fired.

By late afternoon, she was genuinely distressed by the whole situation. Telling herself not to worry, that it would only put off her body's shedding more, only made matters worse.

At seven o'clock, after a day without food, spent pacing and trudging the hall under Jerry's gaze, Nicola decided enough was enough. She'd get a pregnancy test; prove to her body once and for all that it didn't need to put her through this nonsense — jolt it into action.

Nicola grabbed for the keys on the hallstand, but let them go again. This wasn't an anonymous suburb of Adelaide; this was Nowhere Else, where her whole life and the purchases she made were on show.

She swore to herself and returned to the kitchen.

She slumped into a chair, lifted her eyes to the light and began silently making deals with whomever possessed the power she didn't.

The phone rang.

'Works in mysterious ways,' she muttered, getting up. Her body tingled, her sweaty hands shook. Nicola realised she had been getting dangerously close to hysteria.

'Hello?'

'Nicola, it's Graeme, um, your father.'

Nicola sighed. No mention had been made of the inheritance to date, and she really couldn't be dealing with it now. Hopefully gladness for his son and daughter was outweighing any disappointment or resentment he might feel. Anyway, it was likely the last thing on his mind; the poor man had just lost his wife.

'Graeme, how are you?'

'I'm fine, thank you.'

'Good. Something I can do for you?'

'Just ringing to see how you are.'

Well, I'm probably pregnant to my brother with a two-headed child, but other than that I'm just peachy.

'I'm well, thanks.'

Graeme bumbled on, oblivious to her detachment.

'Hear you're going to try your hand at farming.'

Nicola braced herself with a deep breath. The onslaught didn't come.

'Well, I wish you luck…'

Was he being condescending?

'It's a mug's game, no doubt about it – especially now with the drought. And I've been the biggest mug of all,' he added.

Nicola wondered if he was referring to the feud with Bert. Had he become regretful in the face of two recent funerals? Or was he talking about his relationships with Janet and Dorothy?

She knew she should say something, but she couldn't rouse the words; she had a big enough issue of her own to ponder.

Graeme was muttering something about rules and playing the

game, but Nicola wasn't really listening. She couldn't shake the image of a baby screaming at her.

'Graeme, I'm really sorry to cut you short but I've got to rescue the kettle.'

'Yes, sorry, here I am going on like a sentimental old coot. Can you just hang on a minute?' Nicola heard the sound of muffled voices in the background.

'Oh, the other thing, I almost forgot; Janet's here and wants to know if you can come for tea Thursday night – bit of a family get-together. Alex will be here.'

'Great, love to, thanks,' she said, a little over-exuberantly.

Nicola felt a stirring in her abdomen, wondered if maybe she felt a slight dampness in her undies. She crossed her fingers.

'Graeme, sorry, I really have to go.'

'Righto, see you then.'

'Thanks for the call.' Nicola hung up and bolted down the hall like a greyhound after a mechanical bunny.

Chapter Forty-seven

Nicola was weary when she headed off to have dinner with Graeme, Alex and Janet. She'd spent most of the day consumed with finding a strategy for extracting a pregnancy kit from the chemist without being arrested for shoplifting or dying of embarrassment.

The night before she'd even dreamt about it; the towering balding pharmacist bellowing over the public address system – unnecessary in the tiny shop – that Nicola Harvey, single, thirty-something, famous television journalist, was in fact purchasing a pregnancy test. And one of the double packs, just to be sure.

In the dream she'd left the pharmacy and bumped into Richard, who proudly announced that her story had made front page of the *Echo*. Nicola woke, drenched in sweat, knowing there was no way in hell she could go through with it.

A number of other options had also been depleted, including ordering online – the only chemists she could find were in the United States; she'd probably be showing by the time it arrived.

She'd also discarded the option of phoning Sandy. She hadn't told her friend yet, and it was too late now. Anyway, she was far too embarrassed. It wasn't something she could tell anyone. Perhaps Alex; he'd have to know eventually. *Oh God.*

Nicola thought about the complete turnabout her life had made; she so badly wished Ruth was here to share it with, to guide her. Would she be surprised, pleased or disappointed? Or perhaps she knew; had seen what was there all along that Nicola had patently missed. Maybe it was the reason for everything – the plane crash, Nowhere Else, Scott… Was it *that* ordained? She had no way of knowing.

Nicola began to sob, great wrenching gulps rising from her toes, at the realisation of her journey, the toll it had taken – how far the ripples in the pond of her life had scattered.

For the parents who had raised her, their sacrifice had been ultimate. She dried her eyes. Nothing could bring them back. All she could do was make sure she'd learnt from all this and, if she was carrying the next generation, be the best she could. She really hoped nature wouldn't be too harsh.

Nicola wiped her eyes, checked her face in the rear vision mirror and got out. She threw her shoulders back with the force of her presumed extra responsibility and strode past Alex's ute to the front door.

After she rang the bell, Graeme appeared and gave her a hug; a little awkwardly, Nicola thought, but dismissed it. Everything about this evening was a little awkward. His lover was suddenly back in the picture after more than three decades, and practically living there; his wife had recently died; and the biological daughter he hadn't known of for thirty-four years was there for dinner. Poor Alex was the only constant. Yep, there were bound to be a few difficult moments tonight.

'Come on in,' he said. 'Bit nippy out.'

'For you,' she said, offering the bottle of wine. It was Jacob's Creek. Scott would have had a fit. It was the most expensive – and presumably the best – in the bottle shop at the pub.

She was surprised and a little disappointed that Tiffany hadn't been there to serve her. She'd asked the unfamiliar young lad if she was around, feeling bad about not seeing her since she'd left the motel.

'No,' he'd said. 'She left for Adelaide yesterday.'

'Oh, so did she get her uni place then?'

'Dunno,' he'd said with a shrug. 'Just the bottle of wine, then?'

'Yes, thanks.' Nicola said, handing over a twenty dollar note. Tiff must have been so excited. She wished she'd made the effort to keep in touch; she was a nice kid, and Nicola would have liked to have offered her number – maybe given some assistance, suggested some contacts. She'd shaken the thought aside and held out her hand for the change.

'Hello,' Nicola said brightly, walking into the kitchen. 'Something smells divine,' she said, giving Alex a quick hug on her way to the stove where Janet stood stirring a pot of gravy.

'Anything I can help with?' she asked.

'No, it's all under control,' Janet said, beaming back at her.

When she turned around, Nicola noticed that Graeme was standing in the doorway rubbing a hand over his face. Something was off here – Graeme was definitely looking uncomfortable. Had he and Janet had an argument? No, she thought, glancing back at her mother. Janet was cheerful enough.

She looked at Alex. God he was gorgeous, standing there with his hair all over the place, seemingly unaware of how good-looking he was. Nicola's heart sank. How was she going to break the news that she was quite possibly pregnant to him? And when?

'You look weary,' Graeme said. 'Have a seat – take a load off.' He indicated for her to sit at the table that was already draped in white damask and set with shimmering cut crystal wine glasses and shining silver cutlery.

'Are you sure I can't help?' Nicola called, pausing with her hand on the back of a chair.

'No, seriously, it's almost ready,' Janet said, lifting foil to reveal a sizzling brown leg of lamb.

Nicola caught a waft of aroma and suddenly found her mouth watering and her stomach churning at exactly the same time. Oh God, please no. She swallowed hard.

'Are you okay?' Alex asked from his position leaning against the sink. 'You've gone all pale.'

'I just feel a little weak all of a sudden,' she said 'Mustn't have eaten enough today.'

'Well, sit down before you fall down,' Janet said, picking up the carving knife and fork.

Nicola pulled out the chair and sat down, concentrating on breathing through her mouth in case any more smells threatened to turn her stomach. This is not a good sign, she thought. Hopefully she'd just picked up some virus or twenty-four hour bug or something. Yes, that's what it is. Surely it was too early for morning sickness anyway; when was that meant to start?

Nicola suddenly felt her abdomen cramp.

'Actually, could I please use the loo?' She asked, getting back up.

'Of course – just across the hall,' Graeme said.

Another spasm hit Nicola as she entered the bathroom. *Fingers crossed.*

She was so relieved to see the paper stained that she almost wept. Having put the liner in her undies, she buried her head in her hands and took a few moments to compose herself. *Thank God!*

She practically skipped back into the kitchen.

Nicola tried to make conversation with Graeme, telling him

about Alex teaching her to drive the tractor, before giving up. It was obvious his mind was elsewhere.

Perhaps he was having second thoughts about starting things with Janet again. Maybe Beryl had lectured him about how recently he'd lost his wife. He didn't look like he was struggling with his grief. He seemed more troubled, conflicted.

Stop being the nosy journalist, she told herself. *If you're meant to know, you will, Sandy would say.*

'Can I get you a drink – a glass of your wine, or something else? Beer, white wine, or perhaps a glass of water if you're not feeling well.'

'A glass of wine would be great, thanks. I'm feeling much better, but a glass of water would be good too.'

Seconds later Alex placed a glass in front of her. 'Thanks Alex.'

'Pleasure. And your colour does look better. Who else is for a glass of red? Dad? Janet?'

'Yes thanks,' Janet and Graeme said in unison.

Glasses of wine were put on the table and thankfully, just as silence was descending, Janet and Alex reappeared carrying two laden plates each.

'Wow, this looks great,' Nicola said taking a deep whiff.

'Right, before we start, we need a toast,' Janet said. 'Graeme, can you do the honours?'

'Keep room for dessert,' Graeme said. 'Janet's made a lovely-looking apple pie.' He patted her hand fondly. Janet beamed at him.

'Okay,' Graeme said, raising his glass. 'To family – old and new.'

'To family, old and new,' Janet, Alex and Nicola said, smiling at each other. They all clinked glasses.

'Right, tuck in everyone, before it gets cold,' Janet said. They all picked up their cutlery and started eating.

A few minutes later, Nicola looked around the table at everyone. She knew it was clichéd, but she really did feel all warm and fuzzy inside. It was so nice to be part of a family again, and sitting down to dinner together. She felt a momentary twinge at remembering Dorothy's absence. Alex seemed to be coping okay, and didn't seem to have a problem with Janet. Though with grief you never could be sure; the stages came and went in waves, sometimes over and over.

But he had her; he was no longer an only child. Neither was she. *We have each other,* she thought, smiling inwardly, and returned to her meal.

Finally, Janet was congratulated on a fine meal, and the plates were cleared from main course, rinsed, and put in the dishwasher.

'Well, I do hope you've all left room for apple pie – you were warned,' Janet said, bringing a large pie and knife to the table. 'Nicola, could you please get the cream out of the fridge? It's in the white jug.'

Moments later they were again raving about Janet's culinary skills. Obviously governed by nurture not nature, Nicola thought drolly, as she savoured her pie and took note of the light, crispy pastry.

Suddenly something caught her attention; out of the corner of her eye she saw Janet lay a hand on Graeme's – as if to placate him. Nicola now noticed he was quite jittery; his spoon was shaking slightly as he put it to his mouth. And his eating seemed hurried; automatic shovelling, not slow enjoyment like the rest of them.

Seconds later he put his spoon down in his empty bowl. She, Janet, and Alex were still only halfway through theirs. They all looked up and at Graeme as he began clearing his throat loudly.

'Um. Well. There's something you need to know, son,' he said, staring at the table cloth and fiddling with his napkin. Alex gazed expectantly at his father. Graeme frowned. Alex frowned back.

Nicola tried to finish her dessert silently. Janet was continuing to eat as if nothing had happened – or pretending to, Nicola thought. Whatever was about to be said, she already knew.

It seemed like minutes had passed, but it couldn't have been more than a few seconds before Graeme continued.

'Son, I'm not your biological father,' he said, shaking his head sadly.

Nicola stopped chewing and stared at Graeme, the apple pie losing all appeal and becoming a soggy bland mass in her mouth. He looked like he might either burst into anger or tears; his lips were turned in on themselves and his face looked tight and anguished.

She stole a glance at Alex. All colour had drained from his face and his eyes flickered slightly within his frown as his brain processed the magnitude of what he'd just heard.

'It's what your mother wanted to tell me at the hospital, just before she... She had an affair with an itinerant Italian farm worker,' he said, as if choosing his words carefully. He scratched at the gold floral decoration on the edge of the bowl still in front of him.

Was that all he was going to say? Was he more concerned about Alex not being his son or that he'd been duped for so long; that he wasn't the only one involved in deceitful conduct so many years ago.

After what seemed an eternity in which the only sound was the ticking kitchen clock, Alex cleared his throat and got up, croaking that he really needed some space.

He bolted from the house like someone about to throw up. Nicola looked after him, then back to the strained expression of the now sonless man, loss etched in the deep weathered lines of his ashen face.

She twisted in her chair, trying to decide when to follow. She would, it was just a matter of when. They'd known that – it was no doubt the reason she was here. But how long should she give him? He could take the rest of his life to get his head around it.

Nicola pictured Alex sitting on the cold concrete floor of the shed, knees bent, arms protectively around him, no doubt experiencing the same sadness and confusion of identity she had so many years before.

'I'll go,' she announced, and leapt up from the table.

Chapter Forty-eight

'I know you probably don't want company, but I had to know you were okay. You can tell me to leave if you like, but I guess I sort of know how you feel, well not exactly of course, but anyway... I'll just shut up then.' Nicola's words tumbled out in a flurry, and she had to gulp for air when they finally stopped.

Alex offered a weak smile.

'I'm glad you came. Pull up a pew,' he said, patting the hay bale beside him.

'You sure?'

'Just had to get out of there, away from their pity – because I've lost Mum and everything.

'I know it sounds bad, but I'm not really all that sad – about Graeme,' he said, shaking his head. He frowned and looked down at the ground. He scratched in the dirt for a few moments with the piece of straw in his fingers.

Nicola silently waited for him to continue.

'I feel kind of lost, but also found,' he said, looking back up at her. 'You know, it's like something has just clicked for me – finally makes sense?'

Nicola nodded and waited for him to continue.

'Something has been back in the depths of my being, niggling away at me and I haven't ever been able to figure out what it is. Now I see it.'

'What?'

'This.' He opened his arms wide. 'Everything, me. It was those words: "Son, I'm not your biological father". Explains a lot; why it never seemed right calling him Dad, why we never got on all that well.

'There was always something standing between us – like a brick wall. For years I fought it, fought him. You should have heard the barneys we had.

'That's why I went out on my own so early. I hated his whole way of thinking, couldn't understand why he had to be so bloody rip tear aggressive.'

Nicola felt a twinge; this was her father he was talking about. But she stayed silent.

'I'm just disappointed Mum couldn't tell me. I know it's ridiculous and fanciful to think she could tell me without telling Graeme – hindsight eh?'

Nicola returned his wistful grimace.

'I suppose she did the next best thing, sending me to Italy. They were all farmers – olives, grapes, fruit and veg. Market gardeners but still toilers of the land.

'If she'd told me, I could have met them – properly – *really* got to know them.' Alex lapsed into silence, lost in his memories.

'Giovanni picked me up from the airport, organised my classes and everything. He was my main contact. I wonder if he knew. Good bloke, but he couldn't be my father…'

'Why not?'

'Well he seemed way too young. He didn't look much over thirty. Though, if he was sixteen when he met Mum I guess it's possible.'

'Did you keep in touch, ever go back to visit?'

'We wrote for a while, but you know what it's like once you're back on home soil, working.

'Anyway, Graeme wasn't one for daydreaming, didn't give me a moment's peace. He isn't interested in travelling himself, so doesn't think anyone else should.'

Nicola flinched again at his criticism of her father, but still said nothing.

'Thinks it an appalling waste of money. Mum told me once that she used most of her inheritance to send me. Bless her.'

Nicola noticed his eyes glistening with tears. She ached to her core for him, put a hand on his knee and gently squeezed.

'It's not too late. You could go back, get to know them, your heritage.'

'I just wish she'd told me. Now I'll never know – not her story anyway.' Alex sighed deeply. 'I just feel so alone, like I'm losing Mum all over again. Losing my whole family.'

Nicola nodded. 'I know how you feel.' The words slipped quietly from her lips.

He clasped her hand firmly. 'I'm sorry; here I am going on when...'

'Don't be ridiculous. I've had time. You...'

'I'm so glad you're here.'

'I always will be Alex, I'm family... And there's nowhere else I'd rather be.'

As the words left Nicola's mouth, the truth hit her. It hit Alex at the same time. They turned and stared at each other, eyes free to roam, minds already wandering the avenues of possibility. The only sounds were the occasional creaks of the steel shed and corrugated iron contracting in the cold night air.

Chapter One

Claire rolled onto her stomach and peered at the clock radio on what had been Keith's bedside table. She'd woken early, before dawn, and had managed to doze off again. Now she was surprised to find it was after ten. Anyway, it was Sunday: she'd laze about till lunchtime if she wanted.

Even after four months she still found herself aching for Keith's embrace, his sweet musky scent and…

Snippets of dreams came back to her. In one they'd showered together and then made love in the lounge, on the plush rug in front of the gas log fire. It had been beautiful: him tender, giving; she responding, clinging to him.

She'd woken hot and sweating, despite it being chilly outside, instantly feeling embarrassed at her arousal. But it hadn't been Keith's face at all, had it? No, the face had been blank. Who had it been? She shook her head, trying hard to remember. After a few moments she gave up.

In another dream he'd been lying beside her saying he loved her, that it was okay to move on, that it wouldn't mean she loved him any less. 'I know you have needs,' he'd said with a wink, before drifting from her slumbering memory.

That had definitely been Keith. His face now came to her clearly: the slightly crooked, cheeky grin; the fringe he insisted on keeping too long to cover the scar above his left eye – apparently the result of a silly, drunken escapade at university. She'd never heard the full story – he'd always managed to sidestep her question with a well-timed hug. Now she'd never know. And she'd never have another of his comforting, bear-like hugs.

A tear escaped and her throat caught on the forming lump. She'd give her life for just one more hug with Keith. Would she ever find anything so comfortable again? Did she even want to look?

'Oh Keith,' she whispered. If only she'd shown him more affection and not taken their contentment so much for granted.

Claire roughly wiped the tears from her cheeks with the back of her hand, pushed aside her mop of unruly hair, and sat up.

* * *

Claire had a quick shower and stood – towel wrapped around her – studying her reflection in the bathroom mirror. Did her hairstyle make her features appear hard? For years she'd been talking about getting her hair cut like Jennifer Aniston's – chipped into so that it wasn't so full down the back and sides – but had never been brave enough to go through with it. She'd always kept it plain, practical – straight across the bottom and in a ponytail to keep it away from her face. It was the way Keith had liked it. She'd never dyed it either – always stuck with her natural medium-brown shade. Bernadette and her hairdresser had both given up trying to talk her around years ago.

Claire held her hair away from her face and turned left and right, examining the effect in the mirror. Did she dare? Keith was no longer there to complain. She let it down again. Bernie was right: short didn't suit her. Anyway, she'd feel too self-conscious. But she could definitely do with less bulk around her face. She dragged her brush through her hair a couple of times and put it into a ponytail.

She ran her electric toothbrush around her mouth while roaming the bedroom – pulling up the quilt and straightening the pillows. She had her underwear drawer open, about to pull out socks, knickers and bra when her toothbrush buzzed, signalling her two minutes was up. She turned it off, stood it on the edge of the vanity beside Keith's, and rinsed her mouth. Then she added a thin layer of foundation to her face and neck with her fingers, swept the mascara brush once across each set of lashes, added two layers of deep rose pink 'Goddess' lipstick, blotted with toilet paper and returned to the bedroom to get dressed.

Claire McIntyre was conservative through and through. Her uniform rarely varied: navy or grey skirt suit cut just below the knee for work; jeans or tailored pants and shirt or knit for weekends. Evening wear was a lolly pink wrap over a little black dress – if size twelve was still considered little. It ended four inches above the knee and showed just the right amount of décolletage to straddle the fine line between tarty and prudish. Despite the current trend for bare, bottle-tanned legs and towering stilettos, Claire insisted on sheer, smoky-coloured pantyhose and sensible plain black shoes with ample room for her toes.

Even her career was conservative. Yes, she'd had different roles, but she'd been with the same company for twelve years when the done thing was to move on every few. But she was happy enough; why go through the stress of looking for something else, just so your CV would show you were progressive? Anyway, there were leave entitlements to think of. Claire wasn't exactly thrilled with her job but enjoyed the security of a regular paycheque.

She'd joined the national advertising firm Rockford and Associates as a marketing graduate. Hard work and long hours had seen her move into a senior role in account management. Three years ago she'd been promoted to Client Relationship Manager for one of the firm's largest clients, AHG Recruitment.

Since losing Keith, she had been all the more grateful for the familiarity of her open-plan cubicle and routine tasks: a welcome – if mundane – source of stability in her life.

But now Claire felt something within her stirring: a strange kind of yearning, but for what? It wasn't Keith, it wasn't a dull sad ache, this was different – more a restlessness.

She focussed on her hair again. Knowing her luck, the Aniston look was now as fashionable as the mullet. Maybe her hairdresser had better ideas – could she offer free rein? Claire felt excited at the prospect, even a little empowered. Yes, she'd definitely phone for an appointment.

Bernadette was right: if grief was like a brick wall, each step towards recovery was the removal of a brick, then a layer. Eventually she'd be able to step over the top and be free. Then she'd look back at the good times without tears, and remember the not-so-good times with detachment. But it took time. The trick was to allow the bricks to come away when the mortar loosened – and not to stop their progress with a slap of concrete.

Of course, she wouldn't cut her hair without a second opinion from her best friend. She'd mention it when they next spoke.

Claire and Bernie had known each other since Pony Club and primary school. They'd even studied the same course at university and then started their first jobs at the same company – but in different departments. Twelve months in, Bernadette had been fired for rejecting her boss's advances with a swift slap across his face. Claire had considered protesting by leaving with her, but only for a second; she didn't have the courage to quit without the security of another job to go to. Thankfully Bernie had understood.

The episode had sent Claire into a spin of worrying about what her friend would do, but Bernadette had seen it as a sign she was ready to pursue her dream: opening a nursery specialising in old-fashioned plants, design and accessories. Apparently the Adelaide Hills area was full of people wanting old English-style gardens – God only knew why with the water restrictions.

Regardless, and despite only being in her early twenties, Bernadette had built a successful business on box hedges, white gravel and distressed wrought-iron outdoor furniture.

Claire regularly shook her head in wonder and sometimes felt a twinge – but of what she wasn't sure. Not jealousy; she would never wish her friend anything but all the very best. Seeing Bernadette chasing her dream made her wonder about her own choices. Still, Claire was no different to about ninety-five percent of the population.

Besides, there was no way she'd want to deal with the public every day. She'd spent a lot of time at the nursery, occasionally even manning the till. One virtue Claire McIntyre did not possess was patience, and tolerance with other people's indecision was in pretty short supply as well. She would have strangled someone by now if she was Bernadette, and couldn't believe Bernie hadn't.

Bernadette had always been the quintessential redhead. Her uncontrollable curls stood out like a warning, something Claire realised – too late – on the day they met.

It was their first Pony Club rally and they were both eleven. Bernie was on a small cranky grey pony, Claire on a larger bay. Claire had accidently got too close to Bernie's pony and it had darted sideways in fright, almost causing Bernie to fall off. Bernie shouted so loudly that Claire's mother heard the commotion. Grace McIntyre stormed across the arena to tell her daughter off. Mortified, Claire turned her tomato-red face – first to the instructor and then to Bernie – and said she was sorry.

Bernie had smirked, tossing her head in the air before moving her pony away. Claire decided she didn't like this Bernadette girl very much. But later, Bernie had come up to her at the tap while she was filling her water bucket and said it wasn't fair how much Claire's mother had overreacted. They'd been firm friends ever since.

Bernie used to fly off the handle with the slightest provocation. Once she got started, she wouldn't unclamp her teeth from an argument, even if she knew she was wrong. It was probably the reason she was still single and most definitely why corporate life hadn't been for her. You just couldn't scream at your boss that he was a dickhead one day and ask for a raise the next. And slapping him was a definite no no.

But she had mellowed since finding her 'place in the cosmos', as she called it. Now her fire was being fuelled with passion, and she was a lot calmer.

Claire bit her bottom lip. No, when it came to Bernadette, if she was envious, it was of her state of mind. Bernie glowed with contentment and enthusiasm whenever she spoke – and not just about the business. Even late deliveries weren't enough to unsettle her. She'd just shrug and say that they'd turn up when they were ready. According to Bernie, everything would work out in the end. And for her it usually did.

For the thousandth time, Claire wondered at the reasoning behind Keith being taken from her, and then dismissed the thoughts as ridiculous. There was no reason. He'd had a tragic accident and she just had to get over it. And what about her father's accident, why had that happened?

Whatever the reasons, nothing could alter the fact that she was having the worst year possible. Things always happened in threes: she and Bernadette had pointed out so many instances before. Since Keith's death and Jack's accident, it had become a taboo subject. Claire wondered what else she was to be faced with. The doctors had assured her Jack's injuries weren't life-threatening – he'd come out of his coma when he was ready. It was just a matter of time. But how much time? It had already been a month.

Claire was relieved she hadn't been the one to find Jack crumpled in a silent heap on the ground. Thank goodness neighbours Bill and Daphne Markson had thought to invite him over for an early dinner – luckier still they had thought to drop in on their way back from town instead of phoning. She knew she should spend more time with her father. She had visited a lot in the months after her mother's death five years ago, but gradually the pace of work and social life in the city had engulfed her again. In the last year, she was lucky to see him every three weeks.

Until the accident, of course. She was now spending a couple of hours each day after work sitting with him – time she didn't really have to spare. She felt guilty every time she turned up because invariably Bill and Daphne were already there – Bill reading the paper and Daphne knitting. It was a jumper for Jack, made from chunky homespun natural grey lamb's wool.

Claire tried to tell herself it was different for them because they were retired, but felt guilty all over again when she remembered that they'd driven nearly forty minutes to be there, not ten like she had. But they didn't have an inbox full of six hundred emails waiting to be read and responded to. Claire had tried to sit and do nothing, but on the third day had given up and started bringing her laptop to make better use of the time. She didn't think you were allowed to use electronic equipment in hospitals, but no one had told her off yet.

Claire checked her watch – visiting hours at the hospital were starting soon. She ran down the stairs, grabbed her laptop bag from the kitchen bench and her keys from the bowl on the hall table. Having punched the code into the security system, she deadlocked the door and pulled it shut behind her.

Win an Australian outback experience from

7 major prizes to be won across Australia

Plus everyone who enters wins a FREE eBook!

To download your free eBook and enter the competition go to

harlequinbooks.com.au/redballoon

and tell us your most unforgettable experience in 25 words or less.

Enter promo code: RED0112

Competition closes 1 March 2012

*Terms and conditions available online.